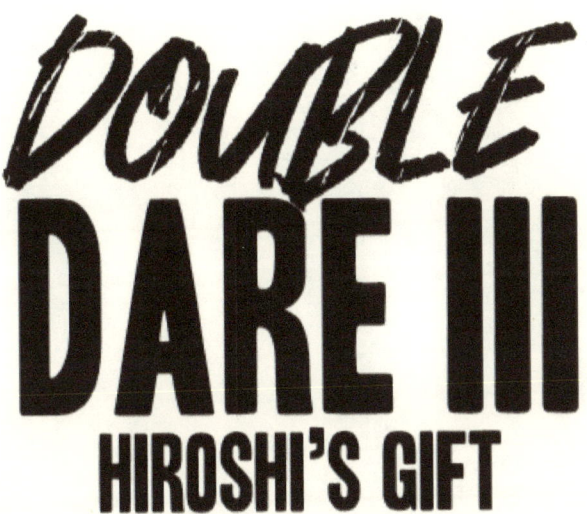

# DOUBLE DARE III
## HIROSHI'S GIFT

# Michael Curless

mAcinSF

Book Cover by Joleene Naylor

Second edition 2024

eBook ISBN 9798215890127

Paperback ISBN 9798990747623

To everyone whose life has gone from joy to overwhelming grief in the blink of an eye. For too many of us, it is a part of this life we are forced to endure. But sometimes, that which brings grief can ultimately open a door to new joy. That is also life.

# A Note to the Reader

The Double Dare trilogy portrays a chosen family of gay men living in 21st Century San Francisco, a city long revered for encouraging its denizens to live their best, authentic lives. The men chronicled here are striving to do just that. Which means there are occasional, frank scenes of sex between men. Loving, devoted men, some of whom enjoy exploring new and growing subcultures in the modern world. As the title should imply, some of these scenes may be, for the uninitiated, a bit daring.

*It was true, what Peter had said. Each of them passed each of the others going in opposite directions. At times, they were walking side by side with another. And sometimes, each of them was alone.*

# One

## THE COLLABORATORS

"Knock. Knock." Alex called out as he stood at Hiroshi's open back door, debating whether to just walk in or wait for an official invitation.

"Come in, my friend," Hiroshi called from inside. "Do not stand on ceremony." Alex wandered in through the mudroom to find Hiroshi in the kitchen, pouring steaming water into a black iron teapot. Hiroshi looked up and smiled. "I'm preparing tea for us, specially blended to promote our creative juices." Alex approached the counter and sniffed.

"Mmmm. I feel more creative already, Hiroshi." Alex smiled as he spied the plate of individually wrapped senbei on the tray with the teapot.

"Well, Alex, we have seen just how creative you can be as a screenwriter, so I am confident you do not need any herbal help. In fact, I have been looking forward to working with you in planning Juan and Ricky's wedding." Hiroshi picked up the tray and headed toward the front of the house. "I thought we would work in the study." Alex followed Hiroshi through the dining and living rooms, across the entry into Hiroshi's study, marveling at the meticulous braiding of the gauzy rokushaku fundoshi Hiroshi was wearing. No matter how many times he'd tried, he could never get his own fundoshi to come out as perfectly as Hiroshi's always were. Which is why he hadn't even tried today and had come through the back garden harnessed and caged, but otherwise naked, as always. Hiroshi set the tray on the desk and poured two cups as Alex pulled up a side chair, set his phone on the desk, and settled in. Hiroshi handed a cup to Alex then placed the plate of crackers between them. As Alex tore open a nori senbei, Hiroshi sat back in the desk chair and sipped from his cup, enjoying the sight of Alex savoring his favorite snack.

"I've done a little research, Hiroshi, but I still don't have a good sense of what a Buddhist wedding ceremony should be. Where do we start?" Hiroshi set his cup down.

"Let us start with what you do know, Alex."

"Well, it's not a religious ceremony, typically there aren't any vows, it's mostly the monk chanting from sacred texts or mantras. Sometimes incense is burned. Not a lot of the pomp and circumstance of weddings here." Hiroshi had peeled open a cracker and munched it while Alex was talking. He picked up his cup and sipped.

"Sounds pretty boring, eh, Alex?" Alex struggled to find a non-judgmental answer.

"It maybe sounds dry on paper ..."

"Was your ceremony for Niki, Steve, Raphael and Luke a typical American wedding?" Alex laughed cracker crumbs onto his lap.

"It was more of an over-the-top production, Hiroshi. I kinda got carried away." Hiroshi nodded.

"From all accounts, your efforts were appreciated by all who were in attendance. I see no reason why we cannot make Juan and Ricky's wedding unique and memorable as well, even if it is a more intimate affair. Alex, I don't think they asked me to officiate because they wanted a traditional Buddhist ceremony or a Japanese ceremony, which are two different things, really. I think they just wanted a simple but meaningful ceremony, blessed by the presence of the people who love them." Alex nodded his agreement. "Here is my suggestion, if I may. We should put together an eclectic ceremony that borrows the best from several cultures, considering the diversity of this unique and wonderful family. What do you think?"

"That's a great idea, Hiroshi. So, we can pretty much do whatever we want?" Hiroshi smiled and nodded. "I mean, within reason. What is the best of the Japanese Buddhist tradition that we should include?"

"Since the setting will be somewhat informal, your garden, I thought the clothing should be rather dramatic. Is it okay with you if the wedding party is wearing clothing, Alex? Unlike your last wedding?" Alex looked self-consciously down at his cage, then back at Hiroshi with a wry grin.

"Like I said, that was something of a spectacle. Intended to honor the kinky lifestyle of the four grooms. If we go multi-cultural, with an emphasis on Buddhist-Japanese influence, I agree, nudity, as much as we all enjoy it, may not be appropriate. Besides, I don't want to be pegged as a one-note wedding planner." Hiroshi laughed. "So, what are you thinking? Will everyone be wearing off the shoulder orange robes?" Hiroshi laughed again, eyes closed, shaking his head.

"No ... no orange robes. Here, what do you think of this?" Hiroshi woke his laptop and the connected larger monitor to display a handsome young Japanese man dressed in a dark, floor length garment. "This is what I was thinking for Juan. It is a yukata, in the keisho kanji print, which represents 'fortunate event.' Not a traditional kimono for a wedding, perhaps, but, as we agreed, this will not be a traditional wedding."

"No," Alex replied, projecting a mix of surprise and joy, "but it will be a fortunate event. We'll see to that, won't we?" Hiroshi nodded with a smile. "That's kind of sexy. I didn't know men wore kimonos. I thought only women wore them ... mostly geishas."

"No, Alex, men and women both wear kimono and yukata, and perhaps you may not have known this, but the first geisha were actually men." Hiroshi lifted one eyebrow to Alex's delight.

"Of course they were," Alex grinned, wiggling his eyebrows in reply. "I like it. Do you think studly Juan will wear that? It's, well ... it's sort of androgynous."

"Only to an American eye, Alex. I am confident Juan and Ricky will go along with whatever we decide. After all, they did put us in charge, did they not?"

"They did!" Alex replied. As he tore open another savory senbei, he looked mischievously at Hiroshi. "Okay, now I'm getting excited." He popped the cracker into his mouth and munched. "So, what do you have in mind for Ricky?" Hiroshi clicked on another tab, bringing up an image of a navy blue kimono emblazoned on the front with two small gold embroidered kanji symbols, one over each pectoral. He clicked to display another image showing the back, with a larger embroidery of the same symbol centered between the shoulder blades.

"Mmmm. Very classy," Alex opined. "What does that symbol represent?"

"Long life and happiness." Alex looked pleased.

"They'll look stunning dressed in these kimono, Hiroshi. Do they have any idea this is what you're planning?" Hiroshi shook his head, delivering his own mischievous smile.

"No, my friend. And not what I am planning. What *we* are planning. We will share the credit, and any blame. Agreed?"

"Agreed," Alex grinned. "Will there be anyone else in the wedding party like we have here ... best man, groomsmen ... maid of honor?"

"I spoke with them about that. In a typical Buddhist ceremony, no. But since we are choosing from different cultures, that is one we will add from the Western world. Alex, it is a testimony to how much love and respect there is in this family that choosing two best men was nearly impossible for them. But they finally decided that since you and Greg had taken Ricky in and protected him from harm, that the two of you should have the honor of 'best men.'"

"Whoa. Really? That's ... I thought they'd pick Raphael and Luke."
Alex looked pleased and humbled.

"As I said, it was not an easy decision for them. But I think they made
the right choice. Here, take a look at what I suggest you and Greg should
wear." Hiroshi clicked on yet another tab to reveal another kimono. He
turned to Alex with an expression silently asking, 'what do you think?'
Alex studied the image a moment longer.

"For both me and Greg?" Hiroshi nodded as he clicked to display
the front and back images of a black kimono decorated with colorful
embroidered dragons, smaller ones over each pectoral on the front, and,
similar to Ricky's, a larger embroidered image on the back. "Very elegant.
I assume there is symbolism behind the dragon?"

"Of course. This is the Kaenryu design, called a flare dragon because
it is flying through a 'flare' cloud, these little red wisps. The dragon is
thought to prevent evil and bring good fortune."

"So, we'll be more than best men, we'll be good luck charms, too?"
Hiroshi laughed again, more heartily than before.

"I *like* that interpretation, Alex. Yes, let us go with that. Would you
like to explore other possible designs?"

"No," Alex shook his head and lingered on the image on the screen. "I
defer to your expertise on kimono. I think we'll all look stunning, not to
mention surprising. Not that we'll have a very big audience. Will these
be hard to get?" Hiroshi shook his head.

"Not if we act soon, Alex. I'll just need shoe sizes for everyone for the
zori, the traditional sandals. Can you do a little sleuthing to find that out
for us?"

"No problem." Alex reached for another senbei. Hiroshi refreshed
both tea cups.

"Now, to your expertise, Alex. Since the ceremony will be outdoors, I
thought we might introduce an element from your culture."

"Hmmm?" Alex queried through a closed but cracker filled mouth.

"I thought we might erect a chuppah as the focal point." Alex's eyes
widened as he swallowed.

"A chuppah? For a Buddhist ceremony?" Hiroshi slowly nodded with
a faint smile. "You weren't kidding about mixing cultures, were you?"
Hiroshi just maintained the smile. "How did you know I was Jewish?
I'm not the only one in the family without a foreskin."

"On one of the days when we were marching for Black Lives, in
all his sweet innocence, Mateo asked me if Buddhism and Judaism are
similar, since neither worships the Christian savior. A deep subject on a
very momentous day. He wants to understand each of us, I think, and
emulate the best of us. A remarkable young man."

"What did you say? This ought to be good ..."

"It was not the best setting for a deep philosophical discussion, as I am sure you recall. So, I simply said that most religions and spiritual philosophies, at their core, are more alike than different. When I asked him why he was asking, he said that I was the only Buddhist that he knew, and that you were the only Jew. And that he wanted to better understand our two cultures." Alex leaned back and sighed.

"I don't remember ever talking about being Jewish with Mateo." Alex held eye contact with Hiroshi for a moment. "He must trust you more than me."

"He reveres you, Alex. Maybe he just felt comfortable enough to ask me what had been on his mind in that moment. With us holding hands and 'making good trouble' in support of his Black brother. As with Ricky, you and Greg provided Mateo with safe harbor and he will always be in your debt. He trusts you Alex, more than almost anyone else in the world." Alex had a studied look as he processed what Hiroshi had said.

"What do you think ... about the chuppah idea?" Hiroshi brought Alex back to the task at hand.

"Aesthetically, I like it. I agree it would be a nice focal point. I can see you, Juan and Ricky standing under it, with flowers twined around the posts. I already have an idea how to embellish it. They don't even have to know it's a Jewish tradition." Hiroshi tilted his head questioningly.

"Why not, Alex? Is it not expected in a Buddhist-Japanese-Jewish-Catholic-Atheist-Black-Latino-Filipino-Caucasian family wedding?"

"Well ... when you put it that way." Alex looked slightly pleased. He leaned toward Hiroshi. "What will you be wearing? A Japanese-Black-Latino-Filipino-Caucasian suit? Or something from the rainbow couture?"

"There is that over-the-top wedding planner I have heard so much about," Hiroshi smiled. "No, my friend, I have a subtle black kimono, with a pale grey obi that I thought I would wear. I do not wish to compete with the wedding party."

"Obi?"

"This," Hiroshi pointed to the wide belt in the image on the monitor. "It serves as a belt on the kimono, but it is actually a long piece of fabric, much like the fundoshi." Alex dunked his head in appreciation.

"That's what I think I most admire about Japanese culture, Hiroshi. Everything is so precise, so beautiful, well planned and executed, yet so very simple." Hiroshi gave Alex a doubtful look. "I mean, look ... no gaudy buckle, no belt loops ... a simple strip of fabric that does the job." Before Hiroshi could respond, Alex's phone vibrated. He looked at it, glanced guiltily at Hiroshi and picked it up. "A text from Raphael. We're supposed to run with Niki this afternoon." He tapped out a reply. "I told him I'm here with you and I'll be home in a few. What else should we discuss today?" Before either of them could speak, his phone vibrated again. Alex looked at the notification displayed without touching the phone. He looked at Hiroshi. "Oh, oh. He says he's coming over."

"We will need more tea," Hiroshi said as he closed his laptop to conceal the display, picked up the teapot and headed to the kitchen. Alex rose and began taking in Hiroshi's study. Unlike the library in the House of the Locked Cock Brotherhood, aside from a couple of bookcases, the door, and the street-facing window, most of the wall space was open, and much of it was covered with framed photos, artwork and ephemera. Some of the photos were of small groups of mostly men in party settings, outdoor venues, tables in restaurants. Many had been taken years ago, yet it was easy to spot a young, bespectacled and studious-looking, but arguably very cute Hiroshi.

"Oh wow," Alex muttered under his breath as he came across a photo of Hiroshi standing next to a taller Caucasian man with shoulder-length hair, his arm slung around Hiroshi's shoulders. They were at a gathering, a demonstration of some sort, both smiling into the camera. Behind them, towering over them on a platform, was a man with a bull horn ... Harvey Milk. So, Alex thought, Hiroshi hadn't just participated in the White Night demonstrations to go along with the crowd. He'd been a supporter of Milk, possibly throughout his career. Perhaps they'd even been acquaintances. Maybe even friends. That could explain why such an otherwise gentle soul clocked a cop. Alex was perusing other photos for familiar faces when Hiroshi returned, teapot and cup in hand and with Raphael by his side.

"Very nice," Raphael remarked, looking around the study while Hiroshi poured tea into the third cup. Hiroshi pulled up a chair for Raphael between his and Alex's, then sat. "Someday you'll have to tell me what other brilliant things you do in here when you're not planning a wedding with your collaborator, Hiroshi." Raphael looked at Alex as he sat and took the tea cup Hiroshi offered him. "I hope you haven't finalized the ceremony yet." Raphael took a sip of tea, glanced at the dwindling plate of senbei, then did his best attempt at a 'Brady' impression. "Please, please, may I have a cracker? I won't tell anyone." Alex rolled his eyes and held the plate toward Raphael.

"If you promise to leave right now, you can have them all," Alex replied. He addressed Hiroshi. "Clearly I knew what I was doing when I cast myself, and not this guy, as Brady." He turned back to Raphael as he set down the plate. "Are you just here for the crackers, or ...?" Raphael slowly munched his cracker, smiling and purposely delaying his answer to irritate Alex. He glanced at Hiroshi a couple of times without turning his head to make sure Hiroshi was appreciating this brotherly standoff. He swallowed.

"I'm not here to interfere. I'm sure Juan and Ricky's wedding is in the most capable of hands. But ... I do have a couple of suggestions, no, requests that I hope you will incorporate into the ceremony. I wanted you to know about them before you finalize everything." Raphael turned to Hiroshi, anticipating more deference from him, since Juan and Ricky had chosen him to conduct their ceremony. And since he wasn't Alex.

"One should always be open to good ideas, eh, Alex?" Hiroshi replied. Alex nodded, a bit apprehensively.

"Good," Raphael began, "because I sort of made a promise to Ricky, well, actually he made a request of me at our second wedding, produced by *you*, Alex. He asked me to be his ring bearer when he and Juan got married. I think he already knew in his heart that this day would come." Raphael momentarily met Hiroshi's gaze. "Hiroshi, he was naked, completely covered in glitter and was wearing a glowing baby blue cage in a room filled with a couple hundred strangers. To honor us on our wedding day. There was no way I could say no. So ... Alex, I need you to make me Juan and Ricky's glitter covered ring bearer." Alex stared at Raphael as if he hadn't understood a word he'd said. "I promised," Raphael pursued. Alex looked to Hiroshi, hoping for support.

"Are ring bearers traditional in a Buddhist ceremony, Hiroshi?" he asked, anticipating a 'no.'

"I believe they are now, Alex," Hiroshi grinned impishly as he reached out and patted Raphael's naked thigh. "Another adopted tradition for what is destined to be the second most memorable wedding of the century."

"Hiroshi," Alex protested, "you guys ... you don't know what you're asking here." He turned to Raphael. "It'll take forever to coat you in glitter. And afterwards, it'll take forever to clean you up. And assuming you want to be the *surprise* ring bearer, you'll miss virtually all of the ceremony." Raphael shrugged.

"I have an idea," Hiroshi said. He looked meaningfully at Alex. "And it will help to prevent marking you as a one-note wedding planner." Alex looked suspiciously at Hiroshi, then Raphael, not sure what was coming. "Maybe this will help you fulfill your promise to Ricky, Raphael. Just give me a minute." Hiroshi pulled his laptop onto his lap and spent a couple of minutes clicking around while Alex and Raphael laid waste to the plate of senbei. "Okay, here," Hiroshi announced as he reactivated the large monitor. On the screen a young Asian man appeared, naked, and completely gold-plated head to toe. At first, Raphael and Alex assumed it was a statue, but as the video advanced, it was clear it was a living, moving human, one who was, in fact, pleasuring himself.

"What the hell?" Alex asked.

"Whoa," Raphael leaned forward. "He's beautiful. How is that possible? Is it permanent?"

"Spray paint?" Alex assumed.

"Not exactly," Hiroshi explained, "he's coated with a mixture of powdered gold paint and coconut oil." Hiroshi brought up another video that showed two men, both completely golden skinned, enjoying sex with one another." Alex and Raphael both watched, rapt. After a moment, Alex turned to Raphael.

"You could never do that coated in glitter." Raphael laughed.

"Is this easy to do," he asked Hiroshi.

"Much easier, I suspect, than coating you in glitter. And easier to remove, as well. Alex, we could gold plate Raphael from the neck down, dress him similarly to how the rest of the wedding party will be outfitted, along with gloves, so the gold is hidden until time for the rings. Perhaps have some role for him in the beginning of the ceremony. Then, while Raphael retreats inside the house to strip and retrieve the rings, we could continue the ceremony. On cue, over an appropriate musical accompaniment ... and the visage of a naked, golden Raphael would certainly demand accompaniment ... Raphael, the ring bearer, could make his entrance and approach the grooms under the chuppah." Alex looked thoughtful a moment.

"Okay," he actually smiled at Hiroshi. "If you think we can pull this off, Hiroshi, it does add a little spice to the ceremony." He glanced at a beaming Raphael. "Looks like this ceremony won't be entirely nudity-free after all."

"No," Hiroshi chuckled, "but it is a sacrifice we will make to honor Ricky's request. Somehow, we will all just have to suffer through having a living, breathing, golden Adonis in our midst." Raphael raised a clenched fist to celebrate his victory.

"But what about Raphael's head?" Alex worried. "Will he have time to coat it in this paint stuff while he's out of sight to strip and get the rings?" He turned to Raphael. "I still think this means you'll miss a lot of the ceremony."

"Not necessarily, Alex. Raphael could wrap a sheer gold lamé scarf around his neck and head to blunt the disparity between his golden body and his flesh-colored head."

"A veil, in other words," Alex agreed. He glanced teasingly at Raphael. "Let's hope no one confuses you for the bride."

"Not much chance of that, since this," Raphael jiggled his cage, "will be on full display. It'll be gold plated, too, I assume?" Hiroshi nodded, wiggling his eyebrows, clearly delighted with Raphael's contribution to the ceremony.

"You had a second request for us to consider?" Hiroshi asked.

"I wasn't sure whether to bring this up to Juan and Ricky or you two. I'd like to invite Mama and Angel. I think Mama will be ready for a little road trip by Valentine's Day. It'll be a good reason for them to finally see the house, and it would be the perfect opportunity for her to thank Juan and Mateo in person for all the support they provided to her and Angel while she was in the hospital."

"I think you should ask Juan and Ricky," Hiroshi counseled, "but I am sure they will be honored. I would love to meet the rest of your family. In fact, I am not sure which I most look forward to ... a gold-plated ring bearer or meeting Raphael and Niki's family. What do you think, Alex?"

"It sounds great to me. Except." Raphael scowled at Alex. "Raphael. You just told us you want to be the bare-assed naked ring bearer. At a wedding attended by your mother."

"Oh. Yeah," realization dawned across Raphael's face. "Well ... she's seen me naked a thousand times."

"As a baby ..."

"An ass is an ass ... even if it's gold plated."

"And a cage is ...?" Raphael's eye widened. "And what about that audacious tattoo above your cage?"

"Oh. Damn ..." Raphael looked down at the tattoo above his cage, teetering on the horns of his dilemma. He painfully looked up at Hiroshi.

"What if ..." Alex proposed, "how about you wear just a fundoshi?" He turned to Hiroshi. "Can we find a gold color fundoshi?"

"Good idea," Raphael smiled, "but, no. I have to be naked, just like Ricky was ... in front of hundreds of strangers. I can't wimp out." Hiroshi, who had been ruminating thoughtfully, smiled and stood.

"Elder has your answer, Adonis. Wait here." Hiroshi left the study.

"Thanks for letting me invade your planning session, Alex," Raphael said. "Ricky will be so surprised."

"Yeah, and so will Mama," Alex cackled. Raphael knitted his brow, then laughed in spite of himself.

"Is this what's known as painting yourself into a corner?" Raphael asked. Alex nodded sagely.

"Ahem." Hiroshi appeared in the doorway, balancing a small toss pillow in both hands at waist level, over which he had draped his unfurled fundoshi, which hung down over the front and back of the pillow, past his knees. He ceremoniously paraded in a circle, approaching Alex and Raphael, then retreated back to the doorway. "Adonis, you said a bare ass was fair game. But, if I was wearing one, would you be able to see my cage?" Raphael shook his head, grinning. He turned to Alex and raised his right hand for a high-five.

"Brady, Elder has once again saved the day. And my ass." Hiroshi laid the pillow and fundoshi aside and approached Raphael and kneaded his shoulders from behind.

"Yours is an ass worth saving, my friend. I think I speak for Alex, and for the grooms, when I say both of your requests will enhance the ceremony greatly. Thank you. Alex, you and I should reconvene soon to continue our planning. But for now, my special powers tell me Niki is eager for the two of you to join him for your run." Alex and Raphael stood and pulled Hiroshi into a brief but firm hug.

## Two

ONE MONTH. FOUR WEEKS.

### Twenty-eight Days

A LITTLE AFTER NINE p.m., Steve quietly entered the library where Niki was engrossed in his laptop, preparing for an upcoming test. He set the bottle of cognac and two snifters on the low table between the two fireplace chairs, pressed the button to activate the gas fire, then walked around behind Niki. As he squeezed and rubbed Niki's shoulders, Niki sat back and sighed deeply.

"Simon says it's time you took a break," Steve whispered into Niki's ear. Niki chuckled.

"Is Simon going to take this physiology test for me?"

"He already did ... and you aced it. Come on ... don't make me drink alone." Steve pulled Niki's chair away from the desk, then spun it around. He grasped both of Niki's wrists and pulled him up and into a hug. Niki groaned but wrapped his arms around Steve, giving in to his very persuasive husband and handler. After they took their seats in front of the fire, Steve poured a mere half inch into each snifter, just enough to relax them both. They touched snifters, eyes locked, then sipped. The fire felt good.

"Thanks," Niki said quietly, licking his lips. "Once I get started, sometimes it's hard to stop."

"I know. And it's paid off for you. Look at you ... finishing last semester with a four point oh." Niki smiled into the fire. "I'm proud of you Niki. We all are." Niki continued smiling, a distant look in his eyes. He took another sip, followed by a heavy sigh.

"I know you're working hard, puppy, but are you having fun too?" Niki resumed eye contact with Steve.

"I wouldn't call it fun, but I'm happy with myself." He read the genuine pride in Steve's face. "It feels great to be accomplishing something worthwhile. I mean, aside from being loved by you, my life before was pretty inconsequential." Steve pulled his head back in reaction. "You know what I mean ..."

"Um, I think I know what you're trying to say, but, Niki, I disagree." Steve set his snifter down and leaned forward to lay a hand on Niki's knee and wiggle it. "Niki, you are worthy just as you are, okay? As a nursing student. As the amazing nurse you will no doubt be. But also as the 'puptender extraordinaire' who had men lined up just for the chance to buy a beer from you. Do you think Mama would love you any less if you weren't in nursing school?" Steve picked up his snifter and sat back, without breaking eye contact. "Although, I have to admit, she does seem to enjoy bragging about you to other nurses now ..." Niki smiled in spite of himself at that and took another sip. Steve paused a moment, debating whether he was accurately reading between Niki's lines. He didn't want to assume Niki had insecurities that didn't exist.

"Niki, I can't fully appreciate what it must have been like for you to find yourself rejected and on the street at fourteen. I really can't ... but I am certain it had to be immensely traumatic for you. I mean, even though Raphael's family immediately took you in and cared for you, you still must have suffered. For a long time. I just hope that my love for you, Mama's love, the love from every member of this family we've created can overcome any hurt you still feel from that awful time."

"Oh, I've healed, Steve. I'm a very lucky guy. And I know it." Niki raised his snifter as he gazed around the room, his room, before resuming eye contact with Steve. "I mean it. I really am happy. And you, mister, are the main reason I am." Steve tilted his snifter toward Niki, then sipped.

"Okay. I believe you. And, yes, I do consider it my solemn duty to make sure you're happy. Wherever that may lead us."

"Yeah," Niki laughed, "you've definitely gone above and beyond on that score. Like I said, I'm pretty lucky." They both sat silently a moment, sipping and playing footsie in front of the fire.

"So," Steve eventually spoke, "it's really none of my business, but ... since I brought the subject up a moment ago ... have you thought any more about calling your mother?" Niki took another sip, holding eye contact with Steve, formulating an answer.

"Every time I walk past the dresser and see the piece of paper Greg gave me ... yeah. But. I don't know. Should I?" Steve looked into Niki's eyes, waiting him out. A technique he'd long ago perfected in dealing with his 'man of few words.' "I guess maybe I should." He made a nearly silent groaning sound. Then it was his turn to wait Steve out.

"Are you afraid she'll hurt you again?" Niki closed his eyes and slightly shook his head.

"No. I don't think she can. Like I said, I've healed."

"Here's what I think, sweetie. She went to some effort to find you and try to see you. It's been a long time. You've changed. Maybe she's changed. You made it pretty clear to her that day we were marching for Black Lives that you are a force to be reckoned with. And, still, she came looking for you. Maybe she has something important to say to you. Something you deserve to hear. She knows where we live. Maybe invite her here, on your turf, to find out what she wants. And to show her what she's been missing all these years." Steve's subtle compliment brought another smile to Niki's face.

"Yeah, but what if she shows up with a bunch of church ladies?" Niki's smile grew coy as he relaxed into the idea of seeing his mother again. "Coming to convert me back to the messed-up kid I was back then?"

"Then she'd leave sorely disappointed. I know you're kidding, but she came alone the first time, Niki. Greg said she seemed really disappointed that she'd missed you. I think she just wants some time with you." Niki heaved another sigh, then slowly drained the last few drops of cognac from his snifter.

"Maybe after this test, Thursday. I'll call her. Get it over with." Steve nodded and reached out for Niki's empty snifter. He held it up as he looked through it at Niki.

"Remember when the thought of sitting here in front of the fire with a glass of cognac was just a wishful dream, Niki? It's not a dream anymore. It's our reality. Remember that. You can do anything you set your mind to."

"What's up, Alex?" Raphael asked on behalf of the group that Alex had assembled in the dining room. It was mid-afternoon, and everyone was present except for Juan, Ricky and Mateo, who were all working. "I'm guessing this is about the wedding?"

"Good guess," Alex replied as he opened his laptop. "I won't take too much of your time, but I wanted to run something past all of you while Juan and Ricky are out. Ryan and I can fill Mateo in later, depending on what you guys think." Alex explained about Hiroshi's suggestion of including a chuppah in the ceremony, and about how most people typically rent them, like so many other accessories that will never be needed again after the ceremony.

"I have a better idea," Alex continued. "But, we would all need to go in on it. *If* you agree it's worth doing." He swung the laptop around to show everyone an image of an octagonal gazebo. Luke glanced at Raphael then back at Alex, looking confused. "No, Luke, this isn't a chuppah. Instead of renting, what if we all go together and get a gazebo for the garden as our collective wedding present to Juan and Ricky? We'd partially assemble it to create the chuppah for the wedding, then, afterwards, reassemble it completely as this gazebo."

"You can do that?" Niki asked. Alex confidently nodded.

"Oh yeah. We'd just drape some fabric over the top of four of these posts to make the chuppah, instead of the roof you see here. Piece of cake."

"It's an interesting idea, Alex," Steve said as he looked around the table for other reactions. "So, this is a kit? We wouldn't need any special carpentry tools? Or skills?"

"Correct. What's really cool is it's recycled redwood, so no new trees have been cut down. And it'll last forever." Alex waited for the inevitable question. His wait wasn't long.

"Recycled redwood is very cool, Alex," Raphael said. "And, I'm guessing, expensive."

"Can we really put a price on Juan and Ricky's happiness?" Alex replied. Luke burst out laughing. He turned to Raphael.

"Alex would make a great used car salesman, if Cynthia ever decides to give him the boot." This time it was Raphael's turn to simply shake his head. He sat back, folded his arms and waited for Alex to elaborate.

"This baby here," Alex pointed at the laptop, playing off of Luke's snide comment, "will only set us back" and then he mumbled inaudibly. Raphael cleared his throat. "Okay, six thousand dollars." Steve coughed. Ryan gasped. Raphael whistled. "Guys ... it'll last forever!"

"So ..." Ryan instantly did the math in his head. "Seven-hundred-fifty dollars each." He looked worried.

"No, that's not what I'm suggesting," Alex said as he took a seat and joined the rest of the group. "Don't worry about the cost, Ryan. Right now, I just want to know if everybody likes the idea. If we're going to do this, we need to place the order right away to get it in time for the wedding. We can make the finances work for everybody."

"I like the idea of a gazebo for the garden," Niki confirmed, "but I don't quite get how it would be a wedding present for Juan and Ricky. I mean, we'd all use it, wouldn't we?"

"Yes, but every time they sit in it, it would bring back memories of their big day."

"That's a bit of a stretch, Alex," Luke said, "but I see your point. I don't really have any other great ideas for a wedding present, I guess."

"I'm a little biased," Greg admitted, "since I'm married to the wedding planner, but I vote yes. It would be a nice addition to the garden. Steve? Raphael?"

"I wish I knew what Ricky and Juan would say," Raphael replied. "If they liked the idea, then, yeah, I'd have to vote yes after the contribution Ricky made to our wedding," He turned to Steve.

"Yeah," Steve chuckled. "Good point, Raphael. We should do whatever we can to make their wedding 'legendary.'"

"Oh," Alex glanced meaningfully at Raphael. "It will be. Rest assured."

"Really?" Luke reacted. "As legendary as ours?" He was looking at Raphael as he spoke. Raphael refused to make eye contact.

"So, you really think we could put this thing together on our own?" Raphael asked Alex, changing the subject.

"Pretty sure. Worst case scenario we get a couple of your friends from the gym to help out. I still have contact information for them from your wedding." Raphael nodded, still not looking at Luke. Ryan hadn't said anything for a while, prompting Greg to mollify what was almost certainly on his mind.

"Ryan, don't worry about the cost. We'll talk later, but I have a suggestion that I think will ease your concerns. With that in mind, what do you think of the idea?" Ryan, who was sitting nearest Alex, reached out and pulled the laptop closer and scrolled down and back up the web page. He pushed the laptop back toward Alex and grinned.

"I think it would be an epic wedding present. It sure beats a blender." He looked mischievously at Niki and then Luke. "After dark it would be a perfect setting for a secret ritual. Or a round of truth serum." Alex nodded at Ryan, then closed the laptop and stood.

"I still want to run this by my collaborator," he concluded, "but thanks for the votes of confidence, guys. I'll keep you posted." Alex and Greg headed into the foyer and up the stairs, with Ryan not far behind. Raphael put a hand on Luke's shoulder as he addressed him along with Steve and Niki.

"Even at six thousand dollars, I'm pretty sure we're getting off cheap compared to what Alex and Greg spent on our 'reception.'"

"I was thinking the same thing," Steve nodded. "Since the ceremony is going to be simple and small ... I have that right, don't I, Raphael? This is one way we can at least make their day go on and on forever, as Alex was saying."

"I honestly don't know much about the ceremony," Raphael said with a clear conscience, "but I think you're right, Steve. It can't possibly be anything like ours' was. Coming up with an 'epic' gift that will be a lasting memento of the ceremony was another stroke of genius by Alex."

"Glowing cages," Luke agreed as he stood and pushed in his chair. "Sarong clad grooms. Convertible chuppahs. What will Alex think of next?"

"Yeah," Niki laughed as he, too, stood. "He really is in the wrong business, isn't he?"

"Luke, maybe I *should* become a car salesman," Alex announced, standing in the doorway to the gym, where Luke, Raphael and Steve were midway through a workout. Raphael was spotting Luke, who eased the barbell into place on the bench supports, then sat up.

"Because …?" Alex entered and sat next to Steve on the other bench.

"Not only does Hiroshi like the idea of the gazebo, he insists on going in on it with us. Greg has a good idea, too. He'll be here in a minute. This isn't going to be as expensive as we thought." As Luke and Raphael switched places, Greg entered and stood behind Alex, resting his hands on Alex's shoulders. Alex looked up and said, "I told them about Hiroshi." Greg nodded.

"What do you guys think of this?" Greg posed. "Luke, I took your advice and have been putting Mateo's rent contributions, both at our old place and here, in a separate account. For when he got a place of his own. But I don't see him leaving the House of the Locked Cock Brotherhood any time soon. And Ryan hasn't begun to eat his way through the check his parents gave us for his room and board. So, I thought we could take five hundred dollars from each of those accounts as their contributions to the gazebo. That way they don't have to come up with any out of pocket, and they'll still feel like they're making a meaningful contribution to Juan and Ricky's wedding." Both Luke and Raphael nodded.

"That sounds good," Steve said. "And that's awfully generous of Hiroshi."

"I guess I'm not surprised," Luke met Steve's gaze. "He and Juan have a history together that none of us fully understands. I think Hiroshi is not so secretly elated to see Juan this happy, marrying Ricky."

"Yeah," Alex agreed. "He's loving his role as their wedding planner. Co-Wedding planner. And, guys, he's also insisting on hosting all of us after the ceremony. It won't just be crackers and tea."

"Any other details you'd like to share, Mr. Co-Wedding Planner?" Steve asked, no doubt fruitlessly.

"Hey, we just saved you a bunch of money. That's all the news you need for now." He stood and wrapped an arm around Greg's waist. "Besides, this guy and I have KP duty today. Something that involves fresh home-made pasta, amiright?" Greg smiled and nodded, then led Alex out of the gym.

"Okay, Sir," Raphael said as he slid into place under the barbell. "If we're eating pasta, I'm going to need you to coach me through an extra set. Or, two."

Ryan heard Mateo bounding up the back stairs after depositing his street clothes in the washer. Mateo, having learned his lesson, didn't try to sneak up on Ryan at his laptop, but he did plant a kiss on Ryan's neck before turning tail and heading into the bath to decontaminate. Newer information from the CDC had downplayed the risk of transmitting COVID through touch and surfaces. However, after Mama's and Angel's experiences, no one in the House of the Locked Cock Brotherhood was taking any chances. Ryan turned when he heard Mateo come out of the bathroom, but, to Ryan's surprise, before he could say anything, Mateo darted out of the room. He turned back to his laptop and resumed reading. It wasn't long before he felt Mateo's left hand on the back of his neck, Mateo's right hand dangling a familiar set of keys in front of the laptop screen.

"Is time!" Mateo declared as Ryan spun around.

"Already?" Ryan grinned as he reached out and pulled Mateo into his lap. The lack of daylight between their lips prevented any further discussion for the moment. When Mateo finally pulled free, he responded.

"Yes. Today is one month." Mateo stood. Ryan looked down at his cage. Luke's cage, technically, but one Ryan had worn far longer than Luke ever had. He realized that he hadn't thought twice about it all day. Nor the collar. Like a pair of glasses, they'd naturally become a part of him. Mateo bent down and slid a key into the padlock on his collar, then pulled it free of Ryan's neck. Ryan reached up and felt the emptiness there. Then, Mateo reached out for Ryan's hand to coax him up and out of the chair.

"Maybe we have Luke unlock you? Like for your cleanings?"

"No, I want you to do it. That was just because we didn't trust either of us to unlock me before. But now ..." Mateo cut Ryan off with another quick lip lock, then dropped to his knees. He fumbled the key briefly, then pulled the brass lock out of the hot pink Holy Trainer. In seconds Ryan was freed. With the cock ring still in place, Mateo immediately swallowed the one part of Ryan that had been denied him for exactly one month. For the first time in more than thirty days, Mateo was serving Ryan. He was almost humming as he sucked, apparently ravenous. His hands gripping Ryan's waist, his thumbs pressing into Ryan's hip bones.

Ryan's cock pressing against the back of his throat. It felt so good. For both of them.

Ryan, eyes closed, buried his hands into Mateo's mane. He loved the feel of Mateo's hair, nearly as long as Juan's, and just as beautiful. As Mateo pulled back far enough to breathe, Ryan pulled out and dropped down to Mateo's level.

"Not so fast, sweet Prince. I've been locked for a month. We need to go slower. You almost made me come already." He stood, pulling Mateo with him, then pushed Mateo backwards, laughing, onto the bed. Ryan crawled on top of him, the two wrestling for position. And possession. Mateo, the Prince, was determined to serve his long denied, self-appointed sex slave. For some reason, this time, Ryan seemed more than willing to submit.


"I have kind of a weird request," Niki said after the first bite of his short stack of Ricky's pancakes. This Sunday's version was new, somehow made with granola mixed in, and the verdict was unanimous. Five stars. Niki looked at Greg, who, along with everyone else, was looking at him expectantly. "I, uh, finally called my mother." He glanced briefly at Steve, then returned his gaze to Greg. "Steve and I agreed I should at least follow up on the conversation she had with you, Greg." He set his fork down with a sigh. "We didn't talk long. I just invited her here to find out what was on her mind. She agreed right away. She's coming tomorrow afternoon, around one." No one said anything, waiting Niki out. He sat back and shared eye contact with Raphael and Ricky, who'd also put his fork down. Niki heaved another sigh. "I don't know what to expect, but, anyway, she's coming. I thought we'd meet in the garden if it's warm enough. In case we start screaming at each other." Niki glanced at Steve with a stifled chuckle. "In case I start screaming again, based on our last encounter. Anyway, if it goes well, maybe I'll show her the house, including our bedroom. Show off a little bit. Rub it in. I don't know ..." Another sigh. "So, what I wanted to ask is, when you hear the doorbell, it might be a good idea if you close your doors until she leaves. So we don't freak her out with our cages and everything." It was clear to everyone that this impending encounter with his mother was already traumatizing Niki.

"Niki ..." Raphael spoke, then stopped, his eyes finishing his sentence.

"I'll be fine, Raffie. It's okay. Like I told Steve, she can't hurt me anymore."

"Do you have any idea what she wants?" Juan asked. Niki shook his head as he picked up his fork and took another bite.

"Wouldn't it be better if we all dressed, and met her, so she could see the rest of your family?" Luke asked. "At least the ones who aren't out working tomorrow?" Niki swallowed.

"Maybe. I don't know. I don't want to interrupt you guys. She'll meet Steve again if I decide on the tour."

"I can hold off on the deliveries for a while, tomorrow, if you want," Ricky offered. "We did a pretty good job impressing Ryan's mom and dad." He flashed a grin at Ryan who grinned back before swallowing.

"Yeah, they couldn't say enough good things about you guys. My mom has even made your Mama's artichoke soup for my dad."

"Well, I guess it's up to you guys," Niki relented. "If it goes well ... I don't know, if your doors are open, and it seems like a good idea, I'll introduce you. I mean, it's not like she's Mama."

"No," Raphael said quietly, resuming eye contact. "But Niki she was ... is ... your mother. I think you're very brave to do this. But, no matter what, Mama is still our Mama, who has always loved you for who you are. And your mother can never take that away from us." Niki nodded and smiled. Steve put an arm around Niki's shoulders as he dug into his short stack again.

Three

## The Reunion

EVEN THOUGH HE WAS expecting it, Niki was startled when the door-bell rang just before one p.m. He was more anxious than he was willing to admit. He and Steve had talked and agreed, at least initially, it would be best for Niki to spend time with his mother alone. Steve's presence would likely inhibit the free flow of whatever it was she wanted to com-municate. Niki closed his laptop and walked anxiously out of the library and over to the front doors. He opened one, half expecting to find the gang of church ladies he'd joked about to Steve. But, no, his mother was alone.

"Hey," Niki greeted her, then stepped aside. "Come in." Gladys hes-itated a moment, slowly taking Niki in, then nodded wordlessly and stepped into the foyer. He seemed taller in this more confined setting than he had appeared at the march, standing next to his even taller ... husband.

"Thank you for inviting me," Gladys said as she looked around the foyer, glancing into the sitting room.

"Of course," Niki replied as he closed the door. "I apologize for not calling you sooner. It's been pretty hectic lately." He felt awkward, seeing and talking to his mother like this. After so many years, she seemed more like a stranger than a family member. "Let's go in here." He motioned to the library, where he'd lit the fire. "I originally thought we might sit in the garden, but it's still a little cool today. I thought the fire might be nice." Gladys nodded and followed him to the fireplace chairs. As they walked, she studied the way his mohawk tapered to a point at the base of his skull, just above the collar of his turtleneck. Niki motioned to Steve's chair. "Can I take your jacket?"

"You may," Gladys replied, unconsciously correcting his grammar. Something she'd always done. She turned her back, inviting Niki to help her out of it. He obliged.

"Have a seat. I'll hang this in the hall closet. We have coffee and tea ... Earl Grey ... which would you like?"

"Oh. I'm fine." Niki nodded and started for the foyer. "Well, maybe coffee. Black is fine." Niki smized and disappeared. Gladys was staring into the fire when he returned with two mugs and set them on the low table. He closed the pocket doors, then sat.

"I know neither of us has been vaccinated yet," Niki said, "but I guess this means we'll have to take our masks off. To drink." Gladys was smiling when she peeled away the navy blue mask that matched her outfit.

"Yes. That's why I changed my mind about the coffee. I wanted to see your face." Niki couldn't help but smile at that, as he peeled his mask off as well. Gladys picked up her mug and sipped. "That's good," she said. "Thank you ... Niki. Forgive me if I accidentally call you Nicholas. You know ..." Niki nodded wordlessly. Gladys didn't take her eyes off Niki as she sipped again. "You've uh ... you've grown into quite the handsome young man." Niki coughed a subtle laugh and set his mug down.

"Thank you, I guess. I can't take any credit for it, but thanks." He hesitated a moment, not sure how to respond further, then said, "You haven't really changed at all."

"Oh," she said, breaking eye contact, looking down at the floor between them. "I'm sure I've changed." Then, resuming eye contact, "But I'll take that as a compliment." Niki nodded. She sipped again, holding her warm mug with both hands, and looked around the room. "This is some room, Niki. Some house." She looked at him, inviting a response. An explanation. "I guess you really meant it when you told me that day at the protest that you live in a 'fabulous home.'" Niki couldn't resist.

"Well, as you know, I always tell the truth." It was Gladys' turn to nod.

"It's not just you and your ... Steve ... who live here?"

"Oh no. You already met Greg. Our whole family is here. Ten of us." Gladys looked startled.

"Ten of you? In one house?" Niki had to laugh.

"It's not as crazy as it sounds. We're five couples; three married couples, another couple getting married in just a few weeks. Mateo and Ryan are still just boyfriends, but very serious. We've all been extremely close for a long time, so when the house became available it just made sense for all of us to move in together. Each couple has our own suite. In fact, Steve and I have a whole floor to ourselves." He paused a moment, seeing that she was processing what he'd said. "If you want, I'll give you a little tour later." She nodded eagerly. "It's worked out really well, all of us living here. We enjoy being together. Actually, I should have said eleven of us. Our next-door neighbor, Hiroshi, is really part of the family, too. He's in our 'bubble' and spends a lot of time here." Gladys was looking around the room again, taking in all the books.

"Well, you all must have done very well for yourselves."

"We've done okay, yeah," Niki replied. He saw no reason to go into too much detail. "Steve, Greg, Alex and Raphael all work from home. The pandemic. Luke goes in a couple days a week and Juan, Mateo and Ricky are all front-line workers, so they're out every day. Juan's an OR nurse. Surgery. Ryan and I are taking our classes remotely mostly, but he has one lab on campus. So, we're all pretty busy, but we do dinner together. Sunday breakfast. It's nice." Gladys set her mug down and looked eagerly at Niki.

"Classes. So, you're in college now?" Niki smiled.

"Yeah. SF State. I'm studying to be a nurse, as well." Gladys smiled, too, wordlessly expressing satisfaction. Maybe undeserved pride.

"You getting good grades?"

"Dean's list."

"I knew it. You got your father's looks, and my brains." Niki's eye roll over his mother's bi-directional compliment was unconscious, automatic. But it triggered a laugh from Gladys. Her first. However, it was brief, before she became reserved again. "You've had your own pandemic experience. Your friend Greg said." Niki screwed up his face.

"Mama and Angel both got COVID, yeah. Angel did okay. Minor symptoms. You remember Angel?"

"I do. Sweet boy."

"He's not a boy any more, but he's still sweet. Mama, though, was really sick. It was very scary for a while. Like Juan said, we were lucky she got it in December, when the docs and nurses knew a lot more about how to treat it. She's still not back to normal, but she's home now and making progress."

"I said a little prayer for her after talking to your friend. I hope you don't mind."

"That was nice of you. Actually, we all did what we could to send good thoughts to Mama and Angel. Juan worked his magic on her nurses so we could visit with her in the ICU over Zoom. We did a video to cheer her up. I think it helped. Helped us." Gladys pondered a moment before replying.

"So that's where you went that night. To Angel's house. I never knew ..." The next words caught in her throat. Niki calmly sipped his tea, making eye contact without speaking, without offering a comforting comment. Gladys recovered a bit and leaned forward. "I cried every night after you left. For a long time. I didn't know if you were alive or dead." She took a deeper breath. "I expected you to come home after an hour. Or two. I never thought you'd stay away for good, Nicholas."

"What did you expect? After everything you and Dad said?" He paused, staring into Gladys' eyes. "It wasn't even my idea to leave." Gladys had no answer for that.

"I know. After a few nights, your father and I started sleeping apart. I took your bed. I guess I was heartbroken. I think we started blaming each other instead of ourselves. Instead of you."

"Me? How was I to blame?"

"You weren't, honey. I know that now. That's what I'm saying. But we surely blamed each other."

"Do you still blame each other?" Gladys gave Niki a strange look and sat back in her chair. She picked up her cup and sipped, then swallowed. Twice.

"That's one of the reasons I wanted to see you again. Now that I knew you were here. Niki. Your father passed. Last summer." Despite everything, Niki felt an invisible blow to his chest. He looked into the fire a moment as he drew a deep breath, then back at Gladys.

"Oh. I'm sorry." Gladys faintly shrugged.

"Don't be. There's nothing you can do about it. I ... I thought you should know."

"How?"

"It was COVID, like your ... Mama. It didn't help that he smoked. Co-morbidity they called it." Niki nodded, lips pursed.

"Well, I'm sorry ... for you."

"Thank you, for that. But it's not like we were all that close the last few years. More like tenants in common than man and wife."

"I just hope you're okay." Gladys could tell from Niki's eyes that he really meant it.

"Well, let me ask you something. Will I get to see you again? After today?"

"Sure. Of course." Gladys nodded with her brightest smile yet.

"Then, I'm okay. I'm fine." She took a last sip and set her mug down. "Nicho ... Niki, after seeing you at the protest I've constantly thought about you. I was so happy to see you again. To see you ... in a good place. To know you hadn't ended up, I don't know ..."

"In a gang? Or homeless?" Gladys closed her eyes and nodded. Niki laughed.

"Last time I looked there weren't any gay gangs, Black or otherwise." He paused, seeing that his insolence wasn't appreciated. He hadn't meant to discount her very real anguish. "No, I couldn't have been in a better place. Mama and Pop were wonderful from that very first night. And Angel and Raphael are the best brothers anyone could ask for. We're still very close to this day." Niki looked up toward Luke and Raphael's room above them. "I mean, Raphael and I still live together."

"You haven't said much about your Pop. Did he not get COVID along with your Mama?" Niki's eyes darkened.

"No, Mama lives alone. Pop died, what? About five years ago. He died too young, too. He didn't smoke, like Dad, but he liked to eat. He had a cute belly on him." Niki paused in thought. "He died of diabetes complications. I think he was happiest when all of us were together. Eating. Maybe that's why I enjoy our family dinners here so much."

"Sounds like you still miss him."

"Oh yeah. A lot. He was a really cool guy. Everybody liked him. He could be pretty funny." Niki paused, staring into the fire a moment. "Whenever one of us kids had a birthday, he'd first give us some really lame, but nicely wrapped present. Like a pair of socks. And pretend that was all we were getting. Every time. It threw me the first time, but fortunately it was Raphael's birthday, so I learned how to just play along with him. Until the real present came out. It sounds corny talking about it, but he always got a kick out of it." Niki looked seriously at Gladys. "He loved Raphael and me just as much as he loved Angel. Our being gay was never an issue for him. Or Mama. He was as proud of us as he was of Angel." Gladys closed her eyes again, longer this time. Then she returned Niki's serious gaze.

"Well, if it isn't already obvious to you, Niki, I'm proud of you, too." She slapped her thigh. "Oh, shoot!"

"What?"

"Hearing you talk about presents reminded me. I guess I was so nervous when I left to come here." Gladys tsked. Three times. "Niki, after you left, I got a birthday present for you. Every year. For when you came back. I saved them all. I was going to bring them with me. To give you now." She looked morose.

"It's okay," Niki replied, feeling oddly guilty. "Um ... next time. Something to look forward to." Gladys visibly brightened. "That was a thoughtful thing to do. Strange, but thoughtful." She smiled.

"I should warn you, though. You've probably aged out of some of them now."

"It doesn't matter. You know ... it's the thought that counts, right?" He wiggled his eyebrows. "Now I'm intrigued." Gladys laughed again, no longer irritated with herself. Niki drained his mug.

"Ready for that tour? It's free." Gladys stood, replaced her mask and smoothed the front of her dress.

"As long as the tour ends back here. In this room. I have one more thing to share with you." Niki's smile faded. "Oh, honey, it's nothing bad. You'll see. Now ... where do we start?"

Niki gave it his all. Adding little anecdotes as they moved from room to room on the first floor, and up the grand staircase, on to the second, where all doors but Ricky and Juan's were dutifully closed. Niki took Gladys into their room so she could see at least one of the other suites. Upstairs, they also entered his and Steve's room, where Steve was working, so Niki could show off their well-appointed bath. Steve was guarded, but gracious, as was Gladys. He was pleased and intrigued to detect an unexpected comfort level between Niki and Gladys. There were no secretive appeals for rescue from Niki, so Steve went back to work as they left the room. After descending the back stairs, Niki showed off the garden, where, he explained, Juan and Ricky's ceremony would be held. Gladys insisted on examining some of the plantings more closely, admiring and identifying some of the plants that Niki had enjoyed, but never bothered to analyze so carefully. As they passed through the kitchen on their way back to the library, Gladys paused.

"They must be some gourmet dinners you all have with a kitchen like this, or is this just for show?"

"Oh, no. We take full advantage of it. Greg makes pasta from scratch. Ricky has a secret recipe for pancakes. Mateo does fresh squeezed OJ on Sundays. We make our own espresso. Raphael's a whiz, too. Curries and seafood. It's a real working kitchen." After Niki led them back to the library, Gladys did a quick circuit around the room, surveying the many volumes on the shelves before ending up before Niki, standing in front of the fire. She just looked at him a moment, wordlessly taking him in, one last time.

"It breaks my heart to say this, Niki, but you were probably right." Niki unconsciously tilted his head, pup-like, not understanding. "That day at the march, when you said we'd done you a favor by forcing you away." Tears began forming in her eyes. "You've done so very well for yourself, on your own, without us. Without me." Gladys sniffed and looked up, organizing her words, then returned to Niki. "I told you earlier I kept thinking about you after that day. I wanted to know more. I mean, there was so much I didn't know. I wanted to believe you ... that you really were living a good life. When I couldn't find any trace of you on social media, I started spending time here in the Castro, just walking mostly, assuming you might live in the neighborhood, hoping I might catch sight of you again. I hope that doesn't sound disturbing to you, but I didn't know what else to do." She laughed. "I can't tell you how many cups of Peet's coffee I've bought before walking around, trying to look inconspicuous. Until finally, one day, I saw you with who I thought was Angel and another man, jogging. Lucky for me, you seemed to be at the end of your run, because you all slowed down enough that I could follow you. When I saw the three of you come into this house, that's when I knew for sure you were doing okay. You really were living in a 'fabulous house.' With people who cared about you. You all had your arms around each other going up those steps." Tears were still brimming in Gladys' eyes.

"Niki, honey ... sweetheart ... we were so wrong. I was so wrong. I thought I was doing the right thing by you. To protect you. To save you." The last words were whispered as Gladys put her hand to her forehead and rubbed, eyes closed a moment, which forced a couple of tears out and down her cheeks. She dropped her hand and faced Niki stoically. "There was nothing wrong with you. I know that now. I've known it for some time. I just wanted to be able to say to you, in person, that I was the one who was so very wrong. I hope someday, somehow, you'll find it in your heart to forgive me. I'm not asking you to forsake your Mama, any of your new family. You belong with them, now. I ... I don't deserve you. But, Nicholas ... Niki, I've never stopped loving you. You were and are ... and always will be my baby. And if you can find it in your heart to forgive me, I'll finally have a little peace."

They faced each other in silence. Niki didn't know what to say. She was asking a lot. Maybe too much. But, then again, he'd said it himself. She and his father had unwittingly done him a favor by throwing him out, at the age of fourteen. Over a self-righteous, doctrinaire, prejudiced, parochial ... lack of understanding. An unwillingness, grounded in religion, to even try to understand. Not to mention, it was an act devoid of even a shred of compassion. It really seemed like a lot to ask. When he realized he was unconsciously torturing Gladys with his silence, Niki broke eye contact and sat back down in his chair. Gladys remained standing.

"I was a little kid." He looked up at her with those brown puppy dog eyes. "I just wanted to be happy." Gladys dropped down on one knee in front of Niki, putting herself on his level.

"And I ... I wanted you to be saved. The things I said that night. I believed them. I thought my beliefs were more sacred than what you might think or believe. In the moment, I really thought I was doing what was best for you. But, like I said, Niki, I have learned how wrong I was. I've learned a lot. You said I haven't changed, but Niki, I have. I have." She put a hand on Niki's knee for support as she stood. It was the first time they had touched. "Well, I've said my piece. I wanted you to know about Dad. And, mostly, I wanted you to know that I will never judge you again. Or any of your new family. Or anyone, really. It makes me happy to know you're happy. And, like your Pop, Niki, and I know I don't deserve it, but you do make me very proud. If you would please get my coat, I should go now, so you can talk to your husband about what we've said. I'm sure he can help you decide if I deserve even a little forgiveness. He seems like a pretty good guy." Niki smized at that as he stood. Gladys was pulling out all the stops, to get Niki to forgive her. To get what she wanted. He'd forgotten how good she was at that. But he hadn't forgotten how to keep her waiting. He walked away and retrieved her coat. He held it up so she could turn and slide her arms in.

"Thank you, Niki. You've been a charming host." He gave her the slightest smize, then walked out into the foyer and approached the front doors.

"You've given me a lot to think about. A lot. Thanks for letting me know about Dad. I guess I should also thank you for putting so much effort into tracking me down. Literally."

"Well, I know you won't necessarily agree, but I believe it was God's plan that I would find you." Niki chuckled.

"It sounds like you're ready to respect my beliefs, so I guess it's only right for me to respect yours."

"That's very Christian of you, Niki." Niki opened his mouth, then wordlessly closed it. He opened the door and stepped outside to usher Gladys out.

"Can I ... may I call you a Lyft ride home?"

"No, thank you. I'll be fine. Give my best to your family. All of them." She turned and slowly descended the steps.

Niki retreated into the foyer and closed the door. He wondered if he should have hugged her. But somehow it hadn't felt right, not yet, anyway. He turned to find Raphael standing at the base of the staircase, clothed actually, in case introductions had been in order. Niki approached Raphael and the two sat together, their feet on the bottom step. Raphael wrapped an arm around Niki's shoulders. For a moment, neither spoke. Niki sighed.

"You okay?" Niki nodded as he peeled off his mask. He turned to Raphael.

"My dad's dead."

"Oh wow." Raphael squeezed Niki. "Is that why she wanted to see you?"

"Partly. She wants me to forgive her. Tell her what she and Dad did was wrong, but it's all in the past. Something like that. No big deal, you know?" He took a deep breath. "Sorry. I'm being a dick. She was very contrite. I think she really regrets what they did. So, maybe not only was it the best thing for me, but maybe she's a better person today because of it, too. Or something. I don't know. Oh ... and get this. One day when she saw you, Alex and me running? She thought you were Angel."

"Yeah. In his dreams," Raphael scoffed. Niki laughed, a very much needed laugh. Raphael slid his hand down Niki's back. "Listen, since we're already dressed, go get Steve. I'll get Luke and the four of us can go get lunch in one of the parklets. My treat. You can fill us all in. As much or as little as you want." Niki landed a peck on Raphael's cheek and dashed up the stairs.

# Four

## ANOTHER MOMENTOUS DELIVERY

"I'LL GET IT!" ALEX shouted as he hopped out of his door, trying to pull on shorts and walk at the same time. He zipped up at the bottom of the stairs and raced to the front door. He knew who it was, thanks to an earlier text message.

"Hi, I'll be right with you," he greeted the driver. "We're actually going to unload it next door." Alex dashed back to his cubby and pulled out an LCB tee and his running shoes. Niki came to the library door. "Niki, if you're not too busy, can you help unload the gazebo? We're going to stash it in Hiroshi's garden." Niki gave the driver a little thrill as he raced, bare-assed, up the stairs. Thirty minutes later Hiroshi, Alex, Niki and Ryan were surveying the many boxes containing what would soon be a makeshift chuppah and eventually a much larger gazebo. At Hiroshi's direction, they'd arranged two of the longer containers a few feet apart, then layered all the other boxes across them, crisscrossed, to minimize contact with the ground. It took a while for Alex to find the box containing the assembly instructions.

"Man, I hope I don't end up regretting this," he looked warily at Hiroshi. "It seemed like a good idea at the time." The assembly instructions ran more than twenty pages. Hiroshi reached out for them.

"Let me take a look at this, Alex," he replied. "You all have work and studies to attend to. I will try to decipher this and make a plan for the chuppah." Niki and Ryan both headed for the gate. "Alex, when you have time later we should convene another meeting of the wedding planners. I will have a suggestion on how to proceed with the chuppah, and I have something else to show you." Alex promised to try to wrap up his day early.

When Alex returned, a little after four p.m., Hiroshi was sitting on his back steps making notes on a drawing pad, an old-school pencil and paper artist's drawing pad. Alex sat next to him.

"Have you figured it out?"

"Yes, I think we can make your concept a reality, Alex." Hiroshi flipped back a couple of sheets to show Alex a perspective drawing of the chuppah, with legends associated with the various components. "We use the posts from box A-Two as the uprights and the slats from boxes D-One and D-Two for the cross beams to stabilize the posts. We should be able to use the angle irons and bolts that will eventually connect the parts for the gazebo, so we should not need to drill any new holes." Alex nodded, then grinned at Hiroshi.

"Thanks for making me look smarter than I am, Hiroshi. This should work." Hiroshi chuckled and clapped Alex on the back. "I'm still a little worried about actually assembling the gazebo itself." He looked over at the stack of boxes. "There's so much to it."

"I have a friend who is very skilled at these sorts of things. He owns a couple of rental properties, and I helped him build a deck in the garden of one of them a couple of years ago. It is still standing." Hiroshi flashed a proud grin. "If you invite him to one of your three-star Michelin dinners, I am sure I can talk him into giving us a hand. He loves a project like this."

"That sounds great." Alex looked wistfully at Hiroshi. "You always have an answer for everything. I wonder how long it will take us to build it ... the gazebo, I mean. It would be nice if we could build it while Juan and Ricky are out working, so it can be a surprise."

"Well, on page two, here, it says a crew of four should be able to finish the job in six hours. If Kim can help, and we get Luke, Steve, Greg, Raphael, you and me, that's seven of us. We should be able to do it even faster, but certainly in fewer than six hours. As for when, I had a thought that you should ask the rest of the family to consider." Alex raised his eyebrows in invitation. "I was thinking we might send Juan and Ricky on a little honeymoon, say to the Ritz Carlton in Half Moon Bay for a couple of days. So many places are not open yet, but they are. It is not far. And romantic. And it would get them out of the house long enough for us to build the gazebo. And short sheet their bed, too." Hiroshi laughed to himself.

"Short sheet their bed?"

"Oh, am I dating myself?" Alex tapped the drawing pad.

"Do you have a diagram for that, too?"

"No, Alex, but I can demonstrate it later. It is pretty silly, I must admit, but first, come with me. I do have a more relevant demonstration to share with you." Hiroshi stood and opened the back door, then followed Alex in. "Follow me upstairs." He laid the drawing pad on the dining table and led Alex up the stairs and into a hall bath. "I wanted you to see first-hand how we will transform Raphael into a golden ring bearer." Hiroshi had spread a sheet out in the middle of the floor where a square white plastic basin was centered, containing a shallow pool of golden soup. Hiroshi opened a liter sized plastic container to show Alex what the gold powder looked like in its raw form. Then, he dipped his left hand in the basin and swirled it around, pulled it out and rubbed both hands together in a washing motion. Soon, both hands and his arms half-way up to his elbows were transformed, gold-plated.

"Alex, turn that blow dryer on low and dry my hands," Hiroshi instructed. Alex did, slowly moving the blow dryer around Hiroshi's hands and arms, back and forth, over and around. After just a few minutes Hiroshi nodded, and Alex flicked the blow dryer off and laid it aside. Hiroshi tested his hands, rubbing them on his chest, leaving nothing behind. Then, he held them out for Alex to admire.

"This is going to be so cool!" Alex cooed. "Wow. It looks amazing. Just like those guys in the videos."

"So, you approve, fellow collaborator?"

"If there's a Halloween this year, I know what I'll be doing. Yeah, I approve, Hiroshi. I can't wait to see how it looks on Raphael."

Before Luke and Raphael's nightly shower and shave, Raphael wandered into Alex and Greg's room. Earlier, while they were cleaning up the kitchen after dinner, Alex had asked him to stop by. Raphael glanced at the TV as he entered, then stopped to watch at the same time Alex hit the pause button.

"No. Let it play," Raphael said. "What are you watching?" He kept his eyes on the screen as he sat on the edge of the bed, while the action resumed.

"Outlander," Greg replied. Raphael remained silent a moment, focused on a character, kilted and bare chested, his hair darker than Luke's and much, much longer. Greg and Alex shared a look.

"Who is that?" Raphael asked. He turned to Alex and Greg, attempting Luke's eyebrow trick.

"That's Jamie," Alex obliged. "You haven't seen this?"

"No, but I think I want to. So, he's Scottish?" Alex pressed pause again, and he and Greg gave Raphael a quick synopsis of the story line. "Can you roll it back a little, again, Alex?" Alex replayed the last several minutes for Raphael, who was clearly enthralled with Jamie Fraser. When the stream returned to the spot where they'd paused earlier, Alex paused again. Raphael continued to stare at the still of Jamie and Claire beginning an amorous embrace.

"Raphael ..." Alex nudged. "What's up? Is it the kilt?"

"No," Raphael replied, grinning as he turned to give Alex and Greg his full attention. "Jamie's pretty hot, isn't he?"

"That seems to be the general consensus, yeah," Greg chuckled. Raphael nodded, still grinning.

"Is that what you wanted to show me?"

"No," Alex pulled away from Greg to better face Raphael. "The gazebo arrived today. It's in about a dozen boxes in Hiroshi's garden. Whenever we can make time, while both Juan and Ricky are out, we should go over and try putting the chuppah together. Make sure it's going to work. Hiroshi thinks he has it figured out."

"Wow. Where was I?"

"You were in a Zoom meeting, I think. Your door was closed. Anyway, let me know." Raphael nodded as he stood.

"Why don't we try to block out a couple of hours over lunch tomorrow. Will that be enough time?" Alex agreed, and Raphael made his exit. When he entered their room, Raphael found Luke stripping the sheets off the bed.

"Perfect timing, baby. It's time to rotate the mattress again. You grab that end."

"This just seems silly," Raphael said as he took hold of a corner and walked in time with Luke to rotate the mattress one hundred eighty degrees. "It's not like when you flipped a mattress over. Back in the last century."

"I'm only following orders, baby. We love this mattress, so if we want it to last, we should at least try to follow the recommendations." Raphael shrugged as he grabbed a corner of the fresh fitted sheet Luke was unfurling. Moments later the bed was made and they headed into the bath. Raphael immediately sat in the shower so Luke could shave him first. Raphael filled him in about the gazebo while Luke stripped away Raphael's day-old stubble. After he'd buzzed the landing strip and blew away a few stray hairs with a sensual blast of warm breath, Luke stepped around and slid into place between Raphael's legs. Raphael squirted a dab of shaving gel onto his palm, rubbed it into foam, and slathered it around the sides of Luke's head. Then, instead of picking up the razor,

Raphael got up, moved around in front of him and sat again, facing him with his legs around Luke's waist.

"All done!" Raphael grinned, immensely self-satisfied.

"What do you mean, 'all done?' You haven't even started."

"Oh, but I have, Sir." Raphael slowly batted those dreamy, almond eyes. Luke furrowed his brow.

Raphael leaned forward and pressed his lips to Luke's, who innocently leaned forward himself, then wrapped his arms around Raphael. A couple of deep breaths later, when Raphael pulled away, he was bearing a mischievous smile.

"Oh, oh," Luke responded. "Is this ... are we ...?"

"Yes, Sir. It's been too long. Don't you think? I have just started your next dare."

"Oh, boy ..."

"It's not exactly a mutual dare, but it will be a sacrifice for both of us."

"Sacrifice, huh? Is Brutus involved?"

"No. Besides, Alex still has possession of him. I think. Anyway, no." Raphael leaned closer and put his hands on either side of Luke's foamy head, brushing his mohawk with the tips of his fingers. Luke closed his eyes and breathed, reveling in Raphael's warm touch. Suddenly Luke's eyes opened.

"Wait a minute. Am I going to sacrifice my mohawk?"

"Yes, Sir," Raphael looked a bit surprised. "Damn. You read my mind."

"Your fingers did the talking. So, you're going to shave me bald, huh?" Raphael closed his eyes and slowly shook his head, then lowered his lathered hands to Luke's shoulders as he resumed eye contact.

"On the contrary, Sir. We will sacrifice me getting to shave you every evening and you enjoying the shave." Raphael leaned back, bracing himself with his hands behind him, staring dreamily at Luke's foamy head. Imagining. His smile grew. "It's time for a new look for my Braveheart. One more in keeping with his true heritage. Instead of shaving you nightly, we're growing it out. At least as long as Mateo's. Maybe as long as Juan's or longer." Raphael tilted his head. "Yeah. At least." Luke's eyes widened.

"That'll take a couple of years. Or more." Raphael slowly nodded.

"Does your hair get wavy when it's longer?" Luke squinted in thought.

"I guess we'll find out." He reached out and grabbed Raphael's thighs. "Are you sure? I thought we both liked the mohawk."

"We do. If we decide the Outlander look isn't right for you, it'll be fun to buzz it all away and recover your mohawk. Don't you think?"

"Outlander look?" Raphael stood and reached down to pull Luke into a standing position.

"Let's scrub each other down, and I'll show you exactly what I have in mind." He landed a quick peck on Luke's lips. "If I wasn't caged right now, Sir, you'd be able to see just how excited I am about your new look."

Freshly showered, Raphael snuggled up next to Luke on top of equally fresh sheets, his tablet in hand. It didn't take him long to find images of Jamie Fraser online. Lots of them. Luke seemed more amused than turned on.

"You think I'll look as sexy as that, huh?" he teased as the images scrolled by. "That is one majestic kilt, I'll admit."

"Oh, is he wearing a kilt? I hadn't noticed." Raphael turned and puckered. Luke delivered. Raphael laid the tablet aside and rolled over onto his back, pulling Luke on top of him in one practiced motion. After sharing a few deep breaths, Luke lifted his head and stared into Raphael's eyes. "Just think, Sir. In a couple of years your honey and ginger colored locks will be falling around my face right now."

"I don't know ..."

"I was right about the beard, wasn't I? And the kilts. Hey, I just realized. This may not be such a big sacrifice after all. I won't be shaving you every night ... but," Raphael reached up and massaged the sides of Luke's stubbly head, "instead I'll be shampooing your luxurious locks. Then brushing them out later. Like Rapunzel." Luke rolled off Raphael and propped his head up on his right hand, brushing Raphael's pecs with his left. He gave each pierced nipple its due, producing a subtle sigh from Raphael. He looked up to find Raphael staring intently at him.

"What?" Luke quietly asked.

"Oh ... just when I think I've exhausted all possible dares for you, fate delivers yet another one. This one could rival the kilt dare, Sir. In fact, we may have to issue you a bodyguard in a year or so."

"Ha!" Luke rolled over onto his back and pulled Raphael, the top half of him anyway, on top of himself. "When we first met your hair fell around my face when we were like this. I don't remember you needing a bodyguard." Raphael sprouted a sly grin.

"You don't remember Cato? No? He did try to stay in the background ..." Luke's chuckling at Raphael's not-very-subtle admission of vanity grew into full-blown laughter, forcing Raphael to lean down and drown it with both lips. When they parted, Raphael repositioned himself at Luke's side, sliding his left arm under Luke's neck, his lips near Luke's right ear. He reached up with his right hand and pretended to smooth Luke's locks away from his ear. "Yeah. I'll bet it's going to be wavy, just like Jamie's." Luke turned to face Raphael.

"You bet, huh? What do I win if it's not?"

"A perm. Obviously." Luke groaned and rolled onto his side to face Raphael, pulling him tight.

"Then this is one bet I hope you win, baby."

"Me, too, Sir. Now ..." Raphael pulled free and curled his body, positioning his head above Luke's lower tattoo. "Since I robbed you of your anticipated shave earlier, it would only be fair if I paid homage to my cock. You know. The one I allow you to wear between your studly thighs." Raphael leaned down and took possession of his cock, without waiting for Luke's answer. Not that he anticipated an objection. Not that he would have obeyed one had it been offered. After all. It was *his* cock.

Alex opened the gate and followed Raphael into Hiroshi's garden, where they found him on his knees, on a weathered tarp, sorting through an assortment of hardware parts for the gazebo. He looked up with a smile.

"Right on time, the construction crew has arrived." Hiroshi stood and indicated a serving tray on the back steps. "Since you are giving up your lunch hour, I picked up sushi burritos for us to enjoy while we work. There is ginger beer, too." Raphael looked down at the assortment.

"Thank you, Hiroshi. I'm guessing you have this all figured out."

"I think so. We will know soon enough. Shall we?" Hiroshi approached the stack of boxes and tapped one in the middle. "Naturally, the boxes we need to open are not on top."

An hour later, Alex was on a step ladder with a socket wrench, loosely tightening a bolt in the last angle iron connecting a cross beam to one of the four upright poles. Proof of concept had been achieved. The chuppah was wobbly, since they hadn't firmly tightened all the bolts. They'd need to partially disassemble it in order to move it through the gate into their own garden, but it was standing on its own. Alex returned to earth, pulled the ladder away from the chuppah and joined Hiroshi and Raphael. Raphael slung one arm around Alex's shoulders, the other around Hiroshi's.

"I think it'll work," Raphael announced. "The wood is beautiful."

"It's bigger than I was expecting," Alex confessed. "But, yeah, it's going to be amazing. Especially after I embellish it." He looked over at Hiroshi. "You made it work, Hiroshi. I can see you three standing under it now." He bumped thighs with Raphael. "And when you show up, gilded and glowing ..." Raphael bumped back.

"I wonder if our fabric consultant at Britex is working? If they're even open? For the topper." Alex slowly nodded. Hiroshi broke away and returned with the tray.

"Gentlemen ... your reward." They each selected a burrito and a bottle of ginger beer and claimed a spot on the back steps. After a couple of bites, Alex took a swig and spoke.

"Another first. I didn't know sushi burritos were a thing. I mean, can it really be a burrito if it's wrapped in seaweed instead of a tortilla?" Raphael turned to Hiroshi.

"You can take the boy off the farm ..." Hiroshi waved toward the chuppah.

"Our boy may not be a culinary sage, but he knows how to stage a wedding, Raphael. For that we should be grateful."

"Yeah," Alex replied, looking at Raphael from the corners of his eyes. "Listen to Elder. He is wise."

Five

## THE COUNTDOWN BEGINS

DAY BY DAY, DETAILS of the wedding were ironed out as the various pieces fell into place. Not that this was going to be an elaborate affair with a cast of hundreds. But with Alex and Hiroshi in charge, nothing would be left to chance. Just as with Alex's double ceremony for Raphael, Luke, Niki and Steve, very few of those details were being shared with the grooms themselves.

"Shouldn't we be having some kind of rehearsal, or something?" Juan asked. Everyone, including Hiroshi, was sitting around the dining table, empty plates and nearly empty wine glasses before them, at the end of another satisfying meal. "I mean, the wedding is next Sunday." Hiroshi laid his napkin across his plate, then, counter to Miss Manners' guidelines, he placed his elbows before him on either side of his plate, hands clasped above it, forming a triangle just below his goatee. Perhaps his way of exhibiting authority.

"An excellent question, Juan." Hiroshi made momentary eye contact with his collaborator several seats away, then directed his smile back to Juan. "Have you prepared your vows?" Ricky laughed.

"He's been working on them. In the bathroom, with the door closed. Either that or he's going crazy." Juan shook his head and cupped the back of Ricky's neck and kept his hand there.

"I'll be ready," he said, almost confidently. "What about you, mijo?" Ricky looked smugly at Juan.

"I'm ready." He turned to Hiroshi. "They don't have to be very long, do they?" Hiroshi smiled and shook his head.

"No, Ricky. Most attendees appreciate a ceremony that is short and sweet. They are there for the party afterward." Hiroshi regained eye contact with Alex. "Alex, please give everyone a brief overview of the wedding day we have planned." Alex took a last sip of wine and cleared his throat.

"First, I have a question for Ricky. Since the wedding will be Sunday, and we're planning the ceremony for four in the afternoon, will you want to host the traditional pancake breakfast? Or will you be too nervous?" Ricky looked at Juan for guidance, then turned to Alex.

"Sunday without pancakes?" Ricky faked a horrified face, then grinned. "I'll be fine."

"Okay. As some of you know, Mama and Angel will be here, too. They're coming up Saturday. Mama will be in Niki and Steve's room and Angel will have the guest room across the hall. Niki and Steve will spend Saturday and Sunday nights at Hiroshi's."

"Are you sure you want Mama climbing all those stairs?" Juan reasonably asked.

"She says she's up to it," Niki confirmed. "She and Angel have been walking daily. When we asked her about it, she thought it would be cool to be staying in the master suite." Juan nodded, satisfied with Niki's answer.

"We'll have the visitor dress code in effect this weekend," Alex continued. He laughed. "We might actually have to do a couple extra loads of laundry next week."

"So ... what comes after breakfast?" Juan prodded.

"All you need to know for now is that Hiroshi and I will be your dressers, Juan," Alex grinned. "We'll meet you two in your room at three."

"I think we can dress ourselves," Juan naïvely chuckled.

"Do you know what you are wearing?" Hiroshi asked, exchanging glances with Ricky, then Juan.

"Oh, oh. I'm flashing on the last wedding I attended," Juan turned to Ricky, grimacing.

"Not to worry, Juan," Alex reached out a calming hand. "This ceremony will be Mama safe. You two will be stunning. Remember, you asked for a Buddhist ceremony. Mostly."

"What does that mean?" Ricky asked. "Mostly?"

"You'll see. As for a rehearsal, Hiroshi and I will coach you on everything you need to know when we dress you. After the ceremony, Hiroshi is hosting an early supper for us and then we'll have a surprise for the newlyweds."

"So far, just about everything that's happening Sunday is a surprise," Juan scoffed.

"Yeah," Raphael looked cunningly at Juan. "I think this is what they call payback." He glanced at Hiroshi, then Alex, then regained Juan's gaze as he draped his arm across Luke's shoulders. "Bwaa ha ha."

"Hey," Juan said in his defense. "I was only the messenger the night of your weddings. I didn't plan any of it."

"Messenger. Co-conspirator. *Collaborator*," Raphael stressed the last word. "You were in on it. We ..." Raphael waved his hand toward Steve, Niki and Luke, "didn't even know we were having another wedding. You already know more about your wedding than we did. So, buck up, Franceesco. Relax and enjoy it. Hiroshi and Alex are going to make you and Ricky proud." Juan and Ricky exchanged a long look. Ricky settled the issue with his signature smile.

"As long as I end up with you as my husband, Juan, I don't care what kind of ceremony we have." Hiroshi laughed and leaned back in his chair, his hand rubbing Juan's back just below the neck, where Juan's mane now ended.

"Wise words from your fiancé, Juan. But I assure you both, Alex and I are committed to making sure the ceremony that introduces you to the world as Ricky's husband will be one worthy of the two of you." Alex got up and walked around to kneel between Juan and Ricky. He placed one hand on Ricky's left shoulder, the other on top of Hiroshi's hand on Juan's back.

"I wish we could offer you the kind of spectacle we gave those guys last year, but ... we can't. Your wedding will be totally different. Really, at your request. An intimate affair with the people who mean the world to you. But just because it will be intimate doesn't mean it won't be memorable. Unique." He glanced over at Hiroshi. "Definitely unique. In a good way." Juan shook his head.

"Okay," he looked sideways at Alex. "You win. Just tell us where to be and what to do. Far be it from us, the grooms, to try to interfere in our own wedding."

"Juan," Greg suggested, "look at it this way. If you were a straight groom marrying a woman, you'd be in the same boat. Your bride and her mother wouldn't allow you to have any input into *their* wedding day, either." Juan closed his eyes and snorted.

"Yeah. You're right." He turned again to Ricky. "At least we still get to write our vows, right mijo?" Ricky nodded, puckered and leaned in for a pre-nuptial kiss.

"After Ricky's pancake breakfast, several of us will prepare the garden for the ceremony," Alex continued his less than detailed overview. "It's customary in the straight world for the groom and bride to not see each other the day of the ceremony until the bride is walked down the aisle. We're not going to enforce that silly tradition, but you might want to take a walk or something, or at least avoid checking out the garden before the ceremony begins, so our preparations have their maximum impact on you."

"Am I one of the 'several of us'," Luke asked. Raphael offered Luke his best mischievous grin.

"To be determined, Luke," Alex stood. "We'll clue everyone in as needed. I'm going to need a couple of volunteers to help with some things on Saturday. If you're free, you know where to find me." He headed back to his seat.

"If I can help, Alex, you can count on me," Ryan offered.

"Should I ask time off?" Mateo suggested. Alex shook his head.

"No, Mateo, no need to change your schedule. But we will have a very important job for you on Sunday afternoon." Mateo nodded and glanced at Hiroshi, happy to be included in the planning.

"Are you two as excited as I am?" Raphael asked as he stood, picking up his plate and silver, signaling an end to dinner. "Are you feeling any butterflies?" Juan looked at Ricky another moment before answering.

"Excited? Maybe. More like at peace. Complete. This will be the bookend to Ricky's proposal." He reached out with his left hand and cupped Ricky's face much like Francisco had done to Pablo. Ricky reprised his signature grin. "On second thought, yeah. I'm excited."

Saturday afternoon was a blur. Alex, Greg, Ryan and Hiroshi were running errands and handling tasks Alex had delegated to each of them and himself. They'd excluded Raphael and Niki, and their husbands, so they, along with the betrothed, would be free to welcome and entertain Mama and Angel. Errands included sourcing the flowers from two different florists that Alex needed to decorate the chuppah. He and Greg also found a giant Pride flag to use as a topper on the chuppah, and no doubt for potential future uses as well.

Ryan and Hiroshi were in charge of the food, including Mexican wedding cookies and six bottles of Schramsberg. They ended up making two trips to shops on Mission and 24th Streets before finding everything they wanted. The ceremony would be somewhat Buddhist, but the feast afterward was destined to be Mexican. They were counting on Mateo to insure it would be authentic.

While they were at Cliff's picking up the Pride flag, Greg was surprised when Alex led them next door to the annex to check out fabrics. He pulled out a bolt of diaphanous gold tulle, carried it to the register and requested two yards.

"Is this going to be part of the chuppah?" Greg asked.

"No," Alex grinned. "Ricky doesn't know it yet, but this is for a part of the ceremony he requested a year ago."

"Um ... he requested it, but he doesn't know it yet?"

"Yeah," Alex's grin devolved into a smirk. "It'll all make sense tomorrow. I don't want to spoil the surprise."

"So, there are other surprises, besides what Juan and Ricky are wearing?" Alex nodded.

"Yeah ... like what you're wearing, Mr. Best Man."

"Tell me I'm not wearing gold tulle. Please."

"Oh, no. Don't be silly. Remember, I told Juan this ceremony is Mama safe. Well, at least most of it. You're going to look very dignified."

Once the errands were completed, everyone else scattered while Alex and Hiroshi put away the food in Hiroshi's fridge and tackled the flowers. They were pruned and stationed in buckets, until they could be affixed to the chuppah once it was reassembled in the garden on Sunday. While they were working, Alex and Hiroshi agreed it might be a good idea to have Greg try on his kimono to ensure a good fit, as well as to allay his concerns. And because Alex was dying to see how it looked on Greg. When Alex returned with Greg, Hiroshi was waiting in his study with two boxes, one large and flat, one shoebox size.

"I found us a guinea pig," Alex chirped as he led Greg into the study.

"Not a guinea pig, Alex," Hiroshi rose from his desk chair. "No. The second-best thing to a groom in a gay wedding. A best man." Hiroshi looked at Alex. "I assume you want this fitting to be as dramatic as possible?" Alex nodded with a cheesy grin. Hiroshi approached Greg, reached up and placed a stocking cap on his head and pulled it down over his eyes. And laughed.

"Hey!" Greg protested and started to reach up. Alex grabbed his hands.

"I seem to remember someone using a blindfold on a certain other someone on his birthday." Greg dropped his arms. "That's better. Let us have our fun, sweetheart." Hiroshi opened the large box and unfurled the kimono and held it up for Alex's approval. Alex gasped and walked over to fondle it. He met Hiroshi's gaze. "It's beautiful," he purred. Hiroshi moved behind Greg with the kimono.

"Greg," Hiroshi quietly requested, "move your arms back just a bit. There, thank you." Hiroshi pulled the kimono up and over Greg's shoulders as his arms slid into the sleeves. He walked around Greg and pulled the kimono closed, temporarily, tilting his head as he judged the fit. He glanced at Alex and winked. "Alex, if you please, hand me the koshihimo in the box."

"The what?"

"The slender belt." Alex complied and Hiroshi folded the kimono closed, then tied the koshihimo in place.

"So, there are two belts?" Alex asked as he picked up the wider obi.

"Yes, Alex. The koshihimo holds everything in place while we manipulate the more challenging obi. Plus, it makes removing the kimono take that much more time. For dramatic effect when undressing the first time with a lover."

"Makes sense," Alex replied, only half joking. In a way, it did make sense for a culture that seemed to always give so much thought to presentation. Now that the kimono was secured, Hiroshi was free to turn and relieve Alex of the obi, then begin to wrap it around Greg's waist. He methodically worked, wrapping the obi around Greg's waist multiple times then tying a knot in front in a more intricate way than Alex could follow.

"This is almost as complicated as putting on a fundoshi," Alex marveled.

"Yeah, really," Greg chimed in. "Am I going to be a wedding present?"

"No, my friend," Hiroshi said. "You are going to be a best man. What kind of best man will he be, Alex?"

"Legendary."

"Precisely. Now, Greg, suck in your gut for me." Hiroshi, having completed knotting the obi, rotated it one hundred-seventy degrees around Greg's waist, positioning the bow just over Greg's right butt cheek. "Now, one last item." Hiroshi opened the shoe box and pulled out a pair of zori. "Greg, almost done. Please lift your left foot." Once he'd guided Greg's right foot into place and Greg had appropriately wiggled his toes, Hiroshi stepped back, rested his hand on Alex's shoulder and asked, "How did we do, Alex?"

"I can't wait until tomorrow. Greg, you look awesome."

"Is that right? Gee, if only I could ..." before he finished, Alex reached up and snatched the cap off.

"Come look," Alex pleaded. He took Greg's hand and pulled him into the entry hall, where a large, oval mirror hung above a console table. Hiroshi followed with a hand mirror, so Greg could also see the back. Greg grinned as he turned slightly in each direction. He reached up and fondled the embroidered dragon over his left pec. He lifted his left foot to better examine the zori. He gave Hiroshi an impish smile. Hiroshi handed him the hand mirror and signaled for Greg to turn around.

"Wow, guys. This looks ... and feels ... incredible. So, what are Juan and Ricky wearing? I don't want to show them up."

"As amazing as you look, my dear, I promise you, you are not the one everybody will be talking about. Right, Hiroshi?"

"I think every member of the wedding party will be memorable, Alex. Including you."

"What are you wearing?" Greg asked.

"The same as you. We'll be a matched pair." Greg nodded as he turned back and resumed admiring his reflection. "So, what do you think, big guy?" Greg turned to Alex and puckered. After the kiss, he turned to Hiroshi and repeated his gesture.

"I think the two of you have probably cooked up yet another wedding for the ages. Not that I'm surprised." He turned to Alex. "You do have a track record."

Dinner that evening was beyond festive, and for good reason. It was a stand-in for the traditional bachelor party. It was the first time Mama and Angel had seen the entire family since Raphael and Niki's weddings; their first meal in the House of the ... you know. It was their first time to meet Hiroshi and Ryan, whom they'd heard so much about. It was the first time most of the family had seen Mama since their Zoom sessions with her in the ICU. And it was the first time all but one of the dining chairs had been pressed into service. Everyone lost count of how many toasts had been offered over another of Greg's hand cranked pastas, fettuccine this time, in a creamy sauce with smoked salmon and dill, along with a mista salad and store-bought antipasti. A compromise, due to limited time.

"One more ... one more," Angel raised his half empty wine glass. "To Juan and Mateo, for guiding me through one of the scariest times of my life. I'm sure I couldn't have done it without you."

"Okay," Mateo countered, his glass aloft. "To Hiroshi, who give me the mantra that help you." Hiroshi nodded his thanks to Mateo, then turned to Mama, his glass raised.

"To Maricel and Angel. Tonight, we celebrate two great achievements. The joining of Juan and Ricky, which we have already toasted. And toasted. But I also wish to acknowledge our joy in having you both here with us, healthy and vibrant. We are grateful for both." The latest round of toasts apparently at an end, everyone grew quiet and enjoyed at least one more sip. Mama sat her empty glass down and addressed Hiroshi.

"I understand you will officiate tomorrow, Hiroshi," she said, then glanced at Raphael and Niki with an impertinent grin before returning her attention to Hiroshi. "You must be very important for such an honor. The last wedding I attended was conducted by the mayor." Hiroshi laughed. Juan and Ricky exchanged grins.

"Important?" Hiroshi responded. "No. Not at all. But you are right. It will be an honor to join these two men, who are very important to me, in the eyes of the law. Tomorrow will be a momentous day. A wedding and two anniversaries. How special is that?"

"Oh my gosh!" Ryan exclaimed. "That's right! I totally forgot. Last year on Valentine's Day." He waved his glass in turn toward Luke, Raphael, Niki and Steve. "The wedding of the Chas ... the wedding of the century! Happy Anniversary guys!" Thankfully, Ryan's mangled toast went right over Mama's head while Angel caught Raphael's eye and winked. It had been a year. A long year. A hell of a year. But tonight, this night, everyone was together, at last. Tonight, everyone was healthy, happy and looking forward to what tomorrow would bring.

True to his word, Ricky pulled off another flawless pancake breakfast with the help, of course, of other members of the family with juice, lattes, espressos and prepared fruit. Once the table was cleared, however, Alex resumed his role as collaborating wedding planner. Raphael, Luke, Niki and Steve were encouraged to take Mama and Angel into the sitting room so they could spend more quality time together. He led them in with a tray bearing a carafe of coffee and a selection of Hiroshi's senbei as bait. He sent Juan and Ricky to their room. Their assignment? To stay away from the garden, even the back of the house, until permission was granted. Or else. Mateo was dispatched to Hiroshi's kitchen and Ryan, Alex, Greg and Hiroshi began the process of converting the garden into an outdoor wedding venue. Their preliminary work on the chuppah paid off. It took less than an hour to assemble the structure and attach the pride flag as the tallit. Alex and Hiroshi began affixing the flowers to the posts with fishing line, while Greg and Ryan transported and arranged chairs from the dining room. In addition to the seven chairs for the audience, Hiroshi had them place two chairs, each a few feet to either side of the chuppah, facing the audience. Although it took another hour to decorate the chuppah, it was worth it. Alex had chosen bird of paradise blossoms as the focal points. These blooms were arranged to emerge from bunches of multi-colored, pastel sweet pea blossoms, much fuller than the bird of paradise, resulting in lush, colorful arrangements on each post. The effect was stunning.

"You turned my simple idea of a chuppah into a work of art, Alex," Hiroshi praised. "I assume you selected the bird of paradise to complement the colors on the kimono you, Greg and Raphael will be wearing."

"Oh yeah, sure." He gave Hiroshi a quick eye roll. "Actually, I chose them because they're Juan's favorite. But, you're right. The real beauty will be revealed with all of us standing under it, wearing your kimono and yukata." He stepped back to better admire their work. "You know ... I just realized. I need to ask Steve to capture a few pictures during the ceremony. This needs to be preserved for posterity, don't you think?"

"Absolutely." Hiroshi looked around, to see if they'd overlooked anything. "While I check with Mateo, to see if he needs any help, I think you should tell Raphael it is time for us to prepare our ring bearer." Alex made a happy face and headed for the back door as Hiroshi slipped through the gate.

No one knew exactly why Alex had pulled Raphael away, but it obviously had something to do with the impending ceremony. As she watched them disappear into the foyer, Mama set her cup down and turned to Angel.

"I always thought yours would be the only wedding I would be able to attend for my boys. I never imagined Raphael and Niki would be married before you."

"Huh," Angel replied, glancing over at Niki, then Luke. "Well, I could claim that I'm just a lot pickier than Raphael and Niki, but obviously that's not going to fly." He nodded to Steve. "Maybe I'm just letting them work out all the kinks before I take the plunge." He seemed unaware of the double entendre buried in that statement.

"All in good time," Mama said as she stood, patting Angel on the shoulder. "I'm going to go up and take a little cat nap before I dress for the wedding."

"Sounds like a good idea, Mama," Luke stood as well. "One of us will come and get you when it's time. Okay?" Mama nodded and headed into the foyer. Just as Luke sat back down, Niki stood.

"You know, Angel, when we gave you and Mama the tour, we forgot to show you the gym." Steve and Luke both issued a short laugh. "Ignore them. We have a little time to kill before we have to dress. Follow me." Needless to say, Angel wasn't the only one to follow Niki, who led Angel through the kitchen and down the basement stairs.

"You call this a gym?" Angel exclaimed upon arrival. "Holy ..." He made a circuit around the dungeon, muttering quietly before turning to his hosts, eyes closed, shaking his head. "And I thought your second wedding ceremony was bizarre. How long did it take you to put this together?"

"It came with the house," Steve smugly smiled. Angel coughed. "Seriously. This was all here when we moved in." He walked over and opened the door to the gym. "Now, this was Raphael's doing." Angel walked over, glanced into the gym, then turned back to the far more interesting dungeon. He walked over to the pup cage, turned to Niki and raised his eyebrows in a silent question.

"Yep," Niki responded. "My home away from home." Angel shook his head again.

"Do you ... have you ..." Angel seemed unable to finish his question.

"The answer to your question," Luke spoke up, "is probably 'yes.'" Niki barked a laugh. "We've taken full advantage of it, yes. On a number of occasions."

"Well, thanks for sharing, guys," Angel ran his fingers up and down one of the chains suspending a sling. "If I wake up screaming in the middle of the night, tonight, you'll know why." Luke walked over and put a comforting hand on Angel's shoulder.

"If you do, we'll just bring you down here and put your mind at ease. It always seems to relax Niki." Angel nodded, not really believing Luke, as he continued surveying his surroundings. A thought suddenly occurred to Luke as he enjoyed Angel surveilling the dungeon. "Angel, last night you and Mama thanked Hiroshi and Mateo for their help while you two were fighting COVID." Angel vigorously nodded. "Being down here with you reminded me. When you have a minute, you should also thank Ryan. He had me lock him up in a chastity cage for a month. To fulfill a promise he made that night when we chanted the mantra around the veladoras. A promise to sacrifice himself if you and Mama would recover."

"He did what?" Luke detailed Ryan's bargain. "Wow. For a month?"

"A whole month. Anyway, he deserves your thanks, too."

"Yeah," Niki chimed in before leading them back up the stairs. "Ryan is the last person any of us expected to survive a month of chastity. It was definitely a sacrifice." Angel looked quizzically at Luke, who simply smiled and nodded.

# Six

## HERE, THERE AND EVERYWHERE

"MAMA, ARE YOU READY?" Angel asked as he entered Niki and Steve's room. Mama was sitting in a wingback chair in the bay widow, soaking up the sunshine. She set her book aside and stood.

"What do you have there?"

"It's a corsage. Hiroshi made it for you." While Angel pinned the corsage on the lapel of Mama's powder blue pantsuit, Mama marveled at the gentleness with which Angel worked. "The orchid is a clipping from a plant Raphael gave Hiroshi last year. He said it bloomed again for just this occasion. There," he said as he stepped back to evaluate his positioning. "You look great, Mama."

"Let me see." She strode into the bath, Angel following. He stood behind her in front of the mirror. "It's lovely. But, Angel, I'm not the mother of the groom."

"Well, Mama, in a way you are. I've learned how much everyone in this house was pulling for you and me when you were in the hospital. These guys are all like brothers to each other. It's really one big, caring family, and ... whether you like it or not ..." he placed a hand on each of Mama's shoulders from behind, making eye contact in the mirror, "you are everyone's Mama here." Mama bit her lip, and batted her eyes, fighting back tears.

"Angel, you are going to make me cry, and the wedding hasn't even started yet." Angel turned Mama around and pulled her into a close, corsage-sparing hug.

"Don't cry. Enjoy it. Just think. You get to have eleven adoring sons and you only had to go through labor twice." Mama chuckled, pulled away, and put a hand on Angel's forearm and squeezed.

"And out of those eleven sons, you will be the one to give me a grandchild. Or two. Or ..."

"Whoa. Mama. Two. Max. But, remember, gay couples are having kids all the time now, too. Raphael and Niki would both make great dads. Wouldn't they?"

"They would," Mama looked playfully into Angel's eyes. "So would Luke and Steve. And so would *you*." Mama let go of Angel and looked down again at the corsage. "Halika, anak. We mustn't be late. We want good seats for the wedding." Angel laughed.

"Don't worry, Mama. I think we have reserved seating." He held out his left elbow and ushered Mama out of the bath and toward the hall and the stairway beyond. When they reached the open back door, they paused to take in the setting Hiroshi and Alex had prepared for the ceremony. Seven chairs were arranged, four on the left, three on the right, in a gentle semi-circle facing the chuppah. An aisle from the back steps to the chuppah had been left open between them. There were also two chairs, a few feet to either side of the chuppah, facing the guest chairs. Each was occupied by a woman. Each of them, dressed in a festive Mexican costume, was playing an acoustic guitar. A love ballad, no doubt. Luke, Mateo and Ryan were seated on the right. Angel led Mama to the open chairs on the left next to Niki and Steve.

"Where is Raphael?" Mama asked Angel as she sat.

"I think he's part of the wedding party," he responded. Mama nodded.

"The flowers on the altar are beautiful," Mama said, turning to Niki.

"Yeah," Niki smiled. "It's called a chuppah. Alex knows how to put on a show. I can't wait to see what he and Hiroshi have arranged for Juan and Ricky." Steve leaned back to whisper around Niki to Mama.

"You look beautiful, too, Mama." She reached up and touched her corsage.

"Isn't it lovely? From Hiroshi and Raphael." Niki leaned over and sniffed, then patted Mama's forearm. She took his hand in hers and held it. The musicians ended their ballad, paused a few beats, then began a new tune, one with more of a cadence. Not exactly Mendelssohn, but clearly telegraphing that the show was about to begin. A few measures into the song, the gate in the wall slowly swung partially open, and Greg passed through, followed by Alex.

"Whoa," Ryan reacted to their kimono. Luke looked over at Angel and grinned. Greg stopped just short of the left post of the chuppah, and Alex stopped just past the right post. Purely for dramatic effect, no doubt, they bowed to each other, then to the musicians, who continued to play, then to the guests, giving everyone the opportunity to see both front and back views of their kimono. Once they were done bowing, a couple of measures later, Hiroshi came through the gate in his more subdued kimono. He also wore a white and red hachimaki, the traditional headband. He positioned himself between Alex and Greg, bowed to each of them, bowed to the guests, then looked straight ahead, at the back door. Without changing tempo, the musicians slightly increased their volume. After a couple of measures, Raphael descended the steps, leading Juan and Ricky, who followed, holding hands. Raphael was dressed exactly like Alex and Greg, except for the thin black gloves that extended up into the sleeves of his kimono. Juan and Ricky wore the yukata and kimono that Hiroshi had originally proposed. Hiroshi had also arranged Juan's locks into the samurai chonmage style, not quite a manbun, but a perfect accompaniment to his yukata.

"Yep," Niki whispered to Mama. "Alex and Hiroshi didn't disappoint." Mama squeezed Niki's hand. When Raphael reached the chuppah, he stepped aside, so Juan and Ricky could stop directly in front of Hiroshi, and between Alex and Greg. They let go of each other, turned and bowed to the best man at their side, then turned again to face Hiroshi at slight angles and bowed to him; they had separated just enough so the guests wouldn't be looking at their backs and so they would also have a clear view of Hiroshi. Raphael turned away and walked in time with the music back toward the house, winking at Angel as he passed. Before Angel could speculate on why Raphael had left the wedding party, the musicians ended their performance and silence fell.

"Today is a most happy day," Hiroshi announced. "Today we bring to a close an engagement that was not too long, as promised." Luke looked at Mateo, who grinned in return. "Today we join Juan Reyes and Enrique Soto together as husbands within the eyes of the law and before the witness of their loving family. A family that deserves a great deal of credit in bringing these two men together. A delightfully diverse family, but one united in giving Juan and Ricky all the support and love they may need to succeed in life as individuals. As lovers. As husbands." Hiroshi paused and gazed at Ricky, and then Juan, in turn. "You are about to embark on a journey that for too long has been denied to too many men ... and women ... who were as deserving as you. And it is a journey you both richly deserve. From this day forward you are more than you were yesterday. Do not take it for granted. Do not take it lightly. To paraphrase a beloved Buddhist prayer, you shall now serve each other for all your days, here, there and everywhere. And may you be grateful for all your days together, here, there and everywhere." Hiroshi, who had been rather staid up until now, smiled broadly at Juan and Ricky. "I know you will. Your love for one another is undeniable. Now, Enrique, have you any words for Juan?" Ricky, resplendent in his navy blue kimono, bestowed his smile on Hiroshi in return, before turning to Juan. He reached out and took Juan's hand in his.

"I vow today that I will serve you for all our days together, here, there and everywhere. Just as I have every day since you pulled me into your arms on the scariest day of my life and told me you had held open the position of your ... lover ... just for me. That you had waited for me to find the courage to submit to you. Wholly. Without reservation. Juan, my Papito, I vow to never make you doubt your decision to take humble little me as your husband. Your husband! Papito, I love you. I adore you. I am yours. And I promise I will treasure every day ... every moment we are together." Ricky glanced at Hiroshi with a sly grin. "Just as Elder has commanded." Ricky's last words brought grins to Juan's and Hiroshi's lips as he released Juan's hand, reluctantly, and took a step back. Juan's reluctance to let go was evident, too, as he slowly lowered his hand, gazing fondly into Ricky's eyes.

"Juan ..." Hiroshi prompted. Juan glanced at Hiroshi, still smiling, before he reached out, summoning Ricky to take his hand again.

"Ricky, it's true. Elder did command me to care for you, to protect you. From this day into eternity. But, my love, I would have done so even without his wise counsel. You see, I am here before you today because I am powerless in your presence. Since the very first moment I saw you. The first time I looked into your eyes and saw that smile. I've never told you this, but I stood in the doorway of my building and watched you drive away that first evening. I watched, hoping you would turn that little scooter around and come back to me. And. The amazing thing is ... you did! Not that night, of course, but you did come back. Again, and again. Each time exerting more of your power over me. Until it was undeniable. You had captured my heart." Juan glanced at Hiroshi, before continuing. "Ricky, you are as wise as Elder. Perhaps more so. You knew, better than me, that I would never be happy, truly happy, without you in my life. You showed me how brave true love can be. By all means, may you serve me for all our days, here, there and everywhere. But Ricky. Mijo, my love, it was you who asked me to marry you. Some here might have seen that as a request. It was, in fact, a command; one that I happily obey today as a man who is powerless in your presence. Enrique, I whole-heartedly take you as my husband. Today and forever, here, there and everywhere." For a moment no one spoke or moved. Juan and Ricky were lost in one another's gaze as Hiroshi paternally looked on. Then, once again, he lifted his eyes to the back door.

"Those were lovely vows. Thank you. Before I officially pronounce you as legally wedded husbands, there is, of course, the time-honored ritual of exchanging rings. And for that, I will need to summon the assistance of a legendary ringbearer." The musicians began playing softly. Since Raphael was coming from behind them, at first the guests' only clue that something extraordinary was happening was Ricky's reaction. He let go of Juan and put both hands over his mouth in gleeful surprise. Juan half turned to Hiroshi, then back toward Raphael, equally touched.

By then Raphael had cleared the arc of guest chairs, his naked, golden frame creating a small uproar from the heretofore silent witnesses. Niki almost bent double in his chair. Luke and Angel exchanged brief shocked looks, brief because neither wanted to take their eyes off the spectacle that Raphael presented. His golden skin, reflecting the sunlight, somehow elevated his chiseled, naked body beyond the appearance of a mere mortal man. As if he were a walking work of art. A statue brought to life. The gold tulle around his face and head trailed a few inches down his back between his traps, adding an element of mystery. Remarkable, also, was the fact Raphael's back tattoos were hidden under the gold paint, making his appearance even more pristine, more like that of a sculptor's fashioned masterpiece come to life. When he reached Juan and Ricky, he stopped and knelt on one knee, offering the pillow to Hiroshi, while giving the audience an inspired view of his well-developed glutes. Once Hiroshi had retrieved the rings, Raphael stood, turned, revealing a pillow draped with a tapestry that insured his appearance would remain R-rated, and walked back to the house in time with the music. Ricky beamed at Juan, then Hiroshi, then, his head tilted slightly, he watched Raphael, his very own naked ringbearer, retreat. Niki, now upright again, turned to Mama, not sure what to say, if anything. She turned to him with an inscrutable smile.

"You boys," was all she said. Which said it all. Hiroshi handed a ring to Juan and nodded.

"Ricky," Juan said, taking Ricky's left hand in his, "like the gold in this ring, my love for you is everlasting. Indestructible. It will be reshaped and reformed as the years pass us by, but it will endure. Forever." Juan slid the ring onto Ricky's finger. Hiroshi handed the second ring, one Juan had been wearing for months now, to Ricky.

"Juan, Papito, this ring says it all. The inscription inside says 'Love you always, Ricky.' Always, and forever, I am yours and with this ring, you are mine." Ricky slid the ring in place, then both turned to Hiroshi.

"And thus, it is with the greatest of joy, and in the presence of those who love you both, that I pronounce you legally wedded husbands." The guitarists began playing a joyful tune. The family stood and clapped. And Juan pulled Ricky into his arms for a long and passionate kiss. They were still entwined when Raphael walked up beside Luke, dressed in his kimono and zori, the tulle abandoned, but with his gilded hands and wrists on display. Luke wrapped an arm around Raphael's waist and pulled him tight. Raphael flashed the Cheshire grin.

"Baby, if it's all right with you, maybe you could keep the golden body for a while?" Raphael laughed and wrapped his arm around Luke. Ryan, grinning, leaned forward around Luke, wiggled his eyebrows and mouthed 'Wow!' The guitarists strummed up a crescendo, then stopped and stood and bowed to the guests, who applauded them. They sat again as Hiroshi placed a hand on each of Juan's and Ricky's shoulders. He leaned in and whispered something, persuading them to conclude their embrace. They turned to face the family, holding hands.

"My dear friends," Hiroshi announced, "it is my honor to introduce you to Mr. and Mr. Juan and Enrique Soto-Reyes." The ceremony concluded, wedding convention was tossed aside as everyone except Angel and Mama surrounded Juan and Ricky for an HLCB group hug. Mama and Angel approached to congratulate Juan and Ricky, and they, too, were pulled into the hug. Hiroshi extracted himself and thanked each of the guitarists. Mateo and Ryan took their cue and pulled away, too, and retreated through the gate to see to the final preparations for Hiroshi's early supper. Steve jogged into the house and immediately returned with a camera and tripod.

"Before we head over to Hiroshi's, this may seem cliché, but I'd like to get some pictures of the grooms as well as the wedding party under the chuppah, and some with everyone else, including our wonderful musicians. You'll thank me later."

"Be sure to get a couple of the ringbearer," Ricky joked while Steve positioned him with Juan.

"It's all on video," Steve replied, pointing up to Mateo and Ryan's window. "In fact, I had Hiroshi mic'd up, so we've got audio of the ceremony as well." While Steve worked, Mama, Niki and Angel examined Raphael's kimono more closely. Niki took Raphael's hand in his and examined it more closely, too.

"You looked amazing, Raphael," he said. "How did you do this? How long will it take to wear off?"

"I could shower it off right away, but I think Luke wants me to keep it a little longer." Raphael glanced at Mama, not wanting to embarrass her with any implied inuendo.

"If I ever get married," Angel smiled at Raphael, "I had always thought you'd be my best man, but now I'm thinking of asking Niki. You make a much more memorable ring bearer. What do you think, Mama?"

"I think you have your work cut out for you, Angel. I thought the sarongs and those fancy pants and shirts at Raphael and Niki's wedding were the most unique wedding clothes I'd ever see. But, today..." Mama again fingered Raphael's sleeve. "Such beautiful outfits on all of you. And off of you, Raphael." Raphael grinned, shyly, but proudly, too. Mama turned to Angel. "I can't wait to see how everyone dresses, or undresses, at your wedding." Angel laughed and shook his head.

"In that case, I guess I'll have to hire Alex, right Niki?"

"Nobody hires Alex," Niki replied. "He just takes over, whether you like it or not. But the good news is, you always like it." It was at that point that Steve recruited Mama, Angel, Niki, Luke and Raphael to join Juan and Ricky for their poses under the chuppah. Once Steve was satisfied with a few more groupings, Hiroshi herded everyone through the gate and into his house for a low key, but culturally appropriate reception. Mateo, along with Ryan's, and Hiroshi's, help, had prepared a small feast. The dining table served as a buffet offering shrimp and avocado ceviche, both chicken and cheese and onion enchiladas, tortillas, spicy rice, black and refried beans and a heaping platter of Mexican wedding cookies. On the side board were flutes and buckets of iced Shramsberg Cremant. Everyone filled a plate and found a seat in the living room, where Hiroshi had done a bit of rearranging to accommodate the relocated dining room chairs. As the host, he was the first to toast.

"Despite repeated pleas, I must inform you that there will be no traditional first dance by our apparently very shy couple of the hour. This despite the presence of two fine musicians, to whom we are very grateful." Hiroshi bowed to the guitarists, who smiled and raised their glasses. Cheers and a smattering of applause accompanied Hiroshi's praise. "Nevertheless, let me be the first to offer congratulations and my most sincere and heartfelt wishes for a long and happy marriage to my dearest friends ... my brothers ... Juan and Ricky Soto-Reyes." More cheers accompanied Hiroshi's raised flute. Then Niki stood.

"So, am I right? Did you two hyphenate your last names?" Juan nodded and Ricky grinned.

"It's something we joked about before," Juan said, "and when the wedding became a reality, we decided, why not? It seemed to work out well for Niki." Niki beamed. He glanced over at Ryan and Mateo.

"Remember that, guys. Just in case." He turned back to Juan and Ricky and raised his glass. "No one deserves to be happier than you two. Your vows to each other said it better than anything I can say. All I can do is add just how happy I am to have been a witness to the beautiful ceremony joining two of the most loving guys I'll ever know. You inspired Francisco and Pablo. You inspire all of us."

After a couple more toasts, everyone got serious about enjoying Mateo's efforts and the conversation lagged for a bit. Until Mama addressed Hiroshi.

"Do all Buddhist weddings include a golden, naked ring bearer?" she asked. "I'm guessing it ensures a good turnout." Hiroshi glanced at Raphael, who was failing at stifling his laughter, then Alex, before meeting Mama's gaze.

"In honor of this delightfully diverse family, Alex and I decided to incorporate elements from each of the cultures represented here. The tradition of the naked ring bearer, sometimes golden, sometimes jewel-encrusted is not Buddhist. Not nearly that ancient, but is rather of a more recent provenance that represents a metaphysical symbolism that is foundational to how some cultures love and support one another. Living art, if you will, reflecting life as lived." Mama nodded thoughtfully. Raphael leaned into Luke and whispered.

"When did Hiroshi become a bullshit artist?"

"Sssh," Luke grinned. "Mama bought it." He glanced over at Angel, who was grinning at Ricky. "Actually, I kind of bought it myself." He planted a quick peck. "Does it seem weird to look down at golden hands?"

"A little." He looked coyly into Luke's eyes. "Will you think it's weird to make love to a golden boy tonight?"

"Hardly," Luke whispered back. "I pretty much do that every night."

When the musicians finished their servings, they stood to leave. Mateo leapt up to take their flutes and plates, while Hiroshi walked them into the entry hall. He handed one of them an elaborately wrapped envelope, reinforcing Alex's observation about the importance of presentation in Japanese culture. After he saw them out, he returned to the living room to make another announcement.

"Juan, there was a reason we asked you to arrange vacation time this week." He glanced at the grandfather clock. "A car is arriving in forty-five minutes to transport you and Ricky to a brief, but hopefully memorable honeymoon getaway." Ricky and Juan exchanged quick surprised glances before returning their attention to Hiroshi. "We have arranged two nights, so you will need to pack a small bag or two. You may change if you wish, or you may choose to make a stunning entrance at the Ritz Carlton Half Moon Bay in your yukata and kimono. In fact, I recommend it. We are not trying to get rid of you, but ... you now have forty-four minutes to prepare." Juan stood, followed by Ricky, both of whom wrapped their arms around Hiroshi for yet another hug. When they released him, Ricky, still attached to Juan, looked around the room.

"Thank you, everyone. For the best day of my life." He looked up into Juan's eyes a moment, as if seeking inspiration there. "I feel like I owe so much to all of you. I really do." He paused, choking up. Finally getting emotional after having gone through the ceremony and the supper on an emotional high. Juan pulled him tight, Ricky's face buried in his chest, in the folds of his yukata.

"We both do," Juan smiled, doing his best not to tear up. "Today was proof there is no better family than this." He leaned back to free Ricky's head. "Come on, mijo, Hiroshi says we need to pack." Hiroshi accompanied them through the house to the back door while Mateo and Ryan cleared away their plates and flutes. When Hiroshi returned, Mama asked him for directions to the bathroom; he led her toward the back of the house. Everyone else remained silent a moment, sipping or munching wedding cookies, grateful for a successful end to a long-awaited day.

"Umm, maybe it's an inside joke," Angel posed, "but I didn't get the references to 'Elder' in the ceremony. And, Niki, who are Francisco and Pablo?" Angel was surprised by the reactions his questions sparked. Everyone else was looking at each other grinning. A little guiltily. Finally, Alex spoke.

"Steve, what do you think? Would it be all right if we showed Angel the movie?" Angel, brow furrowed, looked at Steve. Steve shook his head. "Not without permission. I promised. Raphael promised." Now Angel was really intrigued. He looked at Raphael, who looked conflicted. Raphael stared back at Angel a moment, then turned to Steve.

"I'll ask Juan. Before they leave." He took a deep breath. "He's on a high. I'll bet he says yes." Niki walked over and took Angel's empty plate from him, then placed a hand on his shoulder.

"Angel, we're going to blow your mind." Then he walked away. Angel looked at Luke who merely smiled and nodded. Before he could say another word, Mama returned. Angel wasn't sure, but intuitively he suspected it was best not to explore the topic further with Mama present.

They debated, but ultimately Juan and Ricky decided to change out of their wedding attire before climbing into the car that whisked them away at six. However, they did pack the yakuta and kimono as lounge wear once they'd arrived in Half Moon Bay. They figured they could never tie the obi as well as Hiroshi had done, but they had no intentions of keeping them tightly closed anyway.

After such an early supper, everyone else found themselves at loose ends. Ryan and Mateo stayed behind with Hiroshi to clean up after the supper while the rest of the family carried in the dining room chairs, then gathered in the sitting room. Had it not been for the pandemic, it would have been fun to celebrate the two anniversaries by taking Mama and Angel to one of the neighborhood bars, or to the Castro Fountain for an old-fashioned soda. Or even to the Castro Theatre to listen to a live performance on the magnificent Wurlitzer before seeing a movie. But too much of what makes the Castro the Castro was still off limits. After a while the conversation waned a bit, then Niki made a suggestion.

"Mama, we haven't played Pusoy Dos in forever. What do you say?" Mama laughed, but looked game. Angel had a better idea.

"Niki, since only four can play," he looked over at Greg and Alex, "how about poker instead. You guys play poker, right?"

"Umm, once or twice, maybe," Alex replied. "I'm not sure I remember the rules."

"All the better," Angel grinned. "We'll teach you while we fleece you." He looked over at Steve. "I'm guessing there are cards and poker chips somewhere in this house." Steve smiled and nodded as he stood.

"Shall we reconvene in the dining room?" Steve headed for the foyer, with Mama and Niki already following behind. "Raphael," Steve called out, "why don't you open another bottle of your favorite bubbly. Our only hope for beating Angel is if we get him toasted first." Alex looked at Greg.

"These guys sound serious. How have we gone this long without knowing we live in a house of card sharks?"

"I guess it never came up. If nothing else, this should be fun to watch ... brothers and brothers-in-law taking on their Mama in a high-stakes poker game."

"My money is on Mama," Alex wagered as he stood.


Alex was right. About Mama, that is. Forty-five minutes into the game, and still not clear about which hand beat which, Alex had given all his chips up to Mama and Niki, except for a few to Angel and Raphael, who were more than holding their own. Mateo and Ryan had wandered in, turned down the offer to be dealt in, and had retreated to their room. Greg and Luke were barely hanging on by folding more often than betting. Steve was still solidly in the game. Obviously, the Malaluan family played for fun, and for keeps. But, once it was clear Mama was running hot and destined to win, she did the only decent thing as a guest. She took a last sip from her flute, which she had slowly nursed throughout the game, and set it down. She pushed half her chips to Niki on her left and the other half to Angel on her right and stood.

"This was fun, but it's been a long day, boys. A beautiful day. Thank you. If you don't mind, I am going to turn in early." She squeezed Niki's shoulder. Raphael jumped up.

"I'll walk you up, Mama." After the two had started up the stairs, Greg turned to Steve.

"We didn't stand a chance, did we?"

"Poker isn't even Mama's best game," he smiled.

"I think it's safe to say Mama isn't suffering any Long COVID brain fog," Niki offered as he rearranged his newly acquired stash of chips. He pushed a couple of stacks toward the middle of the table. "Here, Alex, you earned these today. That was a legendary ceremony."

"Thanks, Niki, but most of the credit goes to Hiroshi. Like ninety percent. Even the chuppah was his idea. You can keep the chips. I'd rather just watch you fleece these guys." He glanced over at Luke, then at Greg. Before Niki could retrieve the chips, Raphael reappeared in the doorway. Completely naked, in all his twenty-four-carat splendor.

"Oh, are we playing strip poker now?" Luke asked. Raphael stepped forward, but didn't sit.

"We could ..." he grinned, "or ..." He whipped a hand from behind his back, holding out a familiar looking jewel case. "Or, we could go upstairs and watch a movie!"

# Seven

# A Fairy Tale Wedding Night

Raphael didn't wait for an answer. He turned and headed into the foyer and up the stairs. Everyone but Angel was out of their chairs before he'd made it to the first landing. Luke picked up the nearly empty bottle and smiled at Angel as he took up the rear of the parade.

"Bring your glass, Angel. You may need this," he held up the bottle, "to settle your nerves." Angel gave him a confused look, but scooped up his flute and followed Luke. As everyone was funneling into Alex and Greg's room, Mateo cracked open his and Ryan's door to see what the commotion was. Niki tilted his head toward Alex's doorway and whispered to Mateo.

"We're going to show the movie to Angel. Come on, you guys." Mateo pulled the door open a bit further, looking intrigued.

"We dress first ..."

"No, amigo. You're fine." To illustrate, Niki began stripping in the hall. Once he finished, the three of them entered the room and pulled the door closed. Alex and Luke had also stripped, and Luke's golden boy had nestled into Luke's embrace, his back against Luke's chest, the two of them sitting on the floor, propped up against the bed. Angel was standing off to the side, taking the scene in.

"Do I have to get naked to see this movie?"

"Not if you don't want to, but Angel," Steve said as he loaded the DVD into the player, "we've been wearing clothes for over twelve hours already."

"Yeah," Niki explained, "this is a record for the House of the Locked Cock Brotherhood."

"Locked Cock Brotherhood ..." Angel repeated, as he watched Steve strip. Greg, like Alex before him, merely had to sluff off his kimono. "Is this why you have those shelves in the foyer?"

"The cubbies?" Raphael grinned. "Yeah. No one's allowed past the foyer with clothes on. Including Hiroshi. Today was only the second time all of us have worn clothes in the house since we moved in." Angel shook his head, more amused than judgmental. Greg rolled the desk chair around the bed and positioned it a few feet from the TV, then invited Angel into it with a gesture.

"You get front row, center, Angel," he said. "The rest of us have already seen it." Angel sat and Luke slid the bottle over and nudged Angel's foot with it. Angel looked down and half-laughed. He looked back at Luke who made a 'don't say I didn't warn you' face.

"Okay, Angel," Steve said, as he dimmed the lights, remote in hand, "this should answer your questions from this afternoon. If any other questions come up during the movie, we'll be happy to answer those, too. It may get a little scary at times, but all we ask is, don't cover your eyes. It goes fast." Angel looked blankly at Steve, but Steve pointed to the screen with the remote reinforcing his point. Then, he pressed play.


Juan handed the bellman the $20 bill Hiroshi had given him earlier, just for this purpose. Hiroshi and Alex had thought of everything. He closed the door and turned to see Ricky, still decked out in slacks and sport coat, standing at the sliding door to the balcony. He was gazing at the surf beyond. Because it was already dark out, Juan could see his husband's face reflected in the glass before he turned, beaming.

"Papito, this is ... amazing!" Juan walked over and wrapped an arm around Ricky as he slid open the door, then immediately closed it. The 'sea breeze' was more of a gale than a breeze, but it smelled fresh and moist. The view of the dark ocean was just as romantic through the glass. They turned and held each other, silent, eyes closed, alone at last, luxuriating for a moment, more in the presence of each other than in their ostentatious surroundings. After a couple of slow breaths, Juan released Ricky and glanced around the room.

"What do you think, mijo? Did we choose our wedding planners wisely?" Ricky squeezed Juan's torso, then stepped back to take in the room.

"Like there was ever any doubt." He walked over to the table, near the center of the room, to examine a basket laden with fruit, cheeses and a couple of baguettes, along with an arrangement of more bird of paradise blooms and other flowers. As he fingered one of the blooms, Ricky looked back at Juan. "We even had our very own legendary ring bearer. Everything has been perfect."

The wet bar along the far wall offered a variety of spirits as well as an iced bottle of Dom Pérignon. Juan picked it up and poured into two flutes, since it was already open. The profusion of bubbles dancing upward from the bottom of the flutes confirmed that the bottle had been opened only moments before their arrival. Juan smiled at the precision, revealed by this detail, that had gone into the planning of every moment of their day. He returned to Ricki's side and handed him a flute. They touched glasses.

"Mijo, I am the luckiest man on Earth. I have the World's Best Locked Cock Leather Boy as my husband and the most thoughtful family anyone could ever hope for." Ricky met his gaze and offered the smile Juan had venerated in his vows.

"True ... true. But, you know, Papito, your luck is my fortune. I now have the handsomest husband all the other runner-up Leather Boys would die for. Husband! I still can't believe it!" He leaned up and stole a kiss before either of them had tasted the wine. Once they had, Juan set his glass down and began unbuttoning Ricky's shirt.

"Well, since we're in the honeymoon suite, you have to believe it, Mister Enrique Soto-Reyes. I am your husband. To prove it, I must now insist that the two of us consummate our marriage. Unless you'd rather sample some of that bread and cheese first." Ricky laughed, dropped to his knees and began unbuckling Juan's belt.

"Maybe we should have listened to Hiroshi after all, Papito," he looked up at Juan. "It would be a lot easier to undress you if all you were wearing was your kimono." Juan nodded as he began unbuttoning his own shirt.

"True, Ricky. But, if we had, with you in that sexy kimono, chances are, we would have consummated our wedding in the limo, long before we got here."

"You say that like it's a bad thing," Ricky said as he slid Juan's pants down to the floor. Juan stepped out of them, reached down and pulled Ricky up.

"Let's see if we can find the bedroom, mijo. Here, don't forget your Champagne. We may be there awhile."

As the final credits rolled off the top of the screen, Angel slowly spun his chair around to face the rest of the audience. His expression was hard to read in the dark, and still hard to decipher as Steve spun the lights back up. He looked, in turn, confused, amused and a little doubtful. He glanced at several apprehensive faces around the room and at one impressive erection that was impossible to ignore.

"Now you know who Elder, Francisco and Pablo are," Alex said from his perch on the bed. "What did you think? Any questions?" Angel shook his head rapidly, as if trying to shake something loose. He opened his mouth to speak, but hesitated a moment before any sound came out.

"So ... you guys did this yourselves?" He was looking at Raphael, who sagely nodded. "It was ... it was like a regular movie, like something professionals would have made." Steve cleared his throat.

"Real professionals did make it," Luke clarified. "Professional director, professional writer, professional acting coaches. Professionally trained puppies, too." Niki barked as he elbowed Ryan, next to him on the floor.

"So ...?" Raphael prompted.

"It was ... educational," Angel admitted. "I learned a few things. Even for a straight guy, it was sexy at times. I guess." He met Raphael's gaze again. "Kind of sad at the end, for Adonis, I mean." Raphael nodded again. "It was a pretty interesting story, come to think of it. Why did you guys make it? Was it for a contest or something? Did it win a prize?"

"Tell him, Luke," Raphael leaned his head back to attempt eye contact as he spoke.

"It was a dare," Luke explained, wrapping his arms more tightly around Raphael. "You've heard about our dares. I dared this guy to make a porn flick and post it online. I was expecting a five-minute, hand-held smartphone video like you see on the internet. But with this family, I should have known better. Alex wrote it. Steve produced and directed it. And everybody else made it the Oscar worthy film you just saw. You're right, Angel. It would win awards if anyone ever saw it, but you, my beloved brother-in-law, are the only person, outside of this family, to have had that privilege." Angel looked back at the now dark screen, then back at Luke.

"Wait. You mean you went to all that work, and nobody's ever seen it? Didn't you say it was posted online?" Raphael chuckled and patted Luke's thigh.

"It was a dare, Angel. So, we had to do it. But we also had to protect careers and reputations. I posted it, but in a way so no one would ever see it, since Niki and Ryan were the only ones who remained anonymous. Sort of."

"Yeah," Angel replied, looking directly at Ryan. "That stiffy *is* pretty recognizable. You warned me about that, didn't you, Raphael?" Luke laughed.

"He can' help it," Mateo grinned, with his usual, and unnecessary, explanation.

"Yeah, Niki is our long-time pup, but we're slowly bringing Ryan along," Steve predicted. "Right, Ryan?" Ryan, embarrassed, but still rigid, tilted his head back and forth, non-committal.

"Umm ... maybe," he relented, glancing at his mentor pup. "It is kinda fun."

"He means it's a turn on," Raphael avowed, trying to read Angel, curious about his reaction to all that had been revealed so far this evening. "He's pretty good at it, too." Angel smiled at Ryan.

"I know I already thanked you for your sacrifice with the chastity, Ryan, but seeing you like this. Now I can see just how much of a sacrifice it must have been. For you *and* Mateo." The two held eye contact a moment before Ryan looked down at his rambunctious member, displaying a humble face. "I appreciate what you did, Ryan. I mean that." Angel looked around at the other lounging family members. Some caged, some not, one painted gold to repay a debt to another beloved family member; all of whom had collaborated in producing a film to help the golden one satisfy a dare that apparently couldn't be dismissed. "The wedding Alex created last year was my first clue, I guess. Now, this film. The video of the mantra session you did for Mama. The ceremony you guys and Hiroshi created for Juan and Ricky today. I'm slowly understanding, I think, what you all mean to each other. I mean, you're all couples. That, I always got. But the affection you all have for everyone else is pretty obvious, now, too. Is that common in the gay world?"

Raphael looked up at Alex, then over at Steve and Niki. He rubbed Luke's thigh again.

"I don't know, Angel. We didn't plan it. We just sort of happened ... evolved into a family over time. Each of us brings something different to the party. Even from a distance, you were a catalyst, too. The conversation we had after bad Niki sent you that video. Helping me realize my responsibility for Niki's coming out brought Luke and me so much closer to Niki and Steve." He glanced up at Alex again. "All I know is we all love each other and we love being together." He raised his foot up to tap on Angel's knee. "Angel, I love that you have accepted us and how we live and have even gone along with some of our craziness. For a straight guy, you're all right." Angel shook his head, smiling, then took Luke's advice and drained his flute. Raphael changed the subject. "When are you and Mama leaving tomorrow?"

"I don't know," Angel replied, stifling a yawn. "Maybe after the traffic eases up."

"Well, if you're not in a hurry and you're feeling butch, you're welcome to stick around a while and join our construction crew."

"In your ... dungeon?"

"No, but now we know where your mind is," Raphael smirked. "In the garden. We're going to convert the chuppah into a gazebo. It's our wedding present to Juan and Ricky. You don't have to, but you're welcome."

"Let me ask Mama in the morning. If she's in no hurry, then sure. I guess." Steve handed the jewel case with its precious contents to Raphael, who climbed out of Luke's embrace, then pulled Luke to his feet. Everyone else took their cues and began filing out into the hall. Steve and Niki gathered up their clothes, but didn't bother to put them back on for the short trip over to Hiroshi's. Before heading up another flight to his room, Angel hugged Raphael, then Luke, goodnight in the hall.

"I hope you weren't put off by any of the sex scenes in the movie, Angel," Raphael tentatively said. "What seems normal to us ..." Angel laughed and squeezed Raphael's golden shoulder.

"Raphael, I'm not as naïve as you think. Like I said, I learned some things, but I wasn't offended. Really." He looked at Luke, then back at Raphael. "Like they say on TV ... the more you know. I appreciate you all sharing it with me. I'm honored. And, seriously, I'm impressed." He looked up the staircase. "With everything. Here, in the House of the Locked Cock Brotherhood. Well ... goodnight." He headed up the stairs as Raphael pulled Luke down the hall toward their room.

"Wait!" Ricky commanded as Juan, fully naked now, started to slide onto the bed. He zipped open Juan's overnight bag and pulled out the yukata, spilling socks and underwear onto the floor in the process. "You should be wearing this while I make love to you the first time as your Leather Boy husband." Juan chuckled, but didn't object. He slipped on the yukata as he watched Ricky dig into his own bag.

"Things might get a bit tangled if we're both wearing kimono, mijo." Ricky turned and beamed.

"Oh, I'll stay naked, Papito, like a good Leather Boy. Except for these." He was holding out his wrist and ankle restraints. "I know we don't have a sling, but ..."

"But they feel so good, right?" Ricky nodded and held them out further, encouraging Juan to buckle them on. Once he had, he climbed up onto the bed and stretched out, the yukata splayed open like a super hero cape beneath him. Ricky slowly crawled up from the foot of the bed and planted his wrist restraints on either side of Juan's hips, his knees between Juan's. He lowered his head, briefly glanced up mischievously at Juan, then slowly inhaled Juan's cock. Juan gradually released a long breath and reached down to massage the shaven sides of Ricky's high 'n tight. It wasn't the first time he'd been worshipped this way by his Locked Cock Leather Boy, but it was the first time that Ricky was, indeed, his. Legally bound. It shouldn't have made a difference, but it did. Especially considering the way it happened. At the hands of Hiroshi, and in the presence of a family he'd never dreamed he'd be a part of. Ricky was skillfully working his Leather Boy craft, hardening Juan, on a selfless mission to bring him off. For a while, Juan let Ricky worship him. It felt good, and, to be honest, Juan was a little tired. It had been a long and demanding day. But when he pulled his hands away and slid them behind his head, to better admire Ricky, the sight of him serving Juan selflessly on their wedding night didn't seem quite right.

"Mijo," Juan whispered, using his elbows to raise his head and shoulders, "why don't you ride me so we can see each other." Ricky looked up, still sucking Juan's cock. Juan issued an air kiss that landed just as Ricky let Juan slip free of his moist, kissable lips, revealing that smile. Ricky repositioned himself, his legs now on either side of Juan's, as Juan pulled his closer together. Ricky's ankle restraints pressed near Juan's knees as Ricky guided Juan inside himself. As he slowly welcomed Juan in, Ricky ran his hands up and down Juan's torso. Each of them breathed slowly, taking turns moaning gratefully as Ricky began working Juan's cock to both their advantage. He took his time. Ricky was doing all the work, still, but now they both were being stimulated appropriately. Eyes closed, concentrating on the feeling of Juan's glans and PA on his prostate, Ricky leaned forward a little, just enough to allow Juan to reach up and begin massaging Ricky's ample nipples. Ricky made little cries between gasps, all without interrupting the motion that was fueling them both. This was a sight Juan never tired of, of Ricky transported. It was as close to what Hiroshi's fisting did for Juan as Juan had so far been able to provide for Ricky, and he was grateful the two of them could achieve such sexual compatibility, almost on command. Some nights they could seemingly do this forever. But not tonight. Suddenly Ricky opened his eyes and gave Juan a look that telegraphed 'now, Papito!' Ricky tightened his grip on Juan's cock and a little gasp accompanied the splash of cum jetting out of his Holy Trainer. He slid his hands free of Juan's nipples, as he leaned down, dug his hands into Juan's hair and pressed his lips against Juan's, sliding his tongue in, demanding Juan to join him. Juan had no choice. Ricky clenched again, moaned into Juan's mouth and willed Juan into coming inside of him. To breed him, husband to husband. For a moment neither moved as Juan pulsed. When he finished, Ricky lifted his head enough to look into Juan's eyes. Juan smiled and pursed his lips in another air kiss. Ricky obliged, teasing Juan's lips with his own. He remained on top of Juan, not wanting to release him just yet, reveling in the perfectly natural pleasure of feeling Juan's cock inside of him. Still holding Juan in, Ricky lowered himself completely, torso to messy torso, his head resting on Juan's right shoulder. Ricky's cage was pressed into Juan's abdomen, but Juan wasn't about to complain. Not with Ricky's warm breath flowing just beneath his chin. Juan took hold of the edges of the yukata and wrapped it and his arms around Ricky, sliding his right hand down until it rested atop the left cheek of the perky butt that still held him hostage. It wasn't long before Ricky's little moans and sighs grew less frequent, and his heartbeat slowed, signaling that he was slipping into unconsciousness. The thought of Ricky being so naturally at peace wrapped in Juan's arms and still impaled, caused Juan to swallow hard. This, he thought, just might be the perfect realization of a fairy tale wedding bed. Nevertheless, Juan debated. Let Ricky sleep just a few minutes? It had been a long day, and with more than the usual amount of bubbly for the World's Best Locked Cock Leather Boy. Or, rouse him for a quick shower? The nearly imperceptible vocalizations from Ricky's lips prevented Juan from waking him just yet. Even asleep, he was being adorable. Another minute. Or two. And then, as Juan's hand slowly slid down the side of Ricky's ass he, too, surrendered to his exhaustion.

"What do we have here?" Luke asked upon entering the kitchen with a once again olive complected Raphael trailing him. Mama, Angel and Hiroshi were seated at the island, with a bounty of pastries heaped in the center.

"Fuel for the carpenters," Hiroshi smiled. He took a sip of coffee. "Help yourselves." Raphael picked out a blueberry scone for himself and an almond croissant for Luke, who was pouring coffee for each of them. They sat and munched.

"You think of everything, don't you, Hiroshi?" Raphael said between bites. He looked across at Mama. "Best. Neighbor. Ever." She nodded, enjoying her own butter croissant.

"Hiroshi says the gazebo should go together in four or five hours with my help," Angel said, "so we'll stick around. Mama's going to supervise." Luke looked over at Mama, knowing Angel was kidding. "Then she'll make us lunch."

"Sounds like a plan to me," Luke climbed off his stool. "I'll go round up the stragglers. I'm eager to see if we can really pull this off." Hiroshi nodded confidently.

Half an hour later the crew of Luke, Steve, Greg, Raphael, Alex, Hiroshi and Angel were in the garden, huddled around the instruction manual and the notes in Hiroshi's drawing pad. The first order of business was deciding where to locate the gazebo and how to best orient it. The prime location, of course, was a corner spot already beautifully landscaped, so, before construction could begin, plantings had to be carefully dug up to be replanted around the gazebo. The planned effect would make it look like the gazebo had been in place for years. Niki, Ryan and Mateo offered to help, but were shooed away. Mateo had work anyway, and Ryan and Niki both had online classes and homework to attend to; especially Niki, who hadn't cracked open a text book, nor his laptop, all weekend. While Luke, Steve and Greg dug with the three available shovels, Hiroshi and Angel went next door and removed the tarps that had shielded the gazebo boxes from everyone's view the day before. They unboxed all the parts and arranged them in Hiroshi's garden in the order called for by the instructions. Raphael and Alex disassembled the chuppah. Once the denuded ground was smoothed and leveled, the real fun began.

Three hours later Mama brought out a pitcher of iced tea and a tray of glasses.

"Thank you, Mama," Luke said as he pulled his soaked t-shirt away from his chest. He downed half a glass of tea seemingly in one gulp. "What do you think?"

"It's very impressive," Mama praised as she rubbed one of the uprights. "Beautiful wood. And it's bigger than I expected." Alex laughed.

"Yeah, it's bigger than I expected, too." He gave Hiroshi a rueful look. "I guess that's what happens when you shop online."

"Do not worry, Alex," Hiroshi patted Alex's back. "Once we get the roof on and the landscaping replanted, it will look as if it has always been here."

Mama's tea break was well timed. The short repast was just what everyone needed before tackling the biggest challenge: installing the roof. For the next hour and a half, most of which Alex and Angel spent on step ladders, their arms achingly raised above their heads, everyone else hoisted beams and planks or tightened bolts. Fortunately, the redwood shakes were pre-cut and numbered, which made the final step in the assembly go reasonably fast. Just under Hiroshi's projected timeline, the gazebo was complete. As the crew stood back, rubbing sore shoulders and picking at splinters, they couldn't help but admire what they'd accomplished.

"Wow," Raphael nudged Alex. "We did it. We built a gazebo. It looks even better than the picture. We really did it."

"Yeah," Steve put a hand on each of their shoulders from behind, "and I'm guessing when we wake up tomorrow, our muscles will remind us exactly how much effort it took. Good job, everyone." Mama, Niki and Ryan strolled out and joined the crew.

"It's gorgeous," Niki pronounced. "Is it all done?"

"We just need to replant the landscaping," Steve pulled Niki into a side hug.

"Can that wait until after lunch?" Mama asked. "It's ready and you boys must be hungry."

"I'm starving," Alex grinned. "But, we're all pretty sweaty ..." Niki nodded and held his nose, prompting Steve to push him away.

"Just wash your hands," Mama turned and headed to the back door. Ryan grabbed Steve's elbow as the crew followed Mama.

"Can I help with the plantings? I want to do something for Juan and Ricky." Steve laid a damp arm across Ryan's shoulders as they continued walking.

"Of course, Ryan. Our master gardener, Hiroshi, is going to tell us what to plant where. Right, Hiroshi?" Hiroshi clapped a hand on Steve's back.

"If it means I will not have to wield a shovel, I will gladly assume the role of landscape architect."

Once nearly everyone had seated themselves in the dining room, Mama and Niki began serving. Raphael noticed Niki was beaming, and as soon as he slid a plate in front of him, he knew why.

"Oh man!" Raphael exclaimed. "Crab Louie! Did Niki request this?"

"No," Niki laughed. "It was a surprise." He leaned over and kissed Mama on the cheek as she slid a plate in front of Steve. Raphael looked over at Alex and Greg.

"This is a Niki special. A few weeks after he moved in with us, Mama asked him if there was anything he missed from his mom's cooking. The only thing he could come up with was Crab Louie. So, Mama found a recipe and made it for his birthday. It was his birthday dinner from then on."

"Why hasn't anyone told me this before?" Steve asked, half-jokingly. Niki leaned down as he placed a cup of artichoke soup next to Steve's plate.

"Now you know all my secrets," he stage-whispered. "Woof." Raphael glanced over at Mama, serving soup to Ryan but she didn't react.

"Oh wow!" Ryan did react. "Artichoke soup." He slurped a spoonful, then looked at Hiroshi. "Raphael and Alex made this when my parents were here ... the day we first met." He looked over at Raphael. "You weren't kidding about it being your Mama's recipe, were you?"

"What's that?" Mama asked as she took her place. Ryan repeated his story. Mama looked thoughtfully at Raphael. "So, my curries aren't the only recipes being carried on by the next generation." She looked down at her plate with a smile. "Good to know."

With lunch over, Alex and Raphael insisted on doing clean-up in the kitchen. Steve and Niki carried Hiroshi's Cape Cod chair over so Mama could sit and 'supervise' the planting. Hiroshi penciled a quick schematic, proposing where the plants could go. With no objections, Ryan, Luke and Greg began digging fresh holes. Steve and Niki trimmed root balls and unspooled the hose, ready to nurture the plants once they were set. Hiroshi had suggested planting the largest bird of paradise just to the right of the entrance to the gazebo, and it, along with the other plants surrounding all but the back third of the structure, indeed made the redwood gazebo look right at home.

"I can't wait to see Juan's and Ricky's reaction," Niki said as the crew stood back and admired their newly enhanced garden.

"When do they get back?" Angel asked, squatting down next to Mama.

"We have a car picking them up tomorrow morning at ten," Hiroshi replied. "They'll be here in time to have lunch in their new gazebo." Angel nodded, then stood.

"I'm going to take a quick shower, then we'll head out, Mama. Are you all packed?" Mama nodded.

"Yes, dear. Ready when you are." She looked over at Raphael. "Although, after this weekend, it will seem awfully boring back home. This has been such a wonderful visit." She turned to Niki. "I'm so proud of all of you, and the wonderful home you've made here." She stood and faced Hiroshi. "And I enjoyed meeting you, Hiroshi. I look forward to seeing you again."

"The pleasure was all mine," Hiroshi bowed. Angel stuck out an elbow, inviting Mama to accompany him into the house.

"Yes, indeed, Hiroshi, it was great to finally meet the man behind the mantra." Angel said. "Hopefully next time we visit, these guys won't make us work so hard for our dinner." Raphael shook his head as Luke slung a sweaty arm around Raphael's neck. Mama and Angel disappeared into the house. Everyone turned to admire their handiwork one more time.

"Would it be tacky if I re-attached some of the bird of paradise and sweet peas to the entrance to the gazebo?" Alex asked.

"Isn't that why we put them in those buckets of water last night?"
Greg asked.

"Well, yeah ..."

"It's a sweet idea," Greg agreed. "Pun intended. I'll help. The rest of
you go see Mama and Angel off."


A little after eleven, Tuesday morning, Juan and Ricky entered the foyer.
The library was empty and the house was quiet as they instinctively
stripped, stowed their shoes in their cubbies, and carried their bags and
clothes up to their room. Luke and Mateo were out working, they
assumed, but everyone else should have been working from home or
studying. After all the attention heaped on them over the weekend, it felt
a little disappointing that no one was waiting to welcome them home.
Even more odd, the doors to the other three bedrooms on their floor
were all closed. When they entered their room, they found a single bird
of paradise blossom on the bed next to a note which Ricky picked up
and read aloud. "'Welcome home, lovebirds. This bird of paradise wants
to rejoin the rest of its flock. Can you help?'

"Okay ... this is weird," Ricky looked suspiciously at Juan, who took
the note and read it again. Juan snorted.

"It's not the first weird note I've gotten." He picked up the bloom.
"I guess they want us to take one last look at the chuppah. I figured it
would be gone by now." He reached out and took Ricky's hand. "Shall
we?" They made a circuit on their way to the back door, finding both the
dining room and the kitchen empty. Clearly something was up. As they
approached the back door, even before they opened it, they could see that
the chuppah was indeed gone. But as soon as they stepped through it, a
burst of applause provided the welcome they had expected, but in a very
unexpected setting. Ricky's eyes widened as he wrapped an arm around
Juan's waist. Juan's eyes closed momentarily as he nodded, once again
disarmed by the resourcefulness of this, his chosen family. Almost all of
whom were sitting in a circle on the benches ringing the inside of what
had been, just two days before, an elegant but much smaller chuppah.

"What is this?" Juan exclaimed as he and Ricky approached. Alex leapt
out of the gazebo and gestured dramatically at the structure.

"Juan, Ricky, we wanted the memories of your wedding day to live
on forever. So, we have magically transformed your chuppah into this, a
most beautiful gazebo, where you can dine, relax, make love and maybe
even enjoy truth serum if the opportunity arises. Congratulations, again,
from all of us." Juan and Ricky stared silently a moment, apparently gob

smacked by what had happened in their absence. Juan looked at Ricky, who was still speechless, then pulled him up and into the center of the gazebo. He looked up at the vaulted ceiling, then at the amused family members surrounding them.

"How ... did you ... this was the chuppah?"

"A little bit of it, yeah," Steve explained. "All the rest of this was hidden next door in Hiroshi's garden. We built it yesterday while you two were off honeymooning."

"You ... you guys built this?" Ricky had let go of Juan and moved over to touch one of the posts. "Seriously?" Niki was nearest Ricky.

"These guys built it, with Angel's help. Ryan and I helped with the plants." Juan sat down, cross-legged, in the center of the gazebo.

"You guys are unbelievable," he said, looking into Hiroshi's eyes. "The ceremony, the honeymoon, and now this?" Studly Juan blinked a few times and sniffed, determined not to get emotional. Ricky sat next to him, leaned over and pressed his lips to Juan's neck with a loud smack.

"You know, we didn't just pick the best wedding planners, Papito. We picked the best family, too." He looked around. "Well, I guess they picked me. But ... I picked you!"

Eight

## HIROSHI'S CRAZY IDEA

"I THINK WE'RE OUT of mango preserves, Papito," Ricky said, as he placed the tray in the middle of the round table in the gazebo. "So I brought blueberry. Since it's my favorite." He made a 'so there' face, followed by a sweet smile. The redwood table had been Juan and Ricky's contribution to what they insisted was *everyone's* gazebo. Since early April they'd made a habit of having breakfast together here every Saturday morning, rain or shine. Sadly, it was always shine this forebodingly dry spring. Juan helped himself to brioche toast and a cup of mixed fruit Ricky had prepared while Ricky poured coffee for each of them before he sat, thigh to thigh, with Juan. After a couple of bites, Juan rubbed Ricky's back with his jam-free left hand.

"What do you want to do today? Besides a workout in the gym."

"Well, you know, I should Dash for at least a few hours this afternoon or evening. Tips are usually pretty good on Saturdays. Especially when there's a game. One of these days they'll start letting people eat inside restaurants again, and go inside sports bars, and that may change. But until then ..." Juan heaved a heavy sigh. "Did you have something special in mind?" Juan shook his head wordlessly and took another bite of toast. The creak of the gate caused both to look up and see Hiroshi appear in the opening. Sporting a light green fundoshi and a dark blue mug, he bowed, then approached the gazebo. Juan waved an invitation for Hiroshi to join them.

"Forgive my boldness, but I wanted to speak with the two of you. If I may." He sat and took a sip from his mug.

"Would you like some toast, Hiroshi?" Ricky offered. "We have blueberry jam."

"Tempting, but no thank you," Hiroshi smiled. "I ate earlier. No, I wanted to invite the two of you on a little mystery tour, unless you have something else planned this morning." Juan leaned back and gazed bemusedly at Hiroshi.

"What's up?"

"That would be telling. I know this whole family loves a good mystery. Well, this may not be a *good* mystery, more like a crazy idea, but ..." Juan and Ricky exchanged curious looks. Ricky finished chewing a chunk of pineapple and swallowed.

"I'm in," he said.

"No kidding," Juan replied. "Who could resist an invitation like that?" Hiroshi stood.

"Is ten o'clock good for you?" Ricky and Juan nodded. "I will meet you out front, then. And please do not say anything to anyone else. Not yet, anyway." He smiled goodbye and stepped down to the ground and continued on through the gate. Juan and Ricky looked at each other, definitely intrigued. This was the first time Hiroshi had instigated an outing. And one just for the two of them. Ricky freshened each of their mugs, then set the carafe back down. He took another sip and looked at Juan.

"I'm clueless." Juan leaned over and planted a blueberry scented kiss.

"You're cute when you're clueless. So am I. Clueless, I mean. Totally."

"So, when am I not cute?"

"When you're adorable. Eat up. We don't know what Hiroshi has planned, so we should probably shower before we meet him." Ricky nodded as he cut his piece of toast in half and slid one piece onto Juan's plate.


Hiroshi was waiting on the sidewalk at the bottom of the steps when Juan and Ricky joined him. He was dressed casually, as usual, in nearly knee-length black shorts and a gray sweatshirt with a UC Berkeley 'CAL' logo.

"Thank you for joining me," he said, as he urged them down the hill. "I will not take too much of your valuable weekend."

"Where are we going?" Ricky asked as he slipped one hand into Juan's and insinuated the other into Hiroshi's. Hiroshi squeezed back in response.

"Not far," Hiroshi replied mysteriously. He turned to Ricky. "How long have you been working with DoorDash?"

"I don't know," Ricky met Hiroshi's gaze. "Two and a half, three years. Yeah, about three years." He glanced at Juan, then regained Hiroshi's gaze. "Why?"

"Oh ... just wondering," Hiroshi teased. Juan chuckled.

"Part of the mystery, Hiroshi?" Juan teased back.

"I will let the two of you be the judge of that. Here. We should cross here." Hiroshi directed them across Noe and toward Castro Street. Three blocks later Hiroshi stopped in front of a vacant store front on Castro. One that had been vacant so long Juan couldn't remember what had previously occupied it. Hiroshi broke free of Ricky's grasp and turned to address them, his back to the building.

"I remember the stories you have told, about Raphael and Alex's famous strip shows. And one that included you, Ricky. How popular they were. How excited the crowds were to see two or three caged young men on the stage. Am I remembering that correctly?" Juan met Hiroshi's questioning gaze with a tentative look.

"Yeah, they were a sensation, to say the least. But ..." Hiroshi raised a hand, pausing Juan.

"Would you say the interest in those sexy men," Hiroshi smiled roguishly at Ricky, "was simply gratification from watching a strip show, or was there genuine curiosity about the display of chastity being presented to them?" Juan looked at Ricky for input. Ricky shrugged.

"Lots of guys tried to grab my cage when they handed me money afterwards," Ricky recalled, "so, you know, I'd say some of them were curious, yeah."

"And horny as hell," Juan asserted. "They were probably more attracted to the sexy guy they'd just seen on stage than his cage."

"So, that is a yes and a maybe," Hiroshi pondered.

"Come on, Hiroshi," Juan reached out and gripped Hiroshi's shoulder. "As Raphael and Alex like to say, 'spill.' What are you getting at?" Hiroshi half turned and gestured to the building.

"Imagine, if you will, a store. Or, maybe better, an academy. Dedicated to the science ... the art ... the lifestyle of chastity. A welcoming place for both the novice and the experienced practitioner."

"You're thinking of opening a store that sells chastity devices?" Juan asked, a little incredulously. "Just cages? Other sex shops in the neighborhood already sell them, don't they?" Hiroshi scrunched up his face.

"Yes, Juan, along with hundreds of other sex toys. And that is how they present them. As toys. What I envision is a source for the serious practitioner and, more importantly, a *resource* for the novice. Not just products, but advice and counsel on sizing and the many types of cages and belts. Expert fittings. Discussion groups. Support, like AA, for newly caged men who need motivational support when tempted to unlock. Maybe even social gatherings, once that is permitted again, to meet other locked men, and perhaps even keyholders seeking men to lock. A community space, if you will. Unlike ordering online, the highly informed staff would be able to provide very personal service in selecting and fitting a device." Juan looked over Hiroshi's shoulder at the weathered façade of the storefront.

"Hiroshi, this sounds like a lot of work. Why would you complicate the life you enjoy now with something like this?" Hiroshi chuckled.

"Because I see a need, my friend." Hiroshi put a hand on Ricky's shoulder. "Besides, I would never enter into such an endeavor on my own. I would need a partner. A partner that would not only be caged, but irresistibly so. And, hopefully, eventually a staff." He paused to insure he had Ricky's full attention. "Ricky, I would like to offer you the position of co-owner and Senior Chastity Consultant at the Castro's soon to be famous, or maybe infamous, LCB Headquarters." Ricky's eyes widened, and he looked at Juan for a reaction.

"Whoa," Juan met Ricky's gaze before turning to Hiroshi. "You're really serious ... about starting a new retail business. Here? Now? In a pandemic? And ... with Ricky?" At that, Ricky gave Juan a deflated look.

"Yes," Hiroshi replied, smiling fondly at Ricky. "I have not finalized anything yet, but I have been thinking and doing some ground work. We may be in a pandemic, but soon, hopefully, we will all be vaccinated, along with most, if not all of our potential customers. I feel certain the time is right for something like this. Chastity is booming on social media and in real life. As you said, it is becoming so common devices are being sold over the counter ... but not in a personalized way. And speaking of social media, men experimenting with and fully adopting chastity are desperate for community, and for the most part, they can only find it online. Just as comic book stores provide community for dedicated aficionados, LCB Headquarters would provide a physical space, for those who live and travel here, to gather, discuss, experiment, learn about and try new devices. Especially since this approachable guy in the baby blue Holy Trainer would be there to measure them and help them try on their new purchase." Ricky looked over at the storefront, trying to imagine what Hiroshi was proposing. He looked back at Juan again, his expression uncertain. An expression not lost on Hiroshi.

"I can see I have overwhelmed both of you. You two should take some time to think about what I have said. When you are ready, we can discuss it further. But, yes, I am serious. I think there is a market for this unmet need. More importantly, I think *we* are best suited to fill it. Now that I have revealed the mystery, we can return home." As Hiroshi turned to leave, Ricky stepped closer to the glass front and peered into the empty space. Juan came up behind him and rubbed up and down Ricky's neck and shaved head a couple of times before resting his hand on Ricky's shoulder.

"Wow," Ricky quietly said, without turning away from the window. "I have lots of questions." Juan tugged on Ricky's shoulder and nudged him around and started walking them toward Hiroshi, now several yards ahead.

"Me, too, mijo. Let's write them down. I'm sure Hiroshi will be able to answer them all."

Sunday's breakfast featured Ricky's granola-laced pancakes, always a welcome surprise. He seemed unusually chipper at the stove, his perky brown butt bouncing inside the open back of his apron, in time to a tune apparently playing solely in his head. Not totally out of character for him, but a welcome vibe nonetheless. Everyone seemed in good spirits. Vaccines were rolling out, although only Juan and Hiroshi had been eligible so far. But soon the rest of the family would be able to get in line for the jab. Maybe, just maybe, someday soon face masks would no longer be a mandatory accessory when venturing out.

"You working today, Mateo?" Raphael asked, leaning back in his chair between bites of his short stack. Mateo shook his head, still chewing, then swallowed.

"Off today." He looked meaningfully at Ryan, who tried to look innocent. It appeared they had plans.

"Alex, Niki and I are planning a run later, if you want to join us. It's been a while for you." Raphael zeroed in on Ricky. "You, too, Ricky. Wanna come?" He turned to Niki. "How many miles today?"

"Four," Niki replied, holding up four digits as a visual aid. "But we can cut it back for the novices." He grinned at Ricky. Ricky offered up a single digit to Niki.

"What time?" he asked.

"Whenever everyone can," was Raphael's response. "Three? Four?" Ricky looked to Juan for confirmation. Juan seemed indecisive.

"I should be free by three," Ricky decided. "Sounds like fun." Alex and Raphael exchanged looks.

"Well, if you and Juan were reserving the dungeon ... or whatever ..." Ricky looked offended.

"No, Alex," Ricky scrunched up his nose. "We just have a ... a commitment. The dungeon is all yours."

"Cool," Alex replied before looking at Mateo, eyebrows raised in anticipation. "Shaman Prince?" Mateo nodded and smiled, chewing away. Alex glanced at Niki. "It's a date. Three o'clock. Four miles. Five sexy guys."

"And Alex," Raphael couldn't resist. Without looking up, Alex offered Raphael one of his own digits in response.

While Alex and Raphael, joined this time by Luke, took care of cleanup in the kitchen, Ricky and Juan slipped out the back door. Greg assumed they'd decamped to the gazebo, but when he wandered out a few minutes later, coffee mug and *Chronicle* in hand, the gazebo was empty. He assumed they must have gone back inside when he wasn't looking, so he sat and opened the Sporting Green section to read about the previous night's Warriors game. He didn't notice that the gate was slightly ajar.

"Thank you for granting me a little more of your weekend," Hiroshi said as he led Juan and Ricky into the study. They sat in the two chairs Hiroshi indicated, facing his desk. While he poured tea he continued, "I should tell you that this is the room where many wonderful endeavors have been hatched, including your wedding ceremony." He handed steaming cups to Juan and Ricky. "Alex, and to some extent Raphael, conspired with me here on your behalf." He sat. "And now I have the pleasure to consider a collaboration with you." He took a slow sip, eyes closed, then he opened them, focused on Ricky. "Where should we start?"

"Well, I guess, first of all, I should say thank you for considering me in your plans," Ricky responded. He glanced at Juan. "That's maybe my first question. Why me? I mean, you know, I really don't have any business experience."

"I respectfully disagree," Hiroshi smiled. "You are already running your own business now, Ricky. You decide your hours. You choose and coordinate deliveries, maximizing satisfaction for both your vendors and your customers. Not to mention you managed to acquire a husband as well as an entire family through your professional services. How many business people can say that?" Juan smiled in reaction, while holding back on any commentary thus far. Ricky's smile indicated he had no valid argument.

"Ricky, I approached you because this 'crazy idea' of mine will never work unless potential customers are attracted, not only to the idea of exploring chastity, but to the people offering them the opportunity to explore it as well. There will be a few who feel comfortable sharing such intimate interests with someone like me. But far more of them will be, not just comfortable, but ... let me just say it ... they will be excited by the idea of consulting with you about the prospect of locking up their junk, or that of their lover." He turned to Juan. "How about it, Juan?

You walk into LCB Headquarters compelled, probably from hours spent online, to explore and maybe, if the circumstances are just right, to begin a journey into chastity. And there, behind the display case featuring dozens of devices you are unfamiliar with, is this sexy young man wearing a skin tight crop top with a caged rooster on it and rocking see-through mesh shorts that showcase a baby blue Holy Trainer. The young man greets you with a heart-stopping smile and asks, 'How may I help you?' Are you going to just window shop?" Juan's tumescent cock was all the answer Hiroshi needed. "Exactly," Hiroshi smiled at Ricky as he nodded toward Juan's involuntary response. "They will be lined up around the block." Ricky, humbled by Hiroshi's soliloquy, glanced slyly at Juan as he sipped.

"You are experienced in customer relations, Ricky. I know you are a hard worker, willing to work long hours at times, evenings and weekends. This would be an opportunity to work more regular hours, many similar to Juan's, giving you both more time together. You would have the opportunity to develop new business skills." Hiroshi paused a moment to reinforce his next words. "Most importantly of all, I trust you. Once we have the business up and running, if I wish, I could take time away, knowing that it would be in good hands." Ricky looked into Hiroshi's eyes, seeing the sincerity and confidence there. Hiroshi saw the respect, and the uncertainty, in Ricky's.

"What else concerns you, my friend?" Hiroshi asked. Ricky swallowed, glanced again at Juan, who was once again more or less under control, then met Hiroshi's gaze full on.

"You said I would be co-owner. But I don't have any money to invest. And that store. It would take a lot of money and a lot of work before it's ready, wouldn't it?" Hiroshi nodded.

"Yes. Your investment would be in sweat equity, initially. I am prepared to front the start-up capital needed. Once we are open, you will receive a salary and commission. And half of eventual profit as co-owner."

"That's quite an offer, Hiroshi." Juan finally spoke. "It seems like an awfully big risk for you. With no guaranteed return." Hiroshi sighed, nodded slightly and turned in his chair to fully face Juan.

"Reward always comes with risk, Juan. I could be wrong about the market potential. If so, I am prepared for the consequences. We have both seen many businesses come and go, have we not? But I have considered this carefully." He turned back to face both Ricky and Juan equally. "I am quite certain that your husband, my dear friend Ricky, is the 'point of difference,' the 'secret sauce' that will ensure the success of LCB Headquarters. Which is why I am cheerfully offering him fifty-percent ownership." Hiroshi leaned forward. "If you say no, I will understand,

Ricky. But ... and this is how much I value your involvement ... I will not go forward without you." Ricky took a deep breath. And held it. As he slowly exhaled, he again glanced at Juan.

"What is your timeline, Hiroshi?" Juan asked.

"I have signed a letter of intent on the lease. If you two say yes, we could start renovations fairly soon. I have identified a permit expediter, so it will all depend upon how successfully she can pull strings. With luck, we could be open by mid-July in time for Up Your Alley Fair, if it happens this year. Meanwhile, if you are on board, Senior Chastity Consultant, we can begin working out all the details in your off hours while you continue Dashing." Ricky still didn't look convinced. "More questions?" Hiroshi prodded.

"It just doesn't seem fair," Ricky looked meaningfully at Hiroshi. "To you, I mean. Your time, your money, your experience. And to make me half owner." Once again, he looked to Juan for support.

"Mijo," Juan reached over and squeezed Ricky's thigh. "I have to agree with Hiroshi." He looked at Hiroshi as he continued, "It certainly is a crazy idea." Hiroshi snorted in response. Juan turned back to Ricky, "But, it's a crazy idea that just might succeed, with the right marketing, ambiance and social media presence. But most importantly, if there is a compelling attraction to pull guys in for their first cage. And their second. And no one would be better at that, mijo, than you." Ricky held eye contact with Juan while a tentative smile slowly formed.

"So, you think I should say yes?"

"All I'll say is Hiroshi trusts you to make this a success. Whatever you decide, I think you can put your trust in Hiroshi." Ricky's smile bloomed as he reached out to shake Hiroshi's hand. Then, he stood and bowed as elegantly as Hiroshi ever had. Hiroshi clapped, then stood and bowed in return.

"Ah ha," he grinned. "Interesting. Are you suggesting an Asian motif for the Headquarters? Already the ideas are beginning to flow. I am excited, partner. I hope you are, too." Juan stood and the three finalized the deal with a traditional LCB group hug.

# Nine

## A Truly Grand Opening

Ricky, bare-chested, in boardshorts, had his back to Alex and Greg when they slowly pushed open the door to the shop. Between his ear buds and the drone of the upright sander Ricky was manhandling over the floor boards, they could have been a horde of Mongolian invaders and he still wouldn't have known they were bearing down on him. Greg winked at Alex, who was holding a surprise sack lunch, before he walked over and pulled the plug on the sander. Ricky looked up at the newly installed rack of spots, assuming he'd blown a breaker, then turned to discover the real culprits. He pulled out one of his ear buds.

"I have a burrito here with your name on it, Ricky," Alex held out the bag. Ricky grinned and removed the other bud. He relieved Alex of the bag.

"Thanks, amigos. I guess maybe I am getting hungry. Did you eat already?" Alex nodded as he pulled a dew covered can of Orangina out of his shoulder bag and handed it to Ricky. All three sat on the floor in the still sparse space. Ricky pulled a napkin out of his bag to wipe his forehead and shaved sides of his high 'n tight. He offered the still warm tortilla chips to Greg and Alex, but they declined.

"You're doing a great job," Greg said, rubbing his hand along the hardwood floor between him and Alex. "Are you going to do a clear seal or a stain?" Ricky shrugged, still chewing his first mouthful of burrito.

"Clear, I think," he replied after swallowing. "Hiroshi and I were kicking around the idea of going with an Asian motif. If we do, a lighter floor with some decorated rugs would make sense. There are some cool homoerotic Japanese prints out there that we could hang on the walls, but, you know, we're not sure yet. Asian would represent Hiroshi well, but not so much me."

"What would make sense for you?" Alex asked. He reached over and snagged a chip.

"I don't know. Maybe Leather Boy images? Power dynamics. You know, like Tom of Finland. We'll see." Alex nodded thoughtfully. Greg looked over at the street windows.

"What are you guys thinking for the display windows? You can't really put cages and chastity belts on display for passersby, can you? I mean, Harvey Milk Civil Rights Academy is only a couple blocks over."

"You kidding?" Ricky laughed. "Those kids have seen it all." He glanced over at the windows. "We'll figure something out. Here, let me show you what we have so far." He jumped up and scurried into the back room, returning with a larger sketch pad than the one Hiroshi had used for the gazebo project. He flipped through several pages showing sketches in perspective, and from overhead, showing placement of six cylindrical display cases. There were also renderings of two 'fitting chambers' that would also be free standing structures that obscured the customer from the chest down, instead of providing total privacy. Ricky also shared several potential designs of the LCB Headquarters logo.

"As soon as we finalize the logo, we're going to get some tees made and then have Raphael's friend Allyson tailor some of them into crop tops. Hiroshi thinks, if I wear them in the store, we'll sell as many of them as we do cages."

"He's probably right," Greg poked Ricky in the abs. "I'd buy one." Alex looked around the bare bones space, then back at the sketch pad.

"I like the direction you guys are going with multiple, smaller, free standing display cases. Like a high-end jewelry store. And the free-standing circular fitting booths are cool. Very original. And a little daring. Are you still on schedule for mid-July?" he asked.

"Hopefully. As soon as I finish here, we can install the display cases. The fitting 'chambers,' as Hiroshi calls them, are being fabricated now. He's been placing orders for the inventory. As soon as we settle on the logo, we'll get that etched into the display windows."

"What about advertising? Social media presence?" Greg prodded.

"We're going to work with Steve on that, as soon as we have the logo." Greg nodded. Ricky wiped his lips and stuffed his napkins into the empty brown bag. Greg reached over and appropriated it. "Thanks for lunch guys. That was just what I needed."

"It was the least we could do," Alex said, rising to his feet. "We haven't been able to be much help so far." Greg stood, reached out for the empty Orangina can and steered Alex toward the door.

"We'll be more help when it really matters," Greg said. "You can count on us, Ricky." Alex looked at Greg, then Ricky. He nodded as if he knew exactly what Greg meant.

"I think I was right, Sir," Raphael asserted, his legs wrapped around Luke's waist from behind. He was slowly, lavishly massaging Luke's scalp, his fingers and Luke's hair foamy with the all-natural rosemary mint shampoo Alex had recommended. It had been four months and dozens of foamy scalp massages since Raphael issued his hair dare to Luke. Although his hair wasn't close to the length that Juan's, or even Mateo's, had attained so far, it was still longer than at any time Luke could remember. Long enough to be annoying, except when Raphael was reveling in it.

"I'm sure you were, baby. You always are," Luke responded languorously, half hypnotized by the sensations and smells of Raphael's sensual ministrations. "About what?" Although he missed the mohawk, and the attention it often received, this nightly session with Raphael, more and more, made the dare a fair trade-off.

"Your hair. It's long enough now that I think I can see it's going to be wavy, kind of like Jamie's. Like Alex's." Raphael brushed away a blob of shampoo trickling down the back of Luke's neck, leaned forward and planted a long kiss there.

"Mmmm," Luke reacted. "You're doing everything you can to make me happy about this dare, aren't you?" Raphael held the kiss dramatically before responding.

"The dare is supposed to make *me* happy, Sir. I'll let you know for sure in another four or five inches." Luke snorted. "Or more ..."

"I'll look ridiculous."

"Does Jamie look ridiculous? Does Juan? Or Mateo?" Raphael stopped massaging Luke's scalp and reached around to squeeze Luke's chest from behind. He whispered into Luke's ear, "Did I?"

"No, of course not, baby. You've always been the beautiful one. But I'm not you."

"Juan's not beautiful, Sir. He's handsome. Studly. Suave. Just like you. Now, stand up. Let's rinse you off. Your locked cock boy wants to have his way with you. If that's okay, Sir." Luke stood, turned and reached down to pull Raphael up and into a bona fide embrace, one that lingered. The feeling of Raphael's pecs pressed into his own chest triggered Luke's predicable arousal. As his cock pressed against Raphael's pubic tattoo, Raphael reached behind himself to flick on the shower. Knowing the first second or two of the spray would be chilly, he ducked just in time, swallowing Luke's offering as the spray hit Luke's chest. Luke bucked, but Raphael held tight, one hand grasping each of Luke's hard thighs. The water immediately warmed and Luke bent forward, rinsing the shampoo off his head and onto Raphael, who was too busy to notice or care.

On his walk home from the hospital, Juan made a point to walk past Hiroshi and Ricky's shop to check things out. It had been several days since he'd last seen it, and he was pleased to see that the façade had been sanded and painted, teal with white accents. The door sported new brass fittings and the display windows were papered over from the inside so he, and everyone else passing by, were denied a look inside. He tried the door, but it was locked. Two guys, holding hands, walking from the opposite direction paused upon seeing Juan attempt to enter.

"Is this your shop?" one of them asked. Juan smiled and shook his head. "You know what's going in here?"

"Yeah, I know the guys who own it."

"So, what's it going to be? It's been empty forever." A new business always generated interest among denizens of the neighborhood, even more so when the fallout from the pandemic and lockdowns made closures far more common than openings. Juan considered offering a clever teaser, but decided against it.

"I really shouldn't say." One of the guys made a snarky 'whatever' face, changing Juan's mind. "But just between you and me ..." The other leaned forward a bit. "It's going to be very cool. Very radical. It's going to be the only shop like it *anywhere*. So stay tuned." Juan wiggled his eyebrows, then turned and headed home. At dinner he relayed the incident to the rest of the family.

"It's not too soon to start generating a little buzz in the community," Steve suggested.

"How?" Raphael asked, knowing Steve probably already had something in mind.

"Yeah," Ricky followed up. "Would that be part of the marketing plan we talked about?"

"Yes," Steve replied, his fork midway between plate and mouth. "Have your people call my people for the details." Ricky put his hand to his ear, feigning a phone call.

"People, tell Steve's people we're ready for the marketing plan to start. Pronto." Steve chewed wordlessly.

"How close are you to opening?" Ryan asked.

"Two, three weeks," Ricky grinned. "Hopefully." Steve's eyes widened.

"I couldn't see how much progress you've made with the windows blocked," Juan reported. "But the outside looks great."

"The guy is supposed to etch the logo onto the windows tomorrow, but we don't want anyone to see inside until we're ready. You know, until it's finished."

"Listen, if you're only two or three weeks away, we should get busy," Steve looked serious. "I've dummied up a website, but I was waiting for the final, final on the logo. Tell Hiroshi we should get started. Yesterday." Ricky nodded. "Do you guys have inventory in yet?"

"A lot of it, yeah."

"We're going to need pics. Just the products for the website, and on a body for the in-house promotional screens. Are you going to be the model?" Ricky grinned again and looked slyly at Ryan.

"Me and Ryan. You know, for diversity." Ryan looked blindsided. "Umm ..."

"Relax, Ryan," Steve smiled. "These will be close-ups. No faces. No identifying characteristics."

"Well, okay then," Ryan relaxed. "Cool. Anything I can do to help."

"I'd be willing to model," Alex volunteered. "I want to help out."

"Oh, you will help," Greg ruffled Alex's hair, then wrapped his arm around Alex's neck. "In fact, you'll have a major role in promoting LCB Headquarters to the Castro." Greg looked meaningfully at Ryan and Mateo, prompting Alex to do the same, but the gaze they returned was as inquisitive as Alex's.

"Oh, are you talking about the mannequin idea I had?" Alex looked enthusiastically at Ricky.

"Sure ..." Greg slid his hand down Alex's back, then resumed eating.

"What about a mannequin?" Ricky asked. This was news to him.

"I wanted to do a little more research before sharing the idea, but since Greg brought it up, I had an idea for your display windows." He detailed his idea of placing two mannequins in each window, with their backs to the street, seemingly naked from that angle, but inside, they'd each be wearing a chastity device. "To add to the intrigue from the street, one would be wearing a full Carrara belt in one window, and one would be wearing a chest harness in the other, so people would realize the display wasn't 'in progress.'"

"I like it," Steve enthused. "Guys would be motivated to enter, thinking maybe it's a shop selling leather gear."

"And ..." Juan joined in, "one should be white, one black and the other two each a different shade of brown."

"Yes! Like us!" Niki agreed. "And ... in the opposite window from the one with the chest harness, one should be wearing a pup hood. If the mannequins have heads." Steve ruffled Niki's mohawk.

"You were right, Greg," Ricky beamed. "I think Hiroshi will love it. Alex, your idea is perfect."

"It is now, thanks to Juan's and Niki's suggestions," Alex nodded. "I'll give Hiroshi the info I found on where to source the mannequins." Ricky made the 'okay' sign with his forkless hand.


"Are you ready, partner?" Hiroshi asked, one hand on Ricky's shoulder, the other on the chain attached to the opaque shade covering the left display window. It was nine-fifty-nine Saturday morning, July 17, 2021, right in the midst of a pandemic. The neighborhood, the entire city, was still semi-comatose; it was by all accounts an insane time to launch a new business. But, then again, those same accounts would probably consider LCB Headquarters an insane business model at any time. So it was, in fact, as good a time as any to roll up the shades and welcome the outside world in.

"Ready!" Ricky nodded, his hand grasping the chain on the other shade. "Pull!" Simultaneously with the rising shades, from his room on the third floor of the House of the Locked Cock Brotherhood, Steve was taking their website, Instagram page and Twitter account live as well. As Juan had promised the two curious pedestrians weeks earlier, LCB Headquarters, now finally revealed, was unlike anything anyone in the neighborhood had seen before. First, there were the four mannequins with their bare backs to the street. The black one in the left window, wearing a puppy hood, had his arm draped across the shoulders of the light brown one wearing a metal band around its waist. A Carrara belt. The white one in the right window was wearing a chest harness, his arm draped across the shoulders of a darker brown model. But that was just the initial impression.

Inside, at first glance, the shop appeared to be a jewelry store, with six widely spaced cylindrical display cases, four feet high and about two feet in diameter, with high intensity spots highlighting each one. Nearer the back, behind the display cases were two free-standing circular fitting chambers with light teal curtains suspended a third of the way from the top. The floor was highly polished wood, the walls dark teal. One wall was decorated with what appeared to be ancient Japanese watercolors, which, upon closer inspection, portrayed samurai and other figures, some clad in fundoshi, some wearing even less in distinctly compromising situations. The opposite wall featured four Tom of Finland prints. However, none of that compared to the impression made by the two proprietors themselves. Ricky sported a crop top emblazoned with the

Headquarters logo, his Holy Trainer visible through his mesh Airtex Sport shorts, all complemented by a new pair of 30-Hole black boots. Hiroshi was temporarily caged again in a white Holy Trainer, discretely visible under a white fundoshi, under a loosely tied black yukata and sandals. More subtle than Ricky's uniform, but still compelling. LCB Headquarters was open for business.

In the first thirty minutes dozens of pedestrians walked by. Most glanced in the windows, but all kept walking. A couple of guys paused and peered in, curious, especially about the guy in the crop top, no doubt, but they moved on without entering. Ricky sighed heavily and looked dejectedly at Hiroshi.

"It is still early days, Ricky. We must give it time." On cue, the door opened and Ricky turned to greet ... Greg and Luke. Ricky tried not to look disappointed.

"Hey," he said. "Can I interest you gentlemen in a new cage? For yourselves? Or perhaps for your lovers?"

"Sure!" Greg replied, taking in the ambience. He and Luke walked to different display cases to check things out.

"The place is beautiful," Luke praised as he wandered, examining some of the art more closely, then fingering the curtain on one of the fitting chambers. "You both look stunning. As usual."

"Not stunning enough, not yet anyway," Ricky complained. Greg wrinkled his brow questioningly. "You guys are our first ... and only customers." Greg smiled and nodded.

"You just opened," he said. "Half the neighborhood isn't out of bed yet. And it's going to take a while for Steve's marketing to catch on and build." He glanced out the window as several men passed by, checking out the backsides of the mannequins without pausing. "Umm hmmm." He gave Luke a strange, mischievous look.

"What?" Luke asked. Greg grinned and turned to Ricky.

"Alex's mannequins were a great idea. But I think it's time he made his real contribution to your grand opening." He took out his phone and tapped out a text. He glanced over at Hiroshi. "Get ready to sell some merchandise, gentlemen."

Alex wandered into Raphael's room, where he was dispensing with emails that had accumulated since he'd logged out Friday afternoon. One of the many drawbacks to the 'work from home' environment was that work flowed seamlessly into evenings and weekends.

"Don't laugh," Alex said, "but Greg wants me to borrow a sarong from you and bring it down to Headquarters."

"What?" Raphael turned from his screen. "Why?" he asked with only a hint of a laugh.

"Don't know. Maybe to wrap around one of the mannequins?" Raphael rose and opened a couple of dresser drawers before finding a sarong, one that Alex hadn't seen before.

"How's this?" Raphael held it up and let it unfurl. It was black and white, the white parts almost sheer, in an abstract fish pattern. Alex nodded approval and took it from Raphael and began folding it.

"Aren't you going to wear it down?" Raphael joked.

"And what would I wear back? A new cage?" Alex headed for the door.

"Why don't I come too, Alex? I want to see shop anyway. Just let me get dressed."

"I'll meet you downstairs," Alex called out, already halfway to his room, bringing Ryan to his door.

"What's up?" he asked, eyeing the sarong in Alex's hand.

"Greg asked me to bring this to Ricky and Hiroshi's shop." Ryan's eyes lit up.

"That's right! Today's the big day. Can I come, too?" Alex agreed, and Ryan dashed back into his room to dress.

Twenty minutes later LCB Headquarters was bustling ... with family members. And still no customers. Alex handed the sarong to Greg, then walked to the center of the shop and turned to assess the mannequins in the windows. He nodded, gratified with the result.

"You guys made the mannequin idea work," he praised. "Do you think they're attracting attention?"

"Yeah," Ricky replied, "but nobody's come in yet." He glanced at Hiroshi. "But it's still early days." Greg walked over to Alex, placed a hand affectionately on his shoulder, and squeezed as he held out the sarong.

"Alex," he grinned, "you just need to take your mannequin idea and kick it up a notch." Alex looked confused, not taking the sarong. "Welcome, my dear, to your first flash dare. A revenge, flash dare."

"What?" Alex looked more confused. Greg glanced over at Ryan and winked.

"Remember when you coerced Ryan into wearing a collar when he was caged? To, ah, contrive a circumstance requiring me to submit to a dare? From you?" Alex looked less confused. And a little uncomfortable. "Well, Ryan, Mateo and I decided that because you were cheating, it would only be right if I were the one issuing the dare ... *to you.* Call it a punishing dare." He glanced back at a grinning Ryan, then to Luke and

Raphael, who were clearly enjoying the scene. He pushed the sarong into Alex's gut. Lovingly. "Go strip and wrap the sarong around your waist while Luke and I make room in the window for a living, breathing ... dancing mannequin. One that's going to flash his shiny cage at passersby and lure them into LCB Headquarters on opening day."

"No!" was Alex's fruitless response. Raphael walked up, took the sarong from Greg and grabbed Alex by the biceps. He began pulling him toward a fitting chamber.

"Actually, Alex ... it's a dare, you can only say 'yes.' And it's a damn good one, too. Not bad for your first dare, Greg."

"No," Alex repeated, more meekly, as Raphael dragged him around one of the display cases and over to the chamber. Alex looked helplessly at Hiroshi.

"Thank you for contributing to our grand opening," Hiroshi grinned. "This is very kind of you." Raphael pulled the curtain aside and pushed Alex in. Hiroshi and Ryan began rearranging the mannequins in the right window to make room for the mannequin wearing the Carrara belt that Greg and Luke were lifting out of the left window. Alex would be sharing the spotlight with the mannequin in a puppy hood. Alex watched all this from his side of the half curtain, still fully clothed. Ricky walked up to the chamber.

"Resistance is futile, Alex. We may not be the Borg, but we do outnumber you. If you make us strip you, we'll run away with your clothes and you'll have to walk home naked." He looked over at Greg. "Is there such a thing as a punishing revenge flash dare addendum?"

"We're about to find out, Ricky," Greg replied. "Counting down from twenty. Nineteen. Eighteen."

"All right ... all right ..." Alex disappeared as he bent down and pulled off his shoes and socks, then his shorts and finally his tee. Raphael handed him the sarong over the chest high curtain.

"Don't tie it too tight, Alex," he coached. "Make sure the overlap is front. We want to see that cage." Alex scowled. "Everybody wants to see that cage." While Alex struggled with the sarong, Hiroshi fiddled with the sound system, replacing the quiet, acoustic background music with something a little louder, and with a lot more energy. Raphael walked up to Luke and Greg, who had finished repositioning the three mannequins. "Let's go outside and make sure Alex puts on a good show."

"Good idea," Greg replied. "We should make room for real customers, anyway." With social distancing rules still in place, the shop was legally limited to no more than three customers inside at a time. Raphael motioned to Ryan to join them as they stepped outside. The four of them gathered at the curb, off to the side, so as not to impede any passersby from becoming voyeurs initially, and then, hopefully, customers. A couple of minutes passed before Alex finally stepped up into the window. Hiroshi propped opened the door, making it possible to subtlety hear the music on the street. Alex stood there a moment, starring daggers at Greg, but soon realized others had stopped and were staring at him, sans daggers. Instinctively, he began to perform. Within minutes, several more guys had paused, attracted by the music, by the novelty of being able to finally see inside the shop, but mostly because of the half-naked dancer in the window. Reprising some of the moves from his Chastity Brothers days, Alex was moving gracefully, sensuously. You couldn't see a smile behind his mask, but his eyes looked reasonably happy. So far, so good. What he wasn't doing was revealing any cage. And there weren't any kids around to justify that. Raphael waited until Alex happened to make eye contact, then pulled down the front of his shorts with one hand, flashing his own cage. Alex turned half around in feigned embarrassment, then turned back and finally opened the front of the sarong.

"Whoa!" One guy reacted, turning quickly to his companion. "Did you see that?"

"Ohhhh!" Another exclaimed. "Now I get it!" He walked up to the other window and tried to see what was hidden on the front side of the mannequins in the window. Having failed, he became the first potential customer to cross the threshold into LCB Headquarters. Alex continued dancing, flirting with the onlookers by opening and mostly closing the sarong. Seeing the first guy apparently transfixed by what he was examining in the display cases, with Ricky's help, a couple more pedestrians decided to investigate as well. Greg's punishing dare was paying off. Two more guys entered, overwhelming Hiroshi and Ricky and exceeding max occupancy.

"Ryan," Luke grabbed his arm, "do you have to get back to the house right away?" Ryan shook his head. "Cool. Come with me." He and Ryan hurried into the shop, where Luke conferred with Hiroshi briefly. Hiroshi and Ryan went into the back. A moment later they returned, with Ryan sporting a tight black tee emblazoned with the LCB Headquarters logo. He and Luke exited, but Ryan posted himself next to the door. Luke, bearing a roll of the painter's tape left over from the remodel, bent down and stretched a blue line on the sidewalk six feet away in front of the window with three mannequins. He repeated the act several more times, working his way down the street. Luke then went back inside and ushered out the last two customers and positioned them at the first mark, before rejoining Raphael and Greg. Soon three more guys had joined the line.

"And here I thought I married you for your studly looks," Raphael planted one through his mask on Luke's masked cheek. "Very clever, Sir."

"Thank you, baby. Ryan makes a nice-looking bouncer, don't you think?

"He does, Luke," Greg agreed. "I'm going to get a shot of this and text it to Steve. He should put this up on Instagram and Twitter right now." Not that Greg's idea was an original one. Several of the onlookers were taking photos of the store front, and no doubt Alex, with their phones.

"I love it," Raphael said as he pulled out his phone. "I'm going to take some video to show Juan, Mateo and Niki later. Of all the Saturdays for Juan to be called in."

"Yeah," Luke pulled out his own phone. "Ricky was bummed about that, but this crowd should cheer him up."

"If they actually become customers," Raphael agreed. "Okay, don't talk for a minute, guys. I'm going to try to get audio, too." Raphael moved away and spent several minutes and several angles capturing Alex, Ryan and the rest of the scene. The 'money' shot came just as he was about to stop when two of the first guys walked out of the store, one holding a small bag with the LCB Headquarters logo on it. Raphael moved to a spot in front of Alex and fist pumped in celebration. Then, again, he pulled down his shorts and stuck out his tongue to egg Alex on. Alex flashed him back. Grand Opening Day was looking up.

## Ten

# ET TU, ALEX?

"To ALEX AND GREG, who went above and beyond to make sure our opening day would be a success," Hiroshi said as he lifted his sake ochoko to the table at large, then touched it to Mateo's Modelo on his left and Juan's on his right. To fete Hiroshi and Ricky's opening day, Luke and Raphael had hastily put together a weird fusion feast of sushi and Mexican fare. The sushi was take out, the beans, rice and tacos homemade. Everyone had a little bit of everything.

"So, tell me everything. Don't leave anything out," Juan said, looking first at Hiroshi, then Ricky.

"Yeah!" Mateo seconded.

"Here," Raphael handed his phone to Ricky and nodded to Juan. As Ricky handed it to Juan, Raphael continued, "Those pictures may be worth at least a thousand words." A grin spread across Juan's face as he swiped through the video and several still shots. He looked up at Alex as he handed the phone to Mateo.

"Once a stripper, always a stripper, Alex?"

"It wasn't my idea." Alex didn't look entirely displeased. "They ganged up on me." He was looking at Ryan as he spoke.

"It was a dare, Juan," Greg explained. "My first one, and as Raphael said, a damn good one."

"And your last one," Alex proclaimed, delivering a squinty-eyed glare to Greg.

"Oh?" Greg firmly met his gaze. "So, I don't have to worry about being on the receiving end of any dares from you?" He looked across the table at Raphael and Luke. "Cool."

"Oh. Well ..." Alex reconsidered. He, too, looked across at Raphael and Luke then to Hiroshi, then Ricky. "Let me think about it." Hiroshi laughed and nodded at Alex.

"Alex, you are welcome to share the window with the puppy mannequin anytime, right Ricky?"

"We open at ten tomorrow, Alex," Ricky grinned. He turned to Juan. "He was amazing."

"He was," Ryan agreed, looking at Alex. "A couple of the guys in the line asked if this was the Chastity Brothers' store. They recognized you, Alex. You're famous."

"Not what I was going for," Alex replied. He popped in a spicy tuna roll, chewed, then met Hiroshi's gaze. "The dare aside, if my little impromptu performance contributed to the Headquarters' opening day, I was glad to help, I guess. Honestly."

"As the pro bono Director of Marketing," Steve announced, "I can confirm your contribution was significant, Alex. Your performance was tweeted, retweeted, posted and reposted far and wide. And, yes, Ryan, the subject of the Chastity Brothers was mentioned more than once. The two of you should consider reprising your act. You still occupy a fair amount of mind-share in the community." Raphael looked at Steve, deep in thought for a moment, then furtively glanced at Alex, before turning to Hiroshi.

"Tell you what," he said, including Ricky in his gaze. "If business starts to lag, maybe," and he glanced again at Alex, "maybe we could be talked into reprising the Chastity Brothers on occasion. The road show version in the Headquarters window."

"We?" Alex protested. Raphael turned to Greg.

"You invented the punishing dare today, Greg." He then looked slyly at Ricky. "I don't think you executed the 'addendum' to that dare yet, did you?"

"I did not," Greg affirmed. Ricky laughed and clapped.

"Hopefully it won't be necessary," Raphael continued. "But the addendum is there if you need it."

"What do you think, sweetie?" Greg bumped shoulders with Alex. Alex laid down his chopsticks and stared intently at Raphael.

"I promise you," and he paused for dramatic effect. "if that happens, it will only be fair," and he paused again, "for me to rip off Raphael's sarong, just like he stripped me the first time." He turned to Hiroshi with a satisfied smile.

"That will work," Hiroshi returned the smile and reached across Juan to touch his ochoko to Ricky's Modelo. "An alliance with the Chastity Brothers makes perfect sense, partner. Agreed? Why did we not think of this sooner?" He shared a grin with Raphael, as Alex, across the table from Raphael, rolled his eyes while retrieving his chopsticks.

"I didn't know you were working at the Headquarters, Ryan," Juan grinned as he passed Raphael's phone to Ricky so he could pass it over to Niki after Mateo had handed it back.

"Oh, that was Luke's idea, but a good one. It was fun. I got to keep the shirt." He scooped up a forkful of beans and rice, then turned to Hiroshi with fork in mid-air. "I'd be happy to do it again. I only have the one class this summer." Hiroshi and Ricky exchanged a look while Ryan chewed.

"Well," Ricky leaned forward for better eye contact, "actually, we talked about that. My associate and I. Hopefully we'll be busy enough to need someone posted at the door on the weekends. During the busy hours. Maybe noon to five or six. But ..." Hiroshi chuckled and looked curiously at Ryan as Ricky continued. "We were thinking the official Headquarters bouncer should probably, you know, be caged. In revealing shorts or leggings? The shirt you wore today would be totally fine." Luke was the next to chuckle. Ryan looked over at Luke and smirked.

"Sure. Fine. If Luke will let me borrow his cage again." Mateo squeezed Ryan's thigh, giving him a look of mock disbelief. "Just for when I'm on duty, of course."

"Ryan," Hiroshi leaned forward this time, "I think we can arrange a cage of your very own, as part of your compensation. Do you have an appropriate pair of shorts or leggings?"

"Come by our room later, Ryan," Raphael offered. "I have a few things you can borrow. They're obviously not getting much use these days."

"So, uh, who does a guy have to talk to, to volunteer for guard duty?" Niki asked, swiping back and forth among the pics on Raphael's phone. He looked up at Hiroshi and Ricky. "One who already has his own cage." Steve snorted. "And his own puppy hood."

"You really want to do that?" Ricky asked, grinning first at Hiroshi, then Niki. "As a pup?"

"Yeah," Niki replied, tilting his head a bit. "I only have two classes. Ryan and I could trade off, three hours each, Saturday and Sunday. Pup Niki is almost as famous as the Chastity Brothers." He turned to Steve. "Especially if your social media director makes sure everyone knows it's Pup Niki working the door."

"We could take turns, every other hour," Ryan was grinning at Niki. Mateo glanced down at Ryan's lap, then closed his eyes and shook his head in staged despair. Ryan caught the look, then looked down. "Oh. Sorry."

"You were thinking about manning the door as a pup, too, weren't you?" Alex alleged. "You can't fool us."

"No I wasn't," Ryan responded, seriously. "Honest." He glanced down, then looked up at Alex. "But now I am." Mateo leaned into

Ryan, one hand on his thigh, the other gripping his shoulder. Then he sat up straight and broke up everyone by dramatically delivering one of Cadmael's best lines.

"We really do not need another pup." After the laughter died down, he relented. "Not all the time. Just for work, okay?" Ryan nodded, then glanced conspiratorially at Niki.


Maybe it was because Alex wasn't in the window, luring innocent passersby into the shop, but more likely it was because the Castro sleeps in on Sunday mornings. At any rate, by noon only one customer had entered LCB Headquarters, someone who had been in the day before, curiously browsing with another. Today, alone, with no witness, he was back to buy. Ricky gave him the deluxe treatment. He explained the strengths and features of various cages. Probed how often and how long the guy anticipated being locked. Explained the option of the Headquarters' keyholding service. Walked him through the video Steve had compiled showing various cages on himself and Ryan without revealing he himself was one of the models. Not that he needed to, since he was a walking, talking model in the flesh. When it became clear the guy was tempted, but conflicted, Ricky went for the kill.

"You seemed to like this model, Brian. Why don't we fit you into one and see what you think? No obligation." The guy hesitated. "Of course, I'll have to measure you first, you know, for a perfect fit." Ricky nodded toward the fitting chambers. Barely suppressing a smile, Brian nodded and started for the nearest chamber. Ricky smiled at Hiroshi, who grinned back as he handed Ricky a pair of nitrile gloves.

A casual observer would have had an entirely wrong impression of what was soon taking place behind that teal curtain, with only one head visible above, but two pairs of feet below. One pair clearly attached to someone on his knees. But this was totally above board. Well, there was some touching involved, totally professional. As Ricky called out the measurements, Hiroshi took notes, walked to the back, then returned and handed Brian a small black box bearing the LCB Headquarters logo. Brian opened it and smized. Ricky, still holding the measuring cord, rose to his feet, just inches from Brian.

"Would you like to put it on, or should I install it for you?"

"Umm ... how do I ...?"

"Here, allow me." As Ricky again disappeared from view, Hiroshi turned away, biting his lip. Yes. The fitting chambers had been a masterful idea. Hiroshi busied himself at the point-of-sale terminal, giving

Ricky time to complete the installation. Brian, trying to be nonchalant, didn't know where to look. Hiroshi started to return to the chamber to distract Brian with some idle chatter when another customer entered. Hiroshi detoured and joined the customer at one of the display cases. The new customer kept glancing between the cages in the case and the more compelling activity inside the fitting chamber where Brian was grimacing and looking down, as if he were receiving the worst blow job of his life.

"All done!" Ricky announced as he stood and came into view. The new customer's eyes grew large.

"A first-time fitting," Hiroshi explained, setting the record straight. "Excuse me a moment." He joined Ricky and Brian, from outside the chamber, to quietly inquire about the fit and feel of the cage for Brian.

"It fits perfect," Ricky turned to Hiroshi, then back to Brian. "It looks really good on you." Brian looked back and forth between his locked cock and Ricky's grin. "How does it feel?"

"Good. I ... I guess. I didn't know what to expect." Assured, Hiroshi returned to the new customer. Ricky ducked down again and made sure the cage was snugged up tight against Brian's body. He slid out from under the curtain and stood, now outside the chamber.

"I think you're really going to like it, Brian. Do you want to practice taking it off, or will you be wearing it home?" Brian gave a short laugh.

"I probably should, shouldn't I? Keep wearing it, I mean." Ricky nodded. Brian reached for his underwear.

"Yeah, you should. You'll see. The longer you wear it, the harder it is to unlock."

"How long have you been ... umm ..."

"More than a year now. Kinda permanent. Except for the cleanings I explained earlier. With this cage you'll need to do that, too. About once a week. In a couple of days, you're going to start getting really horny. One of the benefits. Do you have a boyfriend?" Brian nodded. "Will this be a surprise?" Brian nodded again, smizing broadly.

"His birthday is this week."

"Ah. Cool present, Brian." Fully dressed and safely locked up, Brian slid the curtain aside and stepped out of the chamber. He and Ricky walked over to the terminal. After Brian had paid and left, Ricky wandered over to join Hiroshi and the new customer. The customer smized as he looked Ricky up and down.

"Hi, I'm Ricky."

"Mark. This is a nice place you guys have here. So, you don't just sell these? You actually put them on guys, too?"

"The fit is very important, for comfort and security," Hiroshi explained. "So, yes, we prefer to measure and fit each customer precisely.

A unique service at LCB Headquarters. It is not mandatory, for those who are more modest." He looked knowingly at Mark, then said, "But for men of the world such as yourself, we can guarantee a perfect, trouble-free fit if we do the installation." Mark indicated his agreement with a nod.

"Makes sense," he said. "So, Hiroshi, tell me again why this Cobra model is better for long term wear." As Ricky stepped away, Ryan entered the shop, dressed for work in the tight Headquarters tee and even tighter spandex workout shorts, compliments of Raphael. Ricky and Ryan disappeared into the back room. When they returned fifteen minutes later, Ryan's shorts sported a noticeable chastity bump. Otherwise known as marketing. Since Ryan wasn't needed outside yet, they hung out at the terminal to give Hiroshi and the customer some privacy and space. It wasn't long, though, before Hiroshi and the customer walked toward a fitting chamber, Hiroshi signaling Ricky to join them. This time Hiroshi did the fitting and Ricky assisted. While they were engaged, another couple entered, prompting Ryan to do his best to fill in until Ricky was able to relieve Ryan, who headed outside. The shop was officially at capacity.

And so it went for day two at LCB Headquarters. Niki showed up shortly before one, gym bag in hand, and transformed into Pup Niki in the back room before relieving Ryan. It might have been the puppy hood, or the mesh jock barely hiding Pup Niki's steel cage. Or, maybe, it was just the later hours or the growing presence on social media. Or all of the above. Remarkably, the line maintained throughout the rest of the afternoon. Not every prospect became a customer, but everyone who had entered left enlightened, some intrigued. And some destined, no doubt, to return. To help incentivize a return visit, whether they made a purchase or not, Hiroshi and Ricky handed each visitor a card inviting them to their website, where they could learn more, ask questions and even participate in an online forum. All to normalize the practice of chastity, solo or in a relationship, intermittent or long-term, for kicks or a serious lifestyle. LCB Headquarters was prepared to meet each prospect wherever they were in their journey.

"What do you think?" Alex plopped down on the couch in the sitting room next to Greg, who was just getting into one of the volumes from the library he had promised himself he would read. He and Alex had recently declared Sundays 'No Devices Day.' Including TV. They were calling it a 'mid-year's resolution.' Greg looked expectantly at Alex, lowering the biography of Amelia Earhart, who had recently found her way into the news again. Her disappearance was still one of the great unsolved mysteries. "We've been a little lax in the gym lately, and the pancakes this morning were a little more decadent than usual, don't you think?" Alex nodded toward the door. Greg furrowed his brows.

"Decadent?" Greg waited, but Alex didn't elaborate. "They were just like last week's pancakes. Which is a good thing. But I wouldn't call them decadent." Greg returned to his book. Failing at the guilt trip, Alex resorted to the vanity appeal. He lifted his right arm and flexed, while squeezing his biceps with his left hand.

"I think I've lost a little ground already. What do you think?"

"I think you're being really weird." Greg lowered his book again and sustained eye contact with Alex, waiting him out. Foolishly, since this was a maneuver Alex exceled at. Finally, Greg folded in the wrap-around cover to hold his place in the volume and set it on the coffee table. He pulled his legs out from behind Alex and sat up. Alex grinned in victory. This wasn't the first conquest he had planned this afternoon. He stood and held his hand out to Greg, who stood on his own, asserting some semblance of control. He walked past Alex and headed for the back stairs, a triumphant Alex following behind. When he reached the top of the stairs, Alex pulled the door closed behind him.

"Oh, is this going to be a private workout?" Greg asked over his shoulder. Alex waited until both had reached the bottom of the stairs before replying. As Greg moved toward the open gym door, Alex put a hand on the back of his shoulder to stop him.

"This is going to be private, all right. But not a workout, dear." Greg turned around, catching on almost before Alex spoke. "It's a dare. My first dare for you. It may not be a 'damn good one.' It's not even very original, not entirely anyway. But it ought to be fun. For me, at least."

"That didn't take long," Greg half-laughed. "My dare is still making the rounds on the internet."

"Well, this one is just between me and you." Greg just looked at Alex patiently. It was a dare. What else could he do?

"Does it involve a paddle?" Greg finally asked.

"No. We're breaking new ground here ... for us anyway. Step this way, big guy." Alex led Greg over to a sling. "Make yourself comfortable." Greg's face grew a bit more apprehensive. He hesitated a moment, until Alex patted the sling, inviting Greg in. Greg sat on the edge, then laid down. "Scoot up. All the way in. You aren't scared, are you?" Greg snorted and scooted up the rest of the way. He folded his arms across his chest, his legs dangling off the end. It wasn't exactly comfortable. He lifted his head to watch Alex walk over to the collection of ropes, then return.

"You can't do shibari on me if I'm laying down."

"We'll save that for a later dare. Or just a fun sexcapade. No, this is to make sure you're comfortable. And immobile." Alex lifted Greg's left arm off his chest and began wrapping rope around his wrist, which Greg tried to return to his chest. "Hold it up and hold it still. Don't be a baby." Alex looked sternly at Greg. "Raphael submits. Luke submits. I submitted. More than once. Remember the strip act? And the punishing dare? This is only fair, so buck up." Then he flashed a quick Cheshire grin. Greg, chastened, held his arm up higher. So high, Alex pulled it back down so he could execute the restraint Hiroshi had taught him. Tight, but not too tight. With plenty of trailing rope to secure Greg's arm to the suspended chain. As Alex proceeded to restrain Greg's right arm, and then both legs, upright along the bottom chains, he hummed a happy little ditty, occasionally glancing at Greg to monitor his reaction.

"You really seem to be enjoying this."

"Oh, I am," Alex grinned.

"How long have you been planning this?"

"It first came to me ... oh ... well ... I guess it was while I was dancing in a window on Castro Street. Maybe you remember that day?"

"So, this is a revenge dare?"

"No. To be honest, I've been thinking about doing this with you for quite a while, now. Wrapping it into a dare just makes it a little more fun." Having finished restraining Greg, Alex reached down and squeezed his very accessible balls. "Don'tcha think?"

"I'll let you know when it's over." Alex nodded in response, then walked over to the receiver and switched it on, not too high, but as mood-setting background music. The look on Greg's face was priceless.

"You're not going to fist me, are you?" Alex laughed and patted Greg's belly.

"No, no. Just making your experience complete. Are you okay, sweetie? Comfortable?"

"I'm okay. My feet haven't fallen asleep yet. When does the fun start?"

"It starts now." Alex walked away, out of Greg's view for several frustrating minutes. So long, in fact, Greg had relaxed into his predicament, eyes closed, enjoying the music when suddenly he felt something rub up against his balls again. He opened his eyes, lifted his head and yelped.

"Oh no ..."

"Greg, I'd like to introduce you to Brutus." Alex slightly lifted the strap-on he was wearing and sensually ran his hand along Brutus' length. "Brutus, this is Greg."

"It's huge!"

"He is a big boy," Alex affirmed, grinning. "You're a big boy. I'll be gentle. This first time I don't expect you to take him all the way."

"First time?"

"Oh. So, you want the dares to end after this? Already? The last dare is mine?"

"Fine with me." Greg looked genuinely worried. "Alex ..."

"You'll be fine." Alex reached out and gently rubbed up and down the cleft below Greg's balls. "I'll be gentle, Greg. Raphael coached me on how to fuck a confirmed top the first time."

"Oh, so once again, I'm the last to be consulted?" Alex nodded.

"That's usually how dares work, yeah. At least you don't have an audience. This time." Alex issued his best evil laugh, before reaching over for the lube. He slowly coated Brutus, tenderly, treating Brutus as his own flesh, an actual impressive appendage of his own. He breathed deeply, catching his breath a couple of times, enjoying edging this impressive, erect cock. He was certainly enjoying watching Greg's expression. When he felt he had milked it for all it was worth, Alex pumped a little more lube and introduced it into Greg. First one finger, then two. Gently, half an inch at a time. Greg, overacting, screwed up his face. Alex persevered.

Greg laid his head back down, eyes closed now. He decided his best course of action was to divorce himself from the proceedings as much as he could. Deny Alex the satisfaction of seeing him squirm, which was about all he could do at this point. Deny him even eye contact. Alex was right, though. He should at least submit with grace. Prior to this, his greatest submission to a dare had been wearing that kilt to the company holiday party. Which hadn't been that big of deal in the end. But this ... in one sense this scene felt like one of the many hazings he assumed pledges must have endured in their quest to join a fraternity. Which made him think about Mateo and Ryan, their own pledges. Come to think of it, he might just be the only resident in the House of the Locked Cock Brotherhood who hadn't bottomed. Except maybe Steve. Or Mateo. Hmmm. Maybe this wouldn't be so bad after all. Maybe ...

Whoa! That's when Alex initiated his entry. Brutus' entry.

Go slowly, Alex reminded himself. Not inches. Centimeters, Raphael had said. Two centimeters forward, one centimeter back. And pause. Wiggle a little once in a while. Until Brutus makes his way to Greg's prostate there will be little reward for the virgin, and only anxiety. Might as well take my time and enjoy his anxiety. After a bit, Alex grabbed hold of each of Greg's calves and squeezed, massaging a bit as well. This added stability to his stance and made advancing on Greg easier. Soon his eyes were closed, too, as he imagined Brutus was indeed his flesh. With the help of his Thunderplug, humping Greg with Brutus began to stimulate Alex, too. He unconsciously let go of Greg's left calf and reached down and grasped the length of Brutus between his pubic area and Greg's ass. He slowly jerked it as he worked over Greg, not just vicariously but actually edging himself as well. He had not intended to benefit this much from the act of fucking Greg with a strap-on, and the result was astonishing. He might as well have been impaling Greg with his own cock. How about that?

"Oooooh," Greg sighed, bringing Alex back to his surroundings. He'd done it. Brutus had made his way to Greg's prostate without too many protests from Greg. Alex and Brutus wiggled back and forth, side to side, in time with the music. Alex looked down and watched a tentative smile form on Greg's face as his head slowly rocked from side to side. His eyes still closed. His cock slowly growing erect. Gently, slowly, Alex amped up his rhythm. He'd come too far to make a wrong move now. He let Greg's breathing, facial expressions and hardening cock guide him, much as Greg had probably always done when topping him. Except for the cock part. He was frankly surprised the dare had gone this well. It wasn't just himself who was actually enjoying it. Come to think of it, that was true of most, if not all, of the dares between Luke and Raphael that he knew about. It really wasn't a zero-sum scenario, done right. His eyes drifted closed again as he continued pumping, edging and working his plug. It was Greg's next groan, long, low and sweet that did Alex in. Before he could react, Alex came.

This was not in the script.

Alex was supposed to be the one in control. Greg was supposed to come, not him. He looked down to see Greg was oblivious to the orgasm, eyes still closed, but clearly in a state of arousal and relative bliss. But, apparently nowhere close to coming. Not surprising, really. We can't all be Luke, Alex thought. We need another trigger. Reflecting on what other members of the family indulged in, Alex decided Greg needed a secondary source of stimulation. He and Brutus slowly withdrew from Greg, who looked up, clearly relieved.

"Oh no ... we're not done, sweetie," Alex assured. "Not even." He walked away, accidentally bouncing the tip of Brutus off the nearby shelving where he rummaged for what he was seeking. He quickly returned, set something aside and reached again for the lube. After recoating Brutus, Alex began Act Two. Within a couple of minutes, both of them experienced now, Brutus had made his way back to Greg's prostate. Alex slowly pumped, hoping to get Greg close to orgasm again. Several minutes in, he made his next move, reaching over for the first of the nipple clamps he'd encountered. He'd seen Luke use clamps on Juan. Apparently, Juan was using them, or something like them, on Ricky. Why not add them to the mix? He slid Brutus in a bit further so he could bend over and clamp one on Greg's right nipple.

"Ooooowww," Greg reacted, in a most unappreciative voice. "What the ...!" He raised his head, to confront Alex.

"Sorry. Sorry!" Alex yanked the clamp off, producing another scream. "Sorry, Greg." With Brutus still in place, he leaned forward again and caressed Greg's pec. "I guess I need a few dungeon lessons. I was just trying to get you off. I'm sorry." Greg heaved a sigh through gritted teeth. Then nodded, and laid his head back down, closing his eyes again.

"It's okay." He took a deep breath. "Before you try something like that again, please, sign up for those dungeon lessons." Alex looked down at Greg's withering cock. "Maybe you should stick with something tried and true."

Yeah, Alex thought. I should have done that in the first place.

Alex wrapped the fingers of his left hand around Greg's balls and squeezed. Still working Brutus, he began massaging Greg's cock with his right hand. When he felt Greg begin to swell, he let muscle memory take over and gave Greg's balls a thorough workout. It wasn't long, between Brutus' novel attention to Greg's prostate and Alex's experienced ball torture, before Greg was in the zone. Moaning softly and leaking generously. When he could tell he had Greg right where he wanted him, Alex released Greg's cock and leaned back, thrusting Brutus forward while pulling Greg's balls with him. Greg's vocalizations, which probably penetrated the closed door at the top of the stairs, and the spray of his cum all over his chest and belly, brought a satisfied smile to Alex's sweat stained face. Aside from the one misstep, he'd successfully topped Greg up to and through an epic orgasm. Not totally hands-free, but damn close. He felt good. As he slowly withdrew Brutus, Greg raised his head again and looked at Alex. Greg breathed deeply, but said nothing. Alex moved around to the side of the sling, taking care to direct Brutus under the sling as he bent down and pressed his lips to Greg's. Without breaking the kiss, he fingered, gently he hoped, Greg's abused nipple. Greg slid his tongue in on top of Alex's. A good sign. Both of them breathed deeply a couple of times before Alex broke the seal and stood upright.

"Someone made a mess," Alex grinned. He reached over and smeared Greg's jizz around his abdomen. "Tsk, tsk, tsk."

"You seem awfully satisfied," Greg said quietly, with just a hint of a smile.

"I am. For the most part. This first dare wasn't perfect, but, all in all, I'll take it as a win." He patted Greg's sticky belly. "And I guess it's up to you now, whether this was *a* dare, or the last dare. Either way, it was a helluva dare." Alex looked softly into Greg's eyes as the subdued backlighting made his curls glow. Relieved that the dare was over, Greg could only chuckle.

"Yeah, sweetie. A helluva dare. The details of which will go to our graves with us. Right?"

"Right," Alex smiled as he began loosening the rope holding up Greg's left leg. "Sure. Unless."

"Unless what?"

"Well, we can't be responsible for what someone might ask in our next encounter with truth serum, now ... can we?"

Eleven

# BANDIT MAKES A COMEBACK

THE MONDAY AFTER THE highly modified and scarcely promoted Up Your Alley Fair, which wasn't even called that in this second, depressing, summer of the pandemic, Hiroshi and Ricky closed the shop early. They had scheduled a late afternoon meeting with Steve in the gazebo. Once he finished production estimates on a couple of thirty-second commercial scripts, Steve joined them there. He was pleased to find that, in addition to his laptop, Hiroshi had also brought a pot of tea and a plate of senbei. Hiroshi waited until Steve sat and opened his own laptop before pouring a cup for Steve. Ricky was reviewing printouts, looking adorably studious with a pencil parked above his right ear. That is, if you discounted the wrist and ankle restraints he was wearing, a habit he'd adopted more and more often of late, sometimes even in the shop.

"How are we doing in the metaverse," Hiroshi asked, smiling at Steve, who was tearing open his first cracker. Steve munched as he navigated to a dashboard on his laptop.

"We've had just over three hundred unique new visitors to the site in the last week. One thousand and fifty-two in the month of July. Let's see ..." He navigated some more. "We now have almost five hundred followers on Twitter, almost that many on Instagram." Ricky looked hopefully at Hiroshi, then turned to Steve.

"Is that good? It sounds good."

"It's very good," Steve patted Ricky's thigh. "The video clip of Alex in the window has been retweeted over two thousand times. You guys owe Greg a beer. A case of beer." Steve laughed and looked into Hiroshi's eyes. "Which he should share with Alex." Hiroshi nodded. "More importantly, how are sales?"

"Good," Ricky replied, shuffling through the reports Hiroshi had printed. "Almost doubling every week." He looked up at Hiroshi. "This weekend was the best!" He turned to Steve. "We ran out of inventory on some cages."

"A good problem to have," Hiroshi smiled. "But not ideal. We did not anticipate your marketing would be so successful so soon, Steve."

"I don't deserve that much credit," Steve deflected. "Clearly you two are meeting an unmet need in the marketplace. Good marketing doesn't sell a bad product. Not for very long, anyway. Your online reviews are excellent, and that, more than anything, is what drives more business your way. I think the discussion forum you have been moderating on the site has been key, as well. Giving long-time locked guys the opportunity to mentor novices was brilliant."

"What was really brilliant was the fitting chambers," Ricky laid his papers aside. "Who knew?"

"If I may say so," Hiroshi sat back, grinning at Ricky, "choosing a partner who has men lined up for their own personal fitting was truly brilliant. And I take full credit for that decision." Ricky snorted and turned to Steve.

"Don't listen to him. He's fitting more cages than I am."

"Only because your customers linger longer with you in the booth." Hiroshi, hilariously out of character, mimicked a variety of customers: "Oh, Ricky should it be this tight? Oh, Ricky, that feels so good. Ricky, is this the same cage as yours?" Not to be outdone, Ricky put a hand on Steve's forearm and did his own impressions.

"Sir, your touch is so gentle. Hiroshi, how long should I leave it on? What should I say, Hiroshi, if a guy freaks out when he sees me caged like this?" Steve patted Ricky's hand.

"Sounds to me like you both have your fans, and that's exactly as it should be. Your personal touch, pun intended, is your real point of difference from everyone else selling chastity. Like most successful businesses, it's all about relationships. Connections. Don't change a thing." Hiroshi looked meaningfully at Ricky briefly before meeting Steve's eyes.

"Actually, Steve," he said, "we are going to make a couple of changes. Which, unfortunately, means a bit more work for you." Steve raised an eyebrow. "Nothing major, but now that we have a few weeks experience behind us," Hiroshi turned an admiring eye toward Ricky, "and to make the most productive use of our time, we are going to revise our operating hours." Steve nodded. "Beginning next week, we will be closed Monday and Tuesday, with hours from noon to seven p.m. Wednesday through Sunday. Or, by appointment." Steve was typing notes as Hiroshi spoke. "We have had very little business outside of those hours, and my associate here and I both deserve more time away."

"I think this is wise," Steve agreed, smiling at Ricky, and tapping on his wrist restraint. "The 'by appointment' option will accommodate anyone who can't make your new hours, and those new hours will ensure Ricky will have more time to spend with Juan in his quest to remain the World's Best Locked Cock Leather Boy."

"And ... more time for pancakes Sunday mornings," Ricky grinned, reaching over and rubbing Steve's belly. Steve laughed.

"Will this affect Niki's or Ryan's time at the door on weekends?" he asked. Hiroshi shook his head.

"It may mean longer lines, perhaps not. We could probably manage without them, to be honest. With COVID, there are still very few tourists in the neighborhood. However, they both seem to enjoy helping us, so, for a couple more weeks until classes resume, I think it best to leave things as they are." Again, Steve nodded.

"Good. I can't speak for Ryan, but I think Niki looks forward to it. He misses his fan club at the bar." Steve looked mischievously at Ricky. "So ... you don't need me to post any announcements about the Chastity Brothers doing a window performance?" Ricky and Hiroshi both laughed.

"Not yet!" Ricky affirmed. "But we'll let you know." He gave Hiroshi a conspiratorial grin as he reached for another senbei. Hiroshi returned Ricky's smile, then addressed Steve.

"Perhaps we'll save that for our first anniversary celebration and sale." He reached for a senbei himself, then closed his laptop. "Unless you have any other recommendations for our online presence, Steve, I think we can adjourn." Steve shook his head.

"Nothing so far. Everything is still fresh, and seems to be performing well. Just make sure I shoot pics of any new cages as you get them. It's good to keep posting new images. I'll update your hours. Effective next Sunday?" Hiroshi nodded, then stood and collected his teapot.

"I will leave the senbei with you. Make sure Alex gets one." Ricky laughed.

"Raphael and Luke are making dinner tonight," he said as he, too, stood. "Can you come?" Hiroshi grimaced.

"Thank you, no. I am meeting a friend. But, thank you for asking. Steve, as always, we deeply appreciate your help." Hiroshi stepped down to the ground and walked toward the gate. Ricky ran ahead and pulled it open for him. He leaned in with a cheek kiss before closing it.

Niki thanked the FedEx driver and closed the door. He was accustomed to being the in-house mail man, since he was usually studying in the library when the mail tumbled through the slot, but this was the first package delivery since the gazebo arrived. It was addressed to Ryan, so he headed up to his and Mateo's room.

"Special delivery," he announced. Ryan spun around from the desk. Niki presented the package, with the label facing Ryan. "What did you order? Is it a surprise for Mateo?" Ryan shook his head.

"I didn't order anything. I'm guessing it's from my parents." Ryan reached around and pulled the letter opener out of the pencil cup and sliced through the shipping tape while Niki sat at his feet. Ryan pulled a gift-wrapped box out, along with a square envelope. He opened the envelope first and read the enclosed card. He grunted as he handed the card to Niki. "My mom's taste in cards is so cliché." Niki examined the front of the card.

"Hey. It has a rainbow on it. Give her some credit." Ryan wiggled his head, reluctantly agreeing. "I didn't know it was your birthday. You kept that a big ol' secret."

"More like self-preservation, Niki. I've seen how you guys celebrate birthdays around here." He ripped the paper off the box to reveal an Apple logo. Inside was the latest model iPhone. Niki was reading the message inside the card.

"'If this will encourage more regular contact, it will have been worth it. Happy Birthday from your loving parents.' Hah. Not too passive aggressive, are they?" Ryan was fondling the phone.

"No ... they just miss me." He met Niki's smiling gaze. "You've met 'em. You know how cool they are."

"Yeah. So, when exactly *is* your birthday? I can't believe we let you get away with not telling us."

"September five. There was a lot going on last year. I hadn't been here very long. I was still figuring out my place here with you guys, and ... we'd just had that 'birthday ceremony' for Juan that kind of blew everyone away. I, uh, I guess I wasn't ready to be celebrated yet."

"Well, you've seen eight other birthday ceremonies since then, so you should be ready now, like it or not." Niki jumped up and headed for the door. Before he exited, he turned back to Ryan, who was still admiring his phone. "This time I get to be in charge of the committee, and I already have a good idea of how we're going to celebrate." Ryan looked up with a grimace that wasn't totally convincing.

Despite the semester having recently begun with a full schedule of classes for both Niki and Ryan, Niki managed to find time to orchestrate what he deemed a fitting birthday ceremony for Ryan. He had plenty of help. Unlike previous ceremonies that played out in an hour or two in the dungeon, Ryan's would be more expansive, both in time and place. After all, they had to make up for completely missing his birthday in 2020. Since Ryan's birthday fell on a Sunday, it began, of course, with pancakes. Ryan should have known something was up when he was the last to be served.

"Ta da!" Ricky announced as he placed the plate of pancakes, supporting a single lit candle, in front of Ryan. He leaned down and planted a cheek kiss. "Happy birthday, Ryan." Ryan looked around sheepishly, not terribly surprised that Mateo or Niki had shared his secret. Juan raised his coffee mug.

"Yes, happy birthday, Ryan. Congratulations. Today you turn twenty." He turned his gaze to Mateo. "We no longer have any teenagers in the House of the Locked Cock Brotherhood." Ricky slid into place next to Juan. Everyone began sampling pancakes while the two bowls of fruit were passed around. At one point Alex got up and returned with a fresh carafe of coffee. Raphael complimented Ricky on another tasty breakfast. And Ryan kept furtively looking from face to face, anticipating what surely must be coming. Everyone played it cool until Greg sopped up the last bit of syrup with his last forkful of pancake and chewed his last bite. He laid down his fork, and everyone turned to Ryan.

"Lordy," Ryan muttered as he looked to Mateo for support. All he got was a big grin. Niki stood, retreated to the butler's pantry and returned, ceremonially approaching Ryan with a square box topped with a lush, red bow. He removed Ryan's plate and replaced it with the box, then returned to his seat.

"Ryan," he began, "unlike all the other birthday ceremonies that have taken place exclusively in the dungeon, we decided to begin your full day of activities here and now." Ryan reacted to Niki's reference to 'full day.' "Oh, there will be some dungeon time, but, uh, because of the special nature of your ceremony, we'll be spending a fair amount of time outside." Niki leaned forward and smiled. Ryan looked down at the box, then back at Niki, but didn't move. Mateo tapped the box.

"Open it." His grin hadn't faded. Ryan lifted the lid. He laughed as he reached in and pulled out a puppy collar, the same one he'd worn for the movie and at Alex's request while caged. He looked around curiously as he unfurled the chain. Unable to contain his eagerness, Mateo reached over and lifted up the bone-shaped tag. Ryan smiled as he read the engraving: 'Bandit.'

"Go brush your teeth and do whatever you need to do, then meet us back in the dungeon," Niki instructed. "We have the rest of your puppy gear waiting for you there. You'll spend the rest of your day, until dinner, as a pup." Several stood, and began clearing their dishes as Mateo took the collar from Ryan. He wrapped it around Ryan's neck and clicked the lock shut. He stood, held out his hand and laughed out loud as Ryan, at full staff, stood as well.

"Niki, I think Ryan likes the ceremony you have planned," Steve said as he pulled Niki into a side hug.

"We're just getting started," Niki wrapped an arm around Steve. "By the end of the day he'll be one tired puppy." Ryan's boner swayed in anticipation. He reached up and fingered the collar he hadn't worn in nearly a year. It felt familiar. Given Niki's prediction, a little comforting, too.

When Ryan and Mateo entered the dungeon, they were surprised to find only Niki and Steve there. So, Niki wasn't kidding. The 'ceremony' apparently wasn't going to take place right away. Actually, Steve was with Pup Niki, who was on all fours, decked out in puppy hood, tail, mitts and chest harness. Steve was at his side, sitting on the bondage board next to another, larger box. Pup Niki barked and trotted over to Ryan, reaching his fore paws up, begging for attention. Ryan's boner returned as he looked to Steve for guidance.

"Here boy," Steve called out. "Pup Niki, heel." Pup Niki trotted back over to Steve's feet and sat. "Ryan, since Niki has decided you should celebrate your birthday as a pup, we're going to include a crash course, a sort of abbreviated puppy obedience school. If you're in doubt as to what to do at any point, Pup Niki will do his best to show you the way. Without talking, of course. Once you're pupped out, you won't be able to ask questions, but the rest of us will do our best to understand what you need." Ryan remained silent, his arm around Mateo's waist, boner swaying. "Come on over here, and we'll get you geared up." Steve tipped the box over, to spill out the rest of Ryan's birthday loot: a puppy hood, tail, mitts and chest harness. When Ryan didn't move, Mateo did, pulling Ryan with him. Pup Niki barked and eagerly glanced back and forth between Steve and Ryan. Steve nodded down at Pup Niki, wordlessly instructing Ryan to drop to the floor. He reluctantly let go of Mateo and knelt down on his knees.

"Any last words before I slip this in place?" Steve half-seriously asked. Ryan glanced up at Mateo, then shook his head. "Okay, Ryan. See you at dinner." Steve gingerly worked the pup hood into place, then handed the pup tail and lube to Mateo. While Mateo inserted the tail, Steve locked the mitts in place. The chest harness came last. Greg cupped his hand under Bandit's snout and squatted down to address him. "Because it's difficult for human pups to navigate a lot of stairs, you and Pup Niki are allowed to walk up the stairs on two legs. But once we're outside, you'll need to stay in pup head space. Okay, boy?"

"Arff!"

"Good boy." Steve looked up at Mateo while Pup Niki moved around to check out Bandit's tail. "It sounds like Bandit's up for this, Mateo." He stood. "Okay, let's get our puppies outside." Mateo watched as Steve took Pup Niki's left paw and guided him to his feet, then he followed suit with Bandit, following Steve and Pup Niki up the stairs. As soon as the pups hit the ground, the rest of the family piled out of the gazebo, calling, clapping and whistling for the pups. Pup Niki bounded ahead, but Bandit wasn't far behind. Remembering his first encounter with Pup Niki, Bandit rolled over on his back and whimpered, begging for a belly rub. Luke was the closest and the first to oblige.

"I don't think this guy's going to need much obedience training, Steve," he laughed. Ricky bent down and rubbed along with Luke.

"Are you a good boy?" Ricky asked in baby talk. "Are you?" He looked up at Juan. "Boy, some guys will do anything to get out of doing door duty at the shop."

"Like he had a vote," Juan squatted down beside Ricky and rubbed Bandit's thigh. "Now, Niki on the other hand ..." Pup Niki barked, then whimpered in defense. Juan reached over and patted Pup Niki's back. "Just kidding, puppy."

"We'll be fine," Ricky stood. "This will be a good test of how well we do without them, now that the semester is in full swing." Juan stood and wrapped an arm around Ricky's shoulders. "I think I've convinced Hiroshi to take a few breaks today, so he can spend some time here with the pups. If things get out of control, I'll text for help, Papito." Juan squeezed tighter in affirmation.

Steve broke away from the group and walked toward the gate in the privacy fence. He put one hand on the latch and whistled for attention with the other. Pup Niki bounded toward him and Bandit awkwardly rolled over onto all fours and followed a little more slowly. As Bandit neared Pup Niki, Steve pulled the gate open. Three more puppies, fellow BPOS graduates, raced through and enthusiastically greeted Pup Niki and Bandit. For a few moments it was puppy pandemonium. None of the pups had seen each other in nearly two years ... human years at that. Bandit was looking from pup to pup, curious, excited, but uncertain how to react. Pup Niki bounded over and pounced, rolling Bandit over. The other pups joined the pile on, having been briefed on Bandit's ceremony and his lack of training and experience. Steve was capturing it all on his phone for posterity.

"What do you think?" Juan asked Mateo, pulling him into a backwards hug as they both watched the pile on. "Bandit's pretty cute, isn't he?" Mateo nodded, keeping his eyes on Bandit. "I hope you don't feel too left out. This isn't like most of our other birthday ceremonies, is it?" Mateo silently and slowly shook his head. Then he turned in Juan's arms and looked up, smiling.

"Tonight. After dinner. We have a special birthday. Jus' Ryan and me!" Juan pulled him tight and laughed.

"Bueno! You're a good man, muchacho." He released Mateo, who ambled over to the puppy pile and squatted. He was immediately swarmed by adoring pups. Ricky took his place in Juan's arms.

"So," he said, "this will be a perfect birthday for Ryan, don't you think? You know, if he starts it as a puppy and ends it as his Prince's sex slave." Juan laughed.

"Shaman Prince!" Raphael once again asserted. "Yes. He may have missed his celebration last year, but I think Niki and Mateo are more than making up for it."

"And you," Luke chimed in. "Didn't you and Alex volunteer to make dinner, including his favorite ... artichoke soup?"

"Raphael volunteered," Alex sighed. "Like always, I'm just an innocent bystander." Raphael noogied Alex's curls.

"Bystander, maybe, but certainly not innocent. Not anymore, anyway. Besides, you're my favorite sous chef."

"Yeah," Alex countered. "Because, like everyone, I can't say no to you."

"It's my cross to bear. Let's get to it. We can't let our birthday boy down." Everyone but Mateo and Steve headed back into the house, with Alex and Raphael detouring into the kitchen while everyone else headed up the back stairs.

Seven hours later, back in the dungeon, Mateo helped Ryan shed his Bandit paraphernalia, except for the collar. Niki and Steve had gone to their room to do the same, granting Mateo and Ryan some alone time before dinner. They were sitting on the bondage board, thigh to thigh as Ryan placed the gear back into the box Steve had left there from this morning.

"Was today fun?" Mateo asked, oddly a bit shyly. Ryan turned to him and delivered a long kiss, the kind he'd been warned against when he was caged. Mateo met his passion and wrapped an arm around Ryan's chest and eased the two of them down onto the board. Several minutes passed before Ryan was able to answer Mateo's question. He pulled his lips just far enough away from Mateo's to allow his one-word response.

"Wooof!" Mateo giggled, then delivered a quick peck.

"Cool. I am happy you like it." Ryan, his eyes momentarily closed, nodded. "Pup Niki had fun, too."

"Yeah," Ryan resumed eye contact. "He was great. So were the other pups. And Steve. And Hiroshi." Ryan delivered a peck of his own. "And so were you. It was fun, being your pup." Mateo grinned his adorable grin but didn't say anything. "I mean ... I'm nowhere close to where Pup Niki is in the whole pup head space thing, but now I kind of understand what he meant when he told me he loves being Steve's pup." Mateo raised up half-way, supporting himself with his right arm. He tilted his head as he pensively looked down at Ryan.

"Which you like better? To be my pup? Or my servant?" Ryan took a deep breath as he sat up. He reached out and took Mateo's hand in his as Mateo sat the rest of the way up. A confident smile spread across Ryan's face.

"Being your pup is fun. It's, um, kinky play. But, my Shaman Prince, being your servant is my full-time job. It's my destiny." Mateo's grin returned.

"Good. After dinner, your Prince wants to wish you happy birthday some more. Is okay?" Ryan half suppressed a low laugh and squeezed Mateo's hand, holding his gaze.

"Yeah, it's okay. Mateo, my Prince, I can be whatever you want me to be. As long as I get to be your lover." Ryan suddenly looked like he was about to tear up. He swallowed hard. Mateo stood, still holding Ryan's hand.

"Come. Time to shower. Then ... a special dinner. For a special lover. My lover." Ryan nodded compliantly, still looking a bit emotional as he stood, scooped up the box of pup gear and headed for the stairs with his other arm around his Mateo.

There was bubbly, of course, and the artichoke soup was followed with a choice of chicken or eggplant parmigiana (Ryan had a little of each), roasted root vegetables and garlicky toasted sourdough. Niki was more animated than usual, regaling everyone with anecdotes about Ryan's daylong birthday ceremony. Not only had he been able to spend much of the day pupped out, but he'd had four other pups to play with, for the first time in years.

"Ryan," Greg asked, "today was a pretty immersive experience for Bandit. What did you think?" He'd caught Ryan with a mouthful, giving him time to come up with a thoughtful response.

"It was fun, for sure. And I learned a few things." He looked admiringly at Niki. "Pup Niki was incredible. And mean!"

"Mean?" Niki asked incredulously. "Moi!?"

"Yeah. You and all the other pups kept ganging up on me. Don't deny it. You were definitely the alpha pup."

"He's right," Steve agreed, cupping the back of Niki's neck. "You were the ringleader at times. Just like you were at BPOS."

"Well," Niki tried to look innocent. "Don't blame me. Pup Niki hadn't been with his pack for a long time. He probably got a little carried away. Nobody was hurt. Besides," he met Ryan's gaze, "Bandit got off easy. Ryan's ceremony could have been totally in the dungeon, like all the other birthdays." Ryan, eyes closed, nodded.

"Yeah. True. Thanks, Niki, Hiroshi ... everybody, for a pretty awesome birthday." Mateo leaned in with a cheek kiss.

"Rumor has it the celebration's not over yet," Juan asserted, catching Mateo's gaze. "Right, muchacho?" Before Mateo could respond, Raphael interjected.

"That's right! Alex, Niki ..." While Alex began collecting dishes and silverware, Raphael and Niki headed into the kitchen. Moments later the three returned with a stack of dessert plates, a chocolate frosted birthday cake ablaze with twenty candles and a quart of Double Rainbow ice cream. Happy Birthday was hilariously rapped, the candles were blown out and everyone was served. After a few bites had been taken, Raphael again took the floor.

"Ryan," he began, "it's a good thing you now have your own pup gear." Ryan gave him a quizzical look. "It will come in very handy for my next dare."

"Oooooh," Alex reacted. He looked eagerly at Ryan.

"Lordy," was Ryan's response. He looked plaintively at Mateo.

"Oh, Ryan," Raphael continued, "don't worry, it's not a dare for you alone." Raphael turned his gaze to Alex, who was still grinning. "This will be a family dare. A universal dare. Everyone will participate."

"Time out!" Luke exclaimed. He turned to Raphael and ran the fingers of both hands through his increasingly untamed mop of ginger blond hair. "You're out of order, baby. The last dare issued was your dare to me. Remember? To become your Outlander Braveheart?" Both Greg and Alex exchanged 'ah ha' glances. "Sorry, but the next dare is *mine*." Raphael looked up to the chandelier as he grimaced. Luke dropped his hands and turned to Ryan. "Looks like you're off the hook. All of you."

"Okay, I guess it's not a dare, then. A challenge, maybe." Raphael looked at Alex, whose glee had started to fade. "It's definitely cashing in on a promise Alex made."

"Me? What did I do?" Alex reacted.

"You made a promise," Raphael revived his enthusiasm, "a couple of you did. The Folsom Street Fair is happening this year, at the end of the month. Kind of. I mean, it won't be as big as usual, but it *is* finally happening. We get to collect on Alex's promise to do Folsom nude. We should *all* do it nude." Raphael nudged Luke. "Including Luke, who forced me to go nude last time while he was modestly dressed. In a leather codpiece."

Alex was grimacing, regretting his unfortunate promise.

"Oh man," Ryan muttered, "I don't know ..."

"Ryan," Raphael leaned forward, "you and Niki will be going as pups. No one will recognize either of you. Well, Pup Niki's fan club will recognize him, but you'll be anonymous!" A smile instantly spread across Ryan's face. He turned to Mateo who couldn't help but smile back.

"How about it, Mateo?" Raphael prompted. "You said you would if Ryan would. Remember?"

"I 'member. Yeah." Raphael turned his gaze back to Alex.

"A. First of all, we'll all be wearing COVID masks. B. It'll be a much smaller crowd than usual, so you're getting off easy. And C. ...." Raphael held eye contact with Alex, torturing his senior locked cock brother.

"And C.!?" Alex finally replied, staring semi-lethal daggers.

"And C., if everyone doesn't do it, I'll beg Francisco to turn all of you into human pups. Right, Elder?" Hiroshi laughed, but hesitated to agree with Raphael, unable to fully read the room. After a pause, he cleared his throat.

"Since, as Luke says, this is not an official dare," Hiroshi slowly pondered, "Elder decrees that in exchange for everyone agreeing to his mandate Adonis must offer everyone something in exchange. Something of equal sacrifice and magnitude." It was Steve's turn to chuckle.

"And does Elder have something in mind?" Steve asked, scooping up his last spoonful of ice cream.

"Just a suggestion. Perhaps, as a preview of their appearance at the Fair, the Chastity Brothers could offer a well-publicized performance in the windows of LCB Headquarters the day before. A day when the Castro should be replete with energized leather men, both foreign and domestic." Ricky whooped and clapped, then leaned over and planted a big one on Hiroshi's shoulder.

"What?" Alex protested. "Why both of us? I mean ... You said ..." Alex stared appealingly at Hiroshi, who reflected back the placid, beatific smile of Elder.

"Alex, we're a team," Raphael grinned. "A set. A duo. You know ... we really can't let our public down, now, can we?" Alex snorted.

"Nice try. The obligation is yours, not mine. Besides, our public has forgotten us."

"Au contraire," Steve said. "You two come up quite often in online threads about LCB Headquarters. The legend lives on." Alex, almost convincingly, leaned back in despair.

"So, Elder," Juan posed, "you are agreeing to Raphael's mandate? Will we see you naked at Folsom this year?" Hiroshi turned his smile toward Juan.

"Someone has to mind the store. It should be a busy day. I left Ricky on his own much too long today." He smiled at Ryan, still in his puppy collar. "It will be my duty to free my associate to join you and the rest of the House of the Locked Cock Brotherhood in their first naked appearance at Folsom. I look forward to many provocative photos." The two of them held a long, strong-willed but respectful stare before Juan closed his eyes and nodded.

## Twelve

# REPRISE OF THE VELADORA

"THIS IS CRAZY!" RICKY exclaimed to Hiroshi in the back room as they each retrieved cages for their respective customers. Outside, Pup Niki was manning the door where the line stretched out of sight past the right-hand display window. A window where all four mannequins were currently crowded together, which left plenty of room in the left window for the live action reunion performance of The Chastity Brothers. A performance arguably more toned down than their original performances, more street-worthy as it were, with their contrasting sarongs, but still one that attracted its share of attention. And customers. And ultimately sales. Steve had intended to promote the shop by live streaming their initial performance of the day from outside, but it hadn't been necessary. Plenty of bystanders, many in town for the culmination of this year's understated Leather Week, were posting and streaming on their own. Some of them ended up in line, waiting their turn to become potential customers. Ryan, instead of relieving Pup Niki at the door, was running the point-of-sale terminal so Ricky and Hiroshi could devote full time to one-on-one customer service.

"Maybe I should skip Folsom tomorrow and be here with you," Ricky seriously suggested. He moved closer to Hiroshi and bumped him, shoulder to shoulder, as he whispered, "Or, better yet, we close the shop tomorrow and you come with us."

"Oh no, my friend," Hiroshi replied with a resolute smile. "You deserve to experience your first Folsom Street Fair tomorrow, even if it is not as momentous as those of the past. I will be fine here. We really cannot pass up what is destined to be our biggest weekend in our history."

"Which is why I should be here," Ricky countered as the two of them exited the back room and returned to the fitting chambers. Hiroshi placed a hand on Ricky's shoulder.

"A compromise, then," Hiroshi offered. "I will open the store, you partake of the Fair, and once you have had your fill, leave early and join me here." Ricky grinned and nodded ascent, then turned to rejoin the half-naked customer waiting eagerly behind his teal curtain.

"This feels a lot different," Alex turned to Greg as the two of them, along with the rest of the family, ambled away from the clothes check tent Sunday morning. "Doesn't it?"

"What?" Greg tugged Alex close, his arm around his waist. Alex affectionately bumped against Greg. "Oh. You mean being naked on a city street?"

"Duh!" Alex and Greg were following Raphael and Luke, who were similarly entwined. "A nude beach is one thing, but ..."

"Are you forgetting Halloween? Remember? The one where you forced Luke and me to parade around city streets and bars in see-through body suits? I think we're safely in our element here."

"Oh ... well ..." Alex had no good response to Greg's historically accurate retort. "It's just, not everyone's naked here, is all."

"Yes, my dear, but," Greg leaned in to nuzzle Alex's cheek through both masks, "not everyone here looks as good naked as you do." Alex smized, wordlessly accepting the compliment. He turned to look behind them at Mateo and Steve, each leading their leashed pups who were walking on just two legs for now. In a bow to some degree of modesty, Ryan was wearing his regulation Headquarters cage to keep his otherwise rambunctious member in check. Mateo was grinning, despite being naked in public for the first time. Ryan's expression was hidden by his pup hood, but his swiveling head indicated he was enjoying the sight of hundreds of minimally attired leather men and women around him. This was a first for both of them. Juan and Ricky jogged to catch up. Ricky was the most modesty dressed of them all, sporting a crop top emblazoned with the LCB Headquarters logo. Marketing, even in his off hours. Raphael and Luke stopped and turned, waiting for everyone to gather.

"Steve," Raphael asked, "what do you think? Should we leave Pup Niki and Bandit at the puppy park first, then wander awhile? Or, would that be unfair to the pups?" Pup Niki arfed and panted excitedly, and strained at his leash.

"I don't know, Raphael," Steve grinned and took hold of Pup Niki's snout. "Does puppy know the way to the park?" Pup Niki barked again and took the lead, having done his homework. Bandit, not to be out-

done, pulled Mateo ahead of the rest of the family to join Pup Niki and
Steve as they navigated the crowd. Mateo giggled at Luke and Raphael as
he and Bandit passed them.

"Mateo is amazing," Raphael said to Luke. "He's way more comfortable than I was the first time."

"Yeah, but," Luke made eye contact, "you didn't have a pup to distract
you. Not to mention he's been living naked with a kinky family for a
couple of years. This," Luke waved his arm at the crowd, "seems perfectly
ordinary to him by now." Raphael nodded, then looked around at the
bodies around them. He sighed.

"Yeah. Good point. We've raised him well." To which Luke could only
laugh.

Even though they'd arrived before noon, the fair was already crowded,
likely because the pandemic had eliminated the fair entirely the previous
year. The physical size of the fair was reduced significantly this year,
packing attendees into a smaller space. Despite most everyone being
masked, and hopefully vaccinated, the density was a little worrisome,
especially for Juan, who was doing his best to keep Ricky and himself
as distanced from strangers as possible. They lost sight of the others a
couple of times during the trek to the puppy park and were the last to
arrive, just as Pup Niki and Bandit were welcomed into the pack. There
were about a dozen pups bounding around, a couple of whom were
clearly excited to see Pup Niki.

"I think the pups will be fine without us," Steve wrapped an arm
around Raphael's shoulders as they watched Pup Niki wordlessly attempt to introduce one of the pups to Bandit. "Besides, we won't be
gone that long." He looked back the way they had come. "The fair's a lot
smaller this year." Raphael clasped a hand over Steve's at his waist.

"Okay. Let's explore." He released Steve and Luke and reached out to
pull Mateo into a backwards hug. "Come on, muchacho, let's check out
your first Folsom." The eight of them began to work their way through
the crowd with Raphael, Luke and Mateo initially in the lead. Raphael
took cues from Mateo's apparent interest in the booths they passed,
pausing and stopping when he sensed Mateo had seen something, or
someone, that caught his eye. Despite the smaller footprint of this year's
fair, there was still plenty to discover. It was all new to Mateo, so they
moved slowly. After several pauses, Raphael prodded. "See anything you
just have to have, Mateo?" Mateo turned, smizing through his mask.

"Mos' everthing they have here, we already have." Luke nodded.

"Yeah, there is something to be said about having a well-stocked dungeon, muchacho." He tousled Mateo's mane. Mateo wrapped an arm
around Luke's waist, his right hand sliding down until it rested on Luke's
not-so-very-tanned-anymore right butt cheek.

"Si. Yes. We are lucky." He looked up for confirmation from Luke, and got it. A couple of booths later, however, Mateo did make a find. "Look!" he exclaimed, holding up a pink tee emblazoned with "Sex Slave" across the front. "Is good for Ryan, no?"

"I'd say it's perfect for both of you," Luke laughed, unsnapping his leather wrist wallet, and handing Mateo a couple of the bills he'd stashed for everyone earlier. Mateo completed his transaction and slipped the change into his boot sock, the closest thing he had to a pocket.

Eventually, partly due to varied interests as well as the pull of the crowd, the family became more separated from one another, exploring in ones, twos and threes. It was about a third of the way through the main stretch of the fair when Raphael, Luke and Mateo caught up with Alex and Greg.

"Oh look!" Raphael turned to Luke, smizing away. "It's the guy with the cool corsets." He reached out and pulled on Alex's hand. "Come here, Alex." He pulled Alex ahead and into the booth, while Greg, looking questioningly at Luke, followed. Luke and Mateo trailed behind. "Luke and I tried these on last time. I want to see you in one." Alex scoffed and tried to turn away. Raphael's grip held fast. "Sir," Raphael addressed the corset maker, "what do you have in a size Alex?" It had been two years, but the vendor remembered Raphael and Luke, despite Luke's new 'Outlander' look.

"Hmmm," he played along. "Let's see …" He ran his hands along Alex's sides, from just under his arm pits down to his hips. Alex's cage bobbed in reaction. By now, with Greg, Luke and Mateo in attendance, Raphael was able to let go of Alex's hand. "This should look good with your coloring." The vendor pulled out a gold colored back-laced corset, one more elaborate than what Raphael and Luke had modeled before, in a steampunk style that didn't stop at the pecs, but included shoulder straps. He guided Alex's arms through the straps, then stepped behind him and began lacing it up. Very tightly. Alex uttered a slight moan.

Greg looked from Alex to Raphael, who was enjoying the show. Their eyes met and Raphael's eyebrows danced.

"Damn, Alex," Raphael praised, once the corset was fully laced. "Do a three-sixty for us." Alex obliged, running his hands up and down the sides of the corset. "Believe it or not, it makes you look more muscular." Alex scowled, but continued appraising the corset with his hands. "Seriously. Check yourself out." Raphael guided Alex over to a full-length mirror, where Alex turned a bit to each side. The corset maker handed Raphael a hand mirror, which Raphael passed on to Alex. "Check out your back. You'll see what I mean." Raphael looked to Greg for his reaction while Alex took in the exaggerated V-shape the corset now endowed upon him. Greg was grinning and forming a fig leaf with his left hand. Raphael laughed. "You guys should get it, don't you think?"

"I don't know," Greg replied walking over to Alex. He stepped behind him and fondled the corset himself. Alex turned in his arms.

"Feels a lot like Hiroshi's Shibari," Alex cooed.

"Looks just as sexy," Greg replied.

"Yeah, but," Alex turned his head to include the others in his response, "where would I ever wear it? I mean ... you know ..."

"You can wear it when you sign up for your dungeon lessons," Greg whispered, maybe a bit too loudly.

"What's that?" Luke chuckled.

"Oh, nothing," Greg blushed.

"Hmmm," Luke looked seriously at Raphael and Mateo. "Sounds like a good topic for our next session of truth serum."

"See!" Alex turned back to Greg. "Didn't I tell you? I knew it ..."

"Okay," Raphael said. "I'm not sure what's going on, but now I'm certain you should get it. Alex, it was made for you." The corset maker moved behind Alex and untied the sales tag from the back of the corset. He showed it to Greg.

"I'll take a hundred dollars off if he wears it for the rest of the fair. With that face and the cage? It'll be great advertising." Greg briefly looked Alex over in mock contemplation. He reached down and tested Alex's heavier than usual cage.

"I don't think we'll get any argument from this guy. Okay, let's do it. Luke?" Greg turned to Luke, who was already opening his wrist wallet again. Mateo and Raphael moved in to better admire Alex's sexy new bustier. The transaction complete, the five of them re-entered the moving throng.

"Mateo," Luke suggested, "what do you say we retrieve our pups, so they can enjoy some of the fair?" Mateo nodded happily and eagerly led the way back to the puppy park. When they arrived, they found Steve, Juan and Ricky sitting on a nearby curb, munching, sipping beers and watching the pups frolic. Mateo kneeled down, just outside the low barrier, and called to Bandit. Both Bandit and Pup Niki bounded over, panting and barking. Mateo reached over and petted both and apparently urged them to rejoin the family, as they immediately trotted over to the gate and whined to the handler on duty. Once they were out and back on two feet, leaving pup head space behind, they assumed their human personas despite still being in full pup regalia.

"Alex!" Niki purred, caressing Alex's corseted side. "You are stylin', my man." Ricky, too, seemed taken by Alex's new look.

"Papito," he clutched Juan from the side, "I know what I want my next leather boy prize to be." He released Juan and circled around Alex, who looked uncharacteristically self-conscious.

"You wanna try it on?" Alex offered.

"Yeah! But not right now," Ricky smized. "I'm going to head over to the shop in case Hiroshi needs help. Feeling kind of guilty."

"Um, I'll go with you, too," Niki insisted. "If it's busy, I can man the door."

"Me, too," Ryan volunteered.

"No, Ryan," Juan interjected. "This is your first Folsom. Mateo's too. You all should stay and take everything in. I'll go with Ricky and Niki. I've seen enough for today anyway." Ryan protested again, but Luke intervened.

"Come on, guys," he said, hooking Ryan with one arm and Mateo with the other, turning them into the throng. "You, too, Steve. We have to help Alex advertise that corset to everyone here. Greg made a promise." Greg laughed and took Alex's hand, and then Raphael's, following behind Luke as Ricky, Niki and Juan headed in the opposite direction.

Ricky felt genuinely guilty when the three of them approached the shop, and he spotted the line waiting outside. Hiroshi's prediction the evening before, that everyone would be at the fair until late afternoon, was obviously a rare miscalculation on his part. Ricky hurried inside as Niki took control of the door. Juan stood aside, glancing through the window to see how Hiroshi was managing. He had two customers, each at a different display case, and a third in one of the fitting chambers. He was definitely outnumbered, and clearly relieved to see Ricky appear.

"Well, Senior Consultant," Hiroshi said, a bit breathlessly, "perhaps recruiting the Chastity Brothers was not the best idea for this weekend, after all. We may once again run out of inventory."

"Well, you know," Ricky patted Hiroshi's shoulder before turning to attend to the customer in the fitting chamber, "if we do, we'll just ship them their cages later. Doing the fittings seems to be their favorite part anyway."

Once Ricky completed the fitting and sale, and the customer exited, Juan asked Niki to hold the line a moment and slipped inside himself. Once he got closer, he could see that Hiroshi, despite the silent smize he offered Juan, was not his usual, relaxed self. The hachimaki around his head looked damp from absorbing perspiration. Juan now felt a little guilty, too. He moved over to Ricky, who was attending to the customer at another display case.

"Mijo," he said quietly, "I'm going to run down the street and get some cold tea for Hiroshi." Ricky glanced up and nodded. "I'll get some for everyone. Maybe you can talk Hiroshi into taking a break." At the same time Juan exited, and Niki waved the next customer into the shop, Hiroshi headed into the back room to retrieve a cage for his customer. Moments later Ricky heard a muffled crash.

"Excuse me." Ricky turned away from his customer and whipped into the back to see what had fallen. He found Hiroshi on the floor, still grasping a package. His eyes were closed. He wasn't moving. Ricky knelt at his side and gently brushed the top of Hiroshi's head. He didn't react. Didn't open his eyes. Or groan. He remained unconscious.

"NIKI!" Ricky shouted. Niki, confused, looked through the doorway, to see only customers in the front of the shop. He stepped inside as Ricky shouted for him again. Niki rushed into the back to find Ricky kneeling over Hiroshi.

"He fainted or something," Ricky looked up in anguish. Niki knelt on Hiroshi's other side and placed his fingers under Hiroshi's chin. There was no pulse.

"Call 911. NOW! And get Juan!" Niki took a deep breath and began performing chest compressions.

"Dios Mio!"

"Now, Ricky!" Ricky rushed to the POS terminal, where the landline was, and dialed 911. After confirming the address, he hung up and ran, hoping he'd guessed right about where Juan had gone for the tea. The three customers in the shop looked at each other, uncertain what to do.

"Dammit," Ricky muttered as he ran. Of all the times for most of them to be without their cell phones. They hadn't wanted to be burdened with them while fulfilling Raphael's command nude appearance at Folsom. Before he got far, Juan stepped out of a doorway about a block away, bearing a white plastic shopping bag. "Papito!" Ricky shouted, waving his arms. "Hurry! Hiroshi!" Juan began running and Ricky turned, without waiting, and ran back to the shop. Juan was right behind Ricky as they entered the back room. Niki looked up at them, tears falling. He'd ditched his pup hood so he could administer rescue breaths.

"I can't get a pulse," he moaned. Juan knelt next to Hiroshi, opposite Niki.

"Continue with the breaths," he instructed, without taking his eyes off Hiroshi's face. "I'll take over here." As if they'd practiced this together, Juan and Niki coordinated compressions and breaths.

"I called 911," Ricky said as he knelt next to Juan. In confirmation, they could hear the approaching siren.

"Clear the shop," Juan ordered. "Go outside so they'll know exactly where to go." As Ricky retreated, Niki wiped his eyes with the back of his hand between breaths, relieved that Juan was in charge. He looked back and forth between Juan's determined face and Hiroshi's. He wanted a sign of ... anything. But the only movement Hiroshi's head made was in response to the compressions. Neither said a word as they continued administering CPR.

"This way," Ricky said, leading the two paramedics into the back room. They had jumped out of the SFFD pumper double parked in front of the shop. Juan looked up, pausing his breaths.

"He collapsed about five minutes ago. We've been doing CPR." One of the paramedics knelt down, taking Niki's place, who rose and stood aside. "We can't get a steady pulse." The paramedic made eye contact. "I'm a nurse," Juan explained. The paramedic nodded and further parted Hiroshi's kimono so he could attach the electrodes the second paramedic handed him. Niki recognized the AED defibrillator he was carrying. As they began working, an ambulance noisily arrived. Niki caught Ricky's eyes, and he began moving.

"We should get out of the way," he said quietly, wanting to stay, but aware of the need to give the paramedics as much room as possible. They stood aside as a third paramedic met them at the doorway to the back room, guiding a wheeled cot.

"What happened?" Ricky pleaded. "He was ... he was fine a minute ago. I mean ..." Without saying so, they both realized Hiroshi had been stressed, but if anyone knew how to handle stress, it would be Hiroshi. Niki wordlessly shook his head, eyes closed. His cheeks still tear stained. He sniffled. "Good thing you were right here," Ricky squeezed Niki's biceps. "You knew what to do." Niki let out a breath he'd unconsciously been holding, opened his eyes and met Ricky's gaze.

"I don't know. I hope I did everything right."

"You did. I know you did." They listened: to the commands as the paramedics lifted Hiroshi onto the cot, to the hydraulics as the cot was raised, to the electronics of their equipment. Seconds later the responders were wheeling Hiroshi out and toward the street door with Juan right behind.

"Where are you taking him," Juan asked the lead paramedic as they approached the back of the ambulance.

"Davies. It's the closest."

"That's where I work. Can I ride?" The paramedic gave Juan a questioning look. "I know it's not protocol. But ... he's family." By now, the other two were guiding the cot into the van. The paramedic looked down, then up into Juan's pleading eyes.

"Okay, upfront," he agreed as he climbed in the back. The driver closed the doors, looked at Juan and cocked his head toward the front of the vehicle. Juan turned to Ricky and Niki who'd followed them all into the street.

"Close the shop. Go home. Wait for me." Ricky took off his mask and handed it to Juan. As he slipped it on, and opened the passenger door of the van, he added one more command. "And pray."

Most of the waiting customers had dispersed, aware that something terrible had happened. Ricky was able to quickly lock up before he and Niki wasted no time jogging home. They'd hardly spoken on the way, and seemed at a complete loss once inside the foyer. Niki wandered into the library, the room with the strongest gravitational pull for him since that first day. He collapsed into his chair. Ricky joined him, his phone in hand at last.

"I'm texting Alex. I think he took his phone in case of an emergency tech call." Niki didn't react. He was staring into the cold fireplace. As Ricky sat next to him, he looked up and saw the three spent veladoras on the mantle. 'And pray,' Juan had said. Niki rose and rushed out of the room. Before Ricky had finished his text, he was back from the dining room, holding one of the candles from the sideboard candelabra and the matches. It wasn't a seven-day votive, but it would have to do. He selected a veladora and sat in front of the hearth, facing Ricky. He lit the candle, and dripped hot wax into the bottom of the veladora before snuffing it out, so he could secure the candle in the glass. He heard Ricky make a slight moaning sound as he held the candle still until it was set. He looked up to see Ricky's lips smiling, but his eyes in pain. Niki caught his breath as he relit the candle.

"It worked before," he said, half smiling himself. Ricky slid off the chair and sat facing Niki, the veladora between their crossed legs. He reached out and took Niki's hands. They bowed their heads, closed their eyes and began to chant the words Hiroshi had taught them. "Nam Myōhō Renge Kyō."

"I don't know who's cuter," Alex leaned into Raphael. "Mateo leading Bandit around on a leash, or Bandit." Along with Greg and Luke, they'd been hanging a few steps behind Mateo and Ryan, watching them take in the sights of the fair. The 'sights' mostly being other kinksters, of all stripes. Despite living above a bona fide dungeon, there was plenty they hadn't experienced and they were getting an education today, observing men and women, cis and trans, gay and straight, all openly and proudly indulging in fetishes and kinks, some they themselves had experienced, some they'd no doubt imagined and some not previously conceived.

"They're a package deal," Raphael replied, "so, no contest. Who would have thought the two of them might end up as lovers? And so quickly. And easily. And you get half the credit."

"I do?"

"Your idea about the lab course ended the long-distance phase of their relationship."

"Oh. Yeah. Kudos to me. And the other half?"

"Me. I'm the one who introduced them."

"Any one of us could have done that." Raphael's reaction, half hidden by his mask, was mostly revealed by his left raised eyebrow.

"Uh huh. Could have. Maybe. I'm the one who saw the longing in Mateo's eyes. I'm the one who acted. I get the credit. I'll be best man, count on it."

"Oh? Who died and made you wedding planner?" Raphael bumped hips with Alex.

"Like anyone could wrest that away from you. Besides, I'm kidding. My money's on Juan and Ricky sharing that honor, anyway." Alex nodded. Then, he pulled away from Raphael and leaned down and fished his phone out of his boot sock. Raphael turned back to Luke.

"Oh no!" Alex stopped dead, creating a sudden roadblock for the people walking just behind him. "Guys!" Alex looked up from his phone and reached out to snag Greg, who was still moving. "Guys!" Alex shouted over the crowd. Raphael and Luke, who had still been tracking Mateo and Ryan turned. Alex and Greg caught up with them. "Ricky just texted. They took Hiroshi to the hospital."

"What happened?" Raphael cried, lifting his hand to his throat.

"I don't know," Alex looked from Raphael to Greg, then Luke. "We should go." Luke nodded.

"You guys stay right here. I'll get Mateo and Ryan."

"I think I know where Steve is," Greg said. "You guys head back to the clothes check. We'll meet you there." He started back the way they'd come. He turned and shouted, "Don't leave without us!"

Mateo, Ryan and Steve were first in the door, their Lyft just ahead of the one the others had taken. They found Ricky and Niki still seated around the veladora in the library. Ricky, still holding Niki's hands, looked up into Mateo's searching eyes.

"What happen?" Mateo pleaded. Ricky's eyes darted between Mateo's and Niki's, offering no answer to Mateo. His lips parted, but no words escaped. "Tell me!" Niki released his hold on Ricky's hands and twisted his body to face Mateo. By now everyone had made it into the room, or at least the doorway. The concern on Niki's face, and the flickering veladora, said volumes. As Niki spoke, Mateo fell into Niki's chair between Niki and Ricky.

"Hiroshi lost consciousness in the shop. He collapsed in the back room. Juan and I administered CPR." He glanced at Ricky. "Ricky called 911. Paramedics defibbed him, took him away." Niki paused, took a deep breath, and stared into Mateo's terrified eyes. "Juan went with them. To the hospital."

"He will be okay?" Mateo asked, glancing at Ricky, but concentrating on Niki, the budding nurse. Niki, unable to honestly answer Mateo, very slowly shrugged. By now Raphael had knelt down behind Niki, Luke at his back. Raphael placed both hands on Niki's shoulders and squeezed.

"I don't know, Mateo," Niki finally answered. "It was hard to get a pulse." A small sob escaped Niki's lips, terrifying Mateo. Unsettling everyone. Ricky sniffled.

"No!" Mateo cried out. "No. No!" He reached down and picked up the veladora. "We must help Hiroshi. Come." Mateo brushed past Greg, Alex, Ryan and Steve. "The mantra, everbody." Mateo crossed the foyer into the sitting room.

"Has Juan called or texted?" Greg asked Ricky as they crossed the foyer. Ricky shook his head.

"He doesn't have his phone," he replied. "We came straight from the fair to the shop." Greg frowned.

"How long ago did Hiroshi ... collapse?" Ricky drew a deep breath as they entered the sitting room.

"Thirty, forty minutes ago. I don't know. Everything happened so fast." Greg nodded as he sat down between Ricky and Alex in the circle that was forming around the veladora that Mateo had planted in the middle of the room. He glanced across the circle at Luke and Steve, then at Raphael who was taking Mateo's hand in his. Raphael met his gaze, then lowered his head as Mateo began to chant. Before Mateo had finished the first incantation, everyone, in unison, was whispering, "Nam Myōhō Renge Kyō."

# Thirteen

# THE BEST NEIGHBOR

MAYBE HALF AN HOUR had passed with nothing being said aside from the whispered mantra. No one wanted to be the one to break the spell. To risk endangering Hiroshi's recovery. Mateo believed wholeheartedly in its power, and because he worshiped Mateo, Ryan would never allow himself to question it either. The reverence Steve's video had cast upon the first ceremony made it impossible for any of the others to discount it out of hand. Besides, what else could they do? Only wait. And chant. And visualize. And pray.

It was Niki who finally broke the spell, letting go of Steve's and Ryan's hands.

"Guys. Sorry. I really have to pee." Luke glanced up at the mantel clock as the mantra faded with Niki's exit. The time since Hiroshi's collapse was nearing two hours. By the time Niki returned, most everyone had released the hands of the one next to them, although Raphael still held Luke's tightly. Ryan had wrapped an arm around Mateo, who was still silently mouthing the mantra. "I just noticed," Niki said, slipping back into his spot. "We're all still dressed." Steve gave him a wan smile and patted his thigh. "Like when we Zoomed with Mama."

"Maybe this," Raphael said, plucking his locked cock tee, "and the mantra will ensure the same outcome for Hiroshi that Mama and Angel had." He looked hopefully at Niki. "What do you think, Niki? Is it good or bad that Juan still hasn't called?" Everyone focused on Niki.

"I have no idea, Raphael." Niki met Ricky's worried gaze and held it, before turning back to Raphael. "I mean ..." Niki looked over at Mateo, who was silently pleading with him for a promising response. Niki decided against saying what he thought. The fact Hiroshi hadn't responded well to the CPR scared him. That Juan hadn't called could mean anything. Maybe he was tied up with paperwork. Or consoling a recovering Hiroshi. "The EMTs got there fast, and they were excellent.

So, hopefully ..." Niki took a deep breath and offered Raphael a twisted smile. Raphael squeezed Luke's hand harder.

"Why don't I make a pot of tea," Alex offered as he stood. It was then they heard the front door open. Then quietly close. Alex froze. Ricky stood as Juan appeared in the doorway. He took one look at Ricky and everyone knew. Ricky rushed to him and the two slowly sank to the floor, Ricky's arms around him. Juan buried his face in the crook of Ricky's neck and began to weep. Silently at first, his sobs shaking both of them. Then, his cries grew louder.

"Papito ... Papito ..." Ricky quietly cooed as he, too, began to cry.

"Noooo," Mateo wailed. "No ... please ... Hiroshi ..." Ryan wrapped both arms around him and they rocked back and forth. By now everyone was crying. In the blink of an eye, everyone's worst fear had been realized. It was not a shock to Niki, but devastating, still. He had turned in his spot to better embrace Steve as the two of them sobbed. This went on for several minutes, without anyone saying a word. Eventually, Alex rose, walked past Juan and Ricky and returned, not with tea, but with two boxes of tissues. He placed one at Juan's side and the other next to the still flickering veladora. Luke was the first to reach out for one, then another which he offered to Raphael. Still, no one spoke, giving Juan the time he needed to gather himself. It wasn't until Ricky reached over, pulled a tissue and honked into it that Juan raised his head and took in, for the first time, that he had walked into another of Mateo's healing sessions. With a veladora. And Hiroshi's mantra, no doubt. Hiroshi's mantra. When Juan met Mateo's gaze, he lost control again. He rose up from Ricky's embrace and went to Mateo. He crouched down behind him and Ryan and wrapped his arms around Mateo from behind. He struggled to gain control as Mateo whimpered in his arms.

"Thank you, muchacho," Juan finally, quietly spoke. "You did your best." He looked around the circle. "You all did." Steve pulled another tissue and made good use of it without taking his eyes off Juan.

"So, Juan," but he wasn't sure how to ask. "Do we know ... what happened?" Niki was absentmindedly rubbing Steve's thigh while also focused on Juan. Ricky was now behind Juan, standing on his knees, hands on Juan's shoulders.

"They don't know for certain ... yet ... but it was apparently cardiac arrest." Juan dropped Steve's gaze and focused on the veladora. "It was major. Major." Juan sighed deeply. "We'll probably know more after ..." his voice dropped to a whisper, "the autopsy." Mateo whimpered more loudly, distressing Ryan, who felt somewhat helpless with Juan's arms around Mateo. It must have shown on his face, as Niki reached out and rubbed Ryan's back. That's when it hit Niki.

"Oh god," he muttered. With fresh tears streaming, he looked past Ryan into Juan's eyes. "I just realized. I've lost my first patient." Juan released Mateo and reached over to caress the side of Niki's face.

"Niki, no ... you did everything perfectly. There was nothing more you could have done. This was out of your hands. You did your best; I did my best. The paramedics, the docs at the hospital, we all did everything we could. It just. Wasn't. Enough." Juan wordlessly held Niki's gaze to reinforce what he'd said. "If Hiroshi could have been saved, what you did would have saved him. Okay?" Juan continued to hold Niki's gaze until Niki finally closed his eyes and nodded. Juan released Niki's face and caught Steve's eyes, issuing a wordless appeal for him to reinforce with Niki what Juan had just said. Steve nodded. Everyone was silent again. Juan rubbed Mateo's shoulders and sat back, Ricky moving aside without letting go, his arm around Juan's waist.

"I can't believe this. I feel so ..." Raphael finally said to no one in particular. Alex nodded as he met Raphael's teary eyes.

"Yeah," he said. "What do we do now? I mean, what should we do?" Juan slowly shook his head, apparently too grief-stricken to think analytically yet.

"Did you lock up the shop?" Alex asked Ricky. Ricky nodded, sniffling. "Did, uh, Hiroshi leave street clothes or a shoulder bag or something there?" He glanced at Greg, then Raphael. "With his keys? We should probably make sure his house is okay. I mean, locked up and everything turned off."

"Street clothes," Ricky replied softly. "A shoulder bag. He keeps several kimono at the shop that he changes ... changed into. Before we open." The first of a litany of ramifications suddenly dawned on Ricky. Alex watched the alarm mix with grief on Ricky's face. Alex rose again.

"Ricky, can I borrow your shop keys? Raphael and I'll get Hiroshi's keys. You should stay here with Juan." Ricky pulled his keys out of his pocket and handed them up to Alex without leaving Juan's side. Raphael planted a gentle peck on Luke's cheek, then rose and followed Alex into the foyer and out the door. Niki reached forward and slightly rotated the veladora. He was tempted to blow out the candle, but he couldn't bring himself to do it. He wasn't ready for that much finality. Not yet, anyway.

When Alex and Raphael returned, they found the sitting room empty. Greg and Luke were in the kitchen, the others apparently in their rooms.

"Nobody is really hungry," Luke announced when Alex and Raphael walked in, "so we're just putting out some cheese, crackers, hummus and olives. Anything else?"

"No," Raphael attempted a smile. "Sounds good. Alex and I are going to run next door first." Greg followed along as Raphael and Alex headed for the garden. As expected, Hiroshi's back door was securely locked. They made a quick circuit through the house and found nothing of concern. It felt creepy and intrusive to be there without Hiroshi. Genteel, hospitable Hiroshi, who would have insisted on making a pot of tea. But, for now, someone had to be responsible for the house. They finished their rounds in the study where Alex heaved a sigh.

"Remember planning Juan and Ricky's wedding in this room?"

"Yeah," Raphael quietly replied. Then he snorted a subdued laugh. "And Hiroshi demonstrating his solution for the naked ringbearer." He started to laugh, but immediately began crying again. Greg and Alex fought back their own tears as they wrapped their arms around him. They held him tightly until he nodded, signaling his attempt to regain his composure. He took a deep breath. "I guess we should be contacting someone, shouldn't we? His cousin, maybe? In Tokyo, right?" Alex cleared his throat.

"I wonder if he speaks English? Maybe there's an address book here somewhere?" Alex began sorting through items on the desk. Greg, behind him, noticed Hiroshi's elaborate landline phone.

"This might help," he suggested. "Maybe he, or she, is on one of these speed dial buttons." All three of them clustered around the phone.

"Maybe we should start here," Raphael said, pointing to a button on the top row labeled 'Atty.' Alex looked quizzically at Raphael, who continued, "His attorney?" Alex cocked his head and nodded.

"Good guess, Sherlock. It's worth a try." Raphael sat in Hiroshi's desk chair and looked up at Greg for support. Greg nodded. Raphael pressed the button, leaving the handset on the base, activating the speakerphone. The display on the phone read 'Peter Simmons.' The call rang several times, then just as Raphael considered hanging up, someone answered.

"Hiroshi!" a happy male voice exclaimed. "I was just thinking of calling you ..." Alex and Raphael exchanged pained looks. Greg laid a hand on Raphael's right shoulder. Raphael took a deep breath.

"Sir. Peter Simmons?" There was a pause from the other end.

"Yes? Who is this?" The friendliness had instantly gone out of Peter Simmons' voice.

"Forgive us for disturbing you," Raphael tentatively began, "we uh, we're trying to reach someone for Hiroshi ... are you his attorney?"

"I am, yes. And a good friend. Who is this? What's going on?" Peter's voice had gone anxious.

"My name is Raphael Malaluan. I'm also a good friend of Hiroshi's. I'm here with Alex and Greg, we're neighbors ..." Before Raphael could bring himself to continue, Peter interrupted.

"Oh sure, I know all about you guys. Hiroshi has spoken of you many times. Is everything okay?"

"No," Raphael started, but then stopped, a sob catching in his throat. He took another deep breath.

"Hiroshi ...?" Peter seemed to ask.

"I'm sorry. I'm ... I'm calling because Hiroshi died today." It was the first time any of them had said the word out loud.

Died. Hiroshi had died. There was a long, too long, pause from Peter's end. Greg broke the silence.

"Sir, we're not certain whom we should contact. We know he has a cousin ..." Peter didn't seem to hear what Greg had said.

"How did he ... were you with him?" Peter's voice was strained with emotion. It was obvious he wasn't exaggerating about being more than Hiroshi's attorney.

"Juan, Ricky and Niki were," Raphael explained. "They were all at the shop together. They're not here with us right now. They're at our house. Next door." Raphael paused, not sure what the right thing to say was. "Everybody's pretty ..." but another sob caught in his throat.

"Of course," Peter quietly said. "I understand." He took a deep breath of his own, one that quavered at the end. "I appreciate you calling me. It was. It was the right thing to do." Another pause. "Where is Hiroshi now?"

"They took him to CPMC. Davies Campus," Greg said. "Juan went there with him."

"Thank you," Peter said. "I'll follow up with them. I have Hiroshi's directives. I know how to contact his cousin. I, uh, have ... everything necessary." No one spoke for a moment. "Do you know? Did Hiroshi suffer?" Alex spoke for the first time.

"I don't think so. Juan said they will be doing an autopsy. But they think it was cardiac arrest."

"Yes." Peter said. "Yes, of course." It wasn't clear if he was referencing the autopsy or the presumed heart failure. "Listen, can I have a number for one of you? So I can contact you?" Greg offered his number before Raphael or Alex could react. "Thank you, Greg. Would it be all right if I asked you look after Hiroshi's house? I trust you more than anyone I might hire."

"Of course," Raphael volunteered. "We're used to running back and forth anyway."

"Yes, I know," Peter replied with a little more lightness in his voice. "Again, thank you for reaching out. I'll be touch in the next few days, hopefully in person."

"Okay," Greg replied. "You can reach me anytime."

"I appreciate that, Greg. Listen, all of you. Take care of yourselves. And thank you, again. For everything. I'll be in touch." Peter signed off before anyone could reply. Raphael leaned back in Hiroshi's chair, exhaling deeply. Greg patted his shoulder.

"I think our work here is done. For now," he said. "You made the right call on the first try, Raphael." Raphael rose with a tentative smile and slowly pushed the desk chair into place. The three started toward the doorway, but before they reached it Alex veered off and approached a wall opposite the door. Greg and Raphael turned to see him reach up and take down a photo.

"What are you doing?" Greg chastised. Alex joined them, and both Greg and Raphael looked down to see what Alex was holding. It was the photo he'd admired before, of Hiroshi and a friend, with Harvey Milk in the background. Alex looked up at Greg.

"I uh ... it won't hurt to borrow this for a little while, will it? I always wanted to ask Hiroshi the story behind this photo. Who this other guy was? Whether he was friends with Milk. But ..." Raphael wrapped an arm around Alex's waist as he moved to better look at the photo, and in doing so, felt the corset Alex was still wearing under his t-shirt. Which brought a slight smile to his face.

"Hiroshi was so young there," Greg stated the obvious.

"Yeah," Alex glanced at Raphael. "Something tells me he was the original Spicy Asian." Raphael snorted and took the photo from Alex's hands, studied it a moment, then handed it to Greg.

"I just hope I'll be half as wonderful and half as wise when I'm Hiroshi's age."

"Not to worry," Greg said solemnly, still studying the photo. "You're well on your way, Raphael." He handed the photo back to Alex. "So many stories we deserved to hear. And never will."

"I don't think Hiroshi would mind," Raphael met Alex's misty eyes. "Let's put it on the sideboard in the dining room." He looked to Greg for consensus. Greg nodded and reached out for Alex's free hand.

"Come on, guys, let's go home."


At first it was just Luke, Raphael, Alex and Greg around the kitchen island, half-heartedly nibbling on a cracker or olive, speaking in hushed tones. A bit later, Steve and Niki came down and joined them. Before he sat, Steve pulled a bottle of Sauvignon Blanc out of the wine cabinet and held it up, as if asking for approval. Alex got up and retrieved six wine glasses from the butler's pantry in response. Once everyone's glass was poured, Steve held his up and quietly toasted.

"To Hiroshi. The best neighbor and the truest friend any of us has ever had." Crooked smiles and sniffles accompanied the sound of the clinking glasses. There were many long moments of silence.

"I'm worried about Juan and Ricky," Raphael said, staring into the center of the island where the veladoras once glowed.

"And Mateo," Alex offered. "He's taking this really hard." Raphael nodded.

"Juan's lost a dear old friend ... and mentor I guess, and Ricky has lost not just a friend, but his business partner. What will happen to the Headquarters?"

"He probably has no idea how to even think about that right now, Raphael," Luke suggested.

"He's going to need help," Niki slowly rotated his wine glass. "When he's ready to reopen the shop, I could take the rest of the semester off, maybe." Steve cleared his throat disapprovingly.

"Puppy, Hiroshi would not agree to that, and you know it. Neither would Ricky. We'll find a way to help him out without you derailing your studies." Steve leaned over and kissed a spot where Niki's mohawk met shaved scalp. "You and your big heart."

"Well, I'm going to derail my work schedule," Raphael declared. "I'm going to submit a personal time off request before I turn in, so it's there first thing in the morning. Does that make me a bad employee?"

"No," Luke said quietly, "Your boss will understand. Just to be safe, maybe you should copy Cynthia on the request." Raphael nodded his agreement.

"I'll do that, too," Alex chimed in. "At least request to be back up only." He glanced at Steve, then Raphael. "Do you think we're going to see Juan or Ricky tonight?" Steve shook his head. Raphael just sighed. "I was thinking. I could print out a sign to post inside the shop door announcing a temporary closure due to a family emergency. Something like that?"

"That's probably a good idea," Niki met Alex's gaze. "But since the shop is closed on Monday anyway, maybe we should wait and see how Ricky's doing tomorrow." Alex concurred with a smile.

"Ricky's probably not going to be ready to reopen anytime soon," Luke speculated. Raphael leaned his head against Luke's shoulder.

"I'll put a short notice up on the shop's social media accounts about a temporary closure after we talk to Ricky," Steve said. Niki yawned.

"I know it's early, but I'm really beat. So's this guy. We'll see you in the morning, okay?" Alex stood along with Niki and wrapped his arms around him. Niki squeezed back, then followed Steve into the foyer.

"I know this has been a blow to all of us, but it had to be especially traumatic for Niki," Alex said as he carried abandoned glasses to the dishwasher. "I mean, seeing Hiroshi fade away while desperately trying to save his life." Alex's lips started to quiver again. "He was so heroic," he whispered. Greg joined Alex at the dishwasher and wrapped an arm around Alex's shoulders and walked him toward the back stairs. Alex sighed on the way out but said no more. Luke gathered up the remaining food and slid it into the fridge while Raphael finished loading the dishwasher. Then they, too, made an early night of it in the House of the Locked Cock Brotherhood.

## Fourteen

# Nothing Will Be the Same

He had no idea when, but at some point, finally, Ricky had fallen asleep. He must have, because suddenly it was light out. And Juan was gone. Panicked, Ricky sat up, distressed that Juan had left for work without him knowing it. Without them exchanging a kiss. Or even words. He stood to use the bathroom and saw Juan's ID badge on the dresser. Simultaneously relieved and disheartened, Ricky quickly peed, then headed downstairs. Juan wasn't in the kitchen, but the coffee carafe was heavy and felt warm to the touch. Ricky poured a cup, then began wandering. After a quick circuit downstairs, he headed for the back door, which was ajar. He looked out and saw Juan sitting alone in the gazebo. Juan looked up as Ricky approached.

"Did you sleep at all, Papito?" Ricky asked as he slid into place next to Juan.

"A little. I know you did."

"Yeah, a little. Do I look as bad as you do?" Juan tried to chuckle.

"I don't know. I haven't looked in a mirror yet today. But probably not, mijo. You look just fine to me."

"When I first woke up, I was hoping it was a bad dream. A nightmare. But then I saw your badge. And that's when I knew." After a slight pause, Ricky sighed. "Nothing will be the same." Juan drained his mug. Ricky leapt up and ran into the house, returning seconds later with the coffee carafe. Juan smiled as Ricky refreshed his mug.

"Maybe some things will be the same," Juan laid his arm across Ricky's shoulders. "You're still the World's Best Locked Cock Leather Boy as far as I can tell." Ricky looked down at his cage.

"I'd give it up in a second if ..." Juan jostled Ricky's shoulders. Ricky whimpered and turned to face Juan. "It's my fault, you know." Juan pulled away and turned to fully face Ricky.

"What?" Ricky started to tear up again. Juan placed a hand on Ricky's right leg. "Mijo ..."

"I never should have listened to Hiroshi. I should have skipped Folsom. If I'd been at the shop ..." Juan looked like he'd been slapped.

"Ricky, this is *not* your fault. No one's fault. This is ... this is just *life.*" He leaned forward and cupped Ricky face in both hands. He wiped away a tear with each thumb. "And you said yourself, Hiroshi insisted that you do Folsom. You did what he wanted. God, Ricky, please don't blame yourself. It was a medical emergency. You and Niki did everything possible to save Hiroshi."

"So did you, Papito." Ricky tried a sniffly smile. Juan nodded, offering a slight smile of his own.

"Yeah. We all did, mijo." Juan pulled Ricky into a long embrace.

"Is this a private party?" Greg asked as he stepped up into the gazebo, mug in hand. Juan shook his head and pushed the carafe into the middle of the table. As Ricky wiped away his tears, Greg poured and sat. He took a sip and stared at Juan and Ricky a moment, pondering whether or not he was intruding. Not sure if it was just coincidence or had they chosen, the two of them, to memorialize Hiroshi this morning in the gazebo, part of which had also been the chuppah under which Hiroshi had married them.

"How are you and Alex doing?" Juan asked. "Did you sleep?" Greg shook his head.

"We must have. Off and on, I guess. Alex is making another pot of coffee." As if summoned, Alex arrived with the fresh pot which he decanted into the carafe before heading back into the kitchen. He returned with a mug of his own and sat next to Ricky instead of Greg.

"I thought about you guys a lot last night," Alex said. "We're all close to Hiroshi, but I think you two had a special bond. You and Mateo."

"I don't think Hiroshi had favorites, Alex," Juan contended. "You two shared a special bond over senbei, as I recall." Alex raised his eyes, but didn't quite roll them. "And you were great together as wedding planners." Greg raised his mug in affirmation. "We're all going to miss him terribly."

"Last night," Alex said, "when we were securing Hiroshi's house, Raphael, Greg and I made a call." Alex recounted the conversation with Hiroshi's attorney. "We got the impression he and Hiroshi are more than just business associates or even casual friends. Have you met him?" Juan thought a moment and shook his head.

"Maybe ... but I don't think so. So, he's taking charge of Hiroshi's affairs? I guess that's good."

"Well, yeah, it's his job, after all," Greg said. "But, like Alex said, he took the news pretty hard. He knows about all of us. I mean, I don't know how much he knows, but enough to trust us to look after Hiroshi's house."

"What else should we be doing?" Ricky asked, uncoupling himself from Juan and reaching for his mug of now tepid coffee. Alex laid a hand on Ricky's thigh.

"First, we take care of each other," he said slowly, as Ricky turned to make eye contact. "Especially you. You tell us what you need help with at the shop, and we'll do it. Second, we wait to hear back from Peter. He said he'll be in touch in the next few days. He said, 'in person.'"

"Ideally," Greg interrupted. "He said 'ideally in person.'"

"Actually, my dear, he said 'hopefully in person.'" Alex turned back to Ricky and shook his head. "Don't listen to him. It'll be in person. I got the impression he's very smart and capable, and he'll be able to handle any issues that come up. Don't you worry, Ricky."

"Thanks, Alex," Ricky genuinely smiled. "I'm not worried. Not yet, you know. Just ..."

"Just heartbroken," Alex smiled back. "Like all of us." He leaned in and delivered a cheek kiss, then stood and moved over to sit next to Greg. He looked closely at Juan. "Did you guys eat anything last night?" Juan shook his head. Alex stood and held a hand out to Greg. "Come dear, I need an extra hand, or two." He smiled at Ricky. "Give us twenty minutes, then make another pot of coffee." Greg grabbed his mug as he stood and took one last sip before Alex pulled him out of the gazebo and back into the house.

It was closer to thirty minutes when Alex and Greg came through the back door with shopping bags from the French bakery on Church Street. Greg began unloading smaller bags and boxes while Alex ran back into the house to get plates and utensils. By now Luke, Raphael, Steve and Niki had found their way to the gazebo. Alex returned to the kitchen once more and made a tray with two mugs of coffee. He set it outside Mateo and Ryan's door, knocked twice and headed to the kitchen to snag the fresh carafe of coffee on his way back to the gazebo.

"You've been busy," Luke said when Alex set the carafe down.

"Somebody has to feed you guys," Alex replied, matter of factly. "We have three kinds of croissants, rustic tarts, scones, and two kinds of quiche. Make sure you eat some quiche Juan and Ricky." He glanced at Luke. "They haven't eaten since whatever that was they were eating at Folsom yesterday."

"It was a hot dog," Juan defensively replied. "Or a brat, I think. I don't remember ..." He diligently reached for a slice of quiche as Mateo and Ryan wandered up to the gazebo. Juan and Ricky scooted closer to Raphael and Luke to make room for them.

"Alex and Greg made breakfast," Raphael announced as they sat.

"Thanks, Alex," Mateo said somberly. "Thank you, Greg. Ever'thing looks good." A few minutes into the feast, Raphael glanced up at Hiroshi's house, then closed his eyes and slightly shook his head. Alex caught the moment and made eye contact when Raphael recovered.

"I know what you were thinking, Raphael," Alex quietly muttered. Raphael held his gaze.

"Yeah," was all he said.

"For a second you were thinking of inviting Hiroshi over ..." Raphael sniffled and nodded.

"Yeah," he admitted, a bit more forcefully. "Sorry ..." Juan reached over and placed his hand on Raphael's.

"It's okay," Juan soothed. "It's going to be a big adjustment for all of us."

"You know what this reminds me of?" Luke asked the family at large. "All these pastries, I mean." No one volunteered a guess. Luke looked fondly at Juan and Ricky. "When you two were off honeymooning in Half Moon Bay, we were all here, slaving away, building this gazebo. Hiroshi started us off with a carb-laden breakfast just like this."

"Sounds like Hiroshi," Ricky quietly said.

"We saw the picture in the dining room," Mateo glanced at Alex, then Raphael. "Is Hiroshi, no?"

"Yeah," Alex confirmed. "He was pretty cute, wasn't he?"

"Still is," Mateo smiled for the first time. Juan laughed under his breath as Ryan nudged Mateo. Raphael sighed.

"Alex stole it from Hiroshi's study last night when we were checking things out."

"I did not steal it," Alex protested.

"Oh," Raphael responded. "So, it's just on permanent loan. Like in a museum. I see ..." Alex shrugged.

"Are you thinking of working today, Mateo?" Juan asked. Ryan looked pained.

"Dunno," Mateo replied without looking up. "I prolly should ..." Ryan shook his head while meeting Juan's gaze.

"Muchacho," Juan replied. "Do me a favor, por favor. Call in sick. Tell them a family member passed away and you will be gone all week. I need you here. Ricky needs you. We all do." Mateo, looking visibly relieved, laid his fork down and stood.

"Okay, I call now. Be right back." Ryan looked at Juan and mouthed 'thank you.'

"A restaurant kitchen can be a dangerous place when you're distracted," Juan said. "Besides, he won't admit it, but Mateo's hurting. He needs us."

"He does," Ryan agreed. "He cried most of the night. I felt so bad. All I could do was hold him and let him cry."

"I'm glad he has you to hold him," Alex smiled. "I'm so glad he's not sleeping alone anymore."

"Or with just his phone," Greg said, also smiling at Ryan.

"Yeah," Ryan agreed. "I'm glad I'm here." He looked around at the others, ending his gaze on Niki. "For a lot of reasons."


There wasn't much anyone could do over the next couple of days except be there for each other. Appetites, gustatory and sexual, were blunted despite everyone living naked as always. The gym saw a little action, but workouts were perfunctory at best. Raphael and Niki checked in on Hiroshi's house a couple of times a day, running the dishwasher once, dusting in the living and dining rooms, but it still felt eerie to be there. Like they were intruding somewhere they weren't really allowed to be. Still, they felt obligated to look after Hiroshi's things, some of which sparked bittersweet memories. Like the iron teapot he'd used to serve tea to the two of them on their first visit, when he coyly revealed his own cage. The cage he wore while mourning Ben's death.

It didn't take much for Juan and Steve to persuade Ricky to keep the Headquarters closed for at least the rest of the week. Although he felt obligated to Hiroshi, and to the customers, it was clear Ricky wasn't emotionally ready to stand alone behind one of the display cases Hiroshi had designed. Steve posted the closure on the website and the social media accounts, and Alex affixed a sign inside the shop door. After debating, he pulled down the shades on the display windows, obscuring the enticing manikins from the casual glance of passersby.


It was after Greg had received a phone call that he finally found Alex lounging in the sitting room window seat. He was vacantly staring out the window at the street below, a journal in his lap. Greg slid into the opposite corner, interlaced his legs with Alex's and reached out toward Alex's lap.

"Can I see?" Alex turned to Greg but didn't respond. "Can I see what you've been writing?"

"You'll just laugh."

"I could use a good laugh." Greg's fingers wiggled a come-hither gesture. Alex offered a halfhearted smile and held out the journal. Greg paged to the last entry and read aloud.

"First it's cold
"Then it's hot.
"Then it's windy
"Then it's not."

Then he read the title Alex had penned. 'A Walk on Just About Any Day in San Francisco.' Greg smiled and almost chuckled, but he didn't laugh. He looked up at Alex.

"True. Succinct. I'd say you've captured the San Francisco experience in ..." he counted in his head, "... twelve words." Alex shrugged, but briefly flashed a hint of a smile of his own. Greg thumbed a few pages to a previous journal entry, a longer poem that he read silently to himself.

*Spring*

*I lay there near the window
with the drapes undrawn,
the pane parted from the sill.
I see the moon,
more gone than not,
but brilliant still.
It is the means by which
I witness the movement
of an early spring night
that I would otherwise only
hear smell and feel.
A train in the distance
overpowers the cicadas with its
vibrant advance,
but it fails to stop the wind,
which lifts the curtain and
carries it across my motionless form.
A dog somewhere
barks at a movement,
a noise.
Dead leaves, hangers on,*

*left from last fall,*
*skid noisily across the street below*
*signaling to the cicadas*
*to begin again,*
*the train is gone.*
*I can't sleep.*
*Beside me there is no one*
*to share the dawn of spring with.*
*The only touch I feel*
*is that of a windblown curtain*
*trailing back to the window*
*in time to be blown again.*
*I wish I could sleep.*

Greg swallowed hard, and fought back the urge to tear up again, something they'd all been doing better at these last couple of days.

"When did you write this?"

"Which?" Greg tilted the journal toward Alex.

"Spring ..." Alex, closed his eyes and nodded, truly smiling this time.

"A couple of months before we met. Now you know how easy it was for you to sweep me off my feet. I was one vulnerable ... and lonely ... queer boy back then."

"And profound."

"Well, for some reason, I only write poetry when I'm depressed. Which is why you don't see many new entries in there since I met you." Alex rubbed his leg alongside Greg's. He really did smile again. Greg handed the journal back to Alex.

"Okay then. I'll do my best to ensure there'll always be plenty of blank pages in there." He reached down and caressed Alex's foot. "We need to schedule a family meeting. Peter Simmons called a few minutes ago. He wants to meet with us. All of us. In person." His eyebrows danced with the words 'in person,' eliciting another smile from Alex.

"I hope we learn more about what happened to Hiroshi."

"Me, too," Greg replied.

"Mateo seemed a little better today, Sir," Raphael said as Luke snuggled up behind him in the shower. He was preparing to tighten up and perfect Raphael's high 'n tight for the first time since Saturday. It just hadn't seemed all that important lately.

"I think you're right, baby. Getting him to help you cook dinner gave him some purpose. Something to concentrate on. Maybe it was wrong of us to talk him into taking time off from the restaurant."

"No," Raphael disagreed, as he leaned his head forward so Luke could drag the razor smoothly down the back of his head. "It's important to be surrounded by people you love this soon after a death. Juan was right. Same with Ricky. It's going to be so hard for him when he reopens the Headquarters."

"If there's even going to be a Headquarters, going forward," Luke said, turning Raphael's head to better reach his left side. "I guess we'll learn more tomorrow, huh?"

"Maybe," was all Raphael said. Over dinner Greg had announced Peter Simmons' request to meet with the family. He wanted everyone in attendance for some reason, and since everyone was still on bereavement leave, it was easy to mesh with Peter's schedule. "I hope there aren't a bunch of legal hoops Ricky has to jump through."

"Well, if there are, baby, we'll jump through them with him." Raphael nodded. Then shook his head.

"I hope he doesn't have to go back to Dashing, Sir. He's really established a following at the Headquarters."

"Let's stay positive, baby," Luke leaned forward and kissed the back of Raphael's freshly shaved scalp. Raphael pulled free and flipped around to give Luke a more kissable target. After a little tongue wrestling, he pulled free again and slipped behind Luke so he could shampoo, rinse and repeat Luke's now seven-month long locks. Raphael loved digging into them, massaging Luke's scalp, dragging his fingers through Luke's foamy waves. It was something he'd had years of practice doing when his own hair was even longer than Luke's, but, because it was yet another way to make love to Luke, it was a different and far more rewarding experience.

"I've been meaning to ask," Raphael leaned forward and whispered into Luke's ear. For the first time in days, he was feeling a little frisky. "How many guys flirt with you now that you have hair usually found on the cover of a gothic romance novel? Instead of a mohawk?"

"Well, baby, that would be telling." Raphael half laughed.

"That many, huh?" It was Luke's turn to chuckle.

"You have to admit, the mohawk was a little fringe. Maybe too stern of a look for some. Now I come off more as the approachable type, so ... yeah. I work it." Raphael pushed Luke's back forward in feigned jealousy as he turned and flipped on the shower to rinse both of them off.

"Sir, just so they approach, but never actually touch, what is mine ... all mine." Raphael flipped off the shower, wrapped his arms around Luke's chest from behind and leaned back until both of them were half-reclined in the shower. He gently brushed Luke's nipples with his thumbs. They sat, silent, for several minutes, having finished a ritual they'd shared a thousand times. And were appreciating the fact that they were both still here and able to share it.

# Fifteen

# A Very Hiroshi Idea

Two o'clock on the dot, Peter Simmons rang the doorbell. Greg showed him into the dining room where Raphael, Luke and Niki were already in their usual spots. Like the rest of the family, they were dressed for company. Alex placed a glass of ice water in front of Hiroshi's usual chair, which no one had been willing to slide back against the wall, and invited Peter to have a seat. After hesitating, Peter removed his mask, took a sip of the water, and looked around the room while the rest of the family gathered. Steve was the last to take his seat. Greg introduced everyone, starting with Alex and Raphael, since Peter had already 'met' them over the phone.

"Peter Simmons ... why do I know that name?" Steve asked.

"From the letter about the house," Niki replied. He turned to Peter. "You're Grandpa Ben's lawyer, too, aren't you?"

"I just knew him as Ben. But yes, I was," Peter smiled. "I met Ben through Hiroshi. Small world, isn't it?" Niki smized a self-satisfied smile. "Despite the circumstances, let me say it's a genuine pleasure meeting all of you. I want to thank each of you for giving me a little of your time. I feel like I already know a bit about you. Hiroshi often spoke of you." He looked at Ricky. "Especially you, Ricky. I helped Hiroshi with all the legal issues around LCB Headquarters. He was so excited to be going into business with you." Ricky smiled shyly, then glanced at Steve, then Niki.

"It wasn't just me, Sir. Everybody here has helped out, you know."

"Oh, I know, and please ... call me Peter." He looked around the room again. "It looks like you're taking very good care of this grand old house." He paused a moment as he spotted the photo of Hiroshi at the Harvey Milk rally. He quietly chuckled to himself.

"Peter, is that you in the photo with Hiroshi?" Alex asked. "I never got to ask about the story behind it." Peter shook his head.

"No, but I'm flattered you thought that could have been me. My hair, when I had that much hair, was never quite that long. But, in a way, Harvey Milk *was* responsible for us meeting the first time."

"Were you the attorney who got the charges dropped?" Raphael asked. Peter gave Raphael a humorously shocked look.

"Why, yes. Did he tell you that story?" Raphael nodded.

"Yeah, he did." Raphael's eyes began misting up. "He had us all spellbound that night." Raphael cleared his throat, determined to keep his emotions in check, and resumed eye contact with Peter. "He had really nice things to say about you."

"Most friendships don't last as long as ours has," Peter responded. "I think you would all agree, Hiroshi was one of those people who makes friends for life." A tear trailed down Mateo's left cheek and under his mask as he let out an almost silent moan. Ryan had come prepared and slipped him a tissue. Mateo flashed him a little smize. Peter noticed. "Since you've already invited me to unmask for this water, you don't need to stay masked for me. I assume we've all been vaccinated?"

"We have, Peter," Juan spoke for the first time as he peeled off his mask. "We were hoping you might have more information on Hiroshi's ... collapse." The word 'death' was still hard for everyone.

"Yes, Juan, I have several things here I want to share with you." He took a single sheet of paper out of the portfolio he'd placed on the table, glanced at it briefly, then back at Juan. "In layman's terms, Hiroshi suffered major heart failure." Ricky closed his eyes and slumped. Juan wrapped an arm around his shoulders. "Although it was sudden, and apparently without any warning signs, I can tell you it was not unexpected."

"What?" Ricky quietly whispered.

"I'm sure Hiroshi never said a word to any of you, but he was troubled with cardiac problems for years. I think one doctor suspected it was congenital. He was, I guess you could say, living on borrowed time. I was really worried about him after Ben died. He, uh, he seemed to be giving up." Peter stared at the middle of the table, lost in thought for a few seconds, before he brightened and looked around the table. "But then, you moved into this house and into Hiroshi's life. Suddenly he was his old self again. I can't prove it, but I swear you saved his life. Or at least gave him a new lease on life, if you'll pardon the cliché." Juan looked at Ricky and without speaking telegraphed 'see ... it wasn't your fault.'

"Wow," Niki said under his breath. He looked at Steve, then at Peter. "He always seemed fine. He marched with us for Black Lives Matter. He took care of our garden. Helped build the gazebo." Peter nodded.

"Like I said, all of you gave him new life, new energy." Peter opened his portfolio and took out another sheet of paper. He glanced at it and again looked around the table, making eye contact with each man. "And most importantly, you invited him into your family. You made him a very happy man in his last couple of years, and for that, as his friend, I sincerely want to thank each of you." Peter paused, letting his words sink in with everyone around the table.

"But, of course, I'm also here to meet with you as Hiroshi's attorney." Peter turned to Ricky, who looked anxious. Juan squeezed Ricky's shoulder. "Hiroshi updated his will, not long ago, for obvious and important reasons. I'll leave a copy with you, but there are two important codicils for us to discuss. First, Ricky, Hiroshi has left full ownership of LCB Headquarters to you. If you wish, I would be honored to continue as counsellor of record for the business." Ricky looked instantly relieved.

"Yes, please. That would be great. I ... uh, I'm sure I'll need your help."

"Well, hopefully not too much lawyerly help, Ricky. We have some paperwork to handle with the city and county of San Francisco, the bank and so forth, but otherwise everything is in order." Ricky looked at Niki and widened his eyes in an 'oh wow' gesture. Niki smiled back. Peter seemed just as pleased as Ricky. He sat back and looked around the table again, then nodded to himself, a slight smile forming. He took a deep breath.

"Hiroshi has also left something for all of you. At the time he did it, I admit, I wasn't convinced it was a good idea. But it was his decision, of course. Considering how much each of you meant to Hiroshi over the last two years ..."

"I wish we could show you how much Hiroshi meant to us," Raphael interrupted. "All of us. Yeah, he and Juan had known each other for years, but the rest of us, from the very first moment we saw him, we knew he was someone special." Raphael looked around the table at the nodding heads. "I can still see him that first time, peering around that creaking gate. His fundoshi. His tattoo. And the bottle of sake." Raphael regained eye contact with Peter. "He was always sharing. Material things and spiritual." Mateo silently mouthed the words. *Nam Myōhō Renge Kyō.*

"No, Raphael," Peter leaned forward, "I totally understand. But to hear him tell it, Hiroshi benefitted far more from your generosity. Material and otherwise." He sat back.

"As I was saying, Hiroshi has bequeathed, to all ten of you, his house. And everything in it. With the exception of a couple of family treasures I will be shipping to his cousin." Peter was met initially with stunned silence. Juan was the first to speak.

"What? No ..."

"But what about his cousin?" Alex asked.

"In addition to the artifacts, Hiroshi left her some money. He's been helping her out financially for years, so she'll be fine."

"Is this for real?" Niki was looking directly at Peter. "You can't be serious." Peter smiled.

"It's real, Niki. Hiroshi hoped he'd be with all of you for years to come, but, as I said," Peter paused and swallowed, "he knew that might not be the case. Other than his cousin he had no close family, certainly not here in the US. This isn't the first time Hiroshi updated his will. Years ago, he originally named Ben as his primary beneficiary. Then, after Ben died, he established a short list of charities in his place. He really didn't know what else to do. And then, you entered his life. A few months ago he told me, if he were to pass, he wanted to do what he could to ensure that his family, his brothers, as he referred to you, would be well taken care of. So, we revised his will again." Peter looked around the table, noting that there was no glee on anyone's face. No joy. Just thoughtfulness and more silence.

"I can't believe he did this," Steve finally spoke. "But, knowing Hiroshi, I guess it's not surprising. I mean, we always thought of him as family. I guess it only makes sense that he would consider us in the same way. That must sound odd to you."

"Not at all," Peter, surprisingly, placed a hand on Juan's shoulder as he spoke. "I was happy for Hiroshi when he started telling me about some of his escapades with all of you." Juan turned to give Peter his full attention. "Yes, he shared a few stories with me. I might have been a little envious, in fact. He loved you, each of you. That was obvious. You entered his life at a time he most needed you." Peter withdrew his hand and pulled a sheaf of papers out of the portfolio and placed them in front of Juan.

"I'll let you review the will at your leisure. I'm at your service when you have any questions, and I'm sure you will have some. Becoming group owners of a property can be a little complicated, but it doesn't have to be. We'll have paper work and details to work out in the coming weeks. Please know I'm here to help." Peter stood. "Despite the circumstances, it's been a pleasure to finally meet all of you, in person. What you have here is rare. And special. Very special." He picked up his portfolio, as Juan stood.

"We appreciate everything you've done," Juan said. "Today, and over the years, for Hiroshi. This can't be easy for you, either." Peter smiled weakly.

"Well, it's my duty. But, as Hiroshi's friend, it was also an honor. To fulfill his wishes." He waved to the table. "Stay safe everyone ..." First Steve, then Niki then everyone stood and followed Juan and Peter into the foyer to see him out. Once he'd gone, everyone stood awkwardly in the foyer, still a little stunned and at a bit of a loss. Finally, Alex spoke.

"I don't know what to think."

"Yeah," Raphael seconded.

"Are we millionaires now?" Mateo asked. Greg chuckled.

"In the aggregate, yes, most definitely. Divided by ten? No. But it does make each of us a lot more comfortable, muchacho."

"Greg," Juan asked, his face initially devoid of any emotion, "would you mind reading the will Peter left. I ... I can't look at it right now." Emotion returned as he sniffed. Ryan handed him a tissue as Ricky wrapped an arm around his waist.

"Sure," Greg replied. "Happy to."

"Maybe we can get together after dinner," Luke suggested, "and you can share any details we should know."

"Maybe in the turret room?" Ryan asked. "With truth serum? Instead of secrets we could talk about Hiroshi. Maybe tell our favorite stories or something. Does that sound lame?"

"No," Luke replied. "It sounds like a wake. It sounds like a good idea." Juan clasped a hand on Luke's shoulder and nodded before pulling Ricky toward and up the stairs. Everyone but Greg and Alex followed behind while they returned to the dining room to collect the will and tidy up.

"That doesn't look like Scotch," Steve said as he and Niki settled into place in the nearly complete circle that had formed in the turret room. Luke was opening a tall clear bottle adorned with kanji lettering all around. Raphael and Alex appeared at the top of the stairs, each carrying several ochoko they'd pilfered from one of Hiroshi's cabinets.

"No," Luke looked up from his efforts to unseal the bottle. "It's not truth serum tonight. We decided to honor Hiroshi with some of his excellent sake. Which, I guess, is our sake now."

"Hopefully that bottle isn't one of the heirlooms that's supposed to go to his cousin," Niki posed.

"It's not," Greg smiled. "Our consciences are clear." Raphael and Alex took their places. Luke poured a couple of ounces into Raphael's ochoko and handed the bottle to Ryan. Once the bottle had made its round, Luke poured into his own cup and set the bottle down in the middle of the circle. He lifted his ochoko toward the bottle, initially with a smile that immediately fell into a tearful frown.

"To Elder," he choked out. "Dammit. I wasn't going to cry." As everyone sipped, Raphael rubbed his back, tearing up along with him. Luke cleared his throat and turned to Ryan. "Lead us off, Ryan. This was your idea. Give us a reason to smile." Ryan looked across the circle at Niki. Niki did smile, suspecting what might be coming.

"I guess I have one memory that no one else here can talk about. Except Niki." Ryan looked around the circle. Everyone here had many more experiences with Hiroshi than he himself had had. And maybe that's why it was best for him to go first. "On my birthday. When Niki and I were pupped out all day in our garden and Hiroshi's, he was wonderful. He didn't just put water out for us. Early on it was sparkling water. And later ... it was beer." Niki laughed and nodded. "The other pups were amazed, too. I don't think they'd ever seen that before. He played with us. Gave us belly rubs. Had us perform tricks together. The other pups loved him, too. It was a really special day for me. I owe it all to Niki, of course, and you, Mateo, but Hiroshi was a big part of it. Mateo, I always knew you were terribly fond of him. That day, I could really see why." Ryan held eye contact with a smiling Mateo before taking another sip of his sake. Luke placed a hand on Ryan's thigh.

"Thank you, Ryan." Luke looked across at Juan. "Not only was that a nice memory, but he got through the whole thing without springing a boner." Juan couldn't help but laugh, for the first time in days. He gave Ryan an endearing look.

"Yeah, thanks Ryan," Juan smiled. "This *was* a good idea." He turned to his right, to Greg. "Did you finish the will?"

"I did," Greg nodded. "But first I'd like to hear your Hiroshi story. Or stories. You've known Hiroshi longer than any of us." Juan half wiggled his eyebrows and leaned back, supporting himself with both arms. Ricky leaned over and kissed Juan's shoulder, then sat back up, giving Juan his full attention.

"I feel like anything I might say would seem anticlimactic, after my birthday celebration. As you know, Hiroshi and I, and a host of others, over the years, did our fair share of exploring the sensual arts, you might say. So, yeah, I could tell some stories, and maybe someday I will. But, I guess, to properly honor Hiroshi's memory, all I want to say tonight is that when I was a newbie, curious, excited and totally inexperienced, Ben and Hiroshi took me under their wings and guided me. Hiroshi listened more than talked. He prodded and mentored, but never pushed me where I wasn't comfortable going. He always made sure I was enjoying the journey, inching me along at my own pace." Juan turned to Ricky. "Kind of like I'm doing with you, mijo. I hope I'm doing half as well as Hiroshi did." Ricky grinned with his mouth, but his eyes misted, sharing Juan's pain. He unconsciously reached up and fingered his collar, igniting another smile on Juan's face. "If it doesn't sound too trite, I guess you could say, in many ways, I am the man I am today thanks to Hiroshi. I'll forever be in his and Ben's debt." Juan sat up and pulled Ricky closer.

"That doesn't sound trite at all, Juan," Greg said. "Every one of us could say the same thing about Hiroshi. And maybe Ben, too, even though none of the rest of us ever met him."

"Yeah," Niki agreed. "Without Ben we wouldn't be here. And we never would have met Hiroshi."

"You and Raphael get as much credit as Ben for us being here," Steve contended.

"Yeah, maybe," Niki humbly acknowledged.

"So, Greg," Luke leaned forward, "are there any surprises in the will?"

"Not really. We have to agree that each of us is a co-equal owner and that any decisions regarding the house have to be subject to majority rule. You know, selling or renting or whatever. Hiroshi's intent was for us to use the value of the house to ensure our ability to stay together. Most likely to sell it at the right time to enable us to buy this house, if and when Ben decides to sell, or to buy another, similar property where we could continue to live as a family."

"Steve, do you think Ben will ever consider selling to us?" Niki asked.

"Maybe someday," Steve replied. "Maybe if we persuaded him. Carefully and over time. After all, that was his original intent, before you and Raphael made him an offer he couldn't refuse. So, yeah, I think so. If that's what we really wanted."

"How would that work?" Alex asked. "This house is clearly worth more than Hiroshi's. His house is only four bedrooms."

"And no dungeon," Ricky chimed in. Alex involuntarily scowled.

"We're getting a little ahead of ourselves," Greg offered, "but the proceeds from Hiroshi's house would go a long, long way as down payment. The monthly payments on the remaining mortgage would probably be manageable for us. Depending on Ben's terms, of course. Back to the will ... if any of us decides, for any reason, to leave the House of the Locked Cock Brotherhood, he or they forfeit their share of the inheritance, unless we all decide to disband, in which case the inheritance is split ten ways and Hiroshi's spirit will forever haunt us."

"Oh, it doesn't say that," Raphael protested.

"Oh, but it does, Raphael," Alex insisted. "I thought Greg was ad-libbing, too. It's true. Hiroshi's dry sense of humor made it into his will. I bet it's why Peter didn't want to read it to us. He probably thought it would be more fun for us to discover it later."

"So ... basically Hiroshi is ... was ... doing what he could to make sure we stay together," Raphael posed. "I guess he was well cast as Elder. He's more powerful in spirit form than in the flesh."

"He loved us," Niki said, rubbing a sniffle. "He wanted us to always be here for each other. Even if he couldn't be here for us himself."

"But that's the thing," Raphael spoke, holding Niki's gaze. "He *is* here for us. As long as we stay together, Hiroshi's wish endures. He remains with us because his 'will,' and I don't mean the piece of paper, has bound us together." Niki nodded, as did Juan.

"Speaking of remains," Greg said, "that's another thing in the will. It's his wish to be cremated. It's up to us what we do with him. We could literally keep him around. Maybe bury him near the gazebo. I don't think I could handle seeing him on the mantle every day."

"What if ..." Alex started, then stopped. "No. Never mind."

"I know," Raphael locked eyes with Juan. "We could rent a boat and take him to sea. Out to the Farallones at least. And spread his ashes there. Some would drift back to San Francisco, and some might make it all the way to Japan."

"Or at least Hawaii," Ryan speculated. "Amazing idea, Raphael." He nudged Mateo.

"What do you think, muchacho?" Juan asked Mateo. Mateo glanced at Juan, then looked down thoughtfully, before meeting Raphael's gaze.

"I think is good. Kinda romantic. A very Hiroshi idea."

"Yeah, very Hiroshi," Juan agreed. "So, tell us your Hiroshi story. I really want to hear it." Mateo did, as did the rest of the family. Each a different story, each adding a little more depth and nuance to the memory of Hiroshi. Halfway through, Luke opened a second bottle of sake, since one bottle wasn't enough to last through ten remembrances. Raphael had asked to go last, and so he did.

"I'll use Greg's word ... aggregate ... regarding my memory of Hiroshi," he began. "Because it's not any one thing I want to remember and honor him with. Like I said to Peter, from the first moment I saw him I was charmed. As we spent more time together, I slowly began to realize that growing older wasn't something I should dread ... or fear. Not that I'd ever thought much about it, but Hiroshi showed me what I should have already known. He was a beautiful example of how it's possible to be intriguing and vibrant and sexy, and a loving brother, at any age. He made me realize that my reign could extend into my forties and even beyond. I kind of joked once to Luke that I'd still be his locked cock boy when we're in our sixties. Hiroshi showed me that it really wasn't a joke."

"Baby," Luke leaned into Raphael, "I thought you were totally serious. I didn't take it as a joke." Their lips brushed.

"Reign?" Ricky asked. "What do you mean, 'reign'?"

"You know," Raphael turned from Luke to smile at Ricky. "As the sexiest member of the Locked Cock Brotherhood." Groans from Luke and Alex and genuine laughter from Mateo confirmed that Ryan's idea had succeeded in easing some of their grief. Had made losing Hiroshi, for a few moments, anyway, a bit more bearable.

## Sixteen

# WE ARE WORTHY

JUAN WAS LAYING ON his back, his hands behind his head, elbows splayed out on both sides, clearly deep in thought while he waited for Ricky to join him. Ricky slipped under the covers and curled around Juan, slinging one arm across Juan's chest.

"What did you think?" Ricky gently brushed his hand along Juan's pec. Although they'd frequently embraced one another supportively over the past few days, this was the first time either of them had touched the other sensually. "I mean, what Greg said about the will?"

"Hmmm," was all Juan said at first. He lowered his arms to pull Ricky in closer and kissed Ricky's forehead before heaving a sigh. He rolled over to face Ricky and leaned forward. Their lips touched. Ricky slowly wiggled his lips against Juan's. "Are you trying to get me to talk?" Juan whispered through a chuckle.

"No, Papito. Just ... feels nice. To touch, you know?" Juan puckered up and pressed his lips harder against Ricky's, who parted his lips to invite Juan in. Juan took the bait. After a moment they parted and Juan sighed again.

"What did *you* think?" he asked, knowing Ricky wanted to talk or he wouldn't have brought it up.

"I think it was very clever of Hiroshi. Not just the haunting part, which was pure Hiroshi, but basically daring us to stay together and stay here for, like, forever." Ricky fell silent a moment, basking in Juan's embrace. He fingered Juan's left nipple ring, the one he could easily reach. "I guess I never thought about moving anywhere else anyway. Did you?" Juan didn't respond immediately, pondering Ricky's question while allowing himself to enjoy Ricky's tentative foreplay.

"No. Not really. A part of me knew this couldn't last forever. That someday Ben would want to sell. And that we could never afford to buy. But I always hoped that was a long way in the future. I don't know if this means we can stay here forever, but at least it's more conceivable now. I'm still wrapping my head around the fact Hiroshi put us in his will." Juan swallowed hard. "I'm still trying to accept ..."

"I know, Papito. Me, too."

"Are you feeling a little better tonight?" Ryan was facing away, Mateo pressed against his back in a classic spoon. Mateo's arm was draped over Ryan's waist his right hand close to Ryan's cock.

"A little, si." Mateo pressed his lips to Ryan's neck and made a small smacking sound. "It was good ... your idea ... to talk about Hiroshi. Everbody love him so much." When Mateo spoke, his breath warmed the back of Ryan's neck and ignited the inevitable. As his cock rose to graze Mateo's hand, Mateo took hold and gently squeezed. Ryan reached down and placed his hand over Mateo's.

"Everybody loves everybody in this family. I feel as lucky as Hiroshi must have. To be here. With all of you." Mateo snuggled a little tighter. "Most of all you, my Prince." Mateo snort laughed. Ryan twisted around in Mateo's half-embrace to face him. Mateo reached down and adjusted Ryan's erection, guiding it into place, between his thighs, where it belonged. He stared a moment into Ryan's probing eyes, dimly visible in the dark.

"Sorry, Ryan. To not be feeling sexy for you, like always ..."

"Don't be silly. And don't be sorry. I haven't even thought about that since Folsom. All I want, right now, is for you to know I love you, and it kills me to see you suffer this much. And I don't ever want you to suffer like this again, Mateo. Ever." They held eye contact, feeling each other's chests rise and fall. Mateo pursed his lips.

"Then you better never die, too, okay?" Mateo's adorable smile slowly appeared.

"Is that a command from my Prince?" Mateo nodded. "Then, I'd better partake of the secret nectar of the *homo semen* to insure everlasting life." Ryan's lips briefly touched Mateo's before he drew away and trailed his lips down Mateo's body, until they arrived at the source of the nectar. Mateo didn't resist, repositioning himself on his back. Two minutes earlier sex had been the furthest thing from his mind, but just as Ryan had been right about the wake in the turret room, he was probably right about this. Mateo reached down with both hands and gently massaged Ryan's shoulders as Ryan moaned around Mateo's swelling erection. Mateo closed his eyes, sighed, and let his sex slave take him away to a better place.

Juan was spotting Ricky's bench press when Niki walked into the gym. He sat at the end of the other bench and waited until Ricky had finished his set and sat up.

"Ricky," Niki leaned forward, forearms on his thighs, "have you decided when you're going to reopen the Headquarters?" Ricky glanced up at Juan.

"Maybe Sunday? Steve said there've been a lot of inquiries on social media. And a lot of questions. You know ... guys worried about what's going on. I should, but I'm not looking forward to the questions."

"You shouldn't do it alone, Ricky," Niki said, looking very serious. "Ryan and I want to help. We can take turns when we aren't in class." He glanced up to see Juan's smile, and repeated, "You shouldn't do it alone." Ricky reached out and grasped Niki's knee.

"You guys are amazing. I can't ask you to do that. School's too important."

"Number one, you didn't ask. We volunteered. Two, Ryan and I can handle school *and* help you. Like I said, we'll take turns and work around our class schedules." He glanced up at an amused Juan. "You're outvoted Ricky." Ricky snorted and looked up at Juan again.

"I don't remember Hiroshi naming a new board of directors when he made me CEO, do you Papito?" Juan squatted down to the same level as Ricky and Niki.

"I guess we should have read the will ourselves after all, mijo. I'm with Niki and Ryan. You shouldn't go in alone. At least try this for a few days, and see how it goes." Ricky closed his eyes and nodded, then stood and opened his arms inviting Niki into a hug. When he released him, he was smiling, almost like his old self.

"I guess we should talk to Steve. You know, have him update the website to show we're opening again?" Niki nodded.

"I'll tell him it's Sunday," Niki offered. "I'll be there with you. It'll be fine, Ricky. Business will probably be slow, anyway. After being closed a week."


Business wasn't as brisk Sunday as it had been the day of the Folsom Street Fair, but it was steady. Which, in the end, actually made the day easier for Ricky, giving him little time to think about the fact that Hiroshi wasn't there with him. Except for that first time he had to retrieve product from the back room, which almost felt like a crime scene to him. He had to sit on the floor for a moment, breathing deeply and fighting back tears. Niki, noticing the delay, came back, too, and knelt next to him.

"Should we close for the day?" Niki suggested. Ricky shook his head.

"No. I have to do this. I'm ... I'm being silly." Niki huffed.

"Ricky, you're not being silly at all. You're being human. And an adult. You're processing grief and stepping up to what you see as an obligation. Maybe to Hiroshi. Or, maybe to yourself. But. We really don't have to be here. Maybe it's too soon. And that's okay." Ricky gave Niki a broken smile before standing up.

"Thanks, coach, but I can do this." He put a hand on Niki's shoulder. "Let's get out there and sell some cages."

Ricky held it together the rest of the day, but he did agree to close earlier than usual, at Niki's urging, after they'd gone nearly an hour with only two customers. Re-opening on Sunday was probably a good idea, since he'd have the following two days off, in line with the shop's usual Wednesday through Sunday schedule. On their walk home, both Ricky and Niki were silent at first. Then, Ricky turned to Niki.

"Thanks. For coming in with me today. I don't think I could have done it, otherwise. Not yet, anyway." Niki slung his arm over Ricky's shoulders and pulled him closer as they walked.

"Yeah, I can tell you were pretty preoccupied. You're still wearing your see-through shorts and crop top." Ricky looked down, then into Niki's smiling eyes.

"Shit. I wasn't even thinking, Niki. You should have said something."

"And miss the chance to walk through the Castro with a sexy guy flashing his cage? Pass."

"Speaking of ... this was the first time you've worked at the shop without your pup hood on. Did you feel self-conscious, clearly caged and recognizable to everyone?"

"At first a little, maybe, but I decided it's kind of like your first times going to a gay bar. At first, you're worried somebody might see you. Eventually, though, you realize, if *they're* in a gay bar ... So, it was fine. Kind of nice, actually. I didn't realize how much flirting goes on at LCB Headquarters."

"Like no one ever flirted with you at the bar ..."

"Yeah," Niki agreed. "Good times."

By the end of the week, for the most part, everyone in the House of the Locked Cock Brotherhood had begun easing back into their regular routines. Except for Ryan's and Niki's efforts to assist Ricky at the shop. Which meant studying later into the night for both of them. They didn't say anything but their absence after dinner, night after night, didn't escape Ricky's notice. Even though he knew they enjoyed their time in the shop, Ricky felt more and more guilty about them spending time away from their studies on his behalf. Friday evening, he approached the doorway to Mateo and Ryan's room, where Ryan was at the desk and Mateo was lounging on the bed, reading one of the graphic novels Alex had gotten him, to help with his English.

"Muchacho," Ricky whispered. He cocked his head toward the back stairs. "Follow me." Mateo gave Ricky a questioning look, but laid the book face down on the bed, slid to the floor and followed Ricky down to the kitchen. Mateo was surprised when Ricky surreptitiously closed the door between the kitchen and the foyer. He motioned for Mateo to take a seat before he sat on the stool next to Mateo.

"What's up?" Mateo asked, intrigued.

"I wanted to talk, but I don't want Niki or Ryan to hear. Not yet." Ricky looked up at the ceiling, reviewing the monologue he'd already rehearsed.

"Is this a dare?" Mateo assumed. Ricky shook his head.

"No, this is real. I have a serious question for you. How would you like to come work for me ... with me ... at the Headquarters? Ryan and Niki have been great, but I really feel guilty taking them away from school. Business is already picking up again, so I could use someone full time."

"Wow," Mateo was genuinely surprised. "Me?"

"Yeah. You. You'd have a set schedule instead of what you deal with now at the restaurant. You'd be able to work on your English a lot more, and your Spanish would come in handy, too, with some of our customers."

"I don' know. I never been a salesman ..."

"Mateo, the cages sell themselves. All you have to do is help guys pick out the one that's right for them. I can teach you all of that. Besides, guys will love you. Just pretend you're Cadmael again, and they're your captive slaves. Heck, pretend they're Ryan, and they're there to begin their service to you as soon as you fit them into their first cage. Or second cage. We get a lot of repeat customers." Mateo gave Ricky an amused, but highly doubtful look. "You don't have to decide right now, muchacho, but I'd really love working with you, and I think you'd have a lot more fun at the Headquarters than in the kitchen at the restaurant."

"Yeah, prolly," Mateo acknowledged. He stared into Ricky's eyes a moment, absorbing Ricky's offer and appreciating Ricky's trust in him.

"Of course, there is one catch," Ricky confessed.

"Catch?" Mateo wasn't sure he was following.

"When you're on duty ... you'd have to be caged. Like me. And Ryan, and Niki. And Hiroshi was. It's sort of mandatory, you know. It's what we do."

"Mandatory," Mateo repeated, a likely candidate for the word of the day. Mateo thought a moment, then nodded. "Oh. A uniform, right?" It was Ricky's turn to nod. "Is okay. I maybe wear Ryan's."

"Oh no. We'll get you your own cage, Mateo. There might be times when Ryan is helping us at the door or the register, and you'd both be caged." A silly grin appeared on Mateo's lips.

"Both caged? Shaman Prince and his slave. Is weird, no?"

"No, Mateo. Not weird. Kinky. Sexy. Fun," Ricky replied with a somewhat evil grin. "So, think about it. Talk it over with Ryan and let me know." He and Mateo were both smiling. "No pressure."

"A little pressure," Mateo chided. "Is okay. Wow. I would be in Hiroshi's place, no?" His smile faded and his eyes misted. Ricky's immediately did, too.

"Yeah, you're right, Mateo. You would be taking Hiroshi's place. It wasn't in his will, but I think he would be very happy to know it was *you* taking his place. And not somebody else." He reached out and squeezed Mateo's thigh. "Yeah, he'd be very happy, muchacho."


Saturday morning Juan was up early. He'd agreed to a weekend shift to relieve a fellow OR nurse who had helped cover for him during his bereavement leave. He was on his way out when he saw the white slip of paper someone had slid under their door. He picked it up and read the single word, 'OK!' underscored by a smiley face. It was signed with the initials 'SP.' He pondered a moment, then realized, of course. Shaman Prince. So, Ricky's pitch had been successful. He laid the note on his pillow, leaned down to kiss Ricky's forehead, and headed out to a day that had already started on a better note than any other over the past couple of weeks.

That evening, over dinner, Ricky and Mateo made their big announcement. Everyone agreed it was a good move for Mateo, and for Ricky, who was still learning some of the behind-the-scenes responsibilities that Hiroshi had effortlessly handled in the past. With a little help from Peter. Keeping the city, county, state and federal governments happy and up to date was nearly a full-time job of its own.

"Don't take it personally, Niki and Ryan," Ricky joked. "I like having you guys around, but I feel guilty taking your time away from school." Both deflected, insisting it was not a problem. "Well, that's good to know," Ricky replied, "because, being the honorable person that he is, Mateo insists on giving his boss two weeks' notice. So, if you two can hang with me just two more weeks, that'd be great."

"If it helps, I could put in some time on the weekends," Raphael offered. "I'm a quick study. I'm even Asian-American." Ricky fully understood Raphael's implication and took it one step further.

"Thanks! A little Spicy Asian influence now and then might be fun. I'll let you know. Mateo's going to spend some of his free time shadowing me for the next two weeks so he won't be totally green when he starts. That will help, too." He looked around the table. "I appreciate *all* the help you guys have given me. Since day one. I'll never forget it." He started to look a little misty again. Lately everyone, except maybe Niki and Raphael, had been surprised at how easy it was to unexpectedly become emotional with little or no provocation. Juan laid his arm across Ricky's shoulders.

"Mijo, we're all proud of you. One day, when people refer to you as the New Mayor of Castro Street, we'll be able to say we knew you when." Ricky laughed and Mateo looked confused.

"Another weird English idiom," Ryan said to Mateo. "I'll explain later."

"Are these idiom explanations 'hands-on?'" Niki asked, not so innocently.

"How did you know?" Ryan grinned. "Some people learn best visually. Some auditorily. And some kinesthetically. Mateo's definitely a kinesthetic learner." Raphael leaned into Luke.

"Would you say I'm a kinesthetic learner, Sir?" Luke gave Ryan an amused look before meeting Raphael's gaze.

"I'm not sure, baby. I think we should probably do some intensive research into this matter."

"Oh brother," Alex, in classic Alex fashion, was rolling his eyes. "Like you haven't already researched that one to death by now."

"Well," Raphael retorted, "we all know you're definitely on the kinesthetic spectrum, Alex, or should I say, paddle boy?"

"I'm not sure how we got here," Steve smiled first at Raphael, before taking in the group, "but I have to say it's refreshing to hear this kind of banter from you boys. It feels good to smile, just a little." Niki nodded and leaned over with a cheek kiss.

Several days later it was Greg's turn to make an announcement at dinner. Peter had called to say he had some of the necessary paperwork for the property transfer ready to be signed. Due to COVID protocols, and because he was also a notary, they could handle the signing at home with him witnessing.

Saturday morning, before Mateo's shift, Peter was shown into the dining room with the necessary documents along with his notary embosser and stamp. Once the paperwork had been dispensed with, along with a round of Alex's ceremonial lattes, Peter had another item of unfinished business.

"I have an indelicate question I must ask," Peter addressed the ensemble. "Have you thought about what you'd like to do with Hiroshi's cremains? The mortuary is holding them for us."

"A little," Raphael spoke up. "Here's one idea, what do you think?" He relayed his suggestion of burial at sea. A smile formed across Peter's face as he listened.

"That's a much better idea than what I was going to suggest," he replied. "Hiroshi would approve, I'm sure." He sighed deeply. "From stardust to swimming the planet's greatest ocean." He fell silent, looking a bit wistful.

"I'm glad you like it," Raphael smiled. "If we can work something out, would you like to join us? I think Hiroshi would like that."

"Yes, please," Mateo, who was sitting next to Peter, added his encouragement. Peter nodded, looking first at Mateo, then Raphael.

"I would be honored. Thank you." He collected the notarized documents and stood. He briefly looked pensive, then cleared his throat. "I do have a suggestion for you to consider on the day we send Hiroshi on his last voyage. Something he and I have done before. A little ritual I think his family would find meaningful on such a day." Juan, who had stood along with Peter, spoke for everyone.

"We're all about rituals in this house, so, sure. We'd be happy to participate in something you and Hiroshi have shared, right guys?" He looked around for consensus and got it. "Raphael, your idea. Do you want to be in charge of arranging everything? Along with Peter?" Raphael gave Juan a tight smile and nodded. Juan showed Peter out, then returned to find everyone still seated.

"Is it just me, or is this all too weird?" Niki asked. "By weird I mean unbelievable?" He looked at Ricky. "Ricky's a businessman, who has a shop on Castro Street. We own a multi-million-dollar house. That we don't even need." He locked eyes with Steve.

"Is it any weirder than me being married to guy who's well on his way to becoming a nurse?" Steve asked. He looked around the table. "I think it's safe to say the fates have dealt us hands both heartbreaking and overwhelming."

"Maybe we're being tested," Alex suggested. "Can we handle the heartbreak? Will we prove worthy of Hiroshi's generosity and trust?"

"Good questions," Luke replied. "Together, I'm confident we can handle the heartbreak." He sat back and glanced around the table. "And ... I would trust any one of you with my life. I think we'll prove to be worthy, Alex." Alex lifted his empty cup toward Luke.

"No argument from me. We are worthy."

## Seventeen

# LADY GRATITUDE

"WHERE ARE WE GOING, again?" Ryan asked. It was a sunny and temperate October Sunday afternoon, and the family was assembled on the sidewalk, awaiting a limo van big enough to accommodate all ten of them. Raphael and Peter had worked out the details for what they hoped would be a worthy and memorable send off for Hiroshi.

"Grace Cathedral," Raphael replied, before turning to Ricky. "Thanks for being willing to close the Headquarters today, Ricky. Coordinating everyone's schedules, including the boat, was a bigger challenge than I expected."

"De nada," Ricky replied. 'This is way more important. Right muchacho?"

"Si," Mateo agreed. "Why church, Raphael? Will there be Mass?"

"No, Mateo. Something much better. Something much more Hiroshi." Mateo nodded, but didn't pursue the issue as the van pulled up, then whisked them away.

Peter was waiting at the base of the expansive outdoor stairs leading up to the 'Gates of Paradise,' the massive entry doors to Grace Cathedral. Behind him, and above the entry, the giant rose window centered in the façade of the gothic edifice was a focal point. Peter could see the awe in several men's eyes.

"Have any of you been here before?" he asked.

"I have," Niki was the only one to reply. "My mom brought me here once to hear the choir when I was a kid." Peter smiled.

"Did you enjoy it?"

"Oh yeah," Niki smized. "This is nothing like the little church my parents belonged to."

"It's kind of medieval looking," Ryan said.

"English Gothic," Peter affirmed. "Inside are three organs, sixty-eight newly restored stained-glass windows and several chapels, including the AIDS Memorial Chapel, with an altarpiece by Keith Haring."

"You're kidding!" Alex exclaimed. "Keith Haring? In a church?"

"It's an Episcopal Cathedral," Peter explained. "In San Francisco. So, yes. But we're here to take advantage of my favorite feature of Grace Cathedral. Something Hiroshi and I did more than once. Something more metaphysical, and more Zen like, than you'll find in most churches. And it's something best experienced by more than one person. I've never done it with ten other people, so I'm really looking forward to this." Peter nodded toward the entry and turned to begin climbing the steps. The family followed in silence, already feeling reverent before entering the Cathedral. Once they were inside, Peter motioned to the right.

"That's the AIDS Memorial Chapel over there. We can check it out after we're done, if you'd like, but this is what we're really here for. Follow me." Peter walked a few steps into the cavernous sanctuary and stopped. Beyond and around him were the many stained-glass windows depicting biblical characters, of course, and more contemporary figures, like Albert Einstein. The ceiling above, way above, was supported by massive flying buttresses. But it was the floor that Peter motioned toward.

"This is the indoor labyrinth. There's another outdoors, but Hiroshi and I preferred this one. It's bigger, so the experience lasts longer. Have any of you walked a labyrinth before?" Ten men shook their heads. "It's easy. And profound. At least I think so. Here's what we're going to do. One of us starts walking here," Peter pointed to a spot at the edge of the design embedded in the floor, "and you follow the path into the center of the labyrinth. Ten seconds or so later, the next person starts. Walk slowly. It's more about the journey than the destination. Look around at the beauty that surrounds you. After a while, you'll notice that you're walking in the opposite direction of another person. A little later you'll find yourselves walking side by side. Think of it as a metaphor on life. Look down. Look up. Look in the other's eyes as you pass. Think whatever thoughts that come to mind. If praying is something you do, by all means pray. Think of what it would be like to walk the labyrinth with Hiroshi, and what he might be thinking." Mentioning Hiroshi forced Peter to pause his soliloquy a moment. He swallowed and continued.

"If doing this reminds you of happy memories, smile. If it brings you to tears, that's okay, too. Feel what you feel. Be open and honest with yourself and with each of us. I'll meet you in the center." Peter turned, stepped onto the spot he'd indicated, and slowly began to walk. No one else moved at first. Everyone was still processing what Peter had said. Then, not surprisingly, Mateo stepped forward and began to follow Peter, many steps behind. Ryan was next. Then Steve. Followed by Niki.

And so on, until all eleven of them were walking the labyrinth. It was true, what Peter had said. Each of them passed each of the others going in opposite directions. At times, they were walking side by side with another. And sometimes, each of them was alone.

Raphael was fine until, as he passed Luke going in the opposite direction, he saw tears falling behind Luke's mask. It briefly brought Raphael to a halt as his own tears fell. Alex, who was following Raphael, caught up and embraced Raphael from behind. Raphael moaned, nodded quickly and resumed. He hadn't imagined that the simple act of walking a design could feel like this. Granted, their surroundings were monumental. Literally. It was a day dedicated to a man they loved and revered. And missed so profoundly. Maybe that's what was so moving to Luke and to him. Doing this together reinforced, in a way maybe nothing else could, just how much each of them meant to one another. Whether they were in sync or alone, opposed or in step, they were, and always would be, family.

Nearly twenty minutes later Juan was the last to enter the center. Like everyone else, his eyes were misty.

"Together at last," Juan said, attempting to lighten the mood. He was rewarded with a couple of quiet chuckles. "That was really something. Thank you, Peter."

"No, thank you, everyone," Peter replied. "This was very moving for me, as much as it ever was with Hiroshi. Maybe more so. I feel like he was walking with us."

"He was," Ricky agreed. He wrapped an arm around Juan's waist, who put an arm around Niki's shoulders, which led to a classic LCB group hug that included Peter. For a moment no one spoke or moved.

"What happens next?" Ricky asked as the hug unfurled.

"We go back out, the same way we came in," Peter instructed. "One at a time. We could spend more time here, meditating. Praying. Hugging," he chuckled. "But we do have a date with Hiroshi. He's waiting for us on board the boat Raphael commissioned. Juan, why don't you lead us out."

Juan nodded and began his walk. Before Ricky could follow, the choir began a rehearsal from the far end of the Cathedral. They couldn't have timed it better. The music added another layer of majesty to what was already a surprisingly metaphysical experience for each of them. As they made their way, step by step, one by one, they noticed a couple of others walking the labyrinth, heading in as they were heading out. Reinforcing Peter's contention that this was, in a way, a metaphor for life. As each member reached the end of the labyrinth, he stepped away to wait for the others and to take in their surroundings. Juan and Ricky had sought out the AIDS Memorial Chapel, and soon the rest of the family joined them. The altarpiece was, indeed, a Keith Haring original.

"I can't believe this is here," Greg quietly said. "A chapel dedicated to memorializing those lost to AIDS. I want to come back sometime. I need to come back." He looked at Alex, who looked at Peter.

"Greg's uncle died of AIDS. Before ... you know." Peter reached out and gripped Greg's shoulder, nodding.

"You *should* come back. I've come here several times. A couple of times with Hiroshi, after a labyrinth walk. You'll be glad you did." Greg nodded. "Come gentlemen, we have a cable car to catch."


"I didn't know the cable cars were running again," Alex said to Raphael as the entourage trooped down California Street the two blocks to Hyde.

"They just started up again last month," Raphael replied. "Just the Powell-Hyde line so far." Alex nodded and that was end of the conversation. For now.

Maybe because few tourists had yet to return, or because, like Alex, many people were unaware the Powell-Hyde was running again after the pandemic shutdown, the first car to arrive was nearly empty, allowing everyone to nab a seat. Once they were onboard, the gripman wasted no time engaging the cable and beginning their relatively short journey to the edge of the bay. Everyone, except Ryan, had ridden a cable car at one time or another, some many times. Each time was a thrill, though, especially on the Powell-Hyde line, as it rumbled down Russian Hill at what felt like a forty-five-degree angle. Despite the seriousness of the day's events, Raphael was pleased to see the delight on several faces, especially Ryan's.

"Is that ... is that Alcatraz?" he asked as they made their descent.

"Yeah," Mateo grinned. "Pretty cool, huh?" Ryan reached down and wrapped Mateo's hand in both of his. He lifted them long enough to press a kiss on Mateo's hand before dropping them back into his lap.

It wasn't long before they reached the terminus, near the water. As they stepped to the ground and yelled a thank you to the gripman and the conductor, Alex grabbed Raphael's arm to hold him back.

"Are you sure you aren't a secret playwright?" he asked.

"What?"

"A perfect Act Two, Raphael." Raphael furrowed his brow.

"Act One, the deeply introspective labyrinth walk. Act Two, a more lighthearted jaunt on a cable car, before Act Three. The final, and no doubt painful, goodbye to a dearly departed brother. Classic theater, dude. Right down to the costumes. Well done." Raphael wrapped an arm around Alex's neck and aimed them toward the rest, who were following Peter.

"You give me more credit than I deserve," he said. "But I'll take it, and share it with Peter. I just want everything about this day to be special. Memorable. Worthy of Hiroshi." He released Alex, who caught up with Greg while Luke took his place next to Raphael.

"What are you two conspiring about?" he asked.

"Nothing. Alex was just telling me how wonderful I am." Luke snickered.

"Oh, of course. I should have known. So ... how far are we walking this time?

"Not far, Sir. Just over to the Marina. It's a nice day for a walk."

"It's always a nice day for a walk along the bay. We should do this more often, baby. Get out of the neighborhood. Appreciate where we are. It's easy to take all this for granted." Raphael pulled Luke closer as they walked.

"Just say when, Sir. But you're right. Like Joni Mitchell sang," and he melodiously sang a few bars of one of her most famous songs, a song she wrote after suffering a loss of her own. The one about Paradise. Then, Raphael fell silent a few steps. Luke looked at him and could see the pain had returned to Raphael face. He gently nudged him.

"Baby. You never took Hiroshi for granted." Raphael looked up at Luke, with an almost little boy look of longing.

"I hope you're right, Sir."

"You know I'm right." He nudged Raphael again, forcing a smize out of Raphael. They continued walking in silence, taking in the sights and sounds of the bay. Until, eventually, they could see Peter pointing toward one of the piers on their right. They had arrived.

A middle-aged man in a weathered windbreaker, that seemed out of place on such a warm day, approached the gate in the low fence separating the sidewalk from the pier. Unlike the open piers nearer the Ferry Building and other tourist sites, these piers were private property, and many of the craft tied up were worth millions.

"Guys," Peter said, "this is Captain Louis. We'll be sailing on his boat today." Captain Louis nodded and opened the gate.

"See where that lad is standing, near the end of the pier? That's Jeremy, my first mate. He'll help you onboard." Peter led the family down the pier, then stood aside as each one climbed up the short rope and wooden ladder. After Peter boarded, Captain Louis climbed aboard. Jeremy remained on the pier until Captain Louis started the engine and engaged. As the boat slowly started to back away, Jeremy athletically jumped aboard, pulled the rope ladder up and stowed it on the deck before latching the gate. Jeremy was about the same age as the older members of the family, and built similarly to Luke and Raphael, although his muscles were probably acquired here, on board, rather than in a gym. At least that's what Raphael preferred to think. His muscles, that had caught the admiration of more than just Raphael soon disappeared, however, as Jeremy grabbed a heavy sweatshirt off a nearby fixture and pulled it on over his head and arms. He then wriggled into a life vest and buckled in. He began handing more vests to each of the passengers.

"You men are going to get cold, dressed like this," Jeremy grinned as he pinched the waist of Juan's polo shirt. "Cap'n says we're goin' all the way out to the Farrallones. Is that right?"

"That's right," Juan smiled back and tugged on his polo. "And ... you ain't seen nothin' yet." Jeremy gave Juan a skeptical look, but all Juan said was, "You'll see. You have a really nice boat, or should I call it a ship?" Captain Louis continued slowly maneuvering the boat away from the pier, until he could steer it around and point it toward the middle of the Bay.

"Boat is fine, or ketch. Or vessel. We just call her Lady Gratitude."

"Huh," Juan replied. "Lady Gratitude ..."

"Yeah. 'Cause we're grateful for every minute we get to spend on the water. Listen, feel free to ditch the masks. You're going to want to breathe in all that fresh sea air." Juan immediately obliged, stuffing his mask into his pocket. "Excuse me, I better get to work." As Jeremy moved fore, Ricky took his place next to Juan.

"I think he likes you, Papito." Juan laughed and clasped the back of Ricky's neck, pulled off Ricky's mask and planted one, a generous lip-on-lip.

"He's just doing what you do, mijo. Giving friendly, professional service to the paying customers." He looked around as they glided away from the other moored boats and entered open water. "I can't remember the last time I was on a boat." He made eye contact with Ricky. "I wish it was for a different reason, mijo, but I have to say, like every other idea Raphael's had, this was a good one." Ricky smiled and pressed his head against Juan's chest momentarily.

As they motored into the Bay, Jeremy began to hoist the mainsail up the mast. Everyone watched, fascinated. Once it was up and secured, he unfurled the smaller mizzenmast sail and Captain Louis cut the engine. He redirected the boat just a little. As the sails filled with the wind, *Lady Gratitude* began to move toward the Golden Gate. The ride across the Bay was smooth, not surprisingly, and everyone was enjoying the view as they passed Alcatraz and Angel Island. As the Golden Gate Bridge approached, getting bigger and bigger, the waves grew a bit higher and the boat rose and fell in response. Jeremy took over the helm and Captain

Louis joined the family who had separated, some on the starboard side, some on port.

"It's not a bad day out there, but the ride's going to get a lot rougher once we're clear of the Gate. If anyone starts to feel a bit queasy you can lean overboard, or I've a couple of buckets if you prefer. This is why a lot of the regular burials at sea never venture out past the Gate."

"Thanks, Captain," Peter shouted back, over the sound of the wind and the waves slapping the hull. "I think we'll be fine. We have a good reason to make it to the Farallones."

"As you wish. There's cold beverages and an urn of coffee below deck in the cabin. Help yourselves." Peter gave the 'okay' hand signal with a smile, gripping the handrail with his other. Back at the mainsail, Captain Louis periodically shouted commands to Jeremy as *Lady Gratitude* began cutting through bigger waves, beating her way against the wind toward their destination. She was a good-sized ketch, but she wasn't a cruise ship, either, and each wave made its arrival known. Passing under the Golden Gate Bridge gave everyone a thrill, seeing it from a new perspective, and marveling at just how high it actually was.

About an hour into the voyage, with the Golden Gate barely a smudge in the distance, everyone had grown more comfortable with the motion, moving cautiously from side to side, although none of them could claim to have acquired their sea legs. That wasn't their goal. They were on a mission, after all, not a pleasure cruise, although being here on the open sea, was its own source of pleasure. Especially after the first sighting.

"Look!" Steve pointed starboard. At first no one knew what caught his eye, but soon another, then another bottlenose dolphin broke the surface as they frolicked. Everyone moved to starboard to take in the show. Luke looked to Captain Louis, unsure if that was a good idea, but he smiled and waved an okay. Some swam close to the boat and seemed to be escorting them, and some followed them, causing Mateo and Ryan, then Ricky and Juan, to move to the stern to watch. Alex couldn't resist. He moved over closer to Raphael.

"The secret playwright strikes again," he grinned. "Where the hell did you find trained dolphins?"

"Where else? Central casting." For once Alex didn't deliver an eye roll. He just smiled, then landed a quick cheek kiss.

"You wanted memorable." He looked away from Raphael and out toward the open sea and sighed. "You delivered." He pulled his phone out of his back pocket and started capturing some of their escorts. Captain Louis approached and stood next to Alex, both hands on the railing.

"Quite a show, huh?" he asked.

"Unbelievable," Alex replied. "Were we just lucky or are they always here?"

"Always. This is a marine sanctuary, and I reckon they know it, and they feel safe here. There's plenty of prey here for them, too, so there's that."

"Captain," Raphael leaned back to shout around Alex, "I have what's probably a stupid question. Why does Jeremy keep changing course, going to the left, then the right, then left again?"

"You mean port and starboard?" Alex snarked.

"Not a stupid question, lad," Captain Louis came around to stand closer to Raphael. "It's called tacking. We're sailing into the wind, and Jeremy and I are maneuvering the rudder and sails to face the wind at forty-five-degree angles, the closest we can come to sailing into the wind. Tacking back and forth repeatedly is called 'beating,' I like to say we're 'beating' the wind. Once you've paid your respects, with the wind aft of us, we'll be able to just fill the sails and head straight back."

"Wow," Raphael looked over at Jeremy at the helm, then up to the top of the main mast. "It must take a long time to learn how to sail a boat like this." Captain Louis nodded.

"Started with a Sunfish. I'm not going to tell you how many years ago that was, lad. But that's all it took to hook me for life." He looked out at the pod of dolphins once more, then stepped away from the railing. "We'll be at our destination in about another hour. We'll be stopping short of the islands themselves … too dangerous with all the shoals." With that, he returned to his post manning the sail.

Luke crab-walked over to join Raphael and Alex. He placed his left leg between Raphael's as the two gripped the railing, the safest intimate contact he could conjure.

"Let me guess," he said, looking over Raphael with a knowing look at Alex. "You've already decided to invest the proceeds from Hiroshi's house in a sailing yacht." Raphael leaned back against him.

"You know me so well, Sir." Before they could pursue Luke's ruse, Steve and Niki approached, carrying multiple take-out style covered cups of coffee from below to share with Alex, Raphael and Luke.

"Thanks," Alex said. "It is pretty nippy out here. I guess our cruise director forgot to warn us about that."

"We'll have locked cock embroidered sweats on our new boat," Raphael countered.

"What new boat?" Niki asked.

"Ask Luke," Raphael smiled and sipped. "It was his idea."

"Listen, if you're cold, take a break in the cabin," Steve suggested. "It's pretty nice."

"Yeah," Niki agreed. "There's a head down there, too, if you need it." Raphael turned to Luke.

"See ... Niki's already using the lingo. We'll be a legend on the regatta circuit, just you wait."

"While you guys are dreaming, I'm going to go warm up," Alex announced. With his coffee in one hand and the other arm outstretched for balance, he made his way to the hatch. Greg noticed and followed from where he'd been chatting with Jeremy at the helm. At various times over the next hour each of them spent some time in the cabin, warming, using the head, refreshing coffee cups. But most of their time was spent on deck, drinking in the sights and smells of their surroundings in the Farrallones sanctuary, their second sanctuary of the day. Mateo and Ryan were the ruggedest of them all, having taken up residence near the bow, seated on the deck, arms wrapped around each other, the occasional spray from a wave producing shrieks and laughter. The kind of laughter that hadn't been heard in too many days. Everyone knew why they were here, what they were about to do, but in all the conversations over the past couple of hours, no one wanted to speak of it. Not yet. Not until it was time. Everyone knew it was time when Captain Louis dropped the mainsail with the downhaul. Jeremy pointed the boat into the approaching waves, calming the boat as much as possible.

"All right, lads," the captain announced. "If you've prepared a ceremony, now's the time." Peter approached Captain Louis and Jeremy, expecting the family to gather near the stern, which was currently pointed downwind, but instead they all headed for the hatch. One by one, they climbed down into the cabin.

"Maybe they want to spend a few last moments with Hiroshi's remains," he said to them. "They were very close." Captain Louis nodded and Jeremy, one hand casually on the wheel, looked a little sad. Burials were a rarity on *Lady Gratitude*. But it wasn't long before the family climbed back on deck, starting with Ricky, who was carrying the ceramic urn that bore Hiroshi's name in kanji script. He was naked, except for a deep blue fundoshi. Peter was a bit taken aback, but assumed Ricky, being Hiroshi's business partner, was the designated bearer, and had decided to dress accordingly. But he was wrong. As Juan, and then each remaining member of the family emerged, they were equally naked, each wearing a unique fundoshi. Jeremy grinned. So, this was the 'nothin' yet' Juan had hinted at earlier. Peter joined them at the stern, putting his arms around the bare shoulders of Ryan and Steve on either side of him. First Steve, then Ryan wrapped their arms around his waist. Ricky stood at the railing with Juan on one side and Raphael on the other. Raphael opened a small piece of paper and read aloud the eulogy he and Alex had labored over.

"Hiroshi-san, you were here before any of us, and for that we are grateful. We debated with you whether it was chance or the fates that brought you into our lives, or us into yours. Either way, we were the beneficiaries of your wisdom. Your generosity. Your humor. Your very presence in our lives. You were, in more ways than one, our Elder." He paused, laboring to control his emotions. "The fates have spoken again, and they have taken you from us. Although your spirit will live on with us forever ... and ever ... we've come to this place to release what is left of the physical you. So that you may roam the planet as you will, looking after friends and family in San Francisco, Japan, Hawaii or wherever the currents take you. Godspeed, Brother Hiroshi. Godspeed."

Raphael lowered the note and nodded to Ricky, who turned to face the water. He lifted the lid and handed it to Juan, then, with both Juan and Raphael holding his waist, he bent low and poured. Some of the Hiroshi cloud lifted in the breeze and sailed toward shore, but most fell onto the churning surface and soon disappeared. Raphael released Ricky as he straightened up and turned back to Juan, tears streaming on both their faces. Juan placed the top back on the urn and handed it to Raphael so he could envelope Ricky in a badly needed warm embrace. Which immediately became a signature group embrace. They held it for long moment, until they were encouraged by the chill wind to return to the cabin, and their clothes. As Raphael approached the hatch, Jeremy called out.

"That was very beautiful." Raphael smiled and nodded, still too emotional to try to speak, then headed below. Captain Louis patted Jeremy on the shoulder.

"Let's head for home, lad. I'll take the helm." Jeremy moved to unknot the halyard and begin raising the mainsail for a faster return home.

Eighteen

# Something Special

They took three cars home from the pier. Raphael, Luke, Juan and Ricky rode in Peter's car, the others split two Lifts. Juan invited Peter in, and he gladly accepted. He'd learned a little more about this family at Grace Cathedral and on their voyage, and he hoped to learn more. Alex, Ryan and Mateo were the last in the door, where they found everyone but Raphael in the sitting room. Using deductive reasoning Alex headed for the kitchen, where he found Raphael pulling wine bottles out of the wine cabinet: a Cab and a Sauvignon Blanc to start. Alex threaded three wine glasses between the fingers on Raphael's free hand and snagged four more in each of his own, waiter style.

"I don't know about you guys, but I think I'm finally starting to warm up," Alex said as he followed Raphael into the sitting room. Raphael's look of disdain was exactly what Alex was going for.

"Alex," Peter defended, "Raphael put together an awe-inspiring memorial today. We should be praising him."

"He is," Greg replied, "in his own, unique way. They harass each other like this all the time. It's how they show their love." Once freed of wine bottles and glasses, Alex and Raphael hugged to prove Greg's point.

"He praised me three times already, Peter, so I'm good," Raphael smiled before landing a cheek kiss on Alex. "Which would you prefer ... Cab or Sauv?" Peter indicated Cab. Luke finished pulling the cork and handed the bottle to Raphael, who poured and passed before returning the bottle to Luke. He sat on the floor opposite the coffee table in front of the couch where Peter, Juan and Ricky were seated. Luke handed him a glass of the Cab, which he raised toward Peter, then Juan and Ricky. "Thank you for the experience at Grace Cathedral, Peter. It was almost surreal. Something I think I'll do again."

"Yeah, that was ... indescribable," Ryan agreed. "I mean, words can't do it justice." Several others chimed in their agreement.

"Well, thank you, everyone. It was something of a new experience for me, too. I've never done it with more than one other person before. I was hoping you would enjoy it, knowing how much Hiroshi had. He told me enough about all of you over the last couple of years that I felt confident suggesting it. I owe all of *you* much gratitude, pun intended, for including me on Hiroshi's farewell voyage on Lady Gratitude." Juan touched his glass to Peter's, glancing at him, then turned to Raphael.

"Peter ... Raphael ... today could not have better," he said earnestly. "I really mean that. Hiroshi would have been flattered, and I suspect humbled, if he could have seen the kind of sendoff you two gave him." Peter nodded. "In fact, I'm going to add instructions to my will to put the two of you in charge of my memorial when I go." Ricky slapped his hand over Juan's mouth, startling him.

"Papito! Don't even say that!" He then squeezed Juan while giving Raphael the evil eye. Raphael just shook his head while making eye contact with Peter.

"I don't know, Juan," Raphael sighed. "I don't think Peter and I could top today."

"I wouldn't even want to try," Peter agreed. He decided not to mention the fact that he surely would be the one 'to go' long before Juan. At least he hoped so.

"Will you forgive us for being terrible hosts, Peter?" Greg asked. "We should treat you to a homemade lasagna dinner, but after today, I'm exhausted." He looked around the room. "I can tell everyone is. How about, instead, we reach out to Ricky's old network and order Sausage Factory delivery from DoorDash?"

"No argument here," Alex was first to respond. "Salmon piccata and a Caesar for me, please."

"The penne a la vodka and Caesar for me," Niki piped up.

"Hold on," Greg interrupted. "I guess this was a good idea, but let's let our guest go first. Do you need a menu, Peter?" Peter smiled and shook his head.

"No, your mention of lasagna sounded enticing, so I'll go with their vegetarian lasagna, and yes, a Caesar salad sounds good." He sat back and enjoyed watching everyone requesting their favorites from memory as Greg made entries on his phone. Hiroshi hadn't exaggerated the exuberance and respect each of these men shared with one another. And not just within the couples. It was easy to see how they had lifted Hiroshi's spirits when he was at his lowest and gave him the support and love he'd missed after Ben's passing. Once everyone had ordered and Greg was completing the online form, everyone briefly fell silent.

"Okay, guys ... I have to ask," Peter broke the silence. "Whose idea was it to see Hiroshi off wearing only fundoshi?"

"Raphael and I kind of came up with it together," Alex volunteered. "While we were working on the eulogy. Was it weird for you?" Peter chuckled.

"No. Like everything else today, it was very Hiroshi."

"Actually, it was totally Hiroshi," Alex replied. He and Raphael took turns describing their first encounter with Hiroshi and how it led to their first exposure to fundoshi.

"So ... you were all naked when you met Hiroshi, and he was only wearing a fundoshi?" Everyone but Ryan nodded. "So, he wasn't pulling my leg. You live totally naked here."

"We do," Luke smiled impishly. "We only wear clothes when hosting someone, like you, our Mama or Ryan's parents." He looked over at Ryan and Mateo. "In fact ... true story, he was very worried we'd all be naked the day his parents brought him up." Mateo giggled.

"Yeah! He texted 'put on your CLOTHES,' when they got close. In capitals." Ryan gave Peter a look that said 'of course, what would you have done?' Peter sipped and sighed.

"Ah, to be young again."

"Age has nothing to do with it," Steve contended. "Nor should it. Hiroshi observed the dress code, too. Well, after the first couple of dinners."

"Speaking of dinner," Luke looked over at Ryan and Mateo. "Would our pledges be so kind as to set the table for us? Dinner will be here soon." Ryan grinned as he and Mateo stood and headed into the foyer.

"And let's use the good stuff," Alex called out. 'Yes, sir' came the call back.

"Pledges?" Peter asked. "So, you have a hierarchy here?"

"Only as a joke," Luke replied. "With Ryan and Niki's classes at SF State still mostly online, pretending this is a frat house just seemed like a way to help make their college days a little more like they should be." Niki nodded sagely.

"We've all done our share of adapting, haven't we?" Peter said. The conversation circled around the pandemic for a while, with Ricky bragging on Juan's volunteer work in New York, Luke describing Raphael's creation of their private gym in the basement, and Niki's adoption of the library as his Zoom classroom, the envy of all his classmates. While he was talking, Ryan and Mateo appeared in the doorway wearing beaming smiles and nothing else. Peter guffawed.

"You guys all look weird," Mateo scolded.

"Yes," Ryan agreed. "Shouldn't you undress for dinner?"

"Peter, as you can see," Steve stood, "in this fraternity it's the pledges who do the hazing." He headed for the doorway, pulling his polo off over his head as he walked. Everyone followed, stripping and stuffing their respective cubbies. Even wriggling out of their funeral fundoshi.

Like it was perfectly normal. Which it was. Peter stood in the sitting room doorway, watching, smiling, marveling. Thinking once again how cathartic all of this must have been for Hiroshi. The doorbell rang and Alex and Raphael opened the doors, greeted the delivery guy and relieved him of his bags with total nonchalance. Not only about being naked, but about being caged as well. As they closed the doors, Alex turned to Peter.

"You don't have to strip. But you can if you want to. You can use Hiroshi's cubby." Peter watched the parade of butts, of several hues, march toward the dining room. Yet another in a day of memorable moments. From spiritual to breathtakingly corporal. He sighed. He considered it. But decided not to invade the sanctity of Hiroshi's cubby. Not today, anyway.

"This turned out to be quite a day, mijo," Juan softly spoke. He and Ricky were snuggled in bed, earlier than the rest of the house, since Juan had an early wakeup for his shift tomorrow. Which was fine, since Ricky was exhausted anyway. Physically and emotionally. He hadn't said anything to anyone, but all the unknowns about being totally in charge of LCB Headquarters were still weighing on him. And that was on top of saying goodbye to Hiroshi.

"It was, Papito," he looked sweetly into Juan's eyes. "In some ways, really good. But really sad, too. It was hard …"

"I know, mijo, but you were very brave. Hiroshi would have been happy to know yours were the hands that set him free." Ricky looked down a moment in contemplation before resuming eye contact.

"I uh … I didn't free all of Hiroshi. There's a little bit left in the bottom of the urn." He sniffed.

"Oh?" Juan patiently held Ricky's gaze. Ricky sighed.

"I thought, maybe, we could bury the rest next to the gazebo, so he'll always be here with us. At the place where he made us husbands. Here, there and everywhere. Always and forever." Juan swallowed hard.

"Ricky," Juan smiled, misty eyed, as he leaned in to touch lips. "I could never love you more than I do right now." As they kissed, Ricky wrapped an arm around Juan's waist and pulled tight, chest to chest, cage to cock. There would be no sex tonight. It was too late. They were too tired. Tonight would be a night of pure love. Of closure, of sorts. And new beginnings.

The following week felt more normal for everyone except Mateo. Instead of jeans, tee and an apron, when he and Ricky reopened the Headquarters Tuesday, he was sporting Doc Martens, a tight Headquarters t-shirt, and even tighter gold satin short shorts with a pouch clearly molded around his new KINK3D Cobra cage. He was more nervous about the possibility of not understanding everything a customer might want than he was about his appearance. The fact was, he looked stunning, and more than one of the several customers who wandered in that day noticed and mentioned it. Ricky purposely held back whenever a customer entered to encourage Mateo to take the initiative. Because it was a slow day, Ricky was able to keep close tabs on Mateo in case he needed an assist. It was rarely necessary, thanks to the training they'd done over the previous couple of weeks. This was, however, the first time Mateo had actually done any fittings on a stranger. He seemed to enjoy the process, and his customers clearly did. The only difficulty he had was dealing with the sensations he experienced growing erect in a cage. This was new, and unexpected. And surprisingly painful. Sort of. It was also a little thrilling. After his third satisfied customer of the day departed, Mateo looked forlornly at Ricky.

"Amigo, how do you do it?" He adjusted the pouch on his shorts. "Dios Mio."

"What's wrong, Mateo?"

"I think my cage is too small. Ay..." Ricky laughed.

"That cage was fitted by a professional. Me. The fit is perfect. You just need to stop getting turned on by your customers."

"Oh man ..."

"You'll get used to it. At least you get to take yours off after work. Now you know how devoted to our men Alex, Niki, Raphael and I are. We've all been locked for years." Mateo swiveled his head, eyes closed, in real or faux distress.

"Are you sure is not too tight?" Ricky nodded and wrapped his arms around Mateo.

"Maybe we should keep you locked up twenty-four seven for a week, or two, until you get used to it." Mateo pushed him away.

"No, is okay." Ricky laughed again.

"This is actually good, Mateo. It's good for you to feel what your newbie customers will experience. You can empathetically counsel them on what to expect."

"Empa thet ally?"

"Empaticámente." Mateo nodded and groaned.

"What do I say?"

"Like I just said. That it takes time. Like wearing a new pair of jeans. At first it seems too tight. But soon, it feels good. You know what Raphael told me when he first caged me? Just imagine it's Juan's hand squeezing me. So, tell them if it hurts at first, just imagine it's their lover's hand teasing them."

"What if they don' have a lover?" Ricky gave Mateo a look of frustration.

"If they don't have a lover, then imagine a new lover. Or an old lover." The light went on and Ricky smiled as he reached out and placed a hand on each of Mateo's shoulders. "Better yet. I've seen how these guys are around you. Just say, 'Imagine it's *my* hand tenderly squeezing you. Just enjoy it until the feeling passes.'" Mateo actually looked embarrassed.

"No ... I ..."

"Mateo, you're not proposing to these guys. You're just flirting. I mean, come on, you're handling their junk, measuring it. Fitting the ring and tube. Did any of any of these guys start to get hard on you today?" Mateo half-grinned.

"Maybe," Ricky nodded knowingly. "A little."

"They almost always do, muchacho. Go with it. Make them feel good. Help them feel like they've made the right decision. That's our job. You know ... customer satisfaction."

"Okay. I try. Am I doing good so far?" Ricky brushed some of Mateo's mane off his forehead and planted a kiss.

"You're doing great. Are you kidding? Every customer you've helped has bought a cage. You're a natural." Mateo accepted Ricky's praise with a humble smile.

"Thanks, Ricky. I like working for you."

"With me, muchacho. We're a team, you know?" Mateo smiled, then looked over as a couple entered the shop. Ricky faded into the back room momentarily to force Mateo take the lead once again.

By the end of the week, old routines and schedules that had been in place for months were back. Remote work had resumed full time, and Juan was up and out early as before. Niki had regained primary possession of the library, and dinners were fully attended and met with growing appetites and appreciation for the chefs du jour. The atmosphere was still not as carefree and at times silly, as it had been, but the fog of grief was slowly thinning. The one new notable variation was the daily visit to Hiroshi's house, to make sure everything was fine. By now, they took turns, doing it in pairs, so no one had to do it alone, and no one had to do it every day. It was emotionally taxing, often leaving those who'd just done it silent for a while afterward. It still felt a little like an intrusion. But, each day, each visit, it got a little easier. Although Hiroshi's house was beginning to feel more and more familiar to each of them, no one yet felt emboldened to explore closets and drawers, except for kitchen cabinets. They couldn't let good food go to waste, after all. That's where the stash of senbei was found and immediately rescued. So, considering everything, it wasn't a surprise when Ricky announced, toward the end of dinner Saturday evening, the return of another tradition.

"Pancakes tomorrow, amigos!"

"Are you sure?" Niki asked. Steve's eyebrows danced.

"I'm sure. If Alex can handle the espresso machine." Alex, still chewing, made the 'okay' sign with his free hand.

"I will get oranges," Mateo proposed.

"They're in the fridge," Juan smiled. "Ricky texted me a shopping list this afternoon while you two were working."

"Cool," Mateo replied.

"Save a few minutes after breakfast," Ricky advised, "before you head off to study or whatever. We're going to do something special."

"Ooooh," Alex cooed. "Breakfast *and* a performance." Ricky and Juan shared a look, but they didn't share anything with the rest of the family.

"Kinda feels like a dare," Raphael turned to Luke. Luke nodded.

"About time, I'd say," he agreed.

"Excuse me, Sir?" Luke looked confused. "The last dare wasn't that long ago. It was mine. For everyone to attend Folsom naked. It … it kinda got preempted." Raphael's face darkened, as he fell silent. Luke, humbled, gave Ricky a look of dismay.

"I thought that wasn't an actual dare, Raphael," Ricky said, before looking around the table. "And this isn't a dare either, amigos. Something better." He gave Juan a conspiratorial look. "We'll leave the dares to the experts."


Breakfast, tasty as ever and accompanied with a fair amount of kidding and idle banter, was appreciated as much for the sense of normalcy it represented as for Ricky's griddle skills. Unspoken throughout, however, was the anticipation of what might follow the last bite. Ricky hadn't said another word about the 'something special.' So, of course, Alex stepped into the breach when the last fork landed on its sticky, empty plate. He leaned forward, elbows on the table, his head resting on his clasped hands and spoke.

"Thank you, Ricky ... Mateo ... I'm sure I speak for everyone when I say you haven't lost your touch. That was scrumptious. Should we clear our plates, or will you be serving that 'something special' in the sitting room? Hmmmm?"

"You must have driven your mother crazy," Niki observed.

"Yeah," Greg laughed. "He did. Still does. She sends me sympathy cards on a regular basis." Niki smirked knowingly at Greg.

"Excuse me?" Alex gave Greg the evil eye. Greg wrapped an arm around Alex's shoulders and turned to Ricky.

"The floor is yours, amigo." Ricky took a deep breath and stood. Looking serious, he glanced at Juan, then addressed the table.

"Follow me. We'll worry about cleanup later." The lightheartedness he'd been sharing with everyone moments earlier was gone. Raphael, concerned, looked to Luke for a reaction. Luke just shrugged. Counter to Ricky's comment, and out of habit, several of them carried their dishes as they followed Ricky and Juan through the butler's pantry into the kitchen and then out and into the garden. Ricky walked to the gazebo, stepped up onto the first step and turned to face everyone.

"I have a confession to make, and a suggestion, amigos. It wasn't on purpose, but when I released Hiroshi into the ocean, a little bit of him stayed behind in the urn." Ricky reached around the low wall of the gazebo and produced a folded fundoshi. "Juan and I talked, and I thought maybe ..." He looked to Juan for support. Juan nodded and smiled. "Maybe it would be nice if we buried these ashes here, next to the gazebo, so, you know ..." Again, he couldn't finish the sentence. After a quiet pause, Niki spoke.

"Shouldn't we bury him in his own garden?" His voice broke at the end with a sigh.

"Niki," Juan stepped up next to Ricky and pulled him close. "It won't always be Hiroshi's garden. But, if we follow Hiroshi's wishes, this will always be ours. The gazebo will always be here, and he'll always be with us."

"Forever and always," Ricky quietly affirmed.

"We should do it," Steve seconded. A couple more 'yeahs' followed. Juan stepped up into the gazebo and produced a spade and a pair of shoes which he pulled on without tying them.

"I was thinking under this beautiful bird of paradise you guys planted here."

"That's perfect," Raphael walked up to Juan. "Hiroshi did the landscaping. Putting it there was his idea." Juan dropped the spade and pulled Raphael into an embrace. He nodded wordlessly at the family as he released him and retrieved the spade. He scraped an opening in the river rock next to the plant and pushed the spade in at an angle, pulling out a couple pounds of soil. Luke walked up and held out his hand to Juan, who hesitated, then handed the spade to Luke, who pressed the spade in further with his bare foot. Mateo was next, then Niki, then Ricky. By now the hole was deep enough. Ricky carefully placed the fundoshi bundle into the bottom of the hole. He stood and handed the spade to Raphael, who began the process of refilling the hole. In turn, each of them had a hand in digging and refilling the grave. Ryan carefully redistributed the river rock, and that was it. They all gathered in a loose group hug.

"It wouldn't surprise me," Ricky said, "if Hiroshi intentionally held back in the urn, you know? To give us another reason to stay here. To put flowers here to mark his birthday. Or the day we first met him."

"I wouldn't put it past Elder to do everything in his power to keep us together," Juan smiled. "On that score, you're probably right. But I don't think we need to add any more flowers, mijo. This bird of paradise Hiroshi put here would be hard to top."

# Nineteen

# AN EMBEDDED ANTHROPOLOGIST

"READY FOR FINALS?" RYAN had wandered into the library after fixing his third cup of tea of the morning. It was early December and both he and Niki had been sequestering themselves day and night the last couple of weeks, intensely preparing for the gauntlet of finals. Niki looked up from his laptop.

"Ready as I'll ever be, I guess. But never ready enough."

"So you say, Mr. Dean's List."

"What about you?"

"I think so, for the exams, anyway. It's tomorrow's research presentation for Anthro that has me worried." Ryan plopped into Niki's fireplace chair and set his tea on the low table next to it. Niki closed his laptop and joined him.

"Presentation? In front of the professor?"

"In front of the whole class. She's arranged a whole day in an auditorium where we can spread out for COVID mitigation. We each present our work, then take questions from her and the class. Kind of intimidating. It's been a semester long assignment, so ... high expectations. Fifty percent of the grade."

"Wow. You haven't mentioned it."

"Well, there's a reason I haven't. I've been putting it off, but I have to make my case to you guys. Tell everyone what I'm presenting. It's only fair. Tonight, after dinner. Can you make time?"

"Sure, so this will be a rehearsal?"

"More like an admission." Niki looked confused. Ryan reached over and patted his forearm. "I'll serve details after dinner. A weird sort of dessert." He stood, picked up his tea and made his exit. Inspired, Niki headed into the kitchen to make a cup for himself.

The following morning, at nine o'clock, Ryan was in his seat, four rows from the front, nervous as hell. His confession the preceding evening had gone better than he'd expected. He should have known he had nothing to worry about. In his experience, the House of the Locked Cock Brotherhood had always been supportive and affirming to each member. Still, he was taking significant liberties and had finally worked up the nerve to ask for consent at the last minute. Had they objected, he'd have been totally, totally screwed. Now it was all up to him to either ace the course or bomb, blowing a few minds either way. The professor announced the order of presenters. Of the twenty students, Ryan would be number nine, just before the lunch break. Plenty of time to agonize.

Some presenters were clearly nervous, although a couple had obviously rehearsed. Some didn't even offer any visuals. Most presentations lasted ten minutes, fifteen at the most, and the Q&A afterwards was thoughtful, but non-controversial. Probably because most topics were predictable. Prosaic. Not a lot of new ground was being broken. Yet. If nothing else, Ryan was confident his area of research would change that.

"Mr. Riley," the professor finally announced. Ryan stood and walked up the short flight of steps to the proscenium and approached the lectern. He looked up at the audio/visual volunteer, who nodded. He picked up the wireless remote and clicked. His first PowerPoint slide flashed on the screen behind him.

## A Subculture in Our Midst

*Embedded in the House of the Locked Cock Brotherhood*

### Thesis for Anthropology 302

"Excuse me just one moment," Ryan said as he let the class and the professor absorb what was displayed on the screen. He stepped just out of view stage right and quickly kicked off his shoes and pulled off the hoody and sweat pants he was wearing. He returned to the lectern wearing just his fundoshi. He cleared his throat over low tittering from some in the audience.

"Every culture, even seemingly highly homogenous ones, harbor subcultures. Sometimes hundreds of them. We all know that. However, none of us is familiar with most of them. Or even aware of them. Today, I would like to introduce you to one you may not be aware of, but, trust me, is present all around you. Maybe even next door to you." As Ryan spoke over the next twenty minutes, he periodically clicked the remote, advancing photos of the family in all their naked, collared, harnessed and caged glory. Some were photos he had taken over previous months. Others were photos he'd collected from others, like stills Steve had taken of Mateo's mantra session in the kitchen. There were photos Mateo had taken of him and Pup Niki playing with the pups in Hiroshi's garden on his birthday. Some were innocent candid shots of Raphael and Alex cooking, or Greg watering plants. A few included Hiroshi. And a few, in the dungeon, were more intense.

"For the last year and a half, I have been embedded in a gay male household where clothing is not allowed. Where about half the members are kept locked in chastity cages, for reasons I'll explain shortly. Where labor is shared by everyone, both the dominant partners and those who are admittedly and proudly submissive to their partners sexually. They consider themselves equals in all other respects. In some cases, the more submissive partner is actually more accomplished in terms of financial and career attainment, in others they are on equal ground career wise.

"To the outside world these ten men appear quite ordinary, in San Francisco terms. It's a diverse group. White, Asian, Black and Latino. One is an OR nurse, a couple are students, one in nursing school. A couple of them are entrepreneurs. Some are in the tech industry and one is in finance; another works in a large advertising agency. If you saw them out at a restaurant you wouldn't give them a second glance. Well ... they are a handsome bunch, as you can see, so, maybe a second glance would be in order." That comment elicited a few chuckles, Ryan's first discernable feedback. So far, so good.

"For the most part, the more dominant partners are a bit older than the more submissive, but not in every case. And even the more dominant individuals have been known, at times, to submit. Sometimes sexually. Sometimes in the dungeon. Yes. A dungeon. The House of the Locked Cock Brotherhood has a fully equipped dungeon. As well as a high-tech, fully equipped kitchen where everyone takes turns cooking for the others. Again, outside of some sexual dynamics, it's a totally egalitarian family.

"I use the word 'family' intentionally. In the sixties, this might have been characterized as a commune. From our anthropological perspective, we might label it a tribe. A very small tribe. But if you asked these ten men, they would tell you they are, in fact, a family. A chosen family, although two of them are brothers by adoption. One Black, one Asian." Ryan paused for dramatic effect, gaining confidence from seeing his classmates fully absorbing his visuals and his narration. "Like everything else about this family, it's complicated." More chuckles.

"So why does this family exist? Like any tribe that perseveres, the members share an unbreakable bond. Shared values. On the surface one could attribute this family's existence to a shared love of a kink lifestyle. But there are thousands of people in San Francisco interested in that. For this family, there is an even stronger bond. And that bond is love. Not in terms of sex, which I can report is abundant within each couple. Rather, I'm referring to brotherly love. Each member of this family loves the others, just as you would expect in a biological family. They support one another unconditionally. During the Black Lives Matter protests, the entire family marched multiple times. When Mama, the mother of two of the members and mother-in-law to their husbands, became critically ill with COVID, every member of the family provided support. In fact, one member led a spontaneous healing session in the middle of the night, chanting a mantra that we are all convinced contributed to her recovery." Ryan paused as several of Steve's emotive stills dissolved from one to another on the screen. "To this day we refer to him as the Shaman." Ryan wisely chose to keep the Prince part of Mateo's title out of his presentation.

"But, yes, a shared attraction to kink also binds this family together. I promised to address the fact that some members are locked in chastity cages. This is not a form of punishment or denial; on the contrary, each locked member is happier caged. Is proudly caged. It's possible some of you may have seen one or more of them naked and caged at Baker or Marshall's Beaches. Or at the Folsom Street Fair or Halloween in the Castro. A couple are caged to prove their devotion to their husbands, which ironically enough, is absolutely *not* a vow of chastity. If anyone is curious, I can explain that in more detail offline later. Another was first caged years ago in order to save his marriage. Let's just say he had a terrible time *not* saving himself for his husband.

"When I first embedded with this family, I wasn't sure what to expect. I was somewhat anxious, in fact. I thought, as you might guess from the images you've seen, that it would be one big orgy. I mean, everyone's naked. All the time. And ... this is true ... the dungeon was a total surprise when I arrived. But, by then it was too late. I really couldn't back out.

"I'm glad I didn't. Because it wasn't a non-stop orgy. The nudity, the chastity cages, the pup personas, the leather gear ... they're natural for these guys. It's just how they live as a family. An entertaining, crazy, sometimes intense but always supportive, loving, and respectful family.

"I mentioned earlier that this family represents a subculture that is present all around you. I know I was completely unaware of it before meeting, and then becoming embedded with the members of the House of the Locked Cock Brotherhood. If you don't believe me, search the hashtag 'teamlocked' on Twitter. You will find tens of thousands, maybe hundreds of thousands of examples of men and women who have adopted the lifestyle. It's real. If anything, it's growing. All around you. Maybe even next door." Ryan clicked to a blank, black screen. "Thank you for your attention. Any questions?"

About a dozen hands shot up. Ryan looked to the professor, who looked at her watch.

"Go ahead, Mr. Riley. We can take a few minutes. I'll let you know when you're out of time." Ryan pointed to a guy in the front row. He always tried to dominate discussions in Zoom class, too. Ryan wanted to get his question out of the way.

"How did you find this subculture? And why did you decide to embed with it, if that's really what you did?" The snark and disdain in his question was evident to all, and by this late in the semester, not at all surprising to the other students, nor the professor. Ryan decided to tell the simple truth.

"I didn't go looking for it. I basically stumbled upon it when I attended a wedding of four of the members of the family. A double ceremony. I was introduced to a member of the wedding party, this guy." Ryan pressed a slide number on the remote to bring up a candid of Mateo, sitting cross-legged on their bed, looking very sweet and very intent, studying one of Alex's graphic novels. "We connected. We dated. We fell in love. But I soon learned dating him meant dating the entire family. But it wasn't a problem because, again, they're a generous, loving, family and they quickly took me in as if I'd always belonged. Before I knew it, I was 'embedded.'" The guy opened his mouth to say more, but Ryan pointed to a woman in the middle of the auditorium whom he'd noticed had smiled a lot during his presentation.

"Why does this family not allow clothing, and why did you choose to wear that thong instead of giving your presentation naked? You kind of cheated us." Several students laughed and one guy called out, "Yeah!"

"I'm not entirely sure about the nudity, to be honest, because it goes way back before my time. It's my understanding that when Luke and Raphael were first dating, and Luke challenged Raphael to become his locked cock leather boy, part of that act of submission was to always be naked in Luke's presence. It's not uncommon among many who live a strict leather lifestyle. But Luke, being something of an exhibitionist himself, insisted on being naked, too. And whenever other members of the family joined them ... this was before everyone lived under the same roof ... they felt compelled to follow suit. Reluctantly at first, I suspect, but it soon became expected, and then as natural as kicking off your shoes in someone else's home. Naturism exists in other subcultures around the world, so it's not that shocking. Also, it has the added benefit of encouraging the locked members of the family to be proud of their locked status ... at the gym, at the beach, wherever they can be proudly displayed." Ryan stopped talking.

"And my second question?" Ryan smiled back at her shyly.

"Um, well, I didn't want to be a distraction from the content of my presentation, so I thought I'd wear this fundoshi. It's not a thong. It's a Japanese garment worn at festivals, to the beach, at clubs, etcetera. It's not at all risqué in Japanese culture. I wore the fundoshi to honor a cherished member of the family, a Japanese-American who, uh, we lost a couple of months ago." Ryan pressed another number on the remote to display a candid shot Mateo had taken of Hiroshi, smiling, in his garden. Then he pointed to another student near the back.

"Are you one of the locked guys, as you call it? Are you locked now?" Ryan couldn't help himself and broke into an embarrassed grin.

"Am I locked now? Yes."

"I knew it!" the guy stage-whispered.

"I'm not sure exactly why, but I just felt like I should be, while giving this presentation. But, I'm not one of the permanently locked members of the family. It's more situational for me. Here." Ryan pressed couple of buttons on the remote and brought up an image of the LCB Head-quarters storefront, which he hadn't shown previously. "Two members of the family have a shop in the Castro that exclusively sells custom fitted chastity devices. It's kind of unique. Sometimes, when they're really busy, I help out. Wearing a cage is part of the uniform. A pretty skimpy uniform, actually. So, that's why I have one. That's the case for many others in this subculture. They aren't locked all the time. Just for special occasions or challenges. Or to please their partners. Some go for weeks or months between periods of being locked. If you're curious look up 'Locktober' online." Ryan shrugged eliciting more chuckles, then pointed to another student.

"Can we see your cage?" Ryan looked over at the professor, who smiled and shook her head.

"Uh, well ... since this isn't a life drawing class, I better not. I've probably broken a half-dozen rules already." A couple more hands shot up. One asked about the prevalence of collars and harnesses in the slide show. Another asked for details about the dungeon that Ryan choose not to dwell on. His Q&A went on far longer than anyone else's had. Until, finally, the professor stood.

"Thank you, Mr. Riley, for introducing us to a subculture, apparently a very real subculture, that most, if not all of us, were unaware of. Right here, as you say, in our midst. And thank you for doing so in a thorough and most entertaining way." She nodded to Ryan, who laid down the remote and headed into the wing to pull on his sweats. "We've run longer than I'd planned this morning, so let's cut the lunch break short. I still want you back here at one o'clock." When Ryan reappeared and started down the steps, one member of the class began clapping. Others immediately joined in, and by the time Ryan hit the floor, he was awarded with a small but earnest standing ovation. He glanced at the professor who was clapping along with everyone else. Embarrassed, he took a dramatic bow. His decision to offer up the family as worthy of anthropological scrutiny had paid off. He felt confident this fifty percent of the grade would guarantee an A. He might even be giving Niki a little Dean's List competition this semester after all.

"So, how'd it go?" Niki asked Ryan as he slid into his seat for dinner. Everyone knew what he was referring to.

"I owe you guys bigly," Ryan grinned. "I was so worried they'd be freaked out. That the professor would stop me before I even got started. But, not to brag, it went over really well. Thank you for letting me show the photos of all of you. The presentation would have been meaningless without them."

"Tell 'em what the perfessor tol' you," Mateo looked proudly around the table.

"She took me aside after the class. She said I showed the rest of the class exactly what anthropological study is all about. That she hopes I pursue a career in anthropology because the field would surely benefit from my 'astute observational skills.'"

"So," Alex asked, as if he didn't know the answer, "she was cool with you giving a presentation showing a bunch of naked and caged guys while wearing a fundoshi in a college auditorium?"

"Well, our texts have plenty of pictures of naked natives, so ..."

Greg raised his wine glass in Ryan's direction. "As we natives like to say ... to Ryan, no doubt the future Dr. Ryan Riley, Ph.D., in Anthropology. Just be sure to credit us all in your dissertation." As more glasses were raised, Mateo leaned over and planted one while squeezing Ryan's still locked cock. Ryan turned and made it a full lip-on-lip reward. If only the class could see this moment, offering further proof that his assertions in the presentation were honest and valid. He was indeed embedded in a fully supportive and loving family.

After dinner, Ryan and Mateo retired to their room earlier than usual. Everyone knew why. Aside from his month-long stint during Mama's recovery, no one, except perhaps Mateo, had seen Ryan caged outside of his occasional shifts at the Headquarters, and his brief attendance at Folsom. He was clearly still on a high after his performance at school, and no doubt the Shaman Prince was going to show his sex slave just how proud he was of him. Meanwhile, Raphael and Luke had a standing date with a razor and rosemary mint shampoo.

"Sir," Raphael quietly observed as he massaged the foam deeply into Luke's tresses, "we haven't talked about your hair lately. You know, the hair that you were reluctant to grow this long?" Raphael stretched a handful down until it touched Luke's shoulder, then resumed massaging.

"Had I known how good it feels when you do this, we'd have grown it out a long time ago, baby." Raphael leaned down and kissed the foamy spot he'd left on Luke's shoulder.

"Admit it, Sir. You look ravishing now. And with a kilt and the beard, both of which were also my doing, you break hearts every time we leave the house."

"*We* break hearts because *you* are the one holding my hand. You are the heartbreaker, baby. I'm just there for contrast." Raphael barked a laugh.

"So, you're saying I failed at creating the handsomest man to walk these mean streets? Raphael's a failure?" Luke pulled away and turned to face him, his hands on each of Raphael's meaty thighs.

"Fine. Baby, you created a masterpiece. But one rivaled only by *my* creation. Now, rinse me off, so I can perfect that high 'n tight on the perfect locked cock leather boy that is my beautiful, but silly husband. So I can take him to bed. And make love to him. Until begs me to stop." Luke punctuated his command with a kiss. A long, fierce one that strained Raphael's cage for the first time in, well, too long.

When their lips parted, Raphael whispered, "Oh, I will beg, Sir, but never for you to stop."

# Twenty

## A Modest Proposal

RAPHAEL PADDED INTO THE kitchen, hoping someone else had risen earlier and made the first pot of coffee. He lifted the carafe and smiled. He poured and wandered to the back door assuming, correctly, that he'd find Juan and Ricky ensconced in the gazebo. The fog was already lifting, but, Raphael thought, it was still too cool for a naked al fresco breakfast. He almost started up the back stairs but decided ... if they could brave it, so could he.

"May I," he asked as he neared the steps to the gazebo.

"Of course," Juan, who was practically wearing Ricky, smiled in invitation. Raphael sat across from them and shivered as he sipped.

"I don't think I'll stay long. Whose idea was it, anyway, to ban clothes here?"

"Um ... I think it was you," Ricky giggled. Raphael gave him a guilty look. He sat back and looked over the fence at Hiroshi's house. He sighed. Juan watched him as he sipped from his own mug.

"We can't put it off forever, Raphael," Juan said.

"I know," Raphael half-smiled as he met Juan's gaze. "It's just ..."

"Yeah," Juan agreed. "But we have to think practically. Financially. Hiroshi would want us to be looking out for our own best interests."

"I can't imagine anyone else living there," Ricky said as he rubbed Juan's knee. "What if it's ... what if it's someone who hates gays? Or nudity. Or has five kids?" His voice rose with each worried word. Juan rubbed the back of his shaven head.

"What if," Raphael leaned forward, "it was someone we know. And trust?"

"Oooh," Ricky quietly said. "Raphael has a plan." He pulled away from Juan. "What are you thinking?"

"Who do we know who could afford Hiroshi's house?" Juan asked, genuinely intrigued.

"Um ... I don't want to jinx it, so ... and it's probably not feasible anyway." Raphael stood as he took another sip of his rapidly cooling coffee. "Let me get back to you when I know more." He headed back into the house where he planned to crawl into bed next to Luke and shock him into a very chilly consciousness.

"Do you think they bought it?" Alex asked Raphael as they headed down Noe toward Market Street and the street car stop.

"Why not?" Raphael grinned. He was wearing a shoulder bag holding his laptop, and not just to reinforce the reason they'd given Luke and Greg for why they had to appear at the office. In person. "Things are loosening up, bit by bit. A brief command performance at the office is totally believable." After a few steps he continued, "Maybe I'm being silly to keep it secret, but you have to admit this probably won't pan out. If so, you'll be the only one who knew. I won't feel so ... foolish, maybe."

"Raphael, nobody will think you're foolish. Not every scheme you come up with can be a winner."

"Tell that to my ego."

"I've tried. I can't even get an appointment." Raphael laughed and reached down for Alex's hand. Alex made a 'mmm' sound.

"Yeah," Raphael agreed. "I've missed this, too. You and me. Two of the three cagedketeers. Challenging the world."

"We were younger then, and much more innocent," Alex sighed.

"Excuse me ... you were never innocent, Alex. Maybe just more naïve." Alex tried to shake Raphael's hand loose, but failed. So, instead he gripped Raphael's hand more firmly.

"We've been through a lot, haven't we? Mostly good."

"Yeah," Raphael replied after a couple of beats. "Mostly ..."

It felt weird, riding up an elevator the two of them had ridden five and even six days a week until the pandemic had rendered it off limits. They felt like visitors in a place they had considered their territory not that long ago. When they exited on the floor that housed ... had housed ... administrative offices, they found it was empty today, with most of the overhead lights off. Except for a glass-walled conference room in the center of the floor that was illuminated. Raphael led Alex past the dark offices ringing the floor and up to the door of the conference room, where Cynthia was sitting at the head of the table, with a laptop and a collection of documents. Raphael knocked, though the door was open. Cynthia, unmasked, looked up, then stood, smiling widely.

"Raphael! Alex! Come in, please. Have a seat. This is such a treat. To be in a room with colleagues. In the flesh." She sat and waved at the coffee cart. "There's coffee if you like, and tea." She lowered her voice conspiratorially. "It's all right if you unmask to drink. Our ventilation in this room is CDC approved, I'm told." To calm his nerves, Raphael poured a cup of coffee for himself. Since he would be doing most of the talking, it would be best to remove his mask anyway. When Raphael offered, Alex shook his head and sat at the far end of the table.

"Thanks for making time for us," Alex said as Raphael sat and opened his laptop.

"My pleasure. So, tell me, Alex, have you engineered any more wedding extravaganzas lately?" Cynthia thought she was simply making conversation while she refreshed her tea cup.

"Well, as a matter of fact, yes," Alex smized. "Just one. A very special one."

"Oh? Who was the lucky couple, Alex?" He blushed behind his mask.

"Remember Ricky, Raphael's ringbearer?"

"Indeed!"

"He married the love of his life, Juan, who was up on the stage in the wedding party."

"The tall man with the mustache?"

"Good guess."

"Well, we all saw how they looked at each other when Ricky joined the wedding party. It must have been a more intimate affair, considering ..."

"It was," Raphael said. "Just family. And outdoors. But it was another Alex original."

"Well," Alex demurred, "Alex *and* Hiroshi." Cynthia cocked her head, eyebrows raised. She remembered the unusual name from Raphael's and Alex's recent leave requests.

"Which is kind of why we asked to meet with you," Raphael began to explain. "A lot has happened in the last year or so. It's a long story, and I won't bore you with all of it now. Maybe with Patricia over a glass of wine if you're really interested ... it *is* a long story." Cynthia took a short sip.

"I'll hold you to it. But for now ... why are we here? Raphael, you mentioned something about an opportunity of a lifetime." Raphael plugged the video cable into his laptop and pressed a couple of keys. A street view of Hiroshi's house appeared on the screen suspended from the ceiling at the end of the room.

"You may think I'm crazy," Raphael said as Alex studied Cynthia, "but I remember you saying once that you and Patricia would love to find a place in the city. With more room. And a garden for your puppy."

"Well, she's not a puppy any more, and she takes up even more room than ever," Cynthia replied, eyeing the screen. "So, Raphael, are you moonlighting as a realtor now?" Raphael laughed.

"No, I'm busy enough with my responsibilities here. Okay ... a little bit of the long story. This house belonged to our next-door neighbor. And good friend. Very good friend."

"A member of our family," Alex interjected. "Like a brother."

"Hiroshi," Cynthia said, slowly catching on. Raphael sighed and nodded.

"Yeah. We inherited his house when he died a few months ago. He wanted us to sell it at the right time to ensure we could buy the house we all live in. We're renting right now." Cynthia gave each of them a look that silently conveyed her condolences. Then she raised an index finger.

"Just so I understand, you own a house you don't live in, but you're renting the house next door? Why not move into the house you own?"

"Our house ... the one we live in, is much bigger," Raphael responded. "Six bedrooms. There are ten of us. I warned you it was a long story. But Hiroshi's house ... the house I thought you and Patricia might be interested in, is big, too. Four bedrooms. Two and a half baths. A beautiful private garden. A study for your home office. And ten wonderful next-door neighbors that *maybe* not everyone would consider wonderful neighbors." Cynthia looked wryly at Raphael, then Alex who was trying to look innocent.

"Take a look," Raphael eagerly prompted as he began to click through a dozen photos of the garden and the rooms in Hiroshi's house. Cynthia uttered a couple of oohs and aahs as the photos progressed over Raphael's narration.

"It's on Noe," Alex said. "I guess we should have asked if you're even really in the market, Cynthia." Raphael grimaced, realizing in his nervousness he may have assumed too much and jumped the gun.

"Well, Alex, we haven't been actively looking lately." Raphael sat back in his chair. "But we are open to the idea. This house looks very charming." She paused and looked at Raphael and Alex in turn. "However, you say there could be an issue with these ten neighbors to consider." Alex nodded his head, a serious expression coming over his mask.

"You were at our wedding," Raphael said. "So, you know we're a little unconventional. Even for gay men. One reason we haven't put the house on the market is, well, we don't want just anyone living in Hiroshi's house. We don't want just anyone living next door. And to be honest, not just anyone would like living next door to *us*. We're naturists, Cynthia," Raphael explained, using the most conventional term he could reasonably apply to the House of the Locked Cock Brotherhood. "We live naked, twenty-four seven, indoors and out. Some might be offended to look out an upstairs window on occasion and see us. We thought, *maybe*, you and Patricia would be okay with that." Cynthia laughed.

"Forgive me. I can't imagine anyone else in this company saying the words you just said to me, Raphael." She looked back and forth between Alex and Raphael for a moment, without speaking. Raphael feared he'd assumed too much. Had gone too far. Alex was certain of it.

"But knowing what I know about you two, I guess I shouldn't be all that surprised. We've seen the two of you all but naked, already and, well, Ricky's costume left nothing to the imagination, did it?" She paused again briefly. "And somehow, we survived. Are Patricia and I the first to be considered as potential successors to Hiroshi's house?"

"You are," Raphael said, sharing a relieved glance with Alex. "Like I said, it may not be smart financially for us to be so picky, but we want to be very particular about who will live there."

"Well, then, I should feel honored that you've thought of Patricia and me." Raphael pulled a thumb drive out of his pocket and walked it over to where Cynthia was sitting.

"Here's a copy of all the photos, so you can show them to Patricia. We'd be thrilled and privileged to have the two of you, and your pup, as neighbors." Cynthia smiled with genuine appreciation as she picked up the drive.

"As I said, we haven't been actively looking, but these photos could change that. Don't be surprised if we call to arrange a showing." She stood. "Thank you, Raphael. Alex. For thinking of us. And for putting us at the top of the list."

"There is no list," Alex spoke as he stood and moved toward the door. "We've only considered you and Patricia." Raphael had disconnected his laptop and joined Alex at the door.

"Give our best to Patricia," he said. "It was nice to finally see you again. In person, that is."

"Stay safe," Cynthia replied, "and give my regards to Luke and Greg."

"I can't believe she remembered Greg's and Luke's names," Alex said as they rode the elevator.

"She's a pro, Alex," Raphael replied. "You can bet she reviewed our files before the meeting, just as she would for any business encounter." Alex nodded while watching the floors count down on the screen. "Do you think we'll hear from her? Or was she just being nice?"

"I'm going to say, yes. Even if they're not serious, who doesn't like exploring other people's homes? There's not much else to do yet. And besides ..." Alex turned and wiggled his eyebrows as the doors opened on the ground floor. "If they're lucky, they might get to see that 'tall man with a mustache' in all his glory."

"Whatever it takes to clinch the sale," Raphael smized.

Raphael and Alex had stayed mum about the true nature of their meeting with Cynthia. Several days had passed with no word, so they were glad they had. Nothing ventured, nothing gained. Nothing lost.

Then, late Thursday afternoon, Raphael's phone chimed, displaying a call from a local number he didn't recognize. Likely a spam call, but he answered, hoping otherwise. It was Cynthia. They were *maybe* interested. Certainly curious. Would Saturday afternoon work? Could they bring Daisy? Raphael said yes to both, then rushed down the hall to share with Alex. Who introduced a mega-dose of reality.

"What do we say when they ask the price?" Alex posed. Raphael sat on the edge of their bed, facing Alex at the desk.

"Yeah. I've looked at a couple of online sites, I'm sure they have, too. That's going to be the really awkward part. If we get that far. I think it's time for a family meeting." Alex agreed. There were eight other owners who needed to be briefed and heard from.

The conversation at dinner was lively, with lots of questions, a few reservations, but all in all, a fair amount of optimism.

"I have to say, guys," Greg said at one point, "you have guts. I have to hand it to you. Inviting your CEO ... a woman ... to consider buying a property next door to what they might consider a den of iniquity."

"First of all," Alex retorted, "where is this den of iniquity?" He looked around the table. "I've never laid eyes on a more wholesome group." Ricky, collared, harnessed and wearing his wrist restraints, laughed. Alex half turned to address Greg directly. "Come on. You know Cynthia and Patricia are gay. They had a great time at the wedding. Cynthia not only remembered Ricky fondly, but," he turned to Juan, "she remembered you as well, Juan. Raphael and I figure they'll make an offer for sure if you'll just happen to be sunbathing in the garden during their tour Saturday."

"Yeah, that's right," Raphael confirmed. "Since Ricky and Mateo will be working, maybe Ryan can be seen rubbing sunscreen on you at a strategic point in the tour."

"Sure," Ryan grinned, until he looked at Juan, who had one eyebrow raised judgmentally.

"Not even on a dare," Juan definitively said.

"Seriously, though, this could really work," Raphael got serious. "We want neighbors who can accept us and how we live."

"Check," Niki volunteered.

"Ideally they should be gay."

"Check."

"It doesn't hurt that they love pups."

"Check," Niki laughed, aware that loving an Old English Sheepdog wasn't quite the same as accepting human pups.

"The biggest question for now," Alex moved on to the practical, "is financial. Not whether or not they can afford it, but," he looked directly into Greg's eyes, "what should our asking price be?"

"Yeah," Raphael agreed. "We haven't really talked about that."

"No, we haven't," Greg nodded. He looked around the table. "I suppose you want me to come up with a number." Alex continued to look at him sweetly.

"Yes, dear. A big one." Greg leaned back and pondered his empty plate.

"You do know more about finance than any of us," Luke prompted.

"I've done a little searching online," Raphael offered. "Zillow ..." Greg scratched his neck.

"That's not going to get us very far," he smiled at Raphael. "I need to talk to Peter. And a few other people. You do realize that once you start negotiating price, things between you and Cynthia could get a little uncomfortable. This could affect your careers, guys." Alex and Raphael exchanged a long gaze, before Raphael turned back to Greg.

"We don't have to go for top dollar, do we?" he proposed. "Like I said, there are so many benefits to having them next door, instead of some strangers. As long as we get a fair price, one that Cynthia and Patricia think is fair, that is, we should be happy. They'll be happy." Greg sighed. He looked around the table.

"We know what Raphael thinks. What about everyone else? Is everyone comfortable with possibly giving up ... I don't know, let's say, for the sake of argument, a million dollars just to make nice with Cynthia and Patricia? Versus a deep-pocketed stranger?" For a moment no one spoke.

"Could there be that much disparity?" Steve questioned. Greg nodded solemnly.

"The bigger question," Juan contended, "is ... what's the base? If they offer three million and we could have gotten four, I'm okay with three million. That would make a decent down payment on this house."

"I thought housing prices had dropped because of the pandemic," Niki recalled. "Are we really talking three or four million dollars?"

"Prices dropped in a lot of places," Greg met Niki's gaze, "but not really in SF. Prices stopped climbing, though. Again, I need to do some research but our house next door is a gem."

"When I showed this house to that realtor a couple years ago," Steve offered, "before Raphael and Niki forced it off the market, his initial spitball take was four and half. Two years ago."

"This house is worth four and half million dollars?" Luke asked incredulously.

"Well ... probably more now," Greg replied, enjoying the look on Luke's face while Steve nodded.

"Lordy," Ryan spoke for everyone else at the table.

"Numbers like these don't even seem real to me," Raphael looked at Alex. "Now I'm wishing I'd never said anything to Cynthia." Alex offered a sympathetic smile.

"No, no, Raphael," Greg soothed. "Cynthia wouldn't have agreed to see the place if they were scared off by numbers like these. Like you said, she and Patricia have no doubt done their homework. I may not have a hard and fast number as soon as Saturday, and neither will they. Price probably won't even come up this soon. Think of it as a first date. To insulate the two of you," he turned his gaze to Alex, "you two can be the promoters and I'll be the money guy."

"Works for me," Raphael replied. Alex playfully punched Greg in the shoulder to demonstrate his agreement.

"So," Alex concluded the meeting portion of dinner, "does everyone agree with the idea of having Cynthia, Patricia and Daisy as next-door neighbors?" Nine 'ayes' and one 'woof' made it unanimous.


Alex and Raphael wrapped up the tour of Hiroshi's house around four Saturday afternoon. In a neighborly gesture, they invited Cynthia and Patricia next door for tea. Everyone had been briefed to be in 'company' attire, just in case they said yes, which, of course, they did. Ryan and Niki prepared refreshments while Alex and Raphael conducted yet another, but much briefer, house tour. They ended it in the well-ventilated gazebo, where Luke and Greg were waiting. As they sat, and Niki and Ryan delivered the tea and senbei, Alex demonstrated one more amenity. He stepped down from the gazebo, walked over to the nearly invisible gate and opened it. Daisy, who had been lounging in Hiroshi's garden, came bounding through.

"Oh, how clever," Patricia exclaimed. "You and Hiroshi had a secret passage!" Niki and Ryan sat on the ground and got acquainted with Daisy as Alex returned to the gazebo.

"Yeah," Alex smiled. "It got so much use, we often didn't even close it. By the way, we thought about serving cookies but decided, in keeping with the theme, to introduce you to a treat Hiroshi shared with us many, many times." He took four senbei from the platter and placed two next to Cynthia and Patricia's tea cups. They each began unwrapping one.

"This gazebo," Cynthia looked up and around. "It's like something out of a small-town square." Patricia, crunching her first senbei, nodded.

"Not to brag," Raphael grinned proudly, "but we built it. From a kit, of course. We made a chuppah out of some of the components for Juan and Ricky's wedding. Then we put this together with the rest of the parts as their wedding gift." Cynthia looked at Patricia and shook her head in feigned disbelief.

"With Hiroshi's help," Alex chimed in. "He figured out how to create the chuppah from the gazebo parts without drilling any extra holes or anything." Cynthia studied Alex as he spoke. And noted the solemn look on both Raphael's and Luke's faces.

"This gazebo has very special meaning for all of you, then," she said. The four men nodded very slightly.

"Yeah," was all Raphael said. Then he brightened. "It turned out to be a great idea. Juan and Ricky have breakfast together out here every Saturday." He turned to Luke with a laugh. "I think they're afraid we'll return it if they don't use it at least once a week." Patricia laughed along with him and peeled open her second senbei. Cynthia continued to study the men's faces.

"It won't be easy, will it ... to have someone else living next door. In Hiroshi's house." Luke swallowed hard. He hadn't spoken much yet.

"That's why we were all excited when Raphael and Alex told us about your possible interest." He brushed his hair out of his eyes and gave Cynthia and Patricia his best gothic romance cover smile. "We loved Hiroshi, and we'll always miss him, but we also realize we can't hold onto his house out of sentimentality. We have to be realistic. But," he turned to Raphael briefly to include him in his words, "we want our new neighbors to be someone we respect and admire as much as we loved Hiroshi." Luke's words brought smiles back to everyone's lips. Patricia reached for another senbei.

"It is a lovely house," she said. "And I wouldn't change a thing in the garden."

"It was one of Hiroshi's hobbies," Greg said. "He did a lot of the work in our garden, too."

"It shows," Cynthia smiled, watching Daisy roughhouse with Niki and Ryan. "You have an enviable home here, too, the ten of you. How fortunate you are to have one another."

"I know," Alex agreed. "I have to pinch myself some days." He smiled at Greg. "We are so, so lucky." He looked back Cynthia. "To have each other. This house. A great boss ..."

"Smooth, Alex ..." Raphael chided. Cynthia and Patricia both laughed.

"We'll, you're not the only lucky ones, Alex. I second you on the great colleagues. Who knows. Maybe we'll end up being great neighbors, too." She smiled at Patricia out of the corner of her eyes. "Not that I really needed to, after your sensational wedding, but, yes, I did brief Patricia about the possibility ... the likelihood ... of seeing naked men on occasion in the garden."

Picking up on Cynthia's light-hearted take, Luke asked, "And ...?"

"I said," Patricia replied, "well, I should bloody well hope so!"

## Twenty-One

---

# HELLO, NEIGHBOR

RICKY MOANED SO QUIETLY he was almost drowned out by the background playlist coming over the dungeon's sound system. He was in his happy place, in the sling, wrist and ankle restraints locked in place on the suspension chains. More to the point, impaled on Juan's attentive cock. The Leather Boy training sessions had taken a hiatus after Hiroshi's death. Cuddling and kissing, mostly, were what they had required from one another. But, in time, the need, the drive, the hunger they both felt for each other crept back, in bed at first, in the shower, and now, finally, back in the dungeon. Besides Ricky's permanent cage and collar, and the more and more ubiquitous wrist and ankle restraints, tonight Ricky was also sporting the nipple suckers. Nipple training had also taken a back seat, but his efforts prior to Hiroshi's death had been regular enough that he hadn't really lost any ground. They were still plump, still perky and, according to Juan, still *delicioso*. The sensation of the suckers pulling and teasing his nips made Juan's attention to Ricky's prostate all the more intense.

"Mmmmm, careful, Papito," Ricky moaned. "I don't want to come before you do." Juan paused his pumping and leaned down to press his lips on Ricky's, supporting himself by holding onto the chains restraining Ricky's arms. After a moment he rocked his pubic bone slowly against Ricky's impaled ass without breaking the kiss. Ricky sighed through the kiss. Juan rotated his hips ever so slightly, raised up on his toes now and then, to vary Ricky's appreciation of hosting Juan's cock. In response, Ricky did his best to work over Juan's cock with his increasingly talented leather boy ass. Juan's lips, still locked on Ricky's, turned up slightly in a proud smile. Which encouraged Ricky to turn up the tempo down below even more as he drove his tongue further into Juan's mouth. Juan, fearing he would be the one to come too soon, broke the kiss and stood, grasping Ricky's thighs with each hand.

"I could do this with you for hours, mijo." Ricky squeezed even harder.

"Are you sure you could, Papito? I'm slowly learning how to be a bad ass bottom, you know." Juan laughed.

"Bad ass bottom? Where did that come from?" Ricky just smiled coyly. And worked Juan's cock a little more. "Have you been taking lessons from Raphael?" Ricky cackled.

"I'm sworn to secrecy, Papito. Just ... enjoy ... okay?" Juan shook his head in amusement. Then, since he was ready to come himself, he decided to wrest control back from his 'bad ass bottom.' He reached down and squeezed each nipple sucker at the same time he aggressively pumped Ricky's bottom.

"Dios Mio, oh god, oh god," Ricky cried as he exploded through his cage all over his abs and chest. Juan joined him, pumping his load into his leather boy, thrust after thrust. After thrust. While Ricky still moaned, Juan pulled free and bent down to lick Ricky's offering from his glistening abs. Which only made Ricky moan more. Juan trailed his tongue up Ricky's abs to his left nipple first, pulling the sucker off with his teeth, then the right. Then he bathed each nipple in a moist, Ricky scented kiss, causing Ricky to shiver. Finally, Juan found Ricky's lips, where they shared the remnants of Ricky's offering in a long, deep kiss.

"I love you, Papito," Ricky said, as he always did, when Juan broke the kiss.

"Love you more," Juan replied. He placed a hand in the middle of Ricky's chest and stood, and looked down on his very own World's Best Locked Cock Leather Boy. He slowly sighed, then walked away to the lavatory to prepare a couple of steamy, sudsy cloths to cleanse his most prized possession. When he returned, Ricky, eyes closed, was slowly rocking his head in time with the music. He looked up and smiled when Juan began swabbing his abs.

"Mijo, you like the music?"

"Mmmm. It's nice. Why?"

"I just wondered. I bet you're a good dancer." Ricky scoffed a laugh. "Maybe we should have danced for Hiroshi at our wedding after all." Ricky's smile faded, just for an instant, then returned even brighter.

"Yeah, maybe. I want to see *you* dance, Papito."

"No, you don't." Ricky's smile turned just a bit mischievous. Juan had worked his way up to Ricky's chin with the wash cloth, which he used to wipe the smile off Ricky's lips. "Whatever you're thinking ... whatever you're planning, just forget it. Right now." Juan grinned, in spite of himself. He reached up and released each wrist restraint.

"Not that I'm complaining," Ricky rubbed his arms, "but this didn't seem like a training session. Great sex, you know, but we didn't really do anything new." Juan squatted down to Ricky's level and laid his hand on Ricky's chest. He lovingly brushed each nipple, eliciting the desired shivering response. Ricky turned his head to face Juan. "Not that I'm complaining ..." Juan laughed under his breath.

"What were you expecting, mijo?"

"I don't know, Papito." He held Juan's gaze a few seconds. "Wherever you take me, I'll follow. That's one of the best things about us. The surprises." He reached around and dug his fingers into Juan's mane and pulled his face closer. Juan didn't resist, and cupped the back of Ricky's shaved head with his own hand, guiding them into another long, deep kiss.

"How's this?" Niki laid the document next to Ryan's mug and turned to pour his own cup of coffee before sliding onto a stool at the island next to him. Ryan read it aloud:

"'In celebration of a very successful conclusion to another grueling semester, you are invited to join a very select group of admirers to congratulate the recipients of their respective Dean's List honors.

"'Time – Monday at Six P.M.

"'Place – Dining Room of the House of the Locked Cock Brotherhood

"'Attire – Black Tie Optional.'" Ryan slid the proof over to Niki.

"Cute," he smiled. "Bonus points for the calligraphic font."

"Well," Niki averred, "it's kind of my thing. Everyone deserves to get a formal invite now and then. Have you talked to Mateo?"

"Yeah, he's pumped. He's proud of both of us."

"We've all been working hard ... not just you and me. We're overdue for a celebration. Besides, it's kind of the holiday season, anyway." Ryan nodded, a little wanly. Niki noticed. "Hey, Ryan, are you a little homesick? Do your parents want you to come home during break?" Ryan looked down at his mug before meeting Niki's gaze.

"Do you think I should? I know they'd like to see me. But ..." Niki gave Ryan a 'but what?' look. "I don't want to leave Mateo here alone." Niki shook his head as he ruffled Ryan's hair.

"Ryan, use that four point oh noggin. Take Mateo with you."

"But Ricky needs him here. Besides my parents ..." Niki cut him off.

"Ryan, we're on break. I can fill in for Mateo at the Headquarters. If your parents want to see you, just let them know you and Mateo are inseparable."

"You'd do that?" Niki nodded firmly. "Okay, I'll ask. Thanks. You're the best ... brother." Ryan leaned over to deliver a cheek kiss.

"Hey, no biggie, Ryan. It'll be fun for me. I'll do the shifts as Pup Niki." Ryan snorted.

"Of course you will."


"Look at all this," Raphael said as he and Luke led Alex and Greg into the dining room. He turned to Alex. "Kinda nice having someone else take charge, don'tcha think?"

"One hundred percent," Alex agreed. Niki and Ryan had covered all the bases. The good china, candles, bottles of Schramsberg chilling on the sideboard. Juan and Ricky appeared next and stole the show. Each was wearing a black bow tie, offering a bit of a Playboy vibe. As they found their seats, Steve came through the butler's pantry and began opening the wine. Before he finished filling ten flutes, distributed by Alex, since his seat just happened to be closest to the ice bucket, Niki, Ryan and Mateo arrived with platters and bowls they placed down the center of the table. They sat, then Steve took his seat and raised his flute.

"To our scholars," he said looking first at Niki then Ryan, "and to tonight's chef. We celebrate you." He nodded to Mateo. 'Cheers' sounded around the table.

"Dean's list, huh?" Alex said, smiling at Ryan.

"Well," Ryan confessed, "it hasn't come out yet, but with four point ohs, we know we'll be on it." He gave Niki a knowing look. Niki nodded.

"And how much credit do *we* get?" Alex asked. Raphael laughed.

"Well," Ryan played along, "fifty percent of one of five classes, would be ... ten percent. Actually, I'm the one who compiled and delivered the presentation, so ... two percent." Greg turned to Alex.

"Sorry you asked?"

"Nope," Alex confidently replied. "So, what are we eating?"

"Salbutes and panuchos," Mateo eagerly answered as he pointed. "Dese are turkey, dese are pork and dose are vegetarian. Don' forget to add salsa and squeeze some lime."

"We asked Mateo to prepare some traditional Yucatecan dishes for us," Ryan explained as he handed the bowl of black beans to Raphael.

"Because ...?" Raphael prodded.

"Because my next project is going to focus on the peoples of the Yucatan," Ryan dryly replied. "And because I'm taking him home with me to visit my parents. This is a dry run for the dinner to impress that we'll be making when we're there."

"They'll be impressed," Steve waved his napkin toward Mateo. "This is excellent, Mateo." Mateo beamed.

"You've been holding out," Juan agreed. He tousled Mateo's mane.

"Gracias," Mateo gave Juan a shy, grateful smile.

"And, you, Niki," Raphael raised his flute Niki's way. "I know it sounds repetitious, but I've always been proud of you." He turned to Juan. "At this rate, you'll be giving Juan stiff competition for Nurse of the Year in no time."

"Yeah, well," Juan glanced at Raphael as he raised his puffy tortilla to his lips, "be careful what you wish for. Or you might end up in New York in the middle of a pandemic." Everyone got the not-so-self-deprecating joke and laughed. Then he turned his gaze to Niki. "Seriously, we're all proud of you. Both of you." He laid his *salbut* down and leaned back as he patted his lips with his napkin. "To be honest, everyone here is accomplished in his own way. I'll admit, I've probably been taking all of this ... and every one of you ... a little for granted, after living together so long. What are the odds that ten guys could live together this happily ... this successfully, for this long and still be friends?"

"Easy," Niki replied, looking a bit intense. "We're not *friends*. This isn't officially the House of the Locked Cock Brotherhood in name only. We're brothers. We're family. Ryan called me brother just the other day. He meant it. Families, like ours, endure. No matter what." He tilted his face toward his plate, but looked up from the tops of his eyes for Juan's reaction.

"You're right, future Nurse of the Year," Juan met his furtive gaze. "And with the house next door binding us all together, I guess divorce would be out of the question. No matter what."

"About that ..." Greg changed the subject. "Peter called." Alex did a spontaneous drum roll on the edge of the table. "We may be three point two five millionaires in a couple of weeks." Steve drained his flute and set it down.

"So ... they didn't counter?"

"As I understand it," Greg continued, "their lawyer agreed with Peter's real estate attorney friend, who's been assisting him, assisting us, that if we put it on the market, other buyers would undoubtedly bid it up, by hundreds of thousands. Or more. They agreed it was, what Raphael called, a fair price. More than fair, since it's less than we would otherwise get. Peter jokingly referred to it as the company discount, since the three of you work together."

"Plus, we don't have to pay commission to a realtor," Luke pointed out.

"Best of all," Raphael widely grinned, "we get to choose our neighbors. Neighbors who are cool with naked men in the garden." He turned his grin to Juan. "Especially tall, swarthy naked men with mustaches." Juan, chewing away, just shook his head.

"So, what's next?" Niki asked.

"Lots of paperwork for the attorneys, mostly," Greg replied. "Inspections to satisfy their bank. The usual. It could be more than two weeks. We'll see. Oh. Peter said they're considering a separate purchase agreement to buy out most of Hiroshi's furniture. Kind of like how we adopted all of Ben's stuff. Except we'll get paid for it. Enough to pay off Peter and his attorney, plus some."

"And this, my friends," Alex professed, "is how the rich get richer." He caught Niki's eye. "I mean, brothers."

"So then, what?" Ricky looked at the smiling faces around the table. "We can't really touch the money. Right?"

"Good point, Ricky," Greg replied. "Following Hiroshi's wishes, we said we'd use the proceeds to buy this house when and if the opportunity arises. We need to memorialize that, if in fact, that's what we want to do. Peter can manage that for us. Meanwhile we should invest it appropriately. We don't have a timeline, and," he looked at Steve, who was as attentive as everyone else around the table, "we don't know if Ben will ever agree to sell. But ... but, if and when he does, I guess it's my job to make sure our proceeds have appreciated as much as possible. Not an easy ask in an economy battered by a pandemic."

"Like Juan sort of said," Luke smiled at Greg, "each of us here has our talents. I, for one, trust our millions with you." Several heads nodded. Steve rose and walked over to the sideboard to open the second bottle of bubbly. This time he sat, poured into Niki's flute, then his own, and passed the bottle to Greg.

"Just make sure there's a line item for sparkling wine, Greg," he advised. "This family likes to celebrate just about everything." He turned his smile to Niki. "Including potential valedictorians and Nurses and Anthropologists of the Year."


"Alex," Raphael asked, sharing a bench with him, each doing biceps curls, "when was the last time you wore one of your work polos?" Alex grunted through two more final reps before turning to Raphael to answer.

"Umm, I don't remember. Why?" Raphael grinned.

"I think you should try one on." When Alex continued to stare at him wordlessly, Raphael reached over and squeezed Alex's right biceps. "Hasn't Greg said anything?" Alex furrowed his brow. "Alex, maybe you need to clean the mirror in your bath. You're beefing up, dude. As your unpaid trainer, I'm taking half the credit." A smile slowly grew on Alex's lips.

"You think? I mean ... I thought maybe it was just wishful thinking, but in the shower ..."

"Alex, your dancer's bod is safe, for now at least, but yeah ... you've gained." Raphael's self-satisfied smile broadened, causing Alex's cage to grow heavier. "Have you been upping your protein intake like we talked?"

"A little, nothing major. I guess." Alex looked down at his cage, resting between his thighs. Maybe they did look a little beefier. Raphael reached over and squeezed the right one.

"Tomorrow, let's concentrate on your back, okay?" Alex nodded wordlessly, still reveling in Raphael's praise, even though it was, in part, self-congratulatory. Not that Raphael didn't deserve the credit. He had proven to be one hell of a slave driver at times. Thankfully.

"If you want, we could start measuring you ... documenting your progress."

"Would there be rewards along the way?"

"You mean besides posting pics online showing Alex the Caged Boy's progress to all his Instagram fans?" Alex laughed.

"No thanks. I could never compete with most of those guys."

"Oh, so you still look at online erotica? I knew it!"

"Of course. I look. Once in a while, anyway. And thanks to you and your Thunderplug, I still get *some* satisfaction from it." He looked into Raphael's eyes and sighed. "I have to rely on Greg for total satisfaction, like you do with Luke. Which is all for the best, really." Raphael winked.

"Yeah. I haven't jerked off since Luke caged me. I can honestly say I don't miss it." He gazed wordlessly at Alex for a few seconds. "In fact, the idea seems childish. Maybe even dumb now." Alex gave another short laugh.

"I guess you're right. Onanism is so déclassé." Raphael bowed his head in agreement and rose to rack his dumbbell.

"Race you the showers, stud ..."

New Year's Eve, on the cusp of the year 2022, was another subdued celebration in the House of the Locked Cock Brotherhood. Even more so with Ryan and Mateo away. It was nice, a tasty dinner with bubbly, of course. But between the continuing constraints of the pandemic and the empty chairs for Ryan, Mateo and Hiroshi, it didn't feel all that festive.

A marker, but not a very special occasion. There were plenty of people out celebrating in bars, mostly outdoors in jam-packed parklets, but as both Juan and Niki insisted, it was still too soon. Omicron had supplanted Delta as the dominant variant, and it was even more transmissible. America, and the world, simply couldn't catch a break. Little did they know when they bid good riddance to 2020, that 2021 would bring even more pain. And overwhelming grief. All everyone wanted from 2022 was some kind of semblance of normal. And not some stupid 'new normal.'

A harbinger of their new normal arrived early the next day, January 1, 2022, when the doorbell rang, taking everyone by surprise. Innocently enough, Luke, who'd been sitting in the kitchen with Raphael and Alex, opened the door to find Cynthia and Patricia smiling at him. They looked him up and down before Patricia held out a woven basket covered with a gingham cloth.

"Hello there," she grinned. "We're your new neighbors and we wanted to say Hello! And Happy New Year." Luke reached out for the basket as Raphael and Alex walked up.

"Happy New Year, Patricia ... Cynthia," Raphael said as he joined Luke, while Alex held back just a bit.

"Oh come on, Alex," Cynthia called over Luke's shoulder. "We'll be seeing you like this sooner or later, and quite often, I'm sure. Might as well make it sooner, dear." Alex stepped up beside Raphael and automatically put an arm around Raphael's waist.

"Happy New Year," he said meekly. Then more naturally, "Aren't we supposed to be the ones welcoming *you* to the neighborhood with treats?"

"You certainly may," Cynthia smiled, "but we wanted to show our gratitude for finding us our new home." She glanced at Patricia. "We don't officially move in until Monday, what with the holiday, but since the house is furnished, we decided, at the last minute, to spend the first night of the new year here." She glanced again at Patricia. "And apparently to try out our new ovens." Raphael reached over and lifted the cloth.

"Mmmm. Scones," he said as he sniffed. "Still warm. So, you really baked them?"

"Miss British Bake Off here did, yes," Cynthia replied. "I do the clean-up. There are both blueberry and currant in there. Enjoy, gentlemen. Again, Happy New Year." She took Patricia's hand and began to turn toward the steps.

"Can we invite you in for coffee ... and scones?" Alex called out.

"We'll take a rain check," Cynthia said from the top step. "You know where to find us." Patricia smiled over her shoulder as she kept in step with Cynthia.

"Well," Luke said as he closed the door and handed the basket to Raphael. "Now that we've gotten that out of the way."

"Sir?" Raphael asked as he led the three of them back into the kitchen.

"Full frontal nudity with your boss," Luke answered. "And her wife." Raphael placed the scones in the center of the island and pulled the basket out of the coffee maker to start a fresh pot. He turned and spread his arms, striking a pose.

"Can you think of a better way to start your day? Not to mention a new year?" Luke moved around the island to wrap his arms around Raphael's apparently very proud torso.

"No, baby, I wouldn't want to start the year any other way. However ... as for your boss ..."

Alex, already seated at the island, mumbled something through his mouthful of scone. When both Raphael and Luke gave him questioning looks, he quickly chewed and swallowed.

"I said, they knew what they were getting into. Moving in next door. We made that clear from the first meeting." He took a sip of coffee. "I think," he cocked his head, "Cynthia and Patricia are a lot more open-minded than their demeanor might suggest." Raphael took a seat opposite Alex while he waited for the coffee to finish brewing.

"Are you saying they might be ... kinky, too?"

"I'm not ready to go that far, yet," Alex smiled, "Maybe we should have included the dungeon when we showed them the house." Raphael choked on scone.

"Morning," Ricky chirped as he entered from the back stairs. Juan followed. He lifted the cloth on the basket while Ricky poured their mugs of coffee.

"Your fan club delivered these just moments ago," Alex said. "We tried to get them to hang around until you made an appearance." Juan pretended he didn't understand and gave Alex a look that begged a question he didn't feel a need to verbalize. "Cynthia and Patricia baked and delivered 'em." Juan took a seat, and was immediately joined by Ricky, along with their two mugs of coffee.

"I'm still not buying this story of yours." He lifted a scone to Ricky's lips first, then to his own. "Mmmm ... yummy." Ricky nodded.

"It's a good thing we slept in," Ricky said. "If we'd done our usual gazebo breakfast ..." He gave Juan a silly look. Juan asked another word-less question.

"Papito, if they'd seen you and me in the garden, you know, they'd be too distracted to bake these for us." Juan snorted.

"Have your fun, guys. So, they've already moved in?"

"Almost," Luke explained. "They wanted to spend New Year's Eve in the house. Moving day is Monday."

"Hey!" Raphael took the floor. "Let's invite them over for pancakes tomorrow. She said they'd take a raincheck." He looked around the island for reactions. "Ricky can cook and the tall man with a mustache can serve." Juan tossed his napkin at Raphael.

"You really want your boss to have a naked pancake breakfast with us?" Juan seriously asked, still not buying it. Raphael folded Juan's napkin then leaned toward Juan, reflecting his seriousness.

"If you'd asked me that a year ago, I'd have said ... of course not. But here we are. I think they're up for it. If they seem uncomfortable, best to find out now." He glanced at Ricky who looked worried. "Not that we're ever going to change anything. Like Alex said. They. Were. Warned." Ricky looked sideways at Juan with a grin and picked up his scone.

If Cynthia and Patricia were the least bit put off breakfasting with eight naked men, half of them in chastity cages and various other artifacts of submission, they didn't let it show. Indeed, they appeared to enjoy breakfast immensely, praising Ricky's pancakes as well as Alex's skill as a barista. Maybe it was too soon in the neighborly relationship, or perhaps due to the fact that Raphael and Alex were also employees, but the topic of the dress code in the House of the Locked Cock Brotherhood never actually came up. Instead, Cynthia and Patricia peppered everyone except Raphael and Alex, initially, with getting to know you questions. Drawing Niki out on his current studies and future ambitions. Encouraging Juan to talk about his experience in New York, something no one else had had much success in doing. Getting the lowdown on LCB Headquarters from Ricky. And now that so much was literally out in the open, getting Raphael and Alex to provide a little more detail about the dance contests that had raised so much money for the Trevor Project. Money that had been matched by the company. The story was so rich, Luke, Greg and Ricky eagerly took part in telling some of it. Maybe they were just being nice, but Cynthia and Patricia genuinely seemed fascinated.

After breakfast ended, which had gone so long it qualified as brunch, Cynthia and Patricia thanked everyone profusely and stood, prompting everyone else to stand.

"Would it be all right," Cynthia asked, "if we take Hiroshi's route through the garden and the secret gate?" The compassion and understanding in her eyes were unmistakable. Raphael met her gaze and slowly smiled.

"It's ... uh ... your route now. By all means. This way." He led them through the butler's pantry into the kitchen and beyond. When he returned to the kitchen everyone but Ricky was bussing dishes, loading the dishwasher and scrubbing the griddles. As chef, Ricky was exempt from clean up. He was sitting at the island, enjoying the fact that, this being a holiday, he didn't have to rush off to the Headquarters.

"That was amazing," he said to the room. Niki looked at him, inviting elaboration. "You guys must have the coolest boss in the entire universe." Raphael walked over to Alex and draped an arm over his shoulders to include him in his response.

"Yeah, we know. Why do you think we talked them into buying Hiroshi's house? We knew what we were doing, right Alex?" Alex exhaled a burst of pent-up breath.

"Sure. We totally knew what we were doing." He looked at Ricky and rolled his eyes. Then shook his head. And laughed.

"What's so funny?" Raphael asked. Alex turned to Raphael.

"I just realized. Remember when you dared me to show up at work in that toga? Or totally naked? Your 'I will if you will' dares? Had I only known ..." Raphael briefly pressed his lips to Alex's.

"All in good time, Alex." He turned to Ricky and flashed the Cheshire grin.

# Twenty-Two

⚬

# EXCEEDING EXPECTATIONS

"It's been some time since we last sat in a dining room that comfortably seats twelve." Patricia poured steaming water into Hiroshi's iron teapot. "In a private residence, no less." Cynthia gave a short laugh.

"Or even in a restaurant. This damn COVID. But, yes, the boys do have a magnificent house." She assembled the tea fixings on the tray, then followed Patricia and Daisy into the living room. She placed the tray on the coffee table and sat, turning to Patricia.

"A magnificent house," Patricia agreed. "With an extraordinary dress code," she smirked as she poured tea with one hand and milk with the other. Cynthia stirred her cup and took a long sip before responding.

"Were you bothered?"

"By the dress code? Not at all. A little amused, perhaps. But it's not like they were flaunting it. It seems quite ... natural for them." Cynthia nodded.

"I dare say at this point, wearing clothes is what is most unnatural to them. Especially with almost everyone working from home." She sipped again. "They really are totally unabashed. In an odd way, it's disarming." They sat quietly for a moment, sipping, Patricia stroking Daisy behind the ears, until Daisy stood up and sauntered off to explore.

"This house, our house, is rather magnificent, too, Cyndi," Patricia smiled. "Daisy can't get enough of all this room. Not to mention her new garden." Cynthia leaned back, placed her arm on the top of the sofa, and stroked the back of Patricia's hair.

"Yes. We have more room than we know what to do with."

"You know what we should do?" Patricia brightened and turned to face Cynthia, who shook her head. "We should throw a party. A housewarming. Invite everyone that we haven't been able to see in years." Cynthia's eyes widened in disbelief. "With proof of vaccination, of course. Masks optional. Wait! That's it! A costume party, so masks won't seem at all out of place." Cynthia picked up her cup again and sipped, considering Patricia's proposal.

"Better yet," Cynthia suggested, "proof of a booster shot. Not everyone has been willing to get one. Maybe we can incentivize them." She paused a moment, her enthusiasm growing. "To give them time, we could make it a Valentine's Day party. It will be warmer then, so we may be able to coax people into the garden, at least some of the time. I wager our ingenious Alex could put together a stunning garden party for Valentine's. What do you say?" Patricia puckered her lower lip in the way that always signaled an impending, and no doubt impertinent, pronouncement.

"Not just Alex, dear. What if ... oh, everyone will be delirious." Cynthia tilted her head, much like Daisy might do. "What if we get some of the boys to work the party as servers. Naked! Especially the ones in chastity. Cynthia, they'll be talking about this party *for years*!" Cynthia set her cup down and placed a hand on Patricia's knee.

"Patty, I don't think we should do that. What with sexual harassment suits being all the rage these days, after all. Darling, I'm their superior. Corporately speaking, that is." Patricia stared silently at Cynthia a moment before defending her proposal.

"How could they possibly assert harassment after hosting us for breakfast, naked? Wearing sexually explicit do-dads! They just told us Alex and Raphael performed strip-tease in front of hundreds of other men. You didn't make them do that. Did you?" Cynthia half-smiled and shook her head. "We simply have them sign a waiver, saying they will willingly participate in the party. Their attorney friend Peter can make it official." She ruffled the top of Daisy's head, who had returned for another dose of affection. "They can always say no. But, if we sweeten the offer with a promise of also making the party another fundraiser for the Trevor Project, I wager they'll say yes."

"You want to ask our friends to pay money to attend a party?"

"A Valentine's Day housewarming, philanthropic happening. Donations optional. Which we will match, to encourage full participation. If we had the Chippendales perform, who among them would not be pressing money into their G-strings? What I'm proposing is much more tasteful. Wouldn't you agree?"

"Tasteful? They won't even be wearing G-strings." Patricia gave Cynthia a challenging look.

"I'll ask them," she pressed. "I'll tell them it's my idea. Which is true! I'll keep you out of it in case they are reluctant to say no to you." Cynthia heaved a sigh of surrender.

"Very well." She looked down at Daisy a moment then back into Patricia's eyes. "My god, it would be hard to top, wouldn't it?"

"You're kidding," Greg said, after Raphael and Alex shared Patricia's request with him and Luke. The four of them were lounging in Greg and Alex's room after dinner. They hadn't said anything to anyone else yet.

"Isn't that kind of demeaning?" Luke asked. "To be servants at their party. A party you weren't invited to? Naked?"

"That's one way to look at it," Raphael replied. He glanced at Alex. The two of them had debated the idea before approaching Greg and Luke. "As for the naked part ... of course we'd be naked. We always are. Alex and I have talked, and ... by the way, Sir ... who forced us to perform naked in front of a room full of strangers the first time? Hmmm?" Luke gave a Greg a sidelong glance but said nothing. "How would this be so different?" Luke looked pointedly at Alex.

"You weren't supposed to be naked that first time, baby."

"Hey, don't make this about me," Alex defended. Greg gave him an 'oh yeah?' look. "Well, nobody told me I needed to wear a jock, dammit!"

"Anyway ..." Raphael continued, "Patricia said Cynthia doesn't want us to do it if we feel at all pressured. But if Ricky and Niki are up for it ... and you know they will be ... we'll raise more money for the Trevor Project. And that's a good thing."

"So now you're taking dares from your boss and her wife," Luke seemed to relent. "I feel so. Abandoned."

"It's not a dare, per se, Sir." Raphael looked down at his cage pensively, for a moment, then back up into Luke's eyes. He sighed. A broken sigh tinged with lingering grief. "It's been a while, hasn't it?" His voice dropped almost to a whisper. "For a dare." Luke moved closer and wrapped his arms around Raphael.

"When you're ready, baby, I'll have a dare for you. It just hasn't seemed like a good idea. Yet." Raphael nodded and buried his head in the crook of Luke's neck. Alex looked over at Greg, eyes misting. Greg bravely smiled.

Patricia had no idea what she was getting herself into. The easy part was recruiting the servers. Ricky and Niki eagerly agreed, motivated by the opportunity to raise more money for the Trevor Project. What she hadn't counted on was Alex's ability or, more accurately, his compulsion to take charge of an event. It didn't take her long to realize her wisest course of action would be to sit back, listen to Alex, nod along with Raphael at appropriate times and then, if she dared, take credit later for what would be a housewarming to remember. She did get to suggest a trusted caterer, so that was something.

Despite Valentine's Day falling on Monday, the party would be a Sunday afternoon affair, starting at three, while still warm and light out. The guest list would number between twenty and thirty women, so Alex suggested having the gate open, to encourage guests to wander back and forth between both gardens. The gazebo would undoubtedly be a draw. The suggested theme for costumes would be 'lovers,' of course, in keeping with the Valentine's Day timing, but any and all costumes would be welcome.

"So, you're going to close the Headquarters on Valentine's Day to serve drinks and appetizers to our neighbors' lesbian friends?" Juan asked Ricky upon learning about the plan. "I would think that could be a busy day for you."

"I hope it will be, Papito," Ricky replied through gritted teeth. He was on his back, on the bench, pressing the most weight he'd yet pressed. Juan, spotting him, had one of his favorite views of his glistening WBLCLB. At total fatigue, Juan helped him lift the barbell into place onto the supports. Ricky sat up and turned to Juan. "Mateo will be ready to go solo by then. He already is. And Ryan offered to be there to help out, so ... no hay problema. Everybody wants to contribute."

"Well, if you say so. I guess I'll just sit up in Mateo and Ryan's room and watch you all perform for the ladies."

"Oh. So, Alex hasn't talked to you yet?"

"Excuse me?" Juan's left eyebrow elevated in surprise.

"Oh, never mind." Ricky stood and started to pull plates off one end of the barbell. Juan didn't move, waiting for Ricky to relent and resume eye contact. Which he did.

"What about Alex?" Ricky racked the plate he'd pulled, then turned to Juan and placed a hand on Juan's still pumped pec. And gently pressed.

"All I know, Papito, is he has something in mind for you. You know, because you're a 'tall man ... with a mustache.'" Ricky giggled at his own joke. Juan shook his head.

"This is getting really old." He tried to sound gruff, but grinned in spite of himself. "I'm not serving drinks to our neighbor's friends. I don't care if it is a fundraiser." Ricky shook his head and toyed with the ring in Juan's right pec.

"I think Alex has something else in mind. I shouldn't have said any-thing." He leaned up, demanding a kiss to prevent any further discus-sion. He held the kiss long enough to ensure it. He broke free and began pulling another plate off the barbell. Juan, sensing the conversation was over, for now at least, pulled plates from the other end. Ricky then took his hand and led Juan upstairs to their shower.

Juan waited throughout dinner that evening for Alex to broach the subject of Patricia's party, but it didn't come up unprompted. So, Juan prompted. He figured several around the table knew more than he did.

"Alex," Juan said as Alex took the last swig from his wine glass, "I hear you're planning another special event." Alex's eyes fluttered. "Is there anything I should know?" Ricky catching Alex's gaze, mouthed 'sorry.' Alex closed his eyes and took a breath before looking up, first at Raphael for support, then Juan.

"It's no big deal, really. Tell me what you know." Juan did.

"That's really all it is," Alex smiled, somewhat convincingly. "A house warming. Also, a costume party, in part thanks to COVID." At that, he picked up his empty glass and pretended to sip again.

"And?" Juan patiently pursued. Ricky grimaced at Alex.

"I kinda said something about ..." Ricky muttered. Alex reached up and ruffled his own locks. He sighed and met Juan's gaze.

"Juan, sweetheart, baby ..." chuckles erupted around the table. "Didn't I get you the role of a lifetime in the *House of Francisco*? You were fabulous, baby!" The chuckles became hoots and cheers as Juan looked up at the chandelier, fearing what was to come next. Clearly Juan was out numbered, regardless of what Alex had in mind. Juan sat back and folded his arms in a classic, defensive listening posture. He'd already decided how he would respond to any proposal from Alex. After taking a deep breath, Alex spelled out his concept for a short performance to cap Patricia and Cynthia's housewarming. Raphael, Greg and Ricky were the only others who knew about it. When he finished, Alex stared at Juan, daring him to say no. Niki reached over Luke and patted Raphael on the shoulder, grinning. Greg gave Juan a 'wish I could be you' look. Juan glanced at Ricky, who was, of course, beaming. He returned his gaze to Alex and tried to look unimpressed. Alex held his gaze. "Juan," he quietly said, "you could double the donations to the Trevor Project. Easily." Juan, holding Alex's gaze, slowly shook his head.

"You bastard," he said, then smiled. He glanced over at Niki, doing a happy dance in his chair. "But can I wear a codpiece? I've never been on display in front of a house full of lesbians before. There may be shrinkage." That prompted more laughter all around.

"I was thinking the bodysuit," Alex allowed. "Francisco is, and always will be, a man of mystery." He met Raphael's smiling gaze again before giving Juan a sincere look of gratitude. "Thank you, Juan. It'll be fun. You'll be great. And it's all for a good cause."

The day before Valentine's Day would forever be remembered as a day of exceeded expectations. Due, in no small part, to curiosity to see Cynthia and Patricia's new home, turnout exceeded the invite list. More than one 'plus-one' had become 'plus-two.' Then, of course, there was the novelty, after two years, of actually being invited to a party, any party. A costume party at that. Many of the attendees anticipated being the center of attention. Mark Antony and Cleopatra were in attendance. On a more local note, Diego Rivera and Frida Kahlo arrived in splendid, culturally precise dress. Antinous and Hadrian made a grand and believable entrance. As the hosts, Patricia had insisted she and Cynthia appear as the grand salonnières, Gertrude Stein and Alice B. Toklas. It only made sense, she insisted. Cynthia, wisely, quietly assented. Besides, they both knew who the real stars of the show would be, they just didn't know that Alex would exceed even their expectations.

Once a few of the guests had arrived, Raphael entered the living room bearing a tray of bubbling flutes. Naked. Caged. And completely gold-plated from high 'n tight to toe. The buzzing conversation quieted in mid-sentence. Raphael, beaming his best killer smile, approached Cleopatra and offered his tray. Cynthia turned to Patricia, mouth agape. Patricia shook her head, indicating she had not been briefed on this little detail. Before Cleopatra had taken her first sip, Niki, fully coated in gold and silver glitter, entered with a tray of rumaki. With no spot lights, it didn't provide quite the same impact that Ricky had made at the wedding, but he produced a chorus of 'ohs' and 'ahs' nevertheless. A moment later Alex and Ricky entered bearing their trays, Alex in gold, Ricky all aglitter. Since he'd switched some time ago from his inherited Holy Trainer to a KINK3D Cobra cage, it hadn't been possible to illuminate Ricky's cage this time. But, with the glitter, it hardly mattered.

As more guests arrived, whichever of the four bedazzled servants was closest to the door admitted and greeted them, allowing Patricia and Cynthia to mingle and to encourage guests to explore the house and the garden, where Daisy was happily holding court. As soon as everyone had arrived and had been offered at least one serving of food and drink,

Cynthia slipped away and found Alex in the kitchen, receiving a tray of mini-crab cakes from the caterer.

"You are brilliant, Alex. You boys ... all of you ... are stunning!" Cynthia seemed at a loss for words.

"Just wait," Alex coyly smiled as he hoisted his tray. "Let me know when you're ready for the donation appeal later." He winked a golden wink. "We've got that covered, too."

Alex seemed to have it all covered. The gazebo was definitely a draw, once guests found their way outdoors, thanks to the LED light strings he, Greg and Luke had wrapped around the upright posts. He'd even outfitted Daisy with an LED collar of soft pink lights. What he hadn't anticipated was the challenge of just four servers trying to keep up with forty attendees, spread out between two floors and two gardens. It wasn't just the tasty food and bubbly wine that was in demand by the clusters of women chatting animatedly throughout the properties. The servers found themselves captive at times, posing for selfies and answering questions about their gilt and glitter, about their cages and more. The questions were genuine, intelligent, complimentary. And impossible to deflect. They were respectful. A totally different vibe than what Raphael, Alex and Ricky had experienced when performing their striptease in front of hundreds of semi-inebriated horny men. These women weren't titillated, really. They were seeking insight. Most, if not all of them, had close gay male friends, but none had encountered the chastity sub-culture before today. More than one, however, had to wonder if one of their friends was, perhaps, a customer of Ricky's shop on Castro Street.

As the afternoon wore on, the novelty of the decorated servers wore off and the guests invested more of their attention on each other, on their own clever costumes and, of course, on their hosts and their surroundings. The caterer gradually transitioned the offerings from savory to sweet. Once it seemed most had had their fill of bite-sized cheesecakes and vibrantly colored macarons, Patricia sought out Alex.

"Alex, dear, I think this would be a good time for you to reveal your secret plan to solicit the donations. What can I do to help?" Alex handed his tray to Patricia.

"Just invite everyone into the garden, Patricia. We'll be ready in five minutes." He delivered another golden wink, signaled to Niki across the dining room and headed into the living room to corral Raphael and Ricky. As Patricia began moving between clusters of guests, the men slipped quietly out the back door. Ricky headed into the house to fetch Juan, and Alex and Niki ushered the women lounging in the gazebo through the gate and into Cynthia and Patricia's garden. Alex closed the gate. Once Juan and Ricky arrived, Alex plugged in the cord to the spots directed at the other side of the gate that he and Luke had installed earlier in the day. That was Cynthia's cue to make her announcement.

"Friends. Romans. And countrywomen," she began, eliciting laughter and applause, "Lend me your ears. I can hardly think of a better way to warm our new home and to mark what is hopefully a turning point in our battle with a global pandemic. It has been our great pleasure to share food, wine and camaraderie with the most important women in our lives. Patricia and I have missed you! Thank you for your courage in joining us today. We appreciate it, and we most definitely appreciate the effort each of you put forth in meeting the challenges we gave you. Congratulations on getting boosted. San Francisco is leading the nation in vaccination rates and we couldn't be prouder of each of you for contributing to that effort. As for our second challenge, clearly, we are surrounded today by thoughtful representations of some of the most famous ... and notorious ... lovers in history. Well done, everyone, well done." She paused and led the assembled in another round of applause. "And now, it's time for our third challenge. For that, I shall step aside and turn the spotlight over to ..."

As Cynthia moved away from the imperceptible gate and into the group to join Patricia and Daisy at the front of the cluster, the gate swung back into the neighboring garden. It was dark enough now, and the spots bright enough, to fully maximize the glitter and golden skin of the four servers as they filed through the gate and formed a line with space left in the middle. A space immediately filled by a tall, handsome man with a mustache, his swarthy skin and all his admirable features subtly visible beneath a see-through mesh body suit. His long hair fell to his shoulders. And the smile he directed first to Cynthia and Patricia, then to the rest of the assembled, was captivating and infectious. A low rumble flittered among the assembled. Juan cleared his throat.

"Good evening," he began. He'd memorized the appeal Alex had written for him, and for the most part he delivered it as intended. But he adlibbed a bit, too, giving Alex more credit than he'd been willing to claim. "My name is Juan and I want to join Cynthia and Patricia in thanking you for being here today. I hope you have enjoyed the bounty prepared by one very fine caterer and served to you by my husband and my brothers here in Cynthia and Patricia's beautiful home." Applause broke out, interrupting and surprising Juan. Alex glanced across to Raphael. As if they had rehearsed, first they and then Ricky and Niki bowed to the guests in appreciation. Juan laid an arm across Alex's shoulders once he resumed standing. "A couple of years ago this golden boy was inadvertently responsible for initiating a couple of highly successful fundraising efforts for The Trevor Project." Alex gave Juan a surprised look, which Juan deflected without pausing. "He, along with the other beautiful specimens standing with me, raised several thousand dollars, which were generously matched by Cynthia's firm." This time the bedazzled servers led a round of applause directed at Cynthia and Patricia. Cynthia, playing along, raised her clasped hands in a sign of gratitude, as well as victory.

"This evening," Juan continued, "your final challenge is to meet, and perhaps exceed that earlier fundraising effort. You know how important The Trevor Project is. Even here, in the liberal and enlightened San Francisco Bay Area, LGBTQ youth are abused and even turned out by their families every day. As I'm sure you know, the majority of the homeless youth on our streets are queer kids who couldn't remain in their homes and have found their way here. So ... please ... give what you can. There is a red lacquered box on the console table in the entrance hall where you can deposit cash or checks as you depart. If you need any motivation to up your donation just a little, remember ... Patricia and Cynthia will match whatever you give." A few 'whoops' and 'oh-yeahs' burst forth as Patricia turned and embraced Cynthia in what might have been a 'forgive me' hug.

"Oh. One other thing," Juan paused for dramatic effect. "You all look 'mahvelous!'" Laughter and applause broke out again as the servers and Juan headed for Patricia and Cynthia's back door. A moment later they filed out, bearing trays loaded with white and dark chocolate truffles and more bubbly. Not surprisingly, it was Juan who was initially swarmed by guests wanting to meet and thank him. And maybe to get a closer look at what was beneath that mesh body suit. Juan charmed them all in return. It was easy, actually. He just kept thinking of himself as Francisco. Meeting the unsuspecting doyen of San Francisco society, who had no clue that he was not just a mysterious stranger. But that he was, in fact, a different species entirely. That he was immortal. Alex's acting lessons were paying off again. And Cynthia and Patricia were enjoying the show.

Twenty-Three

⟨◦⟩ — · —————— · — ⟨◦⟩

# "YOU'RE DAFT."

IT WAS LATE AFTERNOON when Niki entered their bedroom, laid his laptop on the bed, and walked up behind Steve, who was finessing a shooting script for an upcoming pre-production meeting. He placed a hand on each of Steve's shoulders, pressing his thumbs into the sides of Steve's neck, and began to massage. Steve sighed and rolled his head back and forth gratefully. He let Niki apply his welcome touch for a few moments before logging out and spinning the chair around to face him. Niki sat on the edge of the bed and smiled. Steve reached out and laid his hands on Niki's thighs and squeezed.

"That was nice. All ready for your test tomorrow?" Niki scrunched his face, then smiled.

"I think so." Steve squeezed again, and looked intently into Niki's eyes.

"Maybe we should touch up your mohawk. For luck. It's been a few days. Busy days." Niki unconsciously reached up and rubbed the stubble on the side of his head.

"Actually ..." He paused before leaning forward and taking Steve's hands in his. "I was thinking, maybe it's time to say goodbye to Pup Niki's technicolor dream 'hawk." Steve looked surprised, but said nothing. "Maybe we could buzz it down to zero. Like I used to wear it." Steve tilted his head in tentative agreement.

"Are we saying goodbye to Pup Niki, too?" Niki's eyes widened and he stood and leaned further forward, putting a hand on either side of Steve's head, and pulling him into a kiss. When he released Steve, he sat back, displaying a confident grin. "I think you're stuck with Pup Niki, Steve. At least once in a while. God, when was the last time I pupped out?" He raised his eyes to the ceiling in thought.

"About a month ago, Niki. Just before Cynthia and Patricia's party, when you and Ryan pupped out for Mateo's birthday."

"Yeah. That was fun." Steve nodded, eyes closed, in agreement. "I just think," Niki sat up straighter, "I'll feel more confident shadowing RNs if I look a little more professional." Steve stood and moved forward, pushing Niki onto his back before crawling on top of him. They kissed again, with Steve in control this time. When they parted, Steve looked down into Niki's sweet, brown eyes.

"You'll be fine, puppy. They'll take to you immediately, mohawk or not. Besides, won't you be wearing a dorky hat, anyway, like Juan does?" Niki laughed and pushed Steve off and to the side. He rolled over to face Steve.

"Dorky? Wait 'til I tell Juan." Steve grimaced and shook his head, silently begging Niki not to. "Juan only wears a cap for surgery, Steve. Staff nurses don't wear caps anymore. When was the last time you saw a nurse?" Steve harrumphed as he slid off the bed and stood.

"I guess that would be when we were Zooming with Mama in the hospital. I could swear the nurses were wearing hats." Niki smiled, but shook his head.

"Whatever. Smarty pants." Steve reached down and offered his hand to pull Niki upright, then jiggled his cage. "Or, smarty cage, I mean. Come on. We should probably have a little ceremony as we say goodbye to the sexiest mohawk this town has ever seen." Niki wrapped an arm around Steve's waist as the two ambled into the bath.


"Patricia, come look." Cynthia was sitting on the couch in the living room, phone in hand. Patricia came through the entry from the den, where she'd been writing belated thank you notes to their housewarming guests. She sat and snuggled up to see what Cynthia was viewing. Cynthia turned her phone toward Patricia and cooed, "Isn't she adorable?" She was watching a video of her niece eating cake on her first birthday. The baby was wearing nearly as much pink and white frosting as she was ingesting.

"Yes. What an adorable ... mess," Patricia noted. "Did Olivia's gift make it across the pond in time?" Cynthia nodded, still watching the short video. When it ended, she put the phone down and turned to Patricia. "Yes, they said it fits and Olivia loves it. You have such good taste in toddler's clothes."

"Actually, I relied on the storekeeper's expertise," Patricia confessed. Cynthia huffed.

"You're wonderful with kids. Always have been." Cynthia looked slyly into Patricia's eyes as she finger-walked up Patricia's arm to her shoulder and toyed with her hair. "We haven't talked lately about ..." She stopped, leaving the rest of her sentence unsaid, but held Patricia's gaze.

"You mean?"

"Yes," Cynthia confirmed. Patricia tilted her head as Daisy wandered up and settled in at Patricia's feet. She began absentmindedly petting Daisy's head.

"Feeling jealous, are we?" Patricia smiled, nodding toward the phone. Cynthia gave a short laugh.

"Not jealous, no. Just ..." She looked away toward the dining room, and the kitchen beyond. "It's just, now that we're in this house. There's never been a better time." She turned back to Patricia. "And one of us is not getting any younger." She paused, giving Patricia time to catch up. "We've talked it through, Patty. We both want a child. And with the pandemic eliminating almost all activities, now would be a perfect time." She gave Patricia's hair a final fluff and folded her hands into her lap. And waited. Patricia gave Daisy one last pat and turned to fully face Cynthia.

"Remind me again. Which of us volunteered to risk stretch marks?" Cynthia laughed again.

"I thought we'd renegotiate, seeing as how we have this big house. And we're both working from home, and will be for the foreseeable future."

"Oh?"

"Darling," Cynthia tilted her head down and eyed Patricia coyly, almost guiltily, "I was thinking we should both get pregnant. That way we can each be a biological mother of one of the children."

"You're daft." Cynthia, enjoying Patricia's reaction, calmly smiled.

"Perhaps. Or am I brilliant? We have the room. We have the time. We've talked it over. And over. This way we get it over with all at once. The morning sickness. The diaper duty. The terrible twos." It was Patricia's turn to laugh.

"You make it sound so easy," she delivered her sarcasm with her own smile. Cynthia sat back and glanced at Daisy before challenging Patricia.

"I made my case. You make yours. Why is this not a brilliant idea?" Patricia took a long, deep breath.

"It *is* a brilliant idea. And scary. I mean, it actually won't be easy, will it?" She stared earnestly at Cynthia. "You want to do it now, don't you? Right. Now." Cynthia closed her eyes and nodded. Then she opened them and reached again for the phone and restarted the video. And handed it to Patricia.

"We could have this, Patty. Times two. Or maybe three. Twins run in my family."

"Oh god!" Patricia laughed again. "Don't say that!" She handed the phone back and exhaled another deep breath. "So, what do we do next? Google sperm banks?" Cynthia shook her head.

"No, actually ... I was thinking we have the ideal sperm bank right next door." Patricia's shriek frightened Daisy, who jumped up and looked around for the suspected intruder.

"You *are* daft! And here I thought you were serious all this time." Cynthia maintained her composure.

"Why not? They're all quite clever. They are loving, kind men. Fine upstanding citizens. Each one of them is superior, I dare say, to anyone who may be donating to a sperm bank. We know them. Admire them. Patricia, we owe this house to them. And with them right next door, the father could easily be involved in each child's life going forward."

"And how do you choose the father?" Patricia, still absorbing Cynthia's proposal, bit her lip. "I mean, if you choose Luke, who certainly has Scottish bona fides ... how will that make Raphael feel? Or Juan. His would be a beautiful baby, but how would Ricky feel? Or Mateo?" Patricia paused a moment, then immediately continued her counter-argument before Cynthia could respond. "Assuming, my dear, that any one of them would agree. I dare say that will be a steep hill to climb."

"You may be right," Cynthia motioned for Daisy to come over and give her a little loving. "I hope not. As for sparing anyone's feelings, I have an answer for that." Cynthia flashed a very satisfied smile, which brought Patricia to her feet. "Where are you going?" At the doorway to the dining room, Patricia turned to respond.

"I think it would be best to be well into a generously poured glass of wine before I hear your answer. While I'm still able to indulge. Assuming I go along with this plan of yours. You really are daft. Shall I bring two glasses?"

"And the bottle," Cynthia replied.


"You like that, don't you?" Ricky ruffled Daisy's head after feeding her another bite of his morning glory muffin. They'd taken to leaving the gate open so Daisy could freely wander between the two gardens, and it hadn't taken her long to become a regular at their Saturday morning breakfasts in the gazebo.

"Just don't let Cynthia or Patricia catch you doing that," Juan knowingly warned, having spied Cynthia approaching.

"Doing what?" she asked, stepping up into the gazebo. Ricky innocently looked up from Daisy.

"She said she was hungry," he grinned. "That you never feed her."

"She eats more than you do, I'll wager," Cynthia smiled as she sat opposite them.

"Would you like some coffee?" Juan asked, starting to stand. Cynthia motioned for him to sit.

"No, thank you. I just stopped over to invite you, all of you, for tea. We haven't properly thanked you for your performances at our housewarming. I know you are all busy. Would this afternoon, or tomorrow be better? Or next weekend? Five o'clock?" Ricky grimaced.

"That would probably work for everyone but Mateo and me. You know, the shop." Juan smiled at Cynthia, then leaned into Ricky.

"When was the last time you got an invitation to tea? Close up early for once." Without waiting for a response, Juan turned back to Cynthia. "This afternoon should work. Can we bring anything?" Cynthia shook her head as she stood.

"Just bring your adorable selves." She stepped down to the ground and snapped her fingers to summon Daisy to follow. She looked back up at Ricky and Juan. "On second thought, you might want to bring a sense of adventure." She smiled and walked toward the gate, with Daisy at her side.

"A sense of adventure?" Ricky asked as he picked up his mug. "What do people usually serve with tea, Papito?" Juan shook his head as he lifted his own mug.

"Scones? Little cakes? And maybe a game or two? I guess we'll find out, mijo."

"Is it high tea or low tea?" Alex asked. Juan and Ricky were making the rounds, informing everyone of that afternoon's 'adventure.'

"I don't know," Juan replied. "What's the difference?"

"Alex only attends high teas," Greg replied. For only a second, Juan thought he was serious.

"Just in case, we should dress," Alex continued, ignoring Greg's sarcasm, as usual. "Like we did for Ryan's parents. No tuxes or anything." Juan laughed.

"That's good. My tux is at the cleaners." He saw the look on Alex's face. "Oh. You're serious. Really?"

"Inviting someone to tea is a big deal, Juan," Alex contended. "You can go in one of your leather outfits if you want. They'll probably get a kick out of that. I'm wearing a suit. And a bow tie, the same one I wore to the company party. This is about as festive as things are going to be for the foreseeable future." He headed for the closet, already in costumer head space.

"I guess I'd better warn everyone else," Juan sighed as he headed for the door. He caught up with Ricky in Mateo and Ryan's room and shared Alex's request.

"Will we have time? To dress?" Mateo asked. Normally he and Ricky wore sweats on their way to and from the shop to cover their minimalist uniforms.

"Yeah," Ricky assured him. "We'll close at four-thirty, maybe earlier if no one's in the shop." He grinned at Ryan. "Ryan can be your dresser. We'll be fine."

They were fine, time wise, and they looked fine, too. Alex, in a suit, sported the green bow tie he'd worn to the last company holiday party, back when companies had holiday parties. Gamely taking a cue from Alex, Raphael wore dress pants and his own party bow tie, with one of the locked cock dress shirts Luke had ordered for him as part of a dare. Ryan had dressed Mateo exactly as he'd appeared when Ryan's parents delivered him to the House of the Locked Cock Brotherhood. Everyone else wore variations of business casual. Polos, button downs and khakis for the most part, along with Luke's pinstripe kilt. Just to pimp Alex, Juan wore leather jeans and a leather vest over a dark blue button down. At five o'clock they headed out the front door, rather than take the usual garden route, since, for once, they were wearing clothes. And since this was, according to Alex, anyway, something of a formal occasion.

"Come in, come in," Cynthia greeted them in a pale green dress, cinched at the waist with a darker green belt. Her hair was gathered in a French knot, giving prominence to the tasteful emerald earrings dangling from each lobe. She looked fabulous, which Alex noted wordlessly by giving Juan a 'told you so' look as they passed into the entryway. Before anyone could compliment Cynthia, Patricia stepped into the living room doorway, looking just as stunning in a champagne-colored midi shirt dress with a floral applique at the neck and the hem.

"Thank you for coming on such short notice," Patricia said as she waved everyone into a living room furnished with a few extra chairs. As they began finding spots to sit, she took Cynthia's left hand in hers. "We should take a picture, Cyndi. We may never see them all dressed like this again." Cynthia laughed, along with most everyone else.

"Quite right," she agreed. "From sexy and provocative one minute to handsome and fashionable the next. That's our boys ..." She started for the dining room doorway. "Alex, could you give me a hand with the tea?" Alex jumped up and followed Cynthia. Patricia temporarily took his spot and began small talk, starting with complimenting Juan and Mateo each on their outfits.

"That's Mateo's lucky shirt," Raphael offered. "He wore that the day Ryan's parents met all of us for the first time. They were impressed enough to entrust Ryan into Mateo's capable hands." Patricia nodded as she smiled at Mateo.

"No doubt! Knowing all of you as I do, I'm certain it was an easy decision for them." Cynthia and Alex returned, Cynthia bearing a tray with three tea pots, a creamer and sweeteners. Alex's tray was loaded with twelve stacked cups, saucers and spoons. Patricia rose and headed to the kitchen while Cynthia and Alex began doling out tea on request: Earl Grey, Darjeeling and Chamomile. Before Cynthia had poured the last cup Patricia was back with a three-tiered cake stand loaded with little triangular sandwiches and savory scones. She placed it in the middle of the coffee table and began passing out linen napkins.

"The sandwiches on top are cucumber, below that are salmon and cream cheese, and I made the scones with cheddar and scallions."

"I'll start with a scone," Luke said, reaching in. "I really liked the ones you baked when you first moved in." Niki followed suit, while Steve helped himself to a salmon sandwich. Soon everyone was relatively quiet at first, aside from compliments, as they munched and sipped. Cynthia sipped her tea without eating, while Patricia bit into a scone, exercising a bit of quality control. Cynthia casually looked at each man as they ate, smiling when eye contact was made. She wasn't sizing them up so much as appreciating each of them for their own, unique qualities. Patricia had been right. Choosing one over the others would not just be unfair. It was ... impossible. She rose, picked up the tea tray and returned to the kitchen to refresh the pots. She anticipated at least some in the group might want another cup, maybe even something a bit stronger, once she revealed her true agenda.

"I have a confession," she said as she replaced the tray and sat. Patricia glanced at Cynthia, then sat back and took in the group, ready to gauge their reactions. "We did want to thank you for your phenomenal contributions to our housewarming. Some of them are still talking about it. We also asked you over because we have something important to discuss with you." She paused, nervously anticipating the possible reactions she was about to provoke. Knowing them best, she made brief eye contact with Raphael and Alex, then their husbands. Then Niki, innocently enjoying his second scone. She took a deep breath and proceeded.

"Patricia and I have discussed, for several years now, our desire to have a child."

"Congratulations!" Steve interrupted, assuming the child had already been conceived. Cynthia cleared her throat. Then she gave a small laugh.

"Not quite yet, Steve. But hold that thought." She looked around the group once more. "We are so fond of each and every one of you. We feel very lucky to have you in our lives." She paused as she saw understanding beginning to dawn on a couple of faces, including Greg's, who was making intense eye contact with her. "Yes, Greg. I know it may be presumptuous. Outrageous, perhaps, but you excel in outrageous, do you not?" Ricky looked confused. "Ricky, my dear. We would like to have a child, both Patty and me, with you as the fathers."

"Me?!" Ricky reacted, not quite comprehending. Not that any of them did, yet. Raphael set his cup down and placed both hands on Luke's nearby thigh. They made concerned eye contact but didn't speak.

"Forgive me," Cynthia continued. "I'm not explaining this well. Rather than going to a sperm bank and dealing with ... well, the chances one takes with a total stranger's DNA, Patty and I are proposing that each of us would bear one of your children. Through artificial insemination, of course. A month apart, coinciding with our cycles. Sorry to sound so clinical."

"And so that each of us can care for the other in those initial days in the nursery," Patricia chipped in. Cynthia nodded and placed a hand on Patricia's forearm for support. Greg and Juan, both increasingly wary, made eye contact.

"So ... are you asking Ricky or Greg?" Juan protectively laid an arm across Ricky's shoulders. Cynthia closed her eyes briefly and shook her head. She looked back into Juan's gaze, as endearingly as she could muster.

"Juan, there is no way we could choose one of you." She again made eye contact around the group with everyone but Mateo, who was intently looking down into his lap, intentionally avoiding eye contact. "We would be thrilled to have our children with any one of you. We would like each of you to participate."

"I don't understand," Alex said. "I'm no expert in making babies, but ..."

"Alex ... everyone ... I know this probably sounds crazy, and it is not recommended by the experts, but we are suggesting that each of you contribute to a common donation. And whoever swimmer gets there first will be the father. The biological father. But we would like all of you to participate in the children's lives equally. A father and nine uncles for each child, if you will."

"You're serious?" Steve leaned forward. "I mean, legally, ethically ... this seems very complicated." He sat back up. "Not to mention emotionally." He glanced at Niki, then resumed eye contact with Cynthia. He saw the mix of emotions in Cynthia's face. "I apologize if that sounded harsh."

"It is complicated," Cynthia agreed, shaking off Steve's last comment. "And, maybe outrageous, as I said." Patricia placed a supportive hand over Cynthia's, still resting on her forearm. Cynthia gave a short, uncomfortable laugh. "If we've offended you, please forgive us. Perhaps this seems selfish of us. Asking such a momentous and personal favor of you." Cynthia paused. Patricia stepped in.

"Gentlemen, you don't *have* to do this. If for any reason, and I'm sure there may be many, your answer is 'no,' we will understand, and we will certainly not hold it against you. Ever. This is more than anyone has ever asked of you, I'm sure." She managed a convincingly warm smile. "One or more of you may never want to be a father. Or the father of one of our children." She managed a short laugh of her own. "Whether you say yes or no, nothing between us should change."

"Well," Cynthia countered, "if you say 'yes,' much will change. But, all for the better, I feel. Sitting here, looking at each of you, imagining one of you as the father of my child, is ..." She began to tear up and sniffled. "Sorry," she smiled and blinked away the tears. "It would be a long-awaited dream come true. One that has seemed unattainable for too long." She tried to read the minds of the ten silent men sitting around the now forgotten tea service. Everyone met her gaze; Raphael even smiled gamely. Everyone but Mateo. "Mateo," Cynthia said softly. "Are you okay?" Mateo looked up at last, looking serious and vulnerable.

"'Kay," he replied. When he didn't elaborate, Cynthia pressed him.

"What are you thinking, dear?" she gently asked, hoping to spur more reactions as well. She watched Mateo struggle for an answer, but said nothing more, waiting him out.

"Is just ..." He paused, working up the courage to answer truthfully. "You said ever'one. But ..." He glanced at Juan, then finally made full eye contact with Cynthia. "I am not tall. Not handsome like ..." Patricia let go of Cynthia and was out of her chair and kneeling at Mateo's feet before he could continue.

"My darling, darling Mateo," she took his hands in hers. "Tall men are overrated. As for handsome," she turned to Ryan. "Ryan, what do you say?" Ryan smiled for the first time since Cynthia began her proposal.

"Mateo's not just handsome. He's perfect. He's a Prince."

"A Shaman Prince," Raphael corrected him. Patricia didn't understand the reference but let it go as she released Mateo's hands and sat back, not quite done with him. Meanwhile Cynthia was watching Niki, trying to gauge his reaction to Patricia's encouraging words.

"Yes, a prince," Patricia nodded. "Who wouldn't want a prince for a father?" She refused to let Mateo break eye contact. "I know you are young, Mateo, maybe too young to be a father in your estimation. But my father was about your age when he had me, and he has been a wonderful father. The best." Then, more quietly, "But it will be your decision." She stood and returned to Cynthia's side. Everyone was making eye contact with everyone else, not sure what to say. Cynthia came to their rescue.

"We've given you much to ponder," she smiled before issuing another nervous laugh. "Not to mention ruining your first tea with us, I fear. When you are ready, we can talk about this more. Now, please, eat up. Patricia and I are not ready to be 'eating for two' quite yet."

# Twenty-Four

# THE ELEPHANT IN THE ROOM

GREG CLOSED THE FRONT door after everyone had silently filed in. Niki began automatically unbuttoning his shirt, then realized his cubby already had street clothes in it. He started for the stairs, to undress in his room, when Steve finally broke the silence.

"Luke, do you have any truth serum on hand?" He caught up with Niki and stopped him at the second step.

"Umm ...I think so ..." Luke replied tentatively.

"We do," Raphael confirmed. "Why?"

"I think we should talk, don't you?" Steve looked around. "Honestly. I mean. This is huge, guys. I'd kind of like to know what everyone else thinks."

"Good idea," Juan said, placing a hand on Steve's shoulder as he and Ricky maneuvered past him and Niki on the stairs. After a couple of steps, he looked over his shoulder at Alex. "High tea, huh?" Alex shuddered as if he'd suffered a chill.

A few minutes later Ryan and Mateo were the last ones to climb the stairs to the turret room. Glasses were waiting for them in their usual spots. Luke opened the bottle with a flourish and began pouring once they were seated. As before, the ten of them were assembled in a circle. Comfortably naked. But with each of them not so comfortably contemplating a potentially momentous decision. Luke lifted his glass toward the center of the circle. Rather than offering a toast he simply said, "Who wants to go first?"

"I'll start," Steve spoke, "by saying our next-door neighbors are turning out to be *way* more surprising than I ever would have expected." Several heads nodded while Ricky quietly uttered 'Dios Mio' under his breath.

"This almost feels like a weird dream," Alex said before taking his second sip. He licked his upper lip and continued, "I mean, do you think anything like this has ever happened before? In real life?"

"Probably," Greg replied. "Somewhere, sometime, sure. Maybe not with two mothers and *ten fathers*, but ..." Steve set his glass down.

"Okay, since this was my idea, I'll just say what I'm thinking, then I want to hear everyone's thoughts. I was stunned at first. We all were, I'm guessing. Never in a million years would I have thought we'd be talking about any of us becoming fathers, let alone with Alex and Raphael's boss." At that, Raphael's eyes widened and he slumped into Luke. "Maybe it's the tea talking as much as the truth serum, but I have to say," and he turned, and with his right hand under Niki's chin, gently turned Niki's head until their eyes met. "I have to wonder, now, how amazing it would be to see what kind of child this man might bring into the world." Niki didn't react for a moment, their eyes locked. Then he completely undermined Steve's heartfelt revelation with a simple, short bark. Steve reacted by releasing Niki's chin and looking down at his hands, examining his fingernails for a second, then he looked back into Niki's eyes. "I'm serious. I've always said you have the biggest heart of anyone I've ever known. It's why I fell in love with you. It's why I'll always love you. Now I'm imagining you cradling a little version of you in your arms." Steve really was serious. He rapidly blinked the mist from his eyes.

"Raphael, Alex," Juan took the floor next. "Steve brings up a good point. Do either of you feel pressured to do this because Cynthia is the head of your company?" They gave each other probing looks. Raphael tapped on his lips lightly in thought before meeting Juan's gaze.

"I don't think so," he answered. "I mean, this is bigger than any raise or promotion."

"Hell," Alex chimed in, "it's bigger than any job." He looked between Raphael and Juan. "But, uh, I don't think Cynthia would hold it against us if we said no." He saw Raphael nod. "That's not who she is."

"So, are you thinking ...'no'?" Juan asked Alex. Alex took another sip.

"Umm ... I'm not thinking anything yet," Alex replied. He turned to Greg. "What do *you* think?"

"I'm thinking Steve stole my thunder," Greg smiled. "Alex Junior would probably be pretty cute. A pain in the ass ... but cute."

"Be serious," Alex ignored the back-handed compliment. Greg took a deep breath.

"Seriously? I'm still processing this. There's a lot we don't know. What do they mean 'participate in the children's lives?' Do they mean visitation rights or every day? You know. Changing diapers. Reading bedtime stories. Playing catch. Do they mean financially? Do you know how much it costs to raise a kid today? Especially in this city?"

"Good questions," Raphael said to Greg, still leaning against Luke. "But how do you feel emotionally?" He turned to Luke. "How do you feel?" Luke gave Raphael a knowing smile and cleared his throat.

"Kind of uncertain, but, after what Steve just said, maybe a little less so." Raphael gave Luke a questioning look. "Baby, I've told you before what a wonderful father you would be. When I said it before, it was just because of who you are and how you treat people. But what if it was a real possibility? What Greg said. I can *so* see you reading your baby a bedtime story." He looked over at Alex. "Probably one that Alex wrote. I can see you teaching him or her how to walk. And ride a bike. Then Ricky's scooter. Then how to analyze a database." This time it was Raphael rolling his eyes.

"Uh huh."

"He's right," Niki agreed. "You would be an amazing daddy." Still trying to deflect the praise, Raphael raised his glass in a silent toast to Niki.

"So, it's decided," Ricky announced. "Raphael and Niki will be the daddies and the rest of us will be the uncles." He closed his case by lifting his glass and pretending to take a long draught of truth serum.

"Whoa, Ricky," Alex leaned forward. "Nothing's been decided. Or even discussed, really. Are you saying you don't want to be a donor?" Ricky looked down at his glass, then at Juan, who was intently awaiting his reply.

"No ..." Ricky said tentatively. "I ... I don't know ... I'm thinking of what Patricia said. Maybe I'm too young?"

"Yeah," Mateo quietly concurred. Juan turned to him.

"Mateo. What's really on your mind?" Mateo looked away from Juan and slowly shook his head. Juan pulled back from the circle and crawled over to Mateo. From behind he placed a hand on Mateo's right thigh and shook it. "Come on. You're not too young to be a good father." He chuckled encouragingly. "And you're plenty tall enough." Mateo took a very deep breath without looking at Juan, or anyone else. "Mateo ..." Finally, Mateo turned to Juan.

'Amigo, I am undocumented. What if somethin' happen and I got deported?" The look on Ryan's face tore through several hearts around the circle. Juan was stone-faced.

"Mateo, we would never let that happen," he contended. Mateo gave a short, dismissive laugh. Ryan wrapped both arms around Mateo, leaned his forehead against the side of Mateo's lush mane and swallowed hard.

"The Democrats are in control now," he asserted. "They're going to fix the Dream act. You're not going anywhere, my Prince."

"They better hurry," Mateo half-smiled as he turned to face Ryan. "You know how they are." It wasn't clear who Mateo meant by 'they,' but everyone shared his doubts about the system. Ryan hadn't moved, his forehead now resting on Mateo's. Juan pulled away and rejoined Ricky.

"If we do this," Juan said as he settled into place, "you'd better participate, Mateo. I think Patricia really wants your baby." Ryan laughed in Mateo's face before sitting upright and facing the circle.

"What about you, Ryan?" Luke asked. "You haven't said much." Ryan made a silly face.

"Gee," he began. "I'm kinda busy with school and keeping my Prince, here, happy." He wrapped an arm around Mateo's waist and tugged.

"We're all busy," Luke pressed. "You have your prince and I have my 'baby,' so, besides all that ..." He held eye contact with Ryan while cupping his baby's knee.

"Besides, unlike the rest of you, I'm still living off my parents."

"Huh," Luke replied. "What *would* your parents say?" Ryan laughed.

"I'm guessing my mother would be thrilled to have a grandbaby. Not sure what my dad would think. Probably that I should quit school and get a job to support the kid. Actually, now that I think about it, this is what it must be like, if you were straight, to have your girlfriend say, 'guess what ... I'm pregnant!'"

"I think you can put your worry about support aside," Alex countered. Ryan gave him a doubtful look. "Ryan, we still don't have all the details, but knowing Cynthia and Patricia, you can bet they'll insist on a baby prenup to protect them and us. And the babies. This is all their idea. I'm sure they'll assume all financial responsibility." Ryan nodded slightly and shrugged, tentatively accepting Alex's contention.

"So, you're in?" Luke pressed, smiling half-seriously.

"I don't know," Ryan smiled back. "I'd rather have Mateo's baby." Mateo snickered and shoulder bumped him from the side. Ryan looked at Luke a moment, then asked, "What about you Luke? You're probably their first choice." Raphael flashed Ryan a conspiratorial smile.

"Yeah, Mr. Outlander, Sir," Raphael again leaned into Luke. "Asking all the questions. Let's hear from you. You fit the profile perfectly."

"What profile would that be?" Luke, apparently taken aback, gave Raphael an uncharacteristically stern look.

"You know," Raphael innocently pursued, "you're an Anglo-Saxon from head to toe. Just what the pediatrician ordered."

"Wait a minute," Luke put his glass down and pulled away to confront Raphael. "First of all, I'm not the only one here who fits that profile. More or less." He waived his hand toward Greg, Alex and Steve, sitting near each other, then toward Ryan. "But regardless, Cynthia and Patricia made themselves very clear. They'd love to have any one of our babies. They don't have a *profile* in mind. Quite the contrary." He took a deep breath, maintaining eye contact with Raphael. "So, where did this profile come from, Raphael?" He said 'Raphael' slowly, with emphasis. "Why are you bringing ethnicity into this?" Raphael blinked, but didn't look away. Nor did he respond. "Raphael," Luke said, then realized how harsh he had just sounded and recalibrated. "Baby. Are you thinking they wouldn't love your baby as much as mine?" Niki shifted in place. Luke noticed. He looked around the group that had suddenly become very solemn. He held up his glass and held it high. "Is there an elephant in the room? This is truth serum, remember?" He made a point of looking at Ricky, Juan, Mateo and Niki without lingering on any one of them, then settled his gaze back on Raphael, but he spoke to the room. "Is anyone here thinking of saying no because they're *not white*?" No one knew what to say. No one had ever seen Luke this upset, and certainly never this upset with Raphael, who looked away from Luke and focused on his glass.

He took a deep breath. Without looking up he said, "Sir, that's not fair. I ..." but before he could continue, Niki interrupted.

"Luke's right." All eyes turned to Niki. "I'm thinking of not donating." He shrugged as if it were inconsequential. Luke and Steve shared an instantaneous, silent exchange. Steve pulled Niki's left hand into his own lap and squeezed.

"You gotta be kidding me," Steve said. Niki looked at Steve, his eyes starting to brim.

"Think about it," was all he could conjure.

"Niki," Juan spoke before Steve could. "Has being Black ever been an issue in your classes?" Niki shook his head without looking at Juan. "What about when you helped out at the Headquarters?" Another shake. "How much harassment did Pup Niki get at the bar? Or at puppy school?"

"He was everyone's favorite at BPOS," Steve bragged. "All the pups loved him."

"Same at the bar," Raphael added. "Everyone lined up at *his* station."

"Niki," Juan continued and waited until Niki met his gaze. "You can't let the ignorance and racism of a few other people limit your decisions about how to live your life. I haven't seen you do that before. Why now?" It took a minute before Niki responded.

"Juan ... it wouldn't just be my life."

"You're afraid Cynthia or Patricia would be disappointed if you were a father? Is that what you're thinking?" Luke asked. Demanded.

"That could be an understatement," Niki replied with a sigh, glancing at Luke before looking down.

"Now *you're* not being fair," Luke shot back. "You're judging them unfairly. They said everyone. If they wanted to exclude any of us, they would have let us know, one way or another." He looked around the circle. "Or did I miss something?"

"No. You're right," Juan said calmly. "They said everyone." He glanced at Mateo. "Everyone." Steve was wiping the tears beneath Niki's eyes and muttering into his ear. The glasses were empty. Luke's confrontation, necessary as it turned out to be, had left some feeling drained, even though it was still early evening. Juan proposed shelving the topic for now and offered to treat everyone to takeout in a couple of hours. No one objected and a quick vote for Thai won the day.

After dinner, where there was much discussion, but nothing was decided, Luke was shaving the sides and back of Raphael's high 'n tight from behind, his legs wrapped around Raphael's waist. Raphael was toying with Luke's toes. Uncharacteristically, both were silent. And had been for some time. When Raphael released a long sigh Luke could bear it no longer.

"Baby. Forgive me. Please? I'm sorry."

"Forgiven," Raphael replied without turning. That was it. Just one word. Luke put the razor down, wrapped his arms around Raphael's torso and leaned back against the tile, taking Raphael with him. Raphael didn't resist.

"It's just," Luke began, his lips now near Raphael's right ear, "it really hurts me that you might think my baby could be more desirable than yours. It doesn't even make sense to me. Baby ... Raphael ... you are the most intelligent, most caring, and the most beautiful man I've ever known. And not despite the fact you're Asian American, but probably because of it. Because of the way you were raised by Mama and Pop. Your worth is in your DNA." He lightly brushed his thumbs across Raphael's pierced nipples as Raphael silently breathed, absorbing Luke's thoughts. "Raphael, to me, you're the amazing person you are exactly *because* of who you are. I never thought of it this way before, but I probably wouldn't have fallen in love with you if you looked more like me. Or Cynthia or Patricia. When we met you weren't just this sweet, buff guy. You were you. You were Raphael Malaluan. Beautiful, smart and a little mysterious. With a smile that disarmed me and eyes that pulled me in and never let me go. When I say Cynthia and Patricia would be lucky to have your baby, I'm not saying it to flatter you. I really mean it. I, for one, would be thrilled." Raphael snorted, having sincerely forgiven Luke by now.

"It's out of your hands, anyway, baby. I know for a fact you're going to donate your little swimmers to Patricia and Cynthia." Raphael turned his head as far as he could to try to establish eye contact.

"Oh yeah? Sir?"

"That's right, baby. It's your next dare. You aren't going to let me down now, are you? Or Patricia, or Cynthia?" Raphael snorted again. He pulled free and rolled around to face Luke.

"Hmm, finally ... a dare from you, Sir," Raphael wordlessly stared into Luke's translucent blue eyes a moment. "You know how horny that makes me."

"What should we do about that?" Luke asked, almost seriously.

"I think we should finish up here, and then you should probably fuck my brains out. I got the impression Cynthia and Patricia are on a schedule, so tonight may be our last chance to make out before we have to start saving our 'highly desirable' swimmers for a greater cause."

"Well," Luke grinned, "if you insist. Anything for my baby. And science ... or whatever we're calling it."

Sunday morning, Ryan was cutting oranges in half while Mateo was juicing them, when the doorbell rang. Ryan gave Mateo a surprised look as he laid down the chef knife and headed through the foyer. He opened the door tentatively, half expecting to find a cookie-pushing Girl Scout on the other side. No one was there but, as he was closing the door, he spied the basket at his feet.

"This looks vaguely familiar," he said as he deposited the basket on the island. Then, as he pulled open the gingham cloth, his suspicion was confirmed. "Yes! More scones." Juan and Ricky arrived as he opened the accompanying envelope. "Ricky, you're off the hook, pancake-wise, this morning," he joked. Ricky peeled back the cloth to look.

"Mmmm," he sniffed. He walked over to where Juan was pulling down coffee mugs. "From next door again, right?"

"Where else?" Juan answered for Ryan. "Is that an apology or a further appeal?"

"Yes," Ryan laughed. "Want me to I read it to you, or wait until everybody's here?"

"Let's wait!" Mateo voted.

"Papito, help me out here," Ricky flicked on the espresso machine. "Since I'm not making 'cakes, this is my chance, before Alex comes down, to be the barista."

"Or you could just chill for once," Juan resisted.

"Nah, this'll be fun," Ricky pulled the beans down from the cabinet. "Anybody know where Alex keeps the grinder?" Juan moved over next to Mateo and poured half a glass of juice. Mateo looked at him suggestively and Juan nodded.

"Yeah, show him how it's done, amigo," Juan agreed. Mateo joined Alex while Ryan followed Ricky's example and began cutting up the fruit Raphael and Luke had bought the day before. Juan set the table, and by the time everyone had found their way downstairs, this morning's variation on the traditional Sunday breakfast was ready. Once everyone had taken a seat and had a few bites, Niki held up half a scone and addressed the table.

"So ... is this a bribe?"

"Prob'bly," Ricky mumbled through his mouthful of pastry.

"Ryan has the details," Juan promised.

"Yeah, I think," Ryan picked up the note. "I didn't read it all, yet." He cleared his throat and began. "'Good morning, all,'" Ryan tried adopting a British accent, which no one judged, as they focused more on the content of the note. "'We hope you enjoy these scones as much as we enjoyed entertaining you yesterday. If we frightened or offended you, please consider this a peace offering. If we intrigued you, consider this a token of our gratitude. We are certainly grateful to each of you for everything you've done for us. We are quite aware that we took all of you by surprise yesterday, at the very least. Therefore, we wanted to again stress three important points, two of which we may not have stressed enough. And one we did not address at all.

"'First, none of you should feel obligated to participate if you are not comfortable doing so. We will understand completely. We know how overwhelming our proposal must be. We debated, *seriously!*, before approaching you because of the gravity of our ask.'" Everyone had stopped eating, giving Ryan their undivided attention.

"'Secondly, and this is just as vital to us, we sincerely hope each of you *will* participate. We cannot adequately express how happy that would make us. We have dreamed of having children of our own for too many years now, and we cannot imagine a better way to achieve our dream than with your help. From each of you.

"'Lastly, and just as importantly, we hope all of you would share in the upbringing of the children, regardless of who the fathers should be. We've observed over the months that yours is a home brimming with love, and we sincerely hope our children would be fortunate enough to be enveloped in your love each and every day. Having said that, we also want to assure you, that even though they would, in a very real sense, be 'all our children,' we would contractually insist on no financial support from you, aside, perhaps, from the occasional stuffed animal or super hero jumper. Please do not let that concern be a reason to decline participation.

"'You will surely have questions once you've fully considered our proposal. We look forward to sitting down with you again when you are ready. And, for Heaven's Sake, don't be strangers in the meantime. Please do not let this make things uncomfortable amongst us.' They added a cute smiley face under the word uncomfortable," Ryan concluded.

He placed the note on the table between his and Mateo's plates and looked up to gauge everyone's reactions. They varied from unreadable on Juan's face to uneasiness on Niki's to half a smile on Greg's. But for a moment, no one spoke. Ryan resumed eating.

"They really want this, don't they," Steve finally said.

"I'll say," Alex agreed. "I guess we should feel flattered. Somehow."

"You realize, of course," Greg looked across at Luke instead of Alex, "no matter how many of us participate, helping them have 'our children' would completely change all our lives. Forever."

"That's what I've been thinking about," Raphael met Greg's gaze. "I mean, this reminds me of the night Niki came to our house after his parents threw him out." He turned to Niki. "It was totally unexpected, no way to plan for it, but ... just like that ... I had two brothers instead of one. Life didn't change *completely*, but it changed." Niki didn't say anything. He didn't know what to say to that. He just stared at Raphael, who turned back to Greg. "And you know what? Life turned out better. For everyone." Niki displayed a smile of relief as Steve brushed through what little hair he had grown out so far. Raphael turned back to Niki. "I mean that. You know I do." He turned back to the table at large. "So, this may seem scary right now, but ... who knows? One of us might be the father of the next Steve Jobs."

"Or Barack Obama," Steve countered, giving Niki a full noogie. Niki pulled away, but smiled nevertheless.

"It sounds like you're ready to donate, Raphael," Juan sat back. "Is that your decision?" He alternated eye contact between Raphael and Luke. Raphael rocked his head back and forth, noncommittal.

"Let's just say ... maybe I'm open to the idea," Raphael replied to Juan. Then he turned to Luke. "But it's not just my decision." Luke half-laughed, acknowledging last night's dare.

"Baby, I'm not going to tell you what to do."

"Yeah, but Sir, you do realize, you'd be affected by this right along with me." Luke nodded his head as Raphael looked across to Greg. "Like Greg said, we'll all be affected, no matter who the daddy is. Daddies, I mean."

"Oh wow," Ricky reacted. "I hadn't thought about that. What if only one of us is the daddy for both babies?"

"Unlikely," Alex predicted, "but possible. Want me to work up a probability analysis?" Ricky laughed and shook his head no. "Oh, come on. This is the perfect opportunity to put that Statistics 101 class to good use. Let's see ... ten men. Some are younger, so more fertile ..."

"Eat your fruit, dear," Greg chided. The discussion that had seemed so intense last night was now, somehow, becoming more lighthearted. He looked across at Ryan. "One thing is certain. Ryan, you lost your excuse to avoid participating." Ryan looked lost. "The finances." Ryan smiled and nodded.

"Yeah, I guess," he replied as he turned to Mateo. "I'd still rather have Mateo's baby."

"You may have to wait a while," Juan drily said. "The science still hasn't quite gotten us there yet. Maybe you should change your major to something in the biosciences." Ryan nodded approvingly.

"How about it, Mateo?" Juan pressed. "Since it may be a while before Ryan can have your baby, how do you feel, today, about all this? Now that you've slept on it?"

"Didn' sleep a lot," was Mateo's quiet reply.

"Oooh, Ryan, you dog," Ricky reacted. Both Juan and Ryan shook their heads, but several others seemed amused.

"Mateo," Niki looked compassionately at Mateo, "is it because you really don't want to do it, or because you're afraid if you do, something bad might happen?" He didn't need to be more specific.

"I don' know," Mateo looked miserable. He sighed. Then shook his head.

"Mateo," Juan leaned forward. "The last thing Cynthia and Patricia want, is to make you unhappy. If you're losing sleep over this, then ... don't do it." He looked around the table. "No one here will tell them you didn't, amigo. It'll be our secret." Mateo gave Juan a grateful smile. "Don't give it another thought, okay?" Mateo nodded, still smiling.

"So, we're down to nine, and counting," said the statistician. Alex looked around the table for reactions. "Come on, guys. Do we need to take a secret vote?"

"I need to think a little longer, Alex," Ricky volunteered.

"Me, too," Greg seconded, turning to Alex. "But it sounds like you're in."

"Well, I will if Raphael will." Alex gave Greg a sly grin. "Like you said, Little Alex would be pretty cute."

"What else did I say?" Greg prodded.

"I don't remember," Alex replied, turning his grin to Niki, then Raphael. "I just remember votes for Baby Niki and Baby Raphael. I figure they need a little competition."

"All joking aside," Steve said, "maybe we should set a deadline for a decision. If any of us are going to do this, we'll need to find out from Cynthia and Patricia what timing works best for them for ... um. Optimum results."

"Never in a million years," Luke said as he stood and picked up his empty plate, "would I have thought we'd be discussing ovulation timing over breakfast. Except maybe Ryan's." He wiggled his eyebrows at Ryan and Mateo. Ryan could only smile, as he'd brought this on himself.

"How about," Raphael stood as well, "Wednesday evening. That gives us three more days." No one objected; the deadline was set.

## Twenty-Five

## SPECIAL DELIVERY

As IT HAPPENED, WEDNESDAY was Greg and Alex's turn to helm dinner. Since this was not just any old Wednesday dinner, Greg baked a couple of his now signature lasagnas. They served them along with Alex's mixed greens salad, a baguette of not too garlicy bread and bottles of Soave and Malbec. So, almost totally Italian.

"Which one is meatless?" Niki asked, first in line, with spatula in hand at the sideboard.

"Both," Greg replied. "I used Impossible Italian sausage this time, so have at it." Niki nodded and did exactly that. Soon everyone was seated, digging in, and voicing mumbled expressions of appreciation.

"You sure this isn't meat?" Ricky kidded.

"No, better than," Alex answered around a mouthful. "I'm a witness." The conversation centered on the day's events, personal and national, with everyone studiously avoiding the real topic at hand. Until after everyone had finished seconds and the salad bowl was empty. The topic couldn't be avoided any longer.

"Alex, collect the plates," Greg prompted, "I'll be right back." He returned from the kitchen with a notepad and a fistful of pens, which he began distributing. Once Alex returned and took his seat, Greg picked up his own pen and issued a request. "Maybe this is over-dramatizing things, but I thought one way to get us started on the daddy discussion would be a blind vote on whether, as a family, we should even do this, regardless of who among us may choose to participate. So, write down 'yes' or 'no,' fold your paper and pass it to Alex." Alex's reaction indicated he hadn't been in on the planning of this.

"Me?"

"Well, you are the house statistician." Greg's delivery was so matter of fact it was funny.

"So, to be clear, we're voting for everyone else, not ourselves?" Steve asked. Greg absentmindedly nodded agreement and began to write. What surprised him was how much time it was taking Steve, Ryan and Raphael to decide on their votes. He'd expected everyone had decided by now, at least about their own participation.

"Was this a bad idea, Raphael?" Greg asked. Raphael looked up from his paper.

"I guess I don't understand why it matters what I think you should do," Raphael answered honestly.

"Oh," Greg smiled. "I wasn't clear. Think of it this way. Is it a good idea or not for *any* of us to donate to Cynthia and Patricia. We agreed Sunday, if any of us do this, it's going to change all our lives. I guess my question is, are we willing to do that ... change all our lives? It just seemed to me like a good way to start our discussion. Maybe not ..."

"No," Raphael replied. "I get it now. It's fine." He dashed off his vote, folded his paper and slid it across the table to Greg, who held it until Alex had recorded his vote. Once Alex had all ten votes, Greg took them from him, shuffled as best he could to randomize them and handed them back to Alex.

Alex opened the first one and announced, "Yes." He opened the second, "Yes ... yes ... yes." He continued until all ten ballots had been revealed. "It's unanimous, guys. Hmmm. How about that?" Glances and a few smiles were exchanged around the table.

"I guess there's not much more to discuss, is there?" Greg concluded. "Maybe we're not too set in our ways after all." Juan stopped toying with his pen and laid his arm across Ricky's shoulders, as he often did when he was in a good place.

"Well," he smiled, "after Raphael's comment Sunday morning, it would have been awfully hard to vote no." Raphael and Niki met each other's gaze, both looking a little pleased.

"Now what?" Ricky asked, brushing his hand along Juan's arm.

"That's totally up to Patricia and Cynthia," Steve suggested. "Who wants to tell them? It should probably be Alex or Raphael, right?"

"Go get your little tripod, Steve," Alex said, "we'll all tell them." A few minutes later Cynthia and Patricia each received a wordless text bearing a pic of the ten members of the House of the Locked Cock Brotherhood, some seated, clustered at the end of their dining table, all flashing a thumbs up. Within minutes Cynthia and Patricia appeared at the back door. Pandemic mitigation was tossed as hugs and many, many expressions of gratitude were exclaimed. The celebration adjourned to the sitting room, so everyone could sit. Cynthia couldn't stop smiling.

"I kept telling Patricia we shouldn't get our hopes up ... we are asking so much of you. But somehow, deep down, I knew, I absolutely knew you would say yes." Patricia nodded her agreement.

"You're an amazing lot," she said. "You truly are." She looked around at the men surrounding her. "We could not be more fortunate."

"Says the woman who called me 'daft' when I proposed this," Cynthia smugly turned to Patricia, who made an 'ah well' gesture with her hands.

"So, uh, how do we proceed?" Steve paraphrased Ricky's earlier comment. "And when? Because of ..." Cynthia smiled sympathetically at Steve's reticence to directly address the biological logistics they faced.

"As I said, we were feeling so optimistic," she began, "we've already asked our solicitor to draw up the necessary document to protect you, us, and the babies. She should have that to us tomorrow. You should have your friend Peter, or whomever you trust, review and, if necessary, amend it before we all sign it. As for the 'nitty-gritty,' as it were," she turned to her wife, "Patricia should be ready later this week." She looked back at Steve. "My turn will arrive in about three weeks. I hope everyone can be flexible." She noted a couple of surprised expressions among the men. "Is this happening too fast? We can wait another month ..."

"Actually," Juan spoke up, "it might be better if we act fast. Less time for any of us to get cold feet." He looked meaningfully at Ricky as he spoke. Ricky scowled back at him, but took Juan's comment as his cue.

"How will, you know, we actually do this?" he asked.

"We've already ordered some supplies online," Patricia answered, looking sheepish. "Just in case. Specimen vials for you and additional items we'll need on our end. They should be here in a day or two. We'll explain what you need to do then. I'm reasonably sure Saturday or Sunday will be D-Day." She glanced at Ricky, then Mateo. "We'll stay in touch. Ideally, we will need your donations once Ricky and Mateo get home from their shop. And we won't want to dally once you've ... produced, so we'll leave it to you how you want to coordinate ... your efforts." Now Patricia was having difficulty expressing herself. Cynthia rescued her by standing and bringing the conversation to a close.

"Again, we cannot thank you enough. We'll be in touch. Eat healthy, work out, whatever you need to do to ensure our first effort will be successful." She flashed that smile again as she took Patricia's arm and headed for the foyer.

"Later!" Greg called out. Several others called out their goodbyes.

"This *is* happening fast," Steve said, once they heard the back door close.

"Having second thoughts?" Luke asked.

"No, just ... whoa," Steve half grinned while shaking his head.

"I'm sure I don't have to say this," Juan said as he stood, followed by Ricky, "but we should try to save things up between now and Saturday. It'll make it that much easier to perform on demand."

"Raphael, cancel our regular Friday afternoon orgy," Luke stage-whispered. "You know, the one we have while Juan and Ricky are at work."

"Ha, ha," Juan said, without looking back, as he and Ricky disappeared into the foyer. Luke and Raphael followed Alex and Greg into the kitchen to help with clean up while Mateo, Ryan and Steve headed upstairs. Niki returned to the library to finish up his homework for the day.

It was nearly ten when Niki returned to their room, laptop in hand. Steve was lounging on the bed, reading a trade publication. After depositing his laptop on the desk, Niki joined him. Steve dropped the magazine onto the floor and pulled Niki into a tight embrace. They kissed, a long, deep one, something they realized they hadn't done for a while. Niki breathed deeply without breaking the kiss. When he did, he nibbled Steve's lower lip, then pulled back with a grin.

"Careful, sexy ... remember, Juan said we need to save ourselves for Saturday." A smile broke across Steve face.

"So. Does that mean you've decided you'll donate after all?" Steve was clearly delighted. He cupped Niki's face in his left hand and pressed his lips to Niki's again. When he pulled away the look on Niki's face erased his own smile. Niki sighed.

"I ..." He shook his head. "I can't. I'm sorry." He sighed again. There was real hurt on his face as he met Steve's disappointed gaze. "Please ..." Steve pulled him close again and held him there. Niki sniffed, but said nothing more.

"It's okay ... it's okay, puppy."

"I was thinking more about *your* donation," Niki whispered, his lips near Steve's ear. Steve squeezed Niki in reply. "Our secret, remember?" Steve pulled away, enough to make eye contact.

"I guess we need a plan, then," Steve suggested.

"Way ahead of you," Niki attempted to wiggle his eyebrows. "As the student nurse, I thought I'd volunteer to collect all the donations. I'll do 'us' last." Steve had to smile in spite of himself.

"Brilliant. I seriously doubt anyone will compete for that job." Niki wrinkled his face and nodded. "If you change your mind ..." Steve quietly appealed. Niki humored him with a smile.

A steady stream of customers at LCB Headquarters kept Ricky and Mateo fully occupied Saturday afternoon. It was just by chance, after ringing up a sale, that Ricky checked his phone and saw Juan's text, confirming today would indeed be D-Day. Donation Day. When he told Mateo in an aside, Mateo simply replied with a curt nod which didn't really register with Ricky, given the commotion around them. Ironically, on a day when Ricky would allow Juan to remove his cage to facilitate his orgasm on demand, he had a rewardingly busy day selling chastity devices to prevent, or at least obstruct, just such an occurrence for his customers. The walk home, after ushering the last customer out and pulling on their streetwear sweats, was quick and quiet. Ricky was feeling a bit nervous, preventing him from noticing Mateo's deeper than usual introspection. The ramifications of what the family was about to engage in hung over both of them. When they entered the foyer, they found everyone but Niki gathered in the sitting room.

"Welcome home guys," Alex announced, "to the House of the Unlocked Cock Fatherhood." Greg wasn't the only one who groaned. Mateo just stood there while Ricky looked around the room as he began pulling off, first his sweats, then his Headquarters uniform.

"Where's Niki," he asked

"He's prepping for the donations," Steve replied. "He's in charge of Operation Daddy-O." More groans ensued. Most everyone appeared, if not nervous, subdued. Mateo wandered over to Ryan, who reached out and began pulling Mateo's sweatshirt over his head and arms. By the time he'd stripped Mateo bare, Niki had arrived.

"So, what's the plan, doctor?" Raphael asked. Niki grinned.

"Patricia brought enough specimen vials for each of us. But since we're combining them into one donation anyway, I left one vial in each of your rooms. We'll save the other vials for our donation to Cynthia in a couple of weeks. Since this is kinda embarrassing, I though once you've made both your donations, one of you can bring your vial to our room. I'll decant them into the bigger main vial and run it over to Cynthia, who's in charge of, uh, their end." Steve smiled at Niki, silently supporting his carefully crafted plan. There was still time for one last appeal.

"How much time do we have?" Ryan asked, holding Mateo close and massaging his back. Niki shrugged.

"Whatever it takes, I guess," he replied. "But don't take all night. Ideally Cynthia needs our donation within thirty minutes or less." He half-laughed. "If we take too long, I suspect she'll come over and beat it out of us."

"There's the motivation I needed," Alex said as he stood and reached out to take Greg's hand and pull him up. He looked at Raphael who was rising as well. "I don't know about you, but I can't remember the last time I came, unlocked. This will be a trip." Raphael nodded and grinned.

"Yeah, this is weird," he looked pensively at Luke. "For all kinds of reasons." As everyone headed for the foyer, Steve and Niki held back. Steve wrapped an arm around Niki's waist and began to guide him toward the stairs. Halfway up to the third floor, Niki relaxed to the point he wrapped his arm around Steve's waist, too. He let out a deep breath.

"You're sure?" Steve asked. Niki nodded wordlessly. "Okay, puppy." Steve tugged Niki closer as they approached their doorway. "I love you." Niki nodded again.

"I know," he finally said. Then he looked up into Steve's eyes with a crooked smile. "But it's nice to hear you say it." Steve chuckled as they entered their room. He knew Niki would never hear those words often enough, which was why he was more than happy to deliver them on a daily basis. Niki released his hold on Steve, slid out of Steve's arm and walked over to their bed. He picked up a small tray he'd found in the butler's pantry, set it on the floor outside their door, then closed it. He looked over at Steve. "We'll check every few minutes to see if we have a delivery." He sauntered over to Steve, pressed his body against him and gazed seductively into Steve's eyes. "Speaking of deliveries ..." He dropped to his knees and swallowed Steve before he could react. Niki took Steve's thighs in each hand and squeezed, enjoying the sensation of Steve growing fuller in his mouth. He began sliding his lips and tongue under and around Steve's hardening cock. Unlike a typical night of love-making in the bed, the Jacuzzi or shower, when slower and longer was always better, Niki wanted to keep Steve on his feet, the better to capture every drop of his donation. He hoped everyone else was being equally mindful and regretted, briefly, not having suggested they do so. Steve, too, was aware of the unusual nature of this act.

"Careful, Niki. I don't want to come without the vial." Without releasing Steve, Niki reached behind him and retrieved the vial from where he'd placed it on the bed. While remaining focused on Steve's cock, he brushed it against Steve's left hand which was caressing the side of Niki's head. Steve snickered. "All righty, then. I should have known." He took the vial from Niki, closed his eyes, and relaxed into the blowjob Niki was intent on giving him.

"There," Ryan muttered as he disengaged the Cobra cage from the cock ring still encircling Mateo's package and slid it off. As his Prince's sex slave, he insisted on being the one to remove Mateo's work cage each evening. When they weren't in charge of dinner, this intimate act often led to sex between them. Some evenings Ryan would be caged in the one he wore at the Headquarters as a way of signaling just what kind of sex they might be having that evening. For obvious reasons he was uncaged this evening and rigid already, as he always was when attending to his Prince. He worked Mateo out of the cage's cock ring, licked the tip of his Prince's now free cock, then stood and pulled Mateo into a full body embrace. Their tongues danced together a moment, happy to be together again. It was Mateo who pulled away first, enough to make eye contact and flash his smile.

"Ready for donate?" Ryan shrugged in Mateo's embrace, but smiled back.

"Sure. Can't you tell?" His erection was pressed up against Mateo's belly. Mateo giggled.

"Uh huh, like always." He pulled free and walked over to the dresser, where Niki had left the vial, then returned to Ryan's side. "You wanna do it. Or me do you?"

"Let's both do it at the same time," Ryan said encouragingly. Mateo looked away, then back at Ryan and shook his head. "Please, Mateo? Your baby will be beautiful." Mateo smiled in spite of himself.

"Maybe. Or maybe it will look like me."

"That would be awesome," Ryan continued his plea. "Mateo. You'll never have to go anywhere you don't want to go." He grasped each of Mateo's shoulders. "You'll never go anywhere without me."

"Good," Mateo's smile returned. "I don' want to jinx it. To do this." He glanced at the vial, then shook his head. "So, no, Ryan. We do you. Jus' you." He looked longingly into Ryan's eyes. "Okay?" Ryan closed his eyes and nodded.

"Okay, just me. It's been four days now, so this shouldn't take long." Mateo reached down and grasped Ryan's cock. "No, if you're not going to donate to Patricia ... you're gonna donate to me." Ryan lightly pushed Mateo away. "Lay down on the bed, my Prince. You're going to come in me while I come in this." He waved the vial in the air. Mateo laughed, but jumped backwards onto the bed and scooted up into place. Ryan was right behind him. He straddled Mateo's right leg and bent down to swallow Mateo. Now that Ryan had agreed to Mateo's decision, the pressure was off, and it didn't take long for Ryan's efforts to produce a full-blown princely erection. Mateo, who was closer, lifted the lube off the night stand and placed it near Ryan's right hand. Ryan released Mateo, repositioned his body and impaled himself. He began bouncing on Mateo's cock, vial in one hand and his own cock in the other. For once, he didn't care if he came before Mateo. It had been four days. Four long days, and he was determined to ride Mateo into the sunset, no matter who came first.

After securing Steve's donation, Niki and he collapsed onto the bed, cuddling and kissing, engaged in 'after play' since they, too, had refrained from any serious love making for the previous few days. Steve offered to get Niki off, but he was rebuffed. Niki just wanted to be held. And kissed. And loved. And Steve obliged. They had nothing else to do but wait until everyone else had delivered their donations. Niki's cue came when Steve pulled away, indicating a need to pee. He opened their door to find three vials on the tray. He retrieved them and was in the process of emptying them into the larger specimen vial when Steve returned from the bathroom.

"Ready for delivery, huh?" Steve said, looking only mildly squeamish.

"Not yet," Niki turned to him. "We're still missing one. And time's a wasting."

"Whose?"

"I don't know. Doh! I should have labeled them, but I didn't. I'll go down and see. Here, hold this one upside down until it's done dripping." Steve made a face, but carefully took over holding the smaller vial over the larger one. Niki headed out the door and down the stairs. It was immediately obvious whose vial was missing. Raphael and Luke's door was the only one still closed. He approached, unsure what his next move should be. If he knocked it wouldn't exactly be coitus interruptus, but he really didn't want to waste any more time. After debating a moment, he decided he needed to act and knocked.

"You guys doing okay?" he called through the door. After only a couple of heartbeats Luke opened the door.

"Sorry," he said, looking a little flushed. "Raphael insisted we lock him up immediately before getting this to you, so we had to clean him up first." He looked over his shoulder at Raphael, who was sitting on the side of the bed, rubbing his eyes and yawning. "Here you go." Luke reached over to the top of the dresser out of Niki's line of site. He held the vial out to Niki.

"Jeez ..." Niki reacted as he grasped the half-full vial. He looked up at Luke. "How many times did you guys ...?"

"Oh," Luke laughed. "That's mostly Raphael. He always comes like that."

"Oh ... kay ..." Niki looked again at the vial, smirking slightly, then back at Luke. "If Raphael can get his strength back, we'll see you guys at dinner. I gotta run." Niki didn't dare run with his precious payload, but he wasted no time getting back to his room where he waited and waited while mostly Raphael dripped into the specimen vial. Someday, he thought, this donation would be worthy of a more extended conversation. Finally, satisfied with his efforts, he capped the specimen vial and headed for the stairs. In his hand was a universe of tiny gametes, from all his brothers, that would soon be competing with one another to find and join, hopefully, with one lucky ovum. Patricia's ovum, to produce the answer to her and Cynthia's long sought dream of a child of their own. Although this was a simple task for Niki, ridiculously simple, he felt a rush of emotion as he left the house and crossed into Patricia and Cynthia's garden. What he was bearing could make them the happiest they'd ever been, and he was a part of it. He realized what he was experiencing was the reward of helping others achieve a long-sought health care goal. The thought that maybe this was what he was going to feel every day, as a nurse, brought a smile to his face that lingered as he topped their steps and knocked. He didn't wait long before Cynthia opened the door.

"Darling," she smiled. "Our special delivery?" Niki nodded and held out the vial.

"Oh my." Cynthia's smile widened. She took the vial, then raised her gaze to meet Niki's. "If we don't succeed this first time it won't be for lack of trying, will it?" Niki laughed.

"Yeah, I guess so." He looked down, a bit embarrassed. Cynthia reached out and tugged up on his chin.

"I know we've already said this a dozen times, Niki, but we are ever so grateful to you all. And so very excited. Are you? Excited that is?" Niki beamed.

"Yes. I think so. I mean, we're excited for you and Patricia. And we're all looking forward to being uncles. And daddies, I guess. It's all kind of mind-blowing, really." He stopped talking but didn't break eye contact. He let out a big breath. "I should go. You, too!" Patricia's eyes widened and she nodded vigorously.

"Wish us luck," she called out as Niki headed for the gate. He waved, then disappeared. Cynthia slowly closed the door, then quickly headed for the stairs and a patiently waiting Patricia.

## Twenty-Six

## "It's Time!"

Beth Riley, Ryan's mother, would have been proud. And a little surprised. True, he was using a packaged mix for the cornbread and canned beans, not dried and soaked, for the chili, but he was putting together a dinner for ten without using a microwave. Or a delivery app. It was his and Mateo's turn, and he wanted to surprise even Mateo by getting a head start on things before Mateo and Ricky got home from the shop. Really, before anyone else got home. It was a week before Thanksgiving 2022, and until he'd returned home from classes on campus, where Niki still was, the house had actually been empty. COVID-19 hadn't gone away, but schools, businesses and restaurants were enjoying new signs of life, thanks in part to the vast majority of people in the Bay Area willing to be vaccinated and boosted. On top of that, everyone was bone tired of dealing with the pandemic. Now Juan, Ricky and Mateo weren't the only ones working outside the house. Niki and Ryan were back in the classroom full time, and the rest were back in their respective offices three or even four days a week in what everyone was calling a hybrid mode. Except for Cynthia and Patricia, who were working mostly from home now that they were nearing the end of their last trimester. Cynthia was still going to the office more often than their doctor had advised, but for the most part, they were following orders to protect themselves and the babies. Cases were rising and competing with flu and RSV infections, no doubt due to the gradual reopenings, but the new variants weren't leading to spikes in hospitalizations and deaths like the previous winter surges had. Almost three years into the pandemic, this was, whether anyone liked it or not, the new normal.

Ryan was sauteing diced onions in a big dutch oven when Raphael and Alex came in from the foyer, still shedding their street clothes.

"Something smells good," Alex said, sniffing as he began pulling his polo over his head. Raphael was checking out all the ingredients on and around the cutting board near the main sink.

"This looks like quite a project, Ryan," Raphael examined one of the cans of Italian Roma tomatoes. "Need any help?" Ryan turned to him and shook his head.

"Thanks, guys, but Mateo will be home soon." Raphael leaned over the dutch oven, placing a reassuring hand on Ryan's shoulder. He sniffed approvingly. "Tell you what, if you want, you guys can set the table. And put out soup bowels on the sideboard." Raphael grinned at Alex.

"I can see we're in the way. Okay, Ryan, we'll set the table as soon as we get undressed." Alex led the way as he and Raphael took to the back stairs. Ryan smiled as he turned down the burner and moved back to the cutting board to chop the garlic. Tonight's repast would be a fairly simple one, but one that he could take most of the credit for if he kept moving.

"It's been a long time since I last had cornbread," Greg smiled across the table at Ryan and Mateo. "This is as good as my mom makes."

"Maybe the same brand," Mateo responded, tongue in cheek, before air kissing Ryan. Greg looked confused.

"I used a mix," Ryan admitted.

"So?" Greg shrugged as he reached for another piece. "I like it."

"Me, too," Niki agreed. "The chili's great, too. Just spicy enough. Don't lose the recipe." Steve seemed to be onboard, but was too busy chewing to speak. Several minutes of munching and sipping, with little commentary, seemed to confirm that everyone approved of Ryan's efforts. It was after Raphael finished his second helping of chili that he sat back and surveyed the faces around him.

"Alex and I saw Cynthia in the office today," he said. Alex chewing, nodded. "She looks *really* pregnant. And a little tired."

"Yeah," Alex agreed after swallowing. "We rode the elevator with her and helped her into her Uber. She asked us to ride home with her."

"So, we did," Raphael continued. "We walked her up to her door. We told her she should stop going to the office."

"What did she say?" Niki asked.

"She said, 'I'll think about it,'" Raphael frowned. "We may have to enlist Patricia to convince her. But what I wanted to say is, we're getting really close, I think. We're maybe only a couple of weeks away from becoming uncles and daddies. Remember how we said this would change our lives? Well, here we are." All eyes were now on Raphael, who glanced first at Luke, then Juan. "What changes first?"

"My guess is free time," Juan posited. Everyone turned to Juan. "Remember, they want us all involved in the kids' lives. Which will be limited the first couple of months. But once the babies are more active, we'll have more opportunities to interact with them. And maybe give the moms a break now and then. With ten of us, it shouldn't be a huge challenge, but it'll be a change, Raphael."

"Will it be good or bad for the babies," Ricky asked, "if all of us spend time with them? You know, instead of just the daddies." Juan turned to Ricky with a wide grin.

"That's a very insightful question, mijo." Juan turned back to the table. "Before I answer, what does anyone else think?" Steve spoke first.

"My vote: it should be good. It'll be a little like having a bunch of older brothers. Well, much older."

"Or like in the old days," Alex agreed, "with a big extended family all under one roof. Or, for us, under two roofs." Juan nodded.

"My feeling," he said, "is these kids will be facing some challenges as they grow up, having two moms and probably two different dads who don't live with them. It'll be easier here than in most other places, but still. Having a support system and close relationships with nine 'uncles' who love them, and are a devoted presence in their lives, won't be a bad thing."

"I could coach them at soccer," Luke theorized, "and Alex could coach volleyball."

"If he teaches them to play by the rules," Juan laughed. Alex scoffed at Juan.

"I'll take care of their Halloween costumes," he countered. "We could get arrested if Raphael gets that job."

"I do like the idea," Raphael said, ignoring Alex, "of reading stories to them, like Luke said way back when. In fact, I've already picked up a few picture books." Luke looked surprised at first, then wrapped an arm around Raphael's neck and grinned at Niki.

"Did Raphael ever read stories to you, after you moved in?" he joked. Niki cackled.

"Uh ... no. We just played games," he replied. "Board games," he clarified. "And cards, but you knew that." Niki gave Raphael a sincere gaze. "Raffie, you're really getting excited, aren't you?" Raphael wobbled his head, shyly agreeing. Niki gave Juan an 'uh-huh' look.

"Correct me if I'm wrong," Juan smiled at Niki, "but it seems to me, we have ten potential uncles and daddies ready, and maybe even eager for this." He looked over at Mateo to gauge his state of mind. Mateo closed his eyes, but nodded with a smile. Juan continued smiling himself as he cupped the back of Ricky's neck and squeezed. Initial shock, followed by concern and confusion had clearly evolved over the months into confidence as the dates of the births neared.

"It's kind of exciting, really," Ryan said. "I mean, not knowing who the fathers are. It's a little like playing the lottery." He looked around to see if anyone thought he was being inane. "Only better."

"The odds are certainly better," Steve nodded. "Only one in ... ten," he caught himself. "Hey guys, what do you say we play a little lottery of our own?" Niki gave him a questioning scowl. "Each of us puts in, I don't know, ten bucks. That's a hundred dollars. Each daddy is a winner and gets fifty bucks to spend either on the baby or the mommy." Not everyone looked enthused at first. "Never mind. I guess maybe that's a bit crass."

"No, Steve," Luke came to his defense. "you're on the right track. What if, instead, the money goes into two college funds. Greg can take care of that. Even if he's one of the dads. Then, every year, we add a portion of the interest we're earning on the house money to those college funds." Luke's idea was met with a couple of smiles. "Patricia and Cynthia insisted we have no financial obligation, but we didn't sign anything that says we can't do something like this for the kids." Raphael leaned over and planted a big one on Luke's cheek.

"And you say I'd make a great daddy," Raphael praised, then looked over at Steve. "I vote for Steve's idea, amended by Luke." He looked around the table. "Do I get a second?"

"Second," Niki raised his hand. "All in favor?" Ten ayes and no nays, carried the motion.


Niki and Steve were in the kitchen, contemplating options for a Saturday lunch, when Juan came thundering down the back stairs. Wearing fresh scrubs, he flew through the kitchen into the foyer to retrieve his shoes. On his second pass, on his way to the back door, he turned and announced, "It's time!" Niki turned and wrapped his arms around Steve and bounced a couple of times.

"What should *we* do?" he exclaimed. Steve made a mock pensive face.

"I think we're supposed to boil water." Niki barked a laugh. Alex and Greg rushed in from the foyer at about the same time Raphael and Luke came up the stairs from the gym. They'd all heard Juan's noisy exit.

"Is this it?" Alex asked first. Niki and Steve both nodded.

"Patricia or Cynthia?" Greg asked. Niki shook his head.

"He didn't say, but wouldn't it be Patricia?"

"Probably, Niki," Luke ventured, "but, they're so close, it could be either of them. Or both."

"Whoa, you think?" Raphael's eyes widened. Ryan wandered in at that point.

"It's probably only Patricia," Steve said. "Good thing she started when Juan was right here."

"I'm really nervous," Raphael said as he climbed on a stool backwards, facing the group instead of the island. "I wish they were doing this in a hospital."

"Well," Niki moved closer to Raphael, "they had good reasons. COVID, first of all. Plus, they're really confident in this doula they've been working with, and with Juan right here ... they're in good hands." He said the last few words a little more quietly than the rest.

"You wish you were over there, don't you?" Raphael said tenderly, more as an observation than a question. Niki smiled and rubbed Raphael's shoulder.

"Yes. And no. I mean, I don't have those skills. But it would be amazing to be there."

"You could probably get some kind of extra credit," Greg speculated. Niki barked another laugh.

"Maybe if Steve filmed it, yeah," he agreed. "Otherwise, they'd never believe it."

"Let's get some lunch," Steve suggested. "Chances are, we're in for a long afternoon. Ryan, why don't you text Mateo and fill him and Ricky in." Ryan dashed for the stairs. "What's everyone hungry for?"

Not only was lunch history, but the dinner hour was approaching, and still there was no word. Ricky and Mateo had closed up a couple of hours early, so everyone was home, scattered around the sitting room, or in this case, the waiting room. Juan had left so fast he hadn't even taken his phone, but everyone had their phones handy, just in case.

"Would it be rude to text Cynthia, you know, to check in?" Ricky proposed.

"Yes," was Niki's semi-professional opinion. "With just the doula and Juan there, Cynthia's probably just as busy as Patricia. Or, the other way around." Then, with a bit of exasperation in his voice, "God, we still don't even know who's giving birth."

"We're probably not top of mind right now, even for Juan," Steve ventured. He looked to Niki, who nodded. "This could go overnight, guys." Mateo dropped his head into Ryan's lap as Ryan faked a suppressed scream. Everyone's nerves were taut.

"I don't think so," Niki offered a bit of reassurance. "If things were moving that slowly I think Juan would break away long enough to come home and update us. And get his damn phone." Yes. Very taut.

"Guys," Luke began, "it's not really helping for us to just sit here and stare at each other, despite how handsome you all are. Maybe we should decamp for a while, and if anyone hears anything ..." It was at that moment that Raphael's phone alerted him to a text. It was from Cynthia, inviting everyone to their back door. That's all it said. That's all it needed to say. As one organism the nine of them rose and ran, miraculously not hurting one another, as they made their way through the house, into the garden and to Cynthia's back door. Juan was there, masked, and with the silliest smize anyone had ever seen on him.

"Well?!" Alex exclaimed. Juan, extending the torture, motioned with his head for them to follow him. Once everyone was in the living room, he finally spoke.

"Patricia delivered a beautiful baby boy. She's been through a lot, but she and Cynthia would like each of you to have a look, just a brief look for now, two at a time." He reached down to a box on the coffee table and pulled out a couple of masks. He handed them to Ryan and Mateo. "You two first, and remember, only for a moment. Come with me." He led them to the stairs, leaving the others to wait their turn.

"A boy," Luke grinned. "Do you think it's one of theirs?" he asked no one in particular. "Is that why they went first?"

"That's my guess," Alex replied, with barely veiled dejection in his voice. He sighed, then brightened. "A boy. That's so cool." Raphael wrapped an arm around Ricky's waist, since he seemed a bit lost without Juan at his side. Ricky gave him a nervous smile. It wasn't long before Juan returned with Ryan and Mateo, both of whom were beaming.

"He's so cute," Ryan peeled off his mask.

"And tiny," Mateo followed suit.

Alex and Greg were next. Then Steve and Niki. Then Luke and Raphael. By then Ricky had fallen, silent, into an easy chair, a little miffed that Juan had left him for last. He almost didn't notice Juan standing at his side.

"Mijo," Juan quietly said. "Our turn." He pulled Ricky out of the chair and dipped to grab a mask as they walked across the room and into the entry, before heading up the stairs. Juan held Ricky's hand as they walked through the upstairs hall, past the bedroom that would be the nursery, on their way to the room that had been converted into the birthing room. Cynthia was at the door, looking triumphant. She briefly rubbed Ricky's shoulder as they passed through the doorway. A portable hospital bed was angled from the far corner, where Patricia was resting, holding a bundle at her chest. The doula was nearby, trying to look officious but was clearly mostly amused. By now she'd witnessed eight other naked men come and go and had only wished that she had been warned first.

Juan guided Ricky to Patricia's bedside. She pulled the blanket down far enough to reveal the face of the baby, already nursing. Ricky let out a long gasp. The baby was indeed cute, with a decent head of black hair and a muted olive complexion. Just then he opened his eyes, his dark brown eyes, then closed them again without pausing his suckling. Ricky looked up into Patricia's eyes, which were sparkling, despite the ordeal she'd just been through. She smiled and whispered, "he's lovely." Juan leaned down to Ricky's ear.

"Yes, mijo. One of us is the father." Ricky looked up into Juan's eyes, his lips trembling. On the verge of tearing up, he looked back at Patricia, who was looking down at the baby.

"He *is* lovely," Ricky thickly said, desperately trying to manage his emotions. Patricia returned her gaze to Ricky, who was slightly startled when Cynthia placed a hand on his shoulder from behind.

"We're going to name him Enrique Juan, or Juan Enrique, depending on how the DNA test comes out. Either way, he's adorable isn't he?"

"Dios Mio," Ricky sighed. "He's a little angel, all right." He sniffed. Then sighed. He and Juan wrapped arms around one another, and started to turn away. "I hope you get some rest," he said to Patricia. "You're already an amazing mommy, you know." Juan pulled him toward the door, leaving Cynthia at Patricia's bedside. As they reached the door, Patricia called out.

"Thank you for everything you've done, Juan. And you, Ricky. We dearly love you both."


"What's this?" Juan laughed as Alex and Raphael carried glasses and two bottles of bubbly into the sitting room, where everyone had gathered once again.

"We didn't have much to do while you were keeping us in suspense all afternoon," Alex explained as he handed the first glasses to Juan and Ricky. "We put these on ice, figuring they might come in handy."

"Yeah," Raphael knelt down in front of Juan while carefully opening the first bottle. "We haven't done this in forever, and I can't think of a better reason to revive the old tradition." He poured into Ricky's glass, then Juan's, then scooted over to Steve while Alex began pouring from the second bottle. Once everyone had been served, Steve cleared his throat, stood and took the floor.

"Using words I thought I would never say," he paused and looked around the room at nine expectant faces, "congratulations, pip pip and cheerio to our beloved brother and brand new Daddy ... Juan-or-Ricky." He paused another beat, then finished his toast with, "That would have come off better if I knew which one of you it is." Juan laughed and wrapped an arm around Ricky's waist while Ricky took a long sip, then a deep breath.

"I ... I can't believe it," Ricky quietly muttered. He seemed overwhelmed, and understandably so. He turned to Juan. "I hope it's you." Emotion flowed across Juan's face.

"Why, mijo?" Juan sniffed, then sipped, maybe in an effort to distract from his sniffle.

"Well, you know, you're older. You're taller, so that would be good to inherit. You're almost as handsome as me." Several hoots sounded. "And think how confusing it would be to have the little guy calling *me* Papito." Everyone laughed now, relieved that Ricky was in a good enough place to joke about his possible paternity. When the laughter ended, Ricky pretended to scowl at everyone. "I can't believe one of you didn't tip me off after seeing Juan Enrique before me!"

"You've already named him?" Raphael asked. Juan shook his head.

"Patricia and Cynthia have ... or will, depending. Either Juan Enrique or Enrique Juan."

"Well, Enrique, Juan asked each of us to keep it a surprise when he had us upstairs," Niki explained. He met Juan's gaze. "That was the shortest and probably the hardest secret I've ever kept." Then he caught Ricky's eyes. "I didn't dare look at you when we came back down." Ricky pulled away from Juan and walked over to Niki to pull him up and into a long hug, then returned to Juan's side.

"How long until we find out who the daddy is?" Ryan asked.

"Not long," Juan replied. "At most, four or five days after we submit samples. We'll do that Monday. Right, mijo?" Ricky, looking a little dazed, turned to Juan.

"I don't think I'll be able to sleep. You know, until we know."

"Ricky ..." Luke moved over to sit at Ricky's feet. "Does it really matter whose DNA matches? You and Juan are married." He looked up to see if Juan agreed. "We've been talking about nine uncles, but think about it. Regardless of who the biological father is, you're *both* going to be the little guy's daddies." That trademark smile finally bloomed across Ricky's face.

"Yeah, you're right." He released Luke's gaze and turned to Juan. "But I still hope he ends up being as tall as you, Papito." Juan drained his flute and held it out for someone to refill it.

"I never want you to be disappointed, mijo," he said as Alex poured, "but I won't be mad if it turns out to be you." Ricky accepted the compliment, simply nodding. So many emotions.

"So who will do this? And how?" Alex asked.

"The lab will send someone to the houses to collect the samples," Juan addressed Alex. "A simple cheek swab, easier than the COVID tests we did on Mateo." He then looked around the room. "The plan is to get samples from everyone while they're here, so it'll be even easier after Cynthia gives birth."

"That's it?" Alex looked surprised. "Wow. I thought it would be more ... I don't know, involved." Juan shook his head.

"Well, Papito," Steve said to Juan, "so much for your day off. Not to mention you missed lunch, so you must be starving." He patted Niki's thigh. "And Niki and I are too excited to cook, so dinner will be takeout on us. But you get to choose." Niki looked relieved.

"How about that new dumpling place, mijo-maybe-Papito?" Juan nudged Ricky. Ricky looked at Steve.

"Sure, anything's fine. If I can even eat." Steve chuckled.

"You better eat. You need keep your strength up, Daddy. I'll order for next door, too. Do you think the doula will still be there, Juan?"

"Maybe, but I doubt it. Everything went very well. Margarite will be checking in with them every day, though, especially with Cynthia due next."

"Niki," Steve rose, "if you can text Cynthia and let her know we're ordering dinner for them, I'll take care of the order." He headed into the library so his call wouldn't interfere with conversations in the sitting room. Once he'd left, Raphael returned to the spot at Juan and Ricky's feet. For a moment he just gazed at them.

"It's already happened," he quietly said, with a smile. Juan tilted his head, inviting more.

"It feels like everything *has* changed, and I'm not even the daddy. The fact that one of you is has already affected how I feel."

"Yeah," Alex concurred. Greg pulled him closer.

"I mean," Raphael continued, "I can't imagine how you two feel, but already I feel different, just being the little guy's uncle." He looked to Alex and sniffed. "Is this what verklempt looks like?" Alex nodded, chuckled and sniffed all at the same time, unable to respond.

"Yeah, Raphael," Juan smiled crookedly. "It just got real."

Twenty-Seven

## HIROSHI'S GIFT

THIS THANKSGIVING WAS A little different in the House of the Locked Cock Brotherhood. It was a fuller house than ever, since they had more to celebrate and be thankful for. They had not only insisted Cynthia, Patricia and the baby join them, but they had invited Peter as well. He had sounded so excited when they gave him the news. Since he had played an integral role in making the pregnancies possible, it only seemed right to include him. Patricia already looked more like her old self, physically, and was clearly exuding new mommy vibes. She and the baby were bonding well. Cynthia looked uncomfortable more often than not and more than ready to deliver her addition to the family. Luckily for her, the powder room was just across the foyer from the dining room. Not that they needed to, but in deference to their guests, everyone had dressed for the occasion. It just seemed like the right thing to do.

Juan and Ricky took turns holding the baby during much of the meal so Patricia could enjoy it along with everyone else. She'd hesitated at first, and considered suggesting they retrieve the portable bassinet from home, but she could tell both men wanted their own quality time with the little guy. In fact, they spent most of the meal doting on the baby instead of eating. She took advantage of the fact she had pumped enough breast milk to last the afternoon to have her first glass of wine in nine months. Just a little one.

"I should hate you," Cynthia joked when Patricia took her first sip, "but this *was* my idea, wasn't it?" Patricia nodded slowly, the glass still at her lips.

"Another example of the total inequality between the sexes," Niki observed. It was Cynthia's turn to nod.

"Yes, darling," she responded, "but, going forward, with ten of you and two of us, things should just about even out, I venture."

"What are we talking about?" Juan asked, without taking his eyes off the bundle in his lap. "Bathing, diapering, one a.m. feedings?" When Cynthia didn't respond, he looked up.

"Keep going ..." was all she said. Everyone who wasn't chewing, laughed.

"I'll do anything I can," Ricky earnestly asserted. "Anything you want."

"Good," Juan said as he gingerly slid the baby into Ricky's arms. "I'm pretty sure it's time for a diaper change." Ricky looked a little stunned. Patricia stood and placed her napkin next to her plate.

"Come with me, Ricky. We'll have our first lesson. I left the diaper bag in the sitting room." As they left the room, Raphael exchanged a sly, but knowing look with Niki. Telepathically, they agreed. Everything had changed.

"I'm going crazy," Ricky speared a slice of banana on Juan's plate and popped it into his mouth. They were having Saturday breakfast alone in the gazebo, one tradition still intact. The morning was a little chillier than normal, so Ricky had turned on the radiant electric heaters under the benches that Alex had installed during his summer vacation. The one in which he and Greg hadn't gone anywhere except to the hardware store.

"*Going* crazy?" Juan kidded. Ricky playfully kicked Juan's leg.

"I don't know what's been harder. Waiting for the baby to come or waiting to find out which of us is the daddy."

"We're both daddies, remember?"

"I know, but ... you know what I mean." It was then they could hear rapid panting as Daisy made her regularly scheduled approach.

"Oh no, Daisy!" Ricky lamented as she climbed the stairs and planted herself at his feet. "You're late. I already ate all my cinnamon toast." Daisy tilted her head.

"Here." Juan tore a corner off his second piece and handed it to Ricky. Just like that it was gone.

"Permission to come aboard," Patricia announced as she, too, appeared. She was holding a completely wrapped bundle of baby.

"Of course," Juan grinned widely. "Can we get you a coffee?" Ricky started to rise as she entered the gazebo and sat across from them. She motioned for Ricky to sit.

"Thank you, no." She looked down to confirm the blanket was still well wrapped. "It's still a bit too chilly out here for ... Juan Enrique." She glanced quickly at Ricky, then focused on Juan who sat upright, then leaned forward.

"So ..."

"Yes, we have the results, and Juan, you are the biological father."

"Papito!" Ricky reacted, grabbing Juan's left biceps and shaking him. "I knew it!" He turned his killer smile on Patricia.

"I was worried you might be disappointed, Ricky," she smiled back, relieved.

"No, no ... I wanted it to be Juan. So much. This is wonderful!" She already knew the answer to her next question, simply by the look on Juan's face.

"Juan, are you as thrilled as Ricky?"

"I ... uh ... Patricia ... of course I am." He seemed at a loss as he turned to Ricky. "I probably don't show it as much as Ricky can, but yeah." His smile bloomed. "I feel pretty amazing right now. I never dreamed ..."

"He is a dream, isn't he?" Patricia said, looking down at her bundle as she stood. "A little dreamboat addition to a dreamy family." Then she looked at Juan. "Again ... thank you, Juan. We created a beautiful baby, and you and Ricky, both, have made Cyndi and me so very happy." As she started for the stairs, both Juan and Ricky rose and encircled her and Juan Enrique in a smaller version of the familiar family group hug. The baby gurgled and wriggled from beneath the blanket. As they released her, Patricia smiled again at both of them, then stepped down to the ground. "Come Daisy. You've had enough to eat this morning." Daisy whimpered once, then followed her across the garden and through the gate.

"I'm so happy, Papito. And now you really, really are a Papito." Ricky, still holding on to Juan, sighed. "Now I don't have to go crazy anymore."

"Oh?" Juan gave him a sly look. "Have you forgotten? You may be the daddy of Cynthia's baby." The look on Ricky's face was Instagrammable.

"Oh no! I can't ... that wouldn't be fair. If both of us ..."

"Mijo, life isn't fair. But you have to admit ..." Juan gently caressed Ricky's face with his right hand and touched their buttery lips together and held them there a moment. "You have to admit, it's been pretty good to us lately."

"We're saving the next round of bubbly for the arrival of Cynthia's baby, Juan. But to celebrate you, we've opened a couple bottles of the Turley Zin that Raphael's been hoarding." Alex was pulling a stubborn cork while Greg plated servings of his popular hand cranked cannelloni. After everyone was seated and had begun eating, Juan noticed he was getting a lot of looks from around the table. He laid down his fork and sat back.

"You guys aren't going to get all weird on me, now, are you?"

"Of course we are, *Daddy*," Alex responded. He and Juan held each other's gaze a moment. "You know me, I'm never at a loss for words, but all I can come up with is ... congratulations, Juan. Patricia couldn't have done better." Glasses around the table were lifted again towards Juan.

"I know it wasn't a contest," Juan picked up his fork again, "but I hope none of you are disappointed."

"Are you kidding?" Steve responded. "Speaking only for myself, I'm thrilled for you and Ricky. And of course, Patricia and Cynthia." He placed a hand on Niki's handy thigh and looked around the table with an almost evil grin. "Besides ... we still have one more shot at our own stardom." Niki rubbed Steve's forearm, laughing along with everyone.

"Have you told anyone else?" Luke asked. Juan chuckled and shook his head.

"Yeah, well ..." He looked endearingly at Ricky. "I guess we'll be making a few complicated phone calls tomorrow to some very surprised grandmas and grandpas."

"Maybe you should wait," Luke smiled. "You might need to make the same calls again in a couple of weeks."

"No!" Ricky insisted. "One of you guys gets to go next."

"Like we have any say in the matter," Greg observed.

"Juan," Raphael asked, "does this mean you'll get to take some paternity leave?" Juan looked surprised.

"I ... I hadn't even thought about that, but yeah, I guess I could." He met Raphael's smile. "That'll be another phone call tomorrow."


Paperwork being what it is, Juan's request for paternity leave didn't materialize as quickly as he'd expected. It was the holiday season, plus no one in HR even had a clue he was 'expecting.' He was obligated to work his regular schedule for at least a couple of days, until the bureaucracy had done its thing. No one thought much of it. Until.

"Oh shit!" Niki exclaimed from his seat in the library. It was Tuesday, a day when both he and Ryan had no morning classes. His cry was loud enough that Ryan heard him from his desk upstairs. He came to his door just as Niki rounded the front stairs on his way up to his room.

"Are you hurt?" Ryan asked, following him.

"No! It's Cynthia. The baby's coming!" Niki stopped half-way up the flight and turned, nearly knocking Ryan backwards. "She's a week early.

Help me find some clean scrubs." Niki moved past Ryan and retreated back down the stairs and on to Juan and Ricky's room. Niki spoke excitedly as he pawed through the clothes hanging in the closet. "Ricky texted me from the shop. Patricia couldn't reach Juan ... he's probably in surgery ... so she tried Ricky. Ricky texted me." He turned around and raised both arms in angst. "I've gotta stand in for Juan."

"The doula's there, isn't she?" Ryan asked, pulling dresser drawers open. The third one revealed a stack of scrubs. He pulled out a top and pants and held them up.

"She's there," Niki replied as he began pulling on the scrubs. "But four hands are better than two. Six, I guess, with Patricia there. She must be freaking out." He headed for the foyer, Ryan still following, to retrieve his shoes.

"Should I come, too?" Ryan offered.

"No. Let everyone else know, but keep your phone handy just in case."

"Okay, but please don't keep me in suspense like last time."

"Promise," Niki said as he whipped into the library, grabbed his phone and held it up to Ryan, backing up his promise. Then, just like Juan, he ran for the back door.

Even though Ricky and Mateo's shop was closer, Raphael and Alex were the first to arrive home. Ryan couldn't decide whom to notify first, so he had punted and sent a group text to the family list. Close colleagues at the office knew Raphael and Alex were neighbors with Cynthia, so they were a little surprised, but not shocked, when the two of them dropped everything and ran, shouting brisk explanations as they headed for the elevators. Details would have to come from Cynthia later, if ever.

Ricky and Mateo arrived next, having finished the fittings for the customers already in the shop when Ricky got Patricia's call. It was another hour before Steve could break away, and a bit longer for Greg and then Luke. All of them had been keeping their phones handy as the due date approached, but everyone had been caught off guard. In a reprise of Patricia's delivery day, everyone had gathered in the sitting room.

"It's been what, a couple of hours now?" Luke asked when he arrived.

"Yeah, just about," Ryan replied. "Niki promised to update us when he can. I guess Juan hasn't seen his phone yet."

"We'll hear from him when he does," Steve asserted. "He can be in surgery for hours sometimes. Heck, this may be over before he even knows about it." Raphael smiled at Steve.

"This must be a real thrill for Niki, don't you think?" he said. Steve laughed and nodded.

"You know it, Raphael. He'll be walking on air the rest of the week."

"I've never seen him move so fast," Ryan agreed. "He looked sexy in those scrubs." Mateo gave him a funny look. "Well ... he did!" Mateo smiled and pulled Ryan's hand into his lap.

"Who will be daddy this time?" Mateo asked, voicing what everyone was thinking. The conversation soon lagged, everyone as nervous as the last time. Mateo's question occupied everyone's thoughts until Ryan's phone signaled a text. He unlocked it and read.

"Getting closer, Niki says. He says the doula is doing great. Patricia is doing great. Cynthia just wants it to be over." Ryan looked up at the group. "I'm guessing Niki is great, too." Steve smiled at him and stood.

"I can't just sit here," he said. "I'm going to go make grilled cheese sandwiches. And you can't stop me." Alex rose and followed him. Raphael cuddled up next to Luke. No one was very skilled at waiting. But they had no choice. Steve's patented grilled cheeses did help. They were just finishing up when Niki's text lit up Ryan's phone again. Ryan laughed.

"It says, 'you know the drill,'" he reported. This time their exit was a little less frenzied, but they still arrived at the back door ahead of Niki. And this time everyone was still dressed in street wear. Even Ryan, who'd dressed in case Niki might need his help.

"Come on," Steve opened the door. "We know where to go." They could hear a baby crying before they made it into the living room. It was impossible to know whether it was Juan Enrique or the new kid on the block. From the opposite doorway, Niki entered the living room at the same time as the family. They could tell he was beaming, even behind the mask. His eyes were twinkling.

"How are you doing?" Steve asked.

"I'm doing great, Steve," he said as he walked over and fiercely hugged Steve. "You can probably tell, already, the baby has a great set of lungs. This was incredible. Just amazing." He was staring into Steve's eyes. "I've never felt like I do right now." He cleared his throat and pulled away, ready to assume Juan's role once again. More than one man assumed either Niki or Steve must be the father, given the state of ecstasy he was in.

"Okay," Niki backed up a couple of steps toward the entry. "Let's start with Luke and Raphael." They looked nervously at each other before following Niki. This seemed like more evidence that the father might be Niki. Or Steve. As they disappeared, Alex turned to Steve.

"I bet it's you, Steve," he said confidently. "If it was Niki, he would have been an incoherent puddle."

"I'll take that bet," Greg replied. "Twenty bucks says you're wrong."

Luke and Raphael, squeezing one another's hand tightly, followed Niki to the birthing room. For the second time in just a couple of weeks, they were about to welcome a new member into the family. They held back as Niki entered and approached the bed bearing Cynthia and an apparently unhappy-to-be-here baby. The cries had slowed their approach. Margarite, the doula, was bagging up some items, as she turned and smiled at them.

"You can come in," she said. "This little one just wants everyone to know she has arrived." Niki motioned for them to approach. Raphael walked up next to Niki, with Luke just behind him. Cynthia watched them with a lopsided smile as they neared. They both seemed a bit hesitant to get too close. Niki grabbed Raphael's arm and pulled him closer. Niki, still smizing uncontrollably behind his mask, nodded to Cynthia, who pulled the pink blanket away from the fussy little bundle in her arms. Raphael drew a sharp breath, then fell backwards in a dead faint. Luke caught him, and he and Niki lowered him to the floor.

"He's never done *this* before," Luke looked warily at Niki. Niki's eyes showed he was still grinning.

"He's never been a daddy before," Niki laughed. He patted Raphael's cheeks until he started to come around.

"What ... what happened?" Raphael looked confused as he started to sit up.

"Whoa, stay down," Niki firmly insisted, pressing Raphael's shoulders to the floor. "Just relax a minute, okay? You fainted, Daddy." Luke was leaning over Raphael's face, nodding and sniffling.

"Yeah, baby," Luke said tenderly, "looks like quality *and* quantity won out this time."

"Keep him down," Niki said as he stood and crossed the room to drag a chair over next to Raphael. "Okay, let's pull him up and into the chair."

"I'm fine!" Raphael shook Luke loose, but he did sit. He let out a deep breath as he made eye contact with an apparently amused Cynthia. "Sorry ..." Niki took hold of one of Raphael's hands and squirted sanitizer into it, then handed the bottle to Luke. Raphael, without looking down, automatically rubbed his hands together.

"Don't be sorry, Raphael," Cynthia said. She looked down at the crying baby. "I don't think Lily Rafaela even noticed." Cynthia looked exhausted and uncomfortable, despite the joy in her face. She attempted to reposition herself. Margarite came over and reached down to pick up the baby.

"Thank you, Margarite,' Cynthia sighed and looked instantly better. "She must be starving."

"Hardly," Margarite rocked the crying bundle. "We will try again in a few minutes." She walked around the bed as she explained, "Lily Rafaela hasn't figured out yet what Mommy's boobies are for." She stopped next to the chair and lowered the baby into Raphael's lap. "Just be sure to support her little head." Emotion flooded Raphael's face as he looked down at Lily Rafaela. She had his eyes, no doubt, and hair. A paler version of his caramel complexion. And, apparently, somehow, she'd also inherited the Spicy Asian attitude of Adonis. He gently ran a finger along the tiny chin beneath her open and very vocal mouth. He cooed to her a moment then, inspired by her scrunched up little face, began to sing to her. Haltingly at first. Not a lullaby. Rather, the first stanza of Stevie Wonder's song about a newborn, *Isn't She Lovely*.

Before he got to the fourth line, Lily Rafaela had hiccupped, and begun to quiet. And apparently listen. Her little balled-up fists were still in motion, but her amazingly strong vocal cords had decided to take a break. By the time Raphael got to the end, she almost seemed to be cooing herself, and Luke was fighting back tears. Patricia entered the room with Juan Enrique in her arms. She'd been hanging out in the den, as far from Lily Rafaela's cries as possible, trying to avoid having two babies compete. Which, she knew, could not be avoided for long. Cynthia looked up at Patricia.

"She's already playing favorites, and I'm not it," she said with mock disappointment.

"Not to worry, dear," Margarite patted Cynthia on the shoulder. "As soon as she figures out where her meals are coming from, you'll be her number one."

"Nevertheless," Patricia looked down at a very gay Asian American version of the *Madonna and Child*, "I think we should place a cot in the nursery so Raphael will be comfortable when he sleeps over each night."

"Do I get a vote in this?" Luke laughed, not certain if Patricia was joking.

"Of course, Luke," she bent to get her first good look at a serene Lily Rafaela. "But judging from what I see here, you may be outnumbered. Right Raphael?" Raphael looked up and smized at Patricia.

"Maybe," he posed. "Or maybe we can work out a sleepover arrangement for her." He turned to Luke. "We have room for a bassinet, right?" Luke nodded, still marveling at what he was witnessing.

"We hope you both like the name, Lily Rafaela," Cynthia said. "Luke, Lily was the best we could come up with for a girl's name that honors yours." Raphael and Luke both smiled and nodded as they continued to gaze into Lily Rafaela's eyes. "Now that Raphael has talked some sense into her," Cynthia looked hopefully at Margarite, "should we try again?" As Patricia stepped back, Margarite approached and picked up Lily Rafaela and delivered her back to Cynthia. She picked up a nursing cover from the cabinet nearby, but Cynthia shook her head. No one noticed Niki slipping away.

"Let them watch, Margarite. I've seen all of them naked a thousand times." She looked over at the still seated Raphael. "As long as you promise not to faint again, Daddy." Raphael shook his head, looking a little chagrined as Luke, who had been standing all this time, sat on the floor next to Raphael and took his hand. Raphael leaned over and pressed his lips to Luke's at about the same time Lily Rafaela finally figured things out for herself.

"What the hell is going on?" the never reserved Alex demanded of Niki when he finally reappeared. Niki sat for the first time in several hours and pulled off his mask.

"I promised Ryan I wouldn't drag this out like Juan did." Then, he looked around the room, dragging it out a few more seconds. "Raphael is the father of a beautiful baby girl. We didn't need any DNA test to figure this one out. In fact, if his genes are as dominant as I suspect, she'll probably be as beautiful as him." Ricky was up and out of his chair.

"What's taking so long?" he pleaded. "When do *we* get to see her?" Niki laughed.

"Chill, Daddy. Lily Rafaela is nursing. Finally. Let's give the mommy and daddies a little privacy, okay?" Ricky flashed a momentary pout, but was grinning by the time he sat. Being called daddy made it hard to argue.

Once she got the hang of it, Lily Rafaela wasted no time making the most of her first meal. She started to fuss as soon as she was finished, which was Margarite's cue to hand her back to Raphael. While she was helping Cynthia tidy up, Luke raised up on his knees, and he and Patricia admired Raphael comforting her once again.

"She's so beautiful," Luke whispered. "You're holding your legacy, Raphael." He glanced at Cynthia, to include her. Raphael turned to Luke.

"Well, she may be my legacy, Sir, but more than anything, she's Hiroshi's gift. Her and Juan Enrique, both." Cynthia cocked her head.

"What do you mean, dear?" she asked as Patricia moved around to better see Raphael's face. Raphael glanced up at Patricia, then met Cynthia's gaze.

"Hiroshi was the most generous person we've ever known. If he hadn't become such a good friend and then a member of the family, if he hadn't loved us so much that he bequeathed us this house, so we could sell it to you, you never would have considered creating your family with us. If not for Hiroshi," he looked back up at Patricia, "we wouldn't be holding these two beautiful babies."

"I wish he were here. So we could thank him," Cynthia said quietly, eyeing the bundle in Raphael's arms.

"Oh. You can," Raphael smiled back, a bit knowingly. "He told us how. He will be grateful if we just provide well for our new companions." Raphael turned to Luke, whose eyes had widened. "Right, Sir?"


After the champagne, after yet another celebratory dinner and more than one group hug, Steve and a de-stressed, exhausted Niki retired early. Juan and Ricky slipped next door so Juan could finally see their son's new sister. Raphael and Luke decided to turn in earlier than usual as well. They snuggled awhile on top of the covers, but neither seemed interested in actual sex. In time, Luke found himself on his side, head in hand, silently and proudly gazing at Raphael, who had pulled away and rolled onto his back. He'd tucked one hand behind his head, elbow splayed, and was staring at the ceiling, apparently lost in thought. Luke reached over and rubbed a handy pec.

"Baby. Are you happy? Or worried?" Raphael took a deep breath and turned to Luke with a whimsical smile.

"Yeah," he replied.

"Okay. I know why you're happy." Luke rubbed Raphael's chest a little more roughly. "What are you anxious about?" Raphael smiled as he sighed.

"Lily Rafaela is perfect." His smile grew a little wider. "Isn't she?" Luke nodded but waited for more. "I know Cynthia and Patricia insisted we'd have no financial responsibilities. But. Luke. I want her to have *everything*." Luke issued a low groan as he again snuggled up to Raphael, sliding his arm all the way across Raphael's chest in order to pull him tight. He laid his head down next to Raphael's and quietly spoke into his ear.

"Baby, she has Cynthia. And Patricia. And she has *you*. She already has everything. She's got to be the luckiest little girl in the world." Raphael gave a short little laugh.

"You think?" Raphael turned to Luke, who nodded wordlessly. "You didn't mention her other daddy."

"You mean the one that goes without mentioning?" Raphael laughed harder and pulled his feet towards himself, his knees rising. "Baby, like I said ... she's one lucky girl." Raphael turned and slid one leg between Luke's and one on top, enabling them to fully mesh together in Luke's embrace.

"And you haven't even mentioned the two step-daddies," Raphael's lips brushed against Luke's beard, "if that's what Juan and Ricky are, and the six gay uncles." Luke adjusted position so their eyes and lips met.

"So," Luke whispered, "you agree. Lily Rafaela and Juan Enrique already have everything they need." Raphael batted his eyes, then planted a quick peck.

"I can't argue with that, Sir. For now, anyway." Luke pulled back slightly, enough to better look into Raphael's eyes.

"So, how much paternity leave do you have coming?" Raphael looked startled.

"That's probably not a good idea, Sir," he said after a slight pause.

"Why not?" Luke looked frustrated. "You deserve it."

"That's just it," Raphael replied, displaying an uncharacteristic wispy veil of guilt. "Cynthia will be on maternity leave. If I take paternity leave at the same time, there'll be all kinds of questions. Even though everybody knows I'm gay, a lot of people know we're neighbors. I don't want to make things awkward ... or worse ... for Cynthia." Luke raised that damn eyebrow.

"Baby. The first time Cynthia shows off Lily Rafaela on Zoom, if she hasn't already, everybody will know exactly who the daddy is." Raphael looked perturbed.

"Luke, I'm hardly the only Asian American in the city. Or even in the office."

"Baby, you're the only Asian American who flew out of the office when Cynthia went into labor." That stopped Raphael for a moment.

"Oh. Well. Yeah. But." He met Luke's mischievous gaze. "But we're neighbors. Alex was there, too ..." Raphael knew his argument wasn't as strong as Luke's. Especially given the ubiquitous rumor mill that pervades every office environment. Not to mention Lily's middle name.

"Are you seriously worried, baby? Damn, I should have kept my mouth shut." Luke nuzzled Raphael, wishing he'd left well enough alone. Raphael's emotions were clearly fragile, given the day's events. After a moment of silence between them, Luke tried again. "Don't you think Cynthia has thought this through? Even before she and Patricia approached us?" He tucked a finger under Raphael's chin and tugged. "You know she has, baby." Raphael closed his eyes and chuckled. Then sighed.

"Probably. I just don't want her to get into any kind of trouble. Corporately."

"She won't, baby. She's much too smart for that." Luke pulled away, leading Raphael to impishly reach out for him. Luke slid off the bed, stood and leaned down to pull Raphael with him. "Let's do our ablutions and go to bed. We're going to need a good night's sleep before tomorrow." Raphael gave him a questioning look. "Remember? We've got a couple of ... what did Juan call them? Complicated phone calls to make." Raphael genuinely laughed as he pulled up into Luke's arms.

"Oh yeah. No kidding. And Niki wants to be in on the call to Mama and Angel. We're going to blow their minds."

"And make Mama the happiest she's been in a long time," Luke smiled.

"We'd better clean the guest room before we even call, don't you think?" Raphael suggested. Luke laughed. "You think your parents will come out, too?" Luke nodded.

"Yeah, but I think we can hold them off until the babies are a little older and ready for prime time. They'll have to fly and risk COVID. Better to wait. But they'll love seeing you do your Stevie Wonder impression with Lily Rafaela on Zoom."

"Sorry, Sir," Raphael asserted as he pulled Luke into the bath. "I only do in-person performances. It's in the contract." Luke nodded as if that were actually a thing.

## Twenty-Eight

# "Why me?"

What a difference a baby makes. Never mind two. And not just for Patricia and Cynthia. Or even the daddies. To one extent or another, everyone found themselves adjusting to new responsibilities and schedules. Over the holidays, even more so with COVID lingering, business was slow for everyone. Which made it easier for Mateo to insist on manning the shop alone for hours at a time so Ricky could spend more time with Juan Enrique and Patricia. Which was especially rewarding since Juan was still on paternity leave.

Raphael had not taken paternity leave, despite Cynthia's insistence doing so would not pose a problem for her. But he did take a lot of half-day PTO time, alternating with Luke. The daddies, and even the uncles, became reasonably skilled at diapering, bathing and the occasional bottle feedings, made precise with the help of the instant-read thermometer Alex insisted everyone must use when warming the bottles. It was a rare occurrence for any of them to return home from work or an errand without a case of diapers, a three-pack of swaddles or more disposable liners for the feeding bottles. It was Niki who delighted everyone with the personalized baby-size bodysuits emblazoned with the Golden State Warriors logo. Not that it was a competition, or anything. Cynthia's prediction that the ten daddies and uncles would play a major role had been fully realized.

Mama insisted on being there for the babies' first Christmas. With Cynthia and Patricia's approval, Angel and Raphael couldn't deny her. It took three trips to carry in all the loot crammed into Angel's trunk and back seat, including the bassinet that had served both Raphael and Angel. She had been waiting a very long time to see it put to use again. Raphael tried hard not to rub it in to Angel, but he failed. Miserably.

"Just so you know, Raphael," Angel said as he locked the legs into position in Raphael and Luke's room, "I told Mama a long time ago you guys might beat me in the race to produce a grandkid. Not that I actually believed it, but I did tell her it wasn't that unusual these days, so let's just move on. I gave up ever competing with you after your second wedding in one day, okay?" Luke laughed and Raphael just shook his head. Angel jostled the bassinet to confirm it was stable and solid, then looked over at the two of them. "Do you really think you'll use this?"

"Oh, you bet," Raphael grinned. "We've already figured it out. We'll take turns having sleep overs with Juan and Ricky's baby. We'll give Cynthia and Patricia a break whenever they want. We've seen the benefits of separating Juan Enrique and Lily Rafaela when one of them is out of sorts. You'll see what I mean when you're a daddy." Angel gave Raphael a 'whatever' look.

"So, I meant to ask," Angel looked a bit tentative. "Why Lily Rafaela instead of Rafaela Lily? Like Juan Enrique."

"Lily's not just a sort of honorific for Luke," Raphael answered. "It's also Cynthia's mother's name. I'm good with getting the middle name. Besides, Lily Rafaela rolls off the tongue better. Don't you think?" Angel just smiled, without indicating total buy in.

"We should probably go next door and drag Mama back here," he suggested as both Raphael and Luke nodded. "It's Christmas Eve and we don't want to wear out our welcome." On their way out of the room Angel stopped Raphael, took him by the shoulders and looked into his eyes. "You did good, big brother," he said hoarsely. "She is a beautiful baby." Raphael looked a little embarrassed and smiled.

"Yeah, she is. Thanks. I can only take half the credit." He took advantage of the moment to pull Angel into a hug. "Cynthia did all the work, so be sure to tell her, too, okay?"

"Mm hmm, I will," Angel promised as they pulled apart and caught up with Luke.


Like Christmas morning in households all over the world, Sunday morning was a madhouse in the House of the (covertly) Locked Cock Brotherhood. In addition to having Mama and Angel in house, Ricky had invited Cynthia and Patricia. He couldn't believe it had been so long since they'd last invited them over for pancakes. Mateo, Ryan, Alex and Greg had insisted on eating in the kitchen so there would be more room for Mama and Angel to eat with the mommies and daddies. This also made it easier for Alex to keep the espressos and lattes coming. Feeling a little, but not too, guilty about the segregation, Raphael quietly opened a bottle of Schramsberg and upgraded their freshly squeezed

OJs into mimosas. It was Christmas after all. After breakfast, while Juan and Mama were monopolizing the babies, Raphael ushered Cynthia and Patricia upstairs to get their seal of approval on the bassinet.

"No rush," Raphael insisted, "but whenever you're ready, we can take Lily Rafaela or Juan Enrique for the night. To give you a little breather." They could tell by his face the 'whenever' could be as soon as tonight. Patricia walked over and examined the bassinet more closely. "Was this yours once, Raphael?" she asked.

"And then Angel's," he replied. "Mama kept it, hoping it would come in handy again one day." Luke had quietly wandered in.

"She's quite something, your Mama," Cynthia laughed. "Maricel has given us as much good advice as Margarite." Raphael smiled appreciatively but didn't respond.

"Did Raphael show you these," Luke asked as he crossed the room to the little bookcase and pulled out a handful of thin, colorful books. "Raphael's building a collection of picture books, so he'll be ready for story time when the babies are old enough." Cynthia joined him and took a couple out of his hands to examine them. She looked over at Raphael with gratitude and admiration.

"This is brilliant! You boys are really all in. Not that it hasn't been obvious from day one. I ... I don't know what to say." She sat on the edge of the bed, paging through one of the books.

"Cynthia," Raphael knelt down in front of her, "of course we're all in. These babies have changed our lives just as much as yours. Well. I mean ..." He realized he couldn't possibly put himself in either of their shoes. Cynthia looked up into Patricia's eyes, who was enjoying the moment.

"We just may take you up on that sleep over offer," Patricia said. "Don't be surprised if the first phone call comes at midnight, with two screaming babies in the background."

"Bring it on," Luke laughed. "We're ready." He lifted up a case of diapers in the corner to prove his point. "All we'll need is the baby. And, I guess, a couple of bottles."

"Yeah," Raphael said, rising to his feet, "that's about the only thing we can't do."

"It's a good thing you can't," Cynthia smiled as she rose and handed the books to Patricia. "If you could do that, I fear you would take full possession and we'd have CPS knocking at our door. To investigate child abandonment." Patricia laughed out loud in agreement. Raphael defensively put up his hands.

"If we get carried away, just let us know. Okay? You two," he turned his gaze to Patricia, "get to set all the boundaries." Cynthia took his left hand in both of hers.

"You're doing great." She looked over at Luke, by the diapers. "All of you." Then she met Patricia's gaze. "More and more, each day, we realize we absolutely made the right decision in recruiting all of you into our dream. Into our family." Then she did something very Raphael-like. She planted one on his cheek. And produced a blush, the likes of which Luke had never seen on him before.

It was several weeks before Cynthia relented and offered Raphael and Luke their first opportunity to take Lily Rafaela for a sleep over. Ever so gradually, both babies were sleeping longer between feedings. But the likelihood of getting a full night's sleep was still weeks, if not months, away. Juan and Ricky were a little jealous, but Ricky, for one, was relieved that Raphael and Luke were going first. He was eager to see how the night would go. Cynthia relinquished Lily Rafaela once she'd fallen asleep, after her last evening feeding. She couldn't have done it, had it been with anyone else. But Lily Rafaela had bonded solidly with both Raphael and Luke. And with Niki, as well. For some reason, Raphael's voice and touch always seemed to calm her more quickly than that of anyone else. She seemed to smile more easily, too, when she was in his arms.

You'd have thought Lily Rafaela was a new science experiment. Niki followed Raphael and Luke into their bedroom and showed no signs of leaving. Ricky kept tiptoeing in, confirming everything was okay, then slipping away, only to return again and again. Alex, too, who'd designated himself as the official bottle warmer, had a hard time staying away. At one point. sitting next to Niki on the bed, overlooking the bassinet, he turned to Niki and whispered.

"I just realized, Niki. I don't think we lose our looks as we grow older. We just hand them down to the next generation. And they just keep looking better and better." Niki tried to keep his laugh under his breath as Raphael pounded on Alex's back from behind.

"So," Raphael leaned across the bed to put his mouth to Alex's ear. "Are you saying I'm losing my looks? Already?" Alex shook his head.

"No, she's still a baby. But when she's twenty and a babe, and you know she will be, you'll be this middle-aged guy with a receding hairline and a dad bod."

"And what will you be? Hmmm?" Alex looked at Niki and winked.

"Oh. I'll still be hot. Like Niki. It only happens to guys who have kids." Niki's laugh, as was Luke's, was louder than he'd intended, and Lily Rafaela stirred, but she didn't wake.

"Out," Raphael demanded. "You just lost your visitation privileges, mister." As he rose, Alex leaned down and whispered again into Niki's ear.

"The truth always hits different when you're a daddy." Then from the doorway, "No need to tell me when to heat a bottle. Lily Rafaela will let me know."

And she did. Around two a.m. Raphael was holding her, trying to comfort her, and letting her suck on his finger when Alex opened the door and delivered her late-night snack.

"No charge," Alex muttered as he turned on his heels and exited. Raphael scooted up to lean back against the headboard next to Luke, who sat up as Raphael guided the bottle's nipple into place. The little girl who had no idea what a boob was for in her first minutes of freedom, was now a pro with both boobs and bottles. She almost sucked it out of Raphael's hand.

"I think she was hungry," Luke chuckled, his mussed Outlander locks looking especially sexy in the dim light. Raphael turned to Luke and smiled, then puckered.

"Yeah. Me, too, Sir." He puckered again until Luke got it and leaned over to deliver a lip-on-lip. Raphael turned back to watch Lily Rafaela. Without looking away, he said, "This still seems so surreal."

"There's an understatement," Luke again kissed Raphael, this time on his bare shoulder. "If we were still awake this time last night, it would have been you sucking *my* nipples, or my..." Luke cleared his throat. Raphael's laugh bounced Lily Rafaela as she fed.

"You can say it, Sir. She doesn't know what cock means. Yet." Luke chuckled under his breath. He rested his head on Raphael's shoulder, watching.

"Which brings up a question," Luke said, then paused. "How long before we have to start wearing clothes around them?" Raphael tipped the bottle a little higher.

"Mmmm. Well, Sir, since most toddlers love to rip their clothes off and run around naked themselves, I'd say maybe until they learn how to read our tattoos." That got a real laugh out of Luke.

"So ... two years for her and maybe four for Juan Enrique?"

"Hmmm?"

"Baby, everybody knows girls are more verbal than boys."

"If you say so. Like I said before to Cynthia and Patricia. They get to set the boundaries. When they say 'put some clothes on!' that's when we'll do it." He turned to catch Luke's eye. "I, for one, am all for raising a couple of proud little nudists. So, we'll see."

When Lily Rafaela finished her bottle, Raphael handed it to Luke, who handed Raphael a little cloth so he could tidy up her mouth and

chin. It was like they were old pros at this. Raphael lifted her up and
shouldered her, patting her gently on the back to induce a burp or two.
By the time she'd complied, and Raphael had resumed cradling her,
Luke had returned from rinsing off the used bottle in the kitchen. As she
began to nod off in Raphael's arms, he turned to Luke and whispered.

"Sir, it has been a very long time since your last dare, so I have one for
you. A long distance dare."

"Okay," Luke groggily replied. "It's a little late, but where am I
going?"

"No. Not long distance in space. In time." Raphael turned his adoring eyes back to Lily Rafaela. "If anything should happen to me, you
have to make sure she has everything she needs to live her best life." Luke
groaned quietly.

"Baby, we've talked about this already. We have her and Juan Enrique
surrounded." He sighed a sigh of the sleep deprived. Of a lover whose
lover never ceased to astound him. "Besides, nothing's going to happen
to you. You'll be the one to walk her down the aisle. Unless you want
me to walk with you, too." Raphael turned to him, misty eyed.

"That'll be a later dare, Sir. A reserve dare, I guess." He looked back
at Lily Rafaela. "Oh ... oh," he groaned, "I have a cramp in my leg. Can
you put her back in the bassinet?" Luke planted one on Raphael's cheek,
then slipped out of the other side of the bed to obey.


The cramp had been a subtle clue that Raphael had been slacking off
his fitness routine. And he wasn't alone. Between work and spending
time with the babies, and the extra errands babies are notorious for, the
gym had seen very little action from anyone since the births. It was Niki,
who was more immersed in the topics of health and fitness, for adults
anyway, who took the reins. He corralled Alex, Raphael and Mateo for a
run that was to be the first of a newly revived routine. Just like they used
to do. It was a little late to qualify as a New Year's Resolution, but what
mattered is that they were back at it. And within a couple of weeks, the
runs and the gym began to feel routine again. An enforced little bit of
'me time' for each of them. And somehow, there was still plenty of time
for the babies. At least for the daddies and uncles.

Niki decided the mommies deserved a break from their demanding
routine, too. He got the rest of the family to agree. They planned it for
a day when they would be celebrating three wedding anniversaries that
evening, allowing them to feel a little less guilty for taking time away
from the babies.

"Niki!" Patricia answered the knock at the back door. "Happy Valentine's Day, dear. Come in. You know you don't need to knock."

"Happy Valentine's Day," Niki grinned, a bit sheepishly as he entered. He followed Patricia into the living room where Cynthia and the babies were gathered, a half-consumed breakfast tea service on the coffee table.

"Would you like tea?" Cynthia asked from the couch.

"No thanks." Niki sat on the floor next to Juan Enrique in his baby rocker. "Actually, I came over to give you two a little Valentine's gift."

"Ohhh," Patricia cooed, shaking her shoulders. "What did you bring?"

"Me. When was the last time the two of you did anything together? Just the two of you?" The two of them exchanged looks. Patricia drew down the corners of her mouth in thought.

"Um ..."

"Exactly," Niki nodded. "So today, for Valentine's Day, the two of you are having lunch together at Zuni Café. I'll look after the babies. You have a reservation at twelve-thirty, so I'll be back at noon. Meanwhile, go upstairs, and put on those fabulous outfits you wore the day you conned us into helping you do this." He picked up Juan Enrique to illustrate who 'this' was. "Be sure I have plenty of milk on hand so you can share a bottle of wine with lunch. Which is on all of us, by the way. So don't hold back." Cynthia opened her mouth, and Niki cut her off. "Don't argue. You deserve it." Then he grinned. "See, I can give orders just like Alex and Raphael." He slid Juan Enrique back into his rocker, then stood without giving them an opportunity to protest. "I'll be back at noon!"

True to his words, Niki returned on time for the changing of the guard. At Zuni, it was clear the waiter, in his black slacks, white shirt and bow tie, had been briefed. Despite his earnest and lavish descriptions of several of the wine list's stars, he couldn't sell them a bottle to save himself. However, since they had left Niki well supplied, they did relent and each ordered a glass of wine. Although the mahi mahi was tempting, they decided to split a Caesar salad and the world-famous roast chicken for two, since they hadn't had a meal out in ages. When it came time, the waiter was more successful with the dessert menu. Two and a half luxurious hours later, their Uber delivered them home. Sated, relaxed and almost guilt-free. As had become habit by now, when Cynthia returned from her periodic forays back to the office, they let themselves in quietly in case one or both babies might be sleeping. The living room was deserted, so they crept up the stairs, and could hear Niki talking as they neared the nursery. They stopped short of the doorway, surprised by what they saw, and silently watched.

"Yeah, just like this," Niki said, his back to the doorway, as he swung the brightly colored bird mobile from side to side. Ryan was next to him, and they had both babies lined up sideways in what would be Juan Enrique's crib, once he was old enough. "See? They're both tracking the movement with their eyes. That's a really good sign. In fact, they're a little ahead of some babies their age." Cynthia and Patricia exchanged amazed looks, but remained silent.

"So you've studied this already?" Ryan asked, as he took hold of the mobile and took his own turn.

"From my developmental psych class, yeah. It's not easy to get into it, if you're not in health sciences, but you should think about it. It might be applicable to some of your studies. I can't wait until they're old enough for the hide the toy game." Patricia took Cynthia's arm and pulled her away and back toward the stairs.

"It appears we left them in good hands," she whispered.

"Indeed," Cynthia's eyes widened. After a short pause, and quite seriously, Patricia continued.

"You'll think *I'm* daft, but I think we should do this again."

"You're not daft. Lunch was superb," Cynthia nodded.

"Yes, that, too," Patricia replied confusingly, but she headed back toward the nursery before Cynthia could get a clarification. "What have we here?" she announced as she entered the nursery with Cynthia on her heels.

"Hi!" Ryan let go of the mobile and turned. "Niki's demonstrating how to test the development of the babies. I, uh, hope you don't mind that I came over."

"Of course not, Ryan," Cynthia moved to his side to see two perfectly happy babies, side by side, staring up at the mobile. "Tell us more." Niki did. He seemed as proud of the babies' progress as he hoped Cynthia and Patricia would be. When he finished, as she lifted Juan Enrique from the crib, Patricia talked Niki and Ryan into staying a little longer for tea, to thank them for their little getaway.

"Niki, Ryan, you may have spoiled us," Cynthia admitted, over tea. "I'd forgotten how nice it is to have someone else wait on me. No pressure," she glanced at Patricia, "but if you're up for it, we'd love to do this again. Just the babysitting. We'll take care of the bill next time."

"One thing I learned early on, when I joined this family, is their commitment to routine and tradition," Ryan, the anthropologist, said. "Why not make this a regular thing ... maybe every week?" He looked over at Niki. "We're happy to help. It's actually kind of fun."

"That's very sweet, Ryan," Patricia met Niki's gaze. "Is it fun for you Niki?"

"More than just fun," Niki replied. He glanced at Ryan then back to Patricia. "I haven't said this out loud to anyone yet, but after all this, I'm thinking of changing my focus from respiratory therapy to postnatal

care. And maybe, eventually, neonatal care once I have more experience."
He looked down at Lily Rafaela in her little rocker by his side. "I guess
you could say these babies have had a big influence on my life." Then he
looked sheepish again. "I mean. I know they've affected everyone's."

"Yes, indeed they have," Cynthia laughed. "Let's try once a month, to
start. We very much appreciated our little getaway today. Give our sincere
thanks to everyone." Both Ryan and Niki nodded their agreement as
they stood to go. Niki had trouble taking his eyes off Lily Rafaela, but
finally leaned down and tickled her chin before giving Juan Enrique his
own chin noogie.

"Other than weekends, I have Tuesdays and Thursdays open in the
afternoons this semester," Niki prompted as he led Ryan toward the
back door, "so you just let me know. Okay?" Cynthia and Patricia shared
amused grins and called out their assent as they retook full possession of
their babies.

Cynthia and Patricia had many ... maybe intense is the best description
... conversations over the next couple of weeks. This time it was Patricia
gradually wearing down Cynthia. It was quite the reversal. To her credit,
Cynthia never called Patricia daft. Well, maybe once, but in a fun, loving
way. Cynthia kept raising concerns, and Patricia kept batting them away.
Eventually Patricia realized Cynthia wasn't really objecting any longer,
just testing Patricia's commitment and resolve. It seemed pretty ironclad.
All that remained was to approach Niki.

"How are we doing?" Patricia asked after she and Cynthia had eased
through the front door. It was their second luncheon, one they took to
please Niki as much as themselves. The babies, side-by-side on a blanket
on the living room floor, were apparently taking turns reaching for a
rattle Niki was alternately dangling above each of them. Daisy was su-
pervising from her spot in front of the fireplace.

"We're doing great," Niki looked up.

"Conducting another test, are we?" Cynthia asked as she sat on a
nearby chair to watch. Patricia headed into kitchen to put the kettle on.

"Yeah. Sort of," Niki grinned. "Mostly just playing. It's so cool to see
how quickly they develop new skills." Cynthia chuckled.

"How much longer before you can teach them to do the hoovering?"
she asked. Niki looked confused. "The vacuuming." He laughed.

"I don't know. At least another year," he kidded. She sat down on
the floor next to Lily Rafaela and confirmed that her diaper was fresh.
Lily Rafaela grinned at her and reached. Cynthia picked her up and

began cuddling her. Niki put down the rattle and followed suit with Juan Enrique. He met Cynthia's approving gaze. "So, tell me about your lunch." She did. Then as Patricia entered with the tea tray, Cynthia asked Niki if he had told anyone about his new career plans.

"I did, yeah. Steve was supportive. He's always supportive, no matter what. He's probably the best husband ever. Everyone else likes the idea, too."

"I'm so happy to hear you say that about Steve," Patricia said as she poured. "We have a question for you, Niki. More a proposal, actually, and it's one Steve should be involved in, too." Niki laid Juan Enrique down and sat up on his haunches, focusing on Patricia. She handed him his tea. She took a deep breath as he sipped.

"I'll just say it," Patricia continued. "Niki, we want to have another baby. And we want you to be the father." Niki nearly spilled his tea. He set the cup down and sat upright, looking back and forth between Patricia and Cynthia. Both were giving him open looks, awaiting his reaction.

"I ... really?" He looked at each of the babies, then back up. "You're kidding, right? It's not April Fool's yet." He swallowed hard.

"We're not kidding," Cynthia said quietly, looking at Patricia rather than Niki. "I know it must sound a little crazy." Niki snorted an embarrassed laugh.

"A little, yeah." He gestured to the babies. "I mean, these two are already a handful." He fell silent a moment, then resumed eye contact with Patricia. "Why me?"

"Why not you?" Patricia asked gently. Niki didn't immediately respond. "Niki ..." Patricia glanced at Cynthia who was intently watching Niki. "We were thrilled to have Juan and Raphael turn out to be the fathers of Juan Enrique and Lily Rafaela. We would have been thrilled had it been any of you. I hope that was always clear." She held the little plate of cookies toward him. "Including you, dear." Niki didn't know how to react. What exactly was Patricia saying?

"If you were going to go through all this again, wouldn't it make more sense to choose Luke? Or Steve. Or Alex?" When neither of them answered, Niki pressed. "Were you ... were you disappointed that I wasn't one of the daddies? Is that what you're saying?" A funny little smile formed on Patricia's lips as she set the plate down.

"Niki, I'm trying not to say that." Niki, his tea forgotten, picked up Juan Enrique and looked into his big, brown eyes. He turned him around in his lap, so he was facing Patricia.

"This little guy deserves one hundred percent of your love, Patricia."

"And he will always have it, Niki. From me, from Cynthia, Juan and Ricky. And all of the rest of you." She slid off the couch to sit nearer

Niki. Juan Enrique clumsily reached out for her and she lifted him out of Niki's lap and into her own, turning him to face Niki. "I'm perhaps being a little facetious when I say there's more love around here than any two babies can absorb. But I think you know what I mean." She looked up at Cynthia, who was still silently observing the exchange between Patricia and Niki. "If it were just Cyndi and me, I don't think we'd dare take on a third baby. At least not for some time. If ever." Niki alternated his gaze between Juan Enrique's slobbery smile and Patricia's encouraging one. He swallowed.

"It's my turn to confess something to you. Please don't hate me." Patricia and Cynthia exchanged a look. "I, uh, I didn't donate. That's why I wasn't one of the daddies. I couldn't ..." Finally, Cynthia broke her silence. She reached out and laid a hand on Niki's forearm.

"Darling ... why not?" Niki swallowed hard again. He shrugged his shoulders and turned to Cynthia, a little misty eyed.

"I ... it's ..." He paused, neither Cynthia nor Patricia coming to his rescue. He took another deep breath. "I know what it's like growing up as a little Black kid in this country. You're both really smart, but I don't you can fully understand." He paused, not wanting to offend them. "I didn't want be responsible for the almost certain indignities another kid would have to go through. That the two of *you* would go through. And I guess even for me to suffer, all over again." Niki looked miserable.

"Niki," Cynthia laid Lily Rafaela back down so she could embrace Niki. She looked stricken. "My god, Niki, that's the noblest thing I've heard in a long time. You ... you were trying to protect *us*?" Niki let out a little laugh snort, then sniffled.

"And me. I'm not that noble."

"You do realize," Patricia said, pointing Juan Enrique's right arm at Niki, as if it were him pointing, "that what you were really doing was denying us, and the world, the brilliant and beautiful offspring of one of the most generous, loving, considerate men to walk among us. We shall not let you deny us again." Niki smiled in spite of himself, seeing the innocent glee on Juan Enrique's face. Patricia scooted closer, so he was now encircled. "Niki, don't you think things have changed in the last twenty, thirty years? As I said, don't you agree your baby, our baby, would grow up surrounded by a loving, supportive family?"

"Maybe," Niki conceded. "Most of the time, for sure. But. There's a big, bad world out there."

"Do you not feel safe now, Niki?" Cynthia asked. "You are so confident. So accomplished. Does your youth still haunt you?"

"No," Niki genuinely smiled. "I don't think so. I'm the luckiest guy in the world. I've said so, many times. But, that's just it. I'm really lucky." He took another deep breath. "So many Black kids ... and adults ... aren't so lucky." Patricia leaned back against the couch, rubbing Juan Enrique's belly. She glanced back and forth between Cynthia and the top of Juan Enrique's head. Niki was staring at the empty blanket, not knowing what more to say. Cynthia released her embrace of him and picked up Lily Rafaela again.

"Niki," Patricia finally said, "I do understand what you are saying. And it breaks my heart. For you, for every Black ... and brown person in this country." She sighed. "I'm not as smart as you think I am. It never occurred to me, what you've just said. So. I respect your reason for not wanting to accept our proposal." She glanced at Cynthia, who was clearly surprised at how easily Patricia had conceded. Then Patricia leaned forward and laid a hand on Niki's knee. "But promise me. You will think about it. For a day. Or, two. After all, Niki, we already have two children who are bi-racial or bi-ethnic or whatever. I hope it will never be necessary, but, if so, we'll be the leading experts in dealing with any tossers we, or the children, may encounter. Count on it!" Niki knew in his heart she was serious. A little smile formed on his lips.

"I don't doubt that. For a minute."

"Not to mention, Niki ... *you* will be here to protect her or him, too." The nodding look she gave Niki assured him Patricia wasn't patronizing him.

"One other thing, Niki, since you brought up race," Cynthia again touched his arm. "We don't want you to be the father because you are Black. We want you because you are you. Niki. Maricel. Raphael. Angel. Malaluan-Phillips. See ..." Cynthia looked a little smug. "I remembered. All of it. You may be one of a kind, Niki, but don't you think the world would be a better place with another of you. A Niki two dot oh?"

He stared at Cynthia a moment, a little dumb-struck, before meeting Patricia's gaze. "Okay. I'll think about it."

"Talk it over with Steve," Cynthia suggested. Niki actually grinned.

"To be honest, he would be thrilled." He looked a little embarrassed. "Steve was very disappointed when I refused to donate."

"Of course he was," Patricia quietly said. She reached over and retrieved the little plate and once again offered Niki a cookie. "Thank you for granting us another little getaway, Niki." This time he took a cookie and crunched.

"Yes, Niki," Cynthia concurred. "Thank you. For everything."

## Twenty-Nine

# No Secrets, Indeed

STEVE EASED THE FRONT door closed after a shorter than usual day at the office. He was surprised to find Niki sitting with his back to the doorway, in his fireplace chair, staring into the fire. His laptop sat open on the desk. Steve slipped off his shoes, then walked over and sat in the companion chair, still in his street clothes.

"Tough day?" he asked. Niki turned his gaze to Steve and attempted a smile.

"Sorta, yeah," he sighed.

"Were the babies a challenge?" Niki laughed and truly smiled.

"They were great. Like always. I promised Cynthia I'd teach them how to vacuum by their first birthday." Steve snorted.

"If you can do that, they'll give you a Ph.D. instead of a B.S. So, is it school that's got you down?" Niki thought about lying, but shook his head and again tried to smile.

"No, just trying to work through some things. When I get it figured out, I'll tell you." Steve nodded, knowing that sometimes Niki needed a little introspection before sharing.

"Maybe you ... when was the last time you pupped out?" Steve suggested. "Would it help to get into pup space for a little while?" He glanced over at the laptop. Niki sat up.

"Yeah," he grinned, instantly happier. "This is why I love you. Good idea." He stood and held out a hand to help Steve up. "Just for an hour. Or two."

For the first hour or so in the puppy cage Pup Niki simply occupied pup head space. He tried not to think about school, the babies, the pandemic, the fact he and Steve would have KP duty tomorrow. He was just a pup. And it was cathartic. But then, even though still in the puppy cage, still in pup gear, he drifted away from pup head space and began to contemplate Patricia's proposal. And what it could mean. Would mean.

He mentally began listing the pros and cons. The benefits and challenges. He already knew the benefits of having Juan Enrique and Lily Rafaela in his life. How different would it be to cuddle and nurture his own flesh and blood? He knew all the reasons to decline their request. He had already done so. Twice. And he understood and appreciated the points Patricia and Cynthia had pressed upon him. This *was* an amazing family. Any kid would be lucky to grow up within it. As lucky as him? That's how he'd described himself earlier. Or could this child be even luckier than him, having him as a father. Could he be the kind of father he'd needed, and longed for, as a child? Could he be as good a father as Pop had been in his teens? Could he earn the kind of love and respect from his child he'd had for Pop? Especially considering he wouldn't be present every minute of every day. Although, he would be right next door. And Patricia had basically vowed to be a protective elephant mom, so it wouldn't be up to him, all the time, to protect the child.

Hmmm. It would be ... kind of incredible, wouldn't it? Niki two dot oh, maybe? Whether it was a boy or a girl. Pup Niki laid his hooded head down and sighed. And then he napped.

The sound of the cage door opening woke Pup Niki, who lifted his hooded head as Steve reached in and squeezed his snout. Pup Niki raised up and bounded out, signaling that perhaps Steve's suggestion had, in fact, been a good one. Pup Niki panted excitedly and rubbed up against Steve affectionately. Steve held up the keyring and the pup sat back on his haunches and raised both paws so Steve could unlock the mitts. The hood followed.

"It's almost dinner time. Did Pup Niki have a good nap?" Niki smiled and looked genuinely serene.

"Yeah, oh yeah. This was just what I needed." He leaned forward to deliver a very human kiss. "Thank you for suggesting it."

"Well, Niki, it's been a while. I'm glad it helped." He looked gently into Niki's eyes. "So ... what did you figure out?" Niki looked up at the ceiling and drew a deep breath. When he resumed eye contact, he was sporting a mischievous smile.

"Steve, remember before our wedding, weddings, when Alex wouldn't tell us anything, or almost nothing. And how the day was so amazing we were glad he hadn't told us?" Steve uttered a short laugh.

"I remember the amazing part. But I don't remember ever saying I was glad it was all a mystery." He paused a beat, and when his husband of few words didn't say anything, Steve pressed. "So, why are you bringing that up? Who's getting married?" Niki laughed and shook his head.

"Nobody. No, what I mean is ... sometimes it's better to keep something secret until the right time. Even from you. Because this is maybe even better than our wedding day." Steve's eyes widened.

"Puppy. Don't do this to me! Did you get some kind of national award at school or something?" Niki bounced in place, clearly a hundred times happier than he had been, sitting in front of the fireplace.

"You are so cold. Not even close. And don't keep guessing. I have a feeling you'll find out soon enough. I'm just not sure when."

"Got it. You have a secret, but don't know when it won't be a secret. Do I have that right?"

"Right." Niki looked very satisfied. And happy. And that was all that mattered to Steve right now. Besides, he was counting on Niki letting something slip sooner than later anyway.

Once he'd decided, Niki could hardly wait to share the news with Patricia and Cynthia. Maybe, just maybe, he was afraid that if he didn't act quickly he might talk himself out of it. So, as soon as everyone had left the house for work or class the next morning, he went next door.

"I see you brought your own coffee," Cynthia said as she led him through the house into the living room where Patricia was entertaining the babies on a blanket, alternating between tickles and taking bites of toast. Cynthia was dressed for work.

"I should have texted first," Niki said, nodding to Cynthia. "I don't want to make you late for the office."

"The office can wait," Cynthia said, motioning to a chair for Niki. She sat as well. Patricia lifted Juan Enrique into her lap and turned him so they both fully faced Niki. She was encouraged by what she saw on his face.

"Have you decided?" she asked. She lifted Juan Enrique's little hands and held them over his eyes, causing both Niki and Juan Enrique to giggle.

"Yeah," he replied and immediately became emotional. He was looking at Juan Enrique. He sniffed. "How could I say no?"

"Niki, that's wonderful!" Patricia clapped Juan Enrique's hands.

"What did Steve say?" Cynthia asked as she stood. Niki sat up straighter and sipped from his travel mug.

"I, uh, I didn't tell Steve. Or anybody. Can we keep this between us, until we know everything's going to be okay?" He looked down at his feet, then back at Cynthia. "My mother had a miscarriage, after she had me. It kind of messed her up. For quite a while. I just want to be sure, before we tell anyone." Cynthia and Patricia both looked at him compassionately, their joy momentarily brushed aside. "As for Steve, like I said, he'll be thrilled." A big grin spread across his face, reigniting Patricia's and Cynthia's delight. "I can't wait to tell him."

Years earlier, when they were hoping to establish the House of the Locked Cock Brotherhood, Niki had vowed that none of them would be able to harbor secrets any longer, living under the same roof. Yet, here he was, keeping one of the biggest secrets of his life. Or at least hoping to. One minute he wanted to make the big announcement, but just as quickly he'd change his mind. For him this was big, bigger than the initial donation rounds. This time, there would be no mystery. No DNA test. Juan wouldn't be able to torture anyone, intentionally or not. In a way, he told himself, fair was fair. Steve, Luke and Raphael had kept the secret of his impending foray into puppyhood right up until moments before the van arrived. Until now, that had been the longest week of his life. This secret, if he could keep it, would have to last for months.

The next step required Niki to not only withhold information from Steve, but to go behind his back as well. Not that Steve would have minded for a minute, had he known the reason why. Still, Niki felt guilty when he got the text from Patricia on Friday morning, a couple of weeks later, that 'now would be a good time.' Even though his reason for being caged was far different from Alex's, or even Raphael's, he'd never handled the keys to this newer Cobra cage Ricky had given him for his birthday. Nor to his original steel cage that Raphael had locked onto him that first time. After today he would never be able to say that again. Oh well, he sighed, it's for a good cause. A great cause. He rose from his laptop, ran upstairs and retrieved the keys and his phone and hurried next door. Patricia greeted him with a nervous smile.

"I hope I'm not interrupting your studies, Niki," she said as they walked into the living room. Both babies were upstairs, sleeping.

"No worries," he smiled. "This is way more important than school right now. Besides, we've all been working and studying hard lately, so this probably won't take very long." He laughed, embarrassed. "If you know what I mean."

"Do I ever," she laughed back. "I vaguely remember ..." her words trailed off. She ran a hand through her hair. "There's a vial in the bathroom down here. Before I go upstairs is there anything else you need?"

He held up the keys and the phone containing motivational photos and videos.

"I'm good. I'll come up when I'm done. Want me to look after the babies while you ... umm ..." They both laughed again.

"I'm sorry to put you through this," Patricia looked remorseful.

"It's okay," Niki smiled back. "I'm half a nurse, so, I'm good." She put a hand on his forearm, then turned and headed upstairs. Niki looked at the keys in his right hand, then slowly walked down the hall to the bath.

Keeping the secret turned out to be easier than Niki had feared. School was more challenging than ever, and it was easy to get lost in his studies. School helped so much, in fact, he'd committed to a summer course hoping it would continue to occupy his mind and time. Then, there were the babies. As the weeks passed, he'd made a game out of teaching them to roll over. They were getting better at grabbing things, like his puppy tag and the collars around Raphael's and Ricky's necks. And the straps on the body harnesses they both continued to wear regularly, with concerns about hiding risqué tattoos still a long way away. Another enticement, unfortunately, were Juan's nipple rings.

"Mijo," Juan grimaced one evening on one of Juan Enrique's sleep-over nights, "either I'm going to have to start wearing a shirt or switch out these bead rings for barbells." Ricky laughed as he slid off the bed.

"I guess it's a good thing we still haven't pierced mine, Papito." He looked down at his own well-trained nipples. "Although, he has tried to feed off me a couple of times, so I guess we're even." Then, excitedly, "I'll be right back." He dashed out the door and returned a moment later with Raphael. The two of them climbed onto the bed. Juan Enrique enthusiastically reached out for Raphael. Reluctantly, Juan handed him over.

"Raphael," Ricky asked, "does Lily Rafaela ever pull on your nipple rings?" Before Raphael could answer Juan Enrique underscored the question, to both Ricky's and Juan's amusement. Raphael's face twisted in pain as he pried Juan Enrique's unexpectedly strong fingers free. He looked accusingly at Juan.

"Don't you think he's a little young for World's Second Best Leather Boy training? Jeez." Juan and Ricky both laughed as Juan shook his head.

"No, this is all independent study on his part," Juan assured, proudly grinning.

"She's played with them a little," Raphael said. "I guess they're shiny. Luke's hair gets plenty of attention, but, no, she hasn't learned this trick yet."

"She will," Ricky asserted. "Just you wait. Juan had a good idea. To switch out to barbells. I thought maybe you might want to do the same thing. Maybe you guys should go see Jake together." He looked encouragingly at Juan, then Raphael. Juan Enrique made his move again.

"Owww!" Raphael pried him loose. He looked at Juan. "Is Saturday good for you?" Juan nodded and reached out to reclaim Juan Enrique while Raphael looked down to assess the damage.

By the end of June, there was no way to continue keeping Niki's secret. Patricia was beginning to show. To support Niki, they'd avoided dining in the House of the Locked Cock Brotherhood so often, and when doing so, both had declined wine. They explained they were so out of practice, still, that they didn't want to feel 'buzzed' with the babies in their care. So far, the guys appeared to buy that line. But the loose tops and sweatshirts could only hide so much. Besides, the pregnancy was going well, which had been Niki's sole reason for keeping it under wraps. It was time to come clean.

"When should we do it?" Niki asked over tea and cookies, following another babysitting session. Patricia had insisted they couldn't wait much longer.

"How about today?" Cynthia replied, always the efficient one. "We could come over this evening, after your dinner. Perhaps with a treat." Niki screwed up his face in thought, his eyes tracking back and forth.

"I don't know if you've noticed, but this family loves dramatic announcements and intrigue. What if ..." He paused and looked deviously into Cynthia's and Patricia's eyes. "You know those absurd gender reveal parties?" Both nodded. "What if we have a 'baby reveal' party. July Fourth is next week. We could have a cookout, and then, I don't know, unveil a decorated cake that says 'Congratulations Patricia, Cynthia, Niki and Steve?'" Patricia started laughing, half under her breath. Cynthia dubiously looked at her, then back at Niki.

"Wouldn't that be a lot of work?" Cynthia asked. Patricia reached over and placed a hand on Cynthia's forearm.

"Darling," she said, "remember their wedding? Pardon the pun, but by comparison this would be a piece of cake." She looked at Niki. "You do know where to get the cake?" He nodded, grinning in appreciation of Patricia's enthusiasm.

"I'll take care of everything. We will, I mean. We'll host it, do the cooking. Alex loves planning a party. We just won't tell him about the cake."

"So, we just show up?" Cynthia confirmed.

"Well, you will be bringing dessert," Niki grinned. Cynthia laughed. Relieved, not just about the party planning, but more about how fully and comfortably Niki was embracing his role as the father of their third, and presumably final, addition to the family.

Alex was clearly in charge of the Fourth of July party, but he wasn't working alone, delegating a variety of tasks to other members of the family. He and Raphael worked out the menu, and Mateo was named grill master. In addition to regular and Beyond Brats, he'd also be cooking marinated chicken breasts and skewered prawns. Alex volunteered himself to make the potato salad, his mother's recipe, and Raphael was tasked with the coleslaw, since it was an enduring favorite for everyone. Greg volunteered to make baked beans. When Luke asked to be assigned the dessert, Niki informed him Cynthia and Patricia had beat him to it. He didn't complain.

Alex and Raphael made stops a couple of times on the way home from the office to pick up party favors and decorations. This was the babies' first Fourth, after all, and although they wouldn't have a clue what was going on, it would be fun to share the pictures with them once they were old enough to appreciate them. That was their excuse, anyway, for going all out. Besides, Niki had invited Mama and Angel, not that Mama needed a special occasion to make the trip to spend time with the babies. Everyone was looking forward to the day.

Anticipation dimmed, however, when Mama called Sunday afternoon, to say she'd come down with a cold. Ever since her bout with COVID, she'd seemed especially susceptible to whatever bug was going around. It wasn't a bad cold, she assured Niki and Raphael, but she didn't want to bring any germs around the babies. Niki told her he understood, but he didn't take the news well. Both Steve and Raphael could tell he was more disappointed than they would have expected.

"Puppy," Steve said at one point, "Mama's never been here for the Fourth before. They can come up any time after she's better. At least, back home, they'll actually be able to see the fireworks show."

"Yeah," Niki morosely agreed. The fireworks he was anticipating were of a much different variety than the ones that were usually shrouded in fog along the Embarcadero every July. After he thought about it for a while he told himself it was still going to be a stellar day, springing the news on everyone else in the family. By dinnertime, he'd put his disappointment behind him. He was once again looking forward to surreptitiously picking up the cake the next day.

The fog burned away by late morning on the Fourth. The decorations looked great. By mid-afternoon the weather was almost exactly as ordered, never a sure thing in San Francisco in July. Even though Mama wasn't able to attend, everyone still adopted the company dress code. They wanted to be presentable in all those archival photos to be shared later, when the babies were no longer babies. Mostly, the mommies and babies hung out and ate in the gazebo, to protect them from the sun. Before the first round of grilling was ready, Juan and Ricky had fun toting the babies around both gardens, explaining each plant and letting them touch blossoms and leaves. Later the babies actually did eat a little. They'd recently started on solid food, if you could call pureed sweet potatoes, carrots or butternut squash solid. As usual, they ended up wearing almost as much of the Stage One delicacies as they swallowed. During the meal, daddies and uncles wandered in and out of the gazebo, taking turns with the babies, so the mommies could eat. Otherwise, they lounged and dined on blankets nearby. Daisy did her share of wandering too, reveling in sharing her outdoors with so many humans. She cajoled more than her usual share of bites as well. It was a lazy, tasty, welcome day. A chill kind of day for the unsuspecting. Once everyone had had their fill, Ryan and Alex began collecting plates and utensils.

"What do we need to bring out for the dessert?" Alex asked Cynthia and Patricia. "Spoons, bowls, forks?"

"Oh, no dessert for me," Steve moaned. "Not right now anyway. I'm stuffed." Patricia placed Juan Enrique in his rocker and stepped out of the gazebo. She looked down at Steve on the blanket.

"This is one dessert you won't pass on, Steve," she said confidently. "Alex, we just need small plates and forks. And a big knife." She looked at Niki. "Niki, if you please." He rose and followed her toward the gate, looking back and smiling just before he disappeared.

"This must be some dessert," Steve said to Greg and Mateo. Moments later Ryan and Alex brought out the dinnerware and stacked it on the table in the gazebo. Everyone was ready, curious to see what was coming. Niki came through the gate first, carrying a small table from Cynthia and Patricia's garden. He positioned it between the blanket Steve, Greg, Ryan and Mateo were sitting on and the gazebo. Cynthia followed with a large, round, white frosted cake which she held above waist level until she set it on the table. From their places on the ground, everyone could see there were plastic decorations of some sort rising up from the cake. Steve stood, since Patricia had singled him out, and looked down at the cake. Three plastic cherubs on thin, springy rods appeared to be flying above it, where the lettering spelled out Niki's message: 'Congratulations Patricia, Cynthia, Niki & Steve.' The cake was between Steve and Niki. He looked up into Niki's eyes. Wanting to believe what he thought this meant, but afraid to say anything yet. A big, weepy smile broke out on Niki's face and he nodded. Steve looked at Patricia, next to Niki, who'd now been joined by Cynthia.

"Congratulations, Steve," Patricia smiled. "Our baby is due in January." Steve's breath caught and he moved to Niki and pulled him into his arms, Niki's face pressed into his chest while Steve, Patricia and Cynthia all held eye contact. No words were exchanged, but the three of them alone knew and acknowledged what this moment really meant. What it took for Niki to take this step. Steve didn't yet know why or how this had all come about. He just knew it had been a monumental decision for Niki. He pulled his head back in order to see Niki's face.

"I love you. I'm so proud of you, Niki," he said quietly, but loudly enough for everyone to hear. "And I'm so happy for you." As Niki buried his face in Steve's chest again, Steve smiled at Patricia and Cynthia. "And for you. For all of us." Meanwhile, Raphael had dashed into the house. He was returning with his phone when he saw Patricia about to cut the cake.

"Wait!" he yelled. "Not yet, Patricia." As soon as he realized what was happening, Raphael knew why Niki had been so disappointed that Mama and Angel couldn't attend. He was tapping out a text as he walked toward the cake and the group around it. "I just want to get a pic to send to Mama and Angel." His text to Angel had asked when he and Mama would next be together. The reply, *'I'm at Mama's now. Went grocery shopping.'* came while Raphael was composing his third photo. Raphael texted again, *'Get Mama. Open Facetime. Make sure you're sitting down!'*

"Okay, this is even better than a pic," Raphael said, eyebrows dancing. "Forgive me, Patricia, just one more minute, then you can cut it."

"Take your time, Raphael," Patricia said, setting the knife on the table. "Something tells me this will be worth the wait." She pulled Cynthia into a side hug, one that immediately became a spontaneous family group hug that included everyone but the babies. Even Daisy inserted her nose between Patricia's legs. A few seconds in, Raphael's phone chimed a Facetime call. He pulled away and answered.

"There's something you should know," he said, trying to look serious, and using the very same words he'd used to preface his coming out speech so many years ago. He flipped the phone and held it over the cake for several seconds. When he turned it back to himself, Mama was holding a hand over her mouth, eyes wide.

Angel leaned forward into the camera and exclaimed, "Are you *kidding* me?" Raphael walked around the cake and approached Steve and Niki, who was still enveloped in Steve's embrace.

"Niki ..." Raphael grinned, presenting his phone. "Spill!"

# THANK YOU

I HOPE YOU ENJOYED following the exploits of Raphael, Luke, Niki, Steve, Juan, Ricky and the rest of this adventurous chosen family. If you did, first, I hope you will leave a (spoiler-free) favorable review with your favorite retailer.

I have to admit, I've become very fond of the members of the House of the Locked Cock Brotherhood and the mommies and babies who live next door. This is not a promise, but more of an informed prediction. Wouldn't it be fun to see what develops between Mateo and Ryan? Was it just a phase, or, as she matures, will Lily Rafaela indeed develop a Spicy Asian personality? Will Juan actually write that novel about Francisco and Cadmael, or will Juan Enrique occupy too much of his free time? And will Niki reveal his progeny to Gladys, and if so, when?

So many prospects to explore. If you wish, you can stay informed at macinsf.com.

# ACKNOWLEDGEMENTS

I OWE MUCH TO so many on my journey to where I am today. Too many to list here, a list you may not wish to read, anyway. Nevertheless, as I do at the end of each book, allow me to express my humble gratitude first to Ms. Conner, sophomore English teacher, who took me aside after class and told me I should become a writer. (After reading my short story to every one of her classes that day.) Teachers who inspire their students deserve pedestals. And better pay. Gracias, amigo, to Carlos Hickerson for perfecting my Spanish. Appreciation to Ron Bedford for providing his EMT expertise. And especially the many other early readers, too many to mention, for their encouragement and patience.

Deep gratitude must go to the countless authors whose efforts entertained, fascinated and intrigued me as a reader from a very early age, and who ultimately inspired me as a writer myself.

At lastly, to the men I've known and loved who inspired some of the characters in this trilogy. They are by no means 'too many to mention.' But each of them taught me much and left me a better man.

# About the author

AFTER SPENDING MANY YEARS, maybe too many years, in the advertising game, sometimes writing copy for print, radio and television, which followed a period of feature writing for a periodical during his undergrad years, the author took a break from all that to take over a bed and breakfast, as one does. And where he collected enough anecdotes and personal stories to fill a six-story bookstore.

That was interesting.

Now, he's back to writing. And reading. Full time, as it were. And incorporating a few of the lessons he's learned on the path to the life he dreamed about living all those years when he was doing something else. He doesn't teach writing, like many writers. He just writes. Although he was privileged to sample the offerings at the esteemed University of Iowa Writers Workshop. Maybe it helped. You be the judge.

www.ingramcontent.com/pod-product-compliance
Lightning Source LLC
Chambersburg PA
CBHW030643020726
47493CB00006B/1846